The First Thousand Days

The First Thousand Days

**A STORY ABOUT PAUL'S FIRST
MISSIONARY JOURNEY**

Jack Conroy, Ph.D.

ISBN: 9781096799092

A Note on the Title

χίλια is the Greek word for "Thousand." While the Ancient Greeks understood what it meant numerically, it was also used to mean "a very large number." This is the sense in which it is used in the title.

Table of Contents

For Additional Background Information:

The Sign of the Cross: A Story of Peter and Paul Part One: AD 30 to 43

By Jack Conroy, Ph.D.
Amazon.com

Part I

CHAPTER 1

Memorial Dinner

Antioch in Syria
44 AD (3804)

PAUL SAW THAT THE LARGE room was filled to capacity. He stood at the front of the room on a small raised platform behind a table on which rested an open scroll. The group was settling itself on cushions around three long, low tables set with plates and small cups for wine. He looked out over the still-conversing group (men on his left, women on his right) and took a deep breath. As often as he had preached to this and other Antiochene groups over the last year, he never really felt comfortable in this role. It was the day before Passover, and this gathering of those who followed The Way had become an important tradition. A cold drizzle was falling outside, and the musty odor of rain-dampened wool gave texture to the dim light of the oil lamps.

Barnabas (as his friend Joseph bar Nabas was now called) would preside in his spacious home at the ceremonial reenactment of the dinner that Iēsoûs had had with his friends the night before he died. Nevertheless, Paul had been given the honor of commenting on Isaiah as the first part of the tradition. As he waited for people to take their places, he realized there were probably five other groups in Antioch doing the same thing. Some groups were only six or eight; but some, like this one, reached almost twenty men, women, and children of all ages. These people were friends in the deepest sense. They all lived in close proximity in that part of Antioch that lay close to the wharves that lined the Orontes River. Almost all were poor, barely able to scrape by on the meager wages afforded their class of laborers and artisans. Many of the men worked on the docks or in the warehouses that lined the wharves, where caravans from Damascus or Asia would converge and require their freight to be loaded or unloaded, placed in or removed from the warehouses. As this was an area of convergence of foreign sailors, caravanners, traders and adventurers, brothels and taverns proliferated entertaining both visitors and that ample supply of unscrupulous men and women intent upon fleecing the unsuspecting among them. Fights, knifings, and sudden, violent death were common. The protection of the women of the community while they toiled at the river washing clothes or carrying water from the fountains at street intersections had become an important function for the men.

Paul never ceased to be amazed at the difference in atmosphere within the community and outside. Each family could count on the other families for protection, support and response in need. The community was almost a "place" where fear was absent, where joys and sorrows were shared, and where mutual trust abounded. Outside that place, violence, untruth, promiscuity and the use of others for one's own selfish benefit were the operative standards of behavior.

The group gradually fell into an expectant silence, and Paul opened a scroll to the Prophet Isaiah and began to read the Fourth Song of the Servant wherein the servant's disfigurement and sorrows were highlighted. The prophet wrote that all men despised him, he was crushed "because of our guilt," and he never opened his mouth but, like a lamb, he was silently led to the slaughter. This image had been recognized by the community as referring to Iēsoûs; it foretold his humiliation but also gave the reason for it. The prophet proclaimed that "my servant will justify many by taking their guilt on himself."

When he had finished the reading, Paul looked up, took a deep breath, and began his homily.

"Fourteen years ago, what the Prophet Isaiah foretold actually came about. We, who have been called by the grace of God, know that the Servant was Iēsoûs, the Anointed. He knew he would suffer an ignominious death at the hands of his enemies; he knew he would be despised by men and women as he hung naked on the cross. But he gave his life so that many could be justified. What does this mean? It means that through him, all of us are placed in the right relationship with the Father. And our faith, our constant fidelity to the way of his life, is exactly that which permits us to enjoy his justification."

He continued for another ten or fifteen minutes, focusing on the twofold shift of consciousness that had to occur in that world, first that of seeing Iēsoûs's cross as a sign of glory and honor, the exact opposite from the opinion of virtually everyone else at that time, and secondly, the distinction that a life of faith creates in their community, setting it apart from the rest of the violent and hate-filled world outside.

After he concluded, Barnabas nodded to two assistants, who started passing a basket of unleavened bread and a jug of wine around the tables. After all had taken some of each, he recounted the traditions surrounding the night before Iēsoûs died. He spoke of the dinner, which had been related to him by those who had been there. He then repeated words: "This is my body, which is for you," after which each person ate the bread. He then continued: "This is the New Covenant in my blood. Whenever you drink it, do this as a memorial of me." The group drank silently.

Someone said aloud, "Maran'ATHA," to which the entire group responded, "Marana'THA." The dual meaning of the Aramaic was lost on no one, as the first expression meant "The Lord has come" and the second "Lord, come!" Hence, this short interchange expressed the tension felt in the lives of the community. On the one hand, the End Times had already begun and they were living these days in the presence of the Lord who was somehow present within the community. On the other hand they fully expected that the Lord would return again in glory, descending through the clouds from heaven above.

Imperceptibly, the group lapsed into conversation; the ritual had ended with the acclamation and food began to appear out of hampers. The mistress of each household made sure her food was offered to those around her. It was clear that some families clustered around certain women who were well known for their culinary skills. Children tended to do what children do everywhere, playing, squabbling, laughing, shouting, running and periodically crying to their mothers. After eating, the men knotted up into a group in one end of the room and the women did likewise at the other end. The awkward preadolescents hung around the edges of their respective groups, anxious to be included but not quite old enough to do so. Usually, at thirteen, a male child was expected to begin work as a man. Then he was usually betrothed to a twelve-year old girl, with the marriage anticipated in about a year. That gave her access to the women's world, prior to which time she was kept on the outskirts of the female knots.

The door opened, and a muscular, well-dressed, curly-haired individual in his late twenties with one eye scarred and closed entered the room and looked around. Barnabas went up to him immediately and greeted him warmly.

"Sosipater, welcome," he boomed, his arms open wide.

"Greetings, Barnabas. I hope I am not intruding."

"Of course not. Come in, come in."

Paul recalled that he had seen the man somewhere but could not recall where. He then noticed several of the stevedores go up to the man and greet him with respect. Then he remembered. Sosipater owned a number of warehouses on the docks, and the men constantly transferred goods into and out of the buildings under his watchful single eye.

Paul was summoned over and properly introduced. The workers drifted away, and the three men went to a corner of the room, where Barnabas's wife, Deborah, had placed three cushions where the men could sit.

"As you know, Barnabas, I was born of Jewish parents. But the study of the Law had no interest for me."

"That is true for many of our kinsmen," Barnabas responded.

"And, of course, I married Charis..."

Barnabas and Paul nodded. Charis was a Greek woman, the daughter of one of the leading families of Antioch. Her beauty was legendary, and it was well known that she could have married into any one of the ancient families that traced their ancestry back to Seleucus, one of Alexander the Great's generals who ruled Syria from Antioch. Instead, in a rare act of self-determination, she convinced her family to permit a marriage with Sosipater, the son of a Jewish trading family whose patriarch, Sosipater's father, had been *archon*, or leader of the Jewish community in Antioch. The fact that he had married a Greek had alienated Sosipater from his parents. He was considered an apostate and an outcast.

"I have noticed something different about some of the men who are here today," Sosipater said. "I have never observed any of them attempting to steal from me, which is why I like them to work in my warehouse. They are the only ones I can trust. Also, the fact that they help one another and work so well together sets them apart from other workers on the docks. I know they come together on the Sabbath, as do so many of my kinsmen. But I decided to find out what is different about their community. So I took the liberty of visiting. I hope you are not offended."

"You are welcome, Sosipater, as is your wife."

"My wife? But she is a priestess of Io."

"If she knew of the one who fulfilled the promises of our prophets, maybe she would abandon such myths," Paul suggested.

"I rather doubt it," Sosipater said. "Next year, she will be the *archierae* of the festival of Triptolemus on Mount Casius. That is the highest honor for a woman in this city, and she has been looking forward to this for many years."

Paul nodded, aware that a temple to Io existed on Mount Casius, just behind Seleucia ad Pieria twelve miles away, and that only the most prominent women of the area were permitted to be priestesses, let alone the high priestess in charge of the annual festival. Here they recounted the founding of the area by Triptolemus, who had gone in search of Io. She was beloved of Zeus and was identified with the moon. In other parts of the world, she was known as Isis, but here she retained her Greek identity.

"Well, perhaps you would like to hear what we celebrate," Paul offered.

"Yes, I would."

So Paul and Barnabas began discussing the life of Iēsoûs with Sosipater, beginning with the writings of the prophets, especially Isaiah. They continued as the room emptied, other members of the community waving goodbye but not interrupting what they could see was an important conversation. The connection with Sosipater would be extraordinarily important for the community. To have him as part of the community would provide increased access to more jobs. This reality was not lost upon Paul or Barnabas as they talked late into the night, inviting questions, confidently proposing answers, and building a sense of trust and confidence in the radical idea that the End Times had indeed begun.

A rooster's crow surprised Sosipater. He expressed regret for his many questions, and he left for home. Barnabas and Paul excitedly discussed the biggest opportunity that the community had come upon in many years. The community at Antioch was different from that in Jerusalem, where most people had stopped working in anticipation of the End Times and where the leaders of the assembly provided food for an increasing number of people. In Antioch, it was understood that everyone would continue to work until Iēsoûs returned.

CHAPTER 2

Love

THREE MONTHS LATER, PAUL WAS sitting with Sosipater on a balcony of his home, high on the slope of Mount Silpius. The vista overlooked the broad basin of the Orontes River and the main urban center of Antioch. Sosipater had been baptized over a month ago, amid celebration on the part of the entire community that followed Barnabas and Paul.

Sosipater had invited Paul to his home so that he might meet his wife, Charis. She visualized Sosipater's baptism as a return to his ancestral Jewish faith and had severe reservations about the consequences. While Jews had lived in Antioch for centuries and were nominally afforded the protection of citizenship, the reality was that the Jewish community essentially governed itself as a community-within-a-community. As such, it was permitted to create its own regulations, have its own system of courts for adjudicating disputes within the community, and essentially operate independently of the balance of Antiochene life. This produced a sense of distrust on the part of the Antiochene leading families and was reflected in Charis's attitude.

A commotion was heard in the street below. Sosipater leaned over the balcony rail, waved, and announced to Paul that Charis was arriving, being carried in a sedan chair preceded by a ceremonial group of priests. They had just completed the three-day festival in honor of Io at the port city of Seleucia, the final act of which was the return of the high-priestess to her home.

A few moments later, Charis appeared on the balcony, clothed in a white silk gown, bedecked with necklaces, earrings, and combs sparkling with fine jewels. Both men arose to greet her. Her jet-black hair was piled high on her head; cosmetics highlighted her thin facial features. She was a slender woman, taller than Paul, and carried herself with a sense of confidence and authority. Paul's eyes widened as she approached, her hand outstretched. He mechanically took the slender fingers in his hand, being sensitive to the number of rings worn, bowing slightly as the introduction was made. Her smile was mechanical, almost uninterested. The three returned to chairs on the balcony and sensed the sun sinking in the western sky behind them.

"My parents send their greetings," she said to Sosipater. "They could not understand why you would not accompany me on the trip. Everyone was asking for you."

"We have been over this time and again," Sosipater responded, obviously embarrassed.

"But no one understands," Charis continued. "You may worship your Adonai if you want, just as many men worship Zeus. I don't object. But I don't understand why you won't just accompany me and do what every other husband does on the most important day of his wife's life!"

"Charis, that's not fair," Sosipater insisted.

"I understand how you feel perfectly," Paul interjected to the surprise of both his hosts.

"What do you mean?" they both asked.

"Sharing a common vision of what the world looks like is the most important element in any marriage. My wife and I did not share that common vision, and it drove her to an untimely and tragic death, for which I still suffer. I was unable to reach out to her because of my own stupidity and pride."

Capitalizing upon the looks of inquiry that both gave him, Paul described his own unhappy marriage, concentrating on the gulf that had developed between him and Ruth because they lived in different worlds.

He then began to describe the world into which Sosipater had been born; he began with the account of Creation, continued with the story of the Flood and of God's promise to Noah. He then described the further promise to Abraham. He abbreviated the history of Israel but focused on the promise to David of continued kingship, and then upon the prophecies of Isaiah. Finally, he spoke of Iēsoûs of Nazareth as the one who fulfilled the promises despite the apparent ignominy of his death.

By the time he finished, the moon was high in the sky, and the lamps flickering in the valley below were being extinguished one by one. Charis had listened intently for almost five hours; servants had silently brought food and drink, which the three consumed on the balcony, and the unwashed dishes lay on a table to the side. She had asked a few questions but in each case seemed satisfied with Paul's responses.

"But you have no goddesses," she said at last. "I can relate to Io; she may not have created the world, but she offers women assistance in childbirth and understands us when we have normal womanly problems. How can your Adonai understand us?"

"The Lord is neither male nor female," Paul responded. "There are some who have written that Wisdom is one face of the Lord, with Him at the beginning, but female in character. The Lord is not a man; God made both Adam and Eve, in His own image and likeness. Hence, both men and women can relate to Him. He understands everyone."

As it was getting late, Paul was invited to remain the night, and after some more casual conversation, the hosts summoned a sleepy servant to show their guest to his quarters. Sosipater and Charis bade goodnight to Paul, who had difficulty falling asleep, so intensely was adrenaline pumping through his body.

The next morning, Paul was stunned when he first saw Charis. All the cosmetics had been removed, and her hair was pulled back simply, falling down her back softly in flowing tresses. She was clad in a chiton that was comfortably cut but which revealed more flesh than Paul had been used to. Her beauty was more evident now than last night, when she had worn cosmetics and jewels. Her eyes were intelligent and smiling as she greeted Paul with warmth.

When Paul inquired about Sosipater, she told him that he had left at daybreak for the warehouses. Servants brought fruit and bread for breakfast, and Charis immediately launched into more questions about the previous night's stories. She was fascinated by the Law that Moses had described, as having come from God. So, for hours on end, Paul described the basis for the legendary sense of Jewish morality. The idea that a person's actions should have a divinely revealed standard she found remarkable and attractive. So, in addition to the precepts that Moses had written, Paul introduced the interpretations that the Jewish sages had added, clarifying and interpreting the Mosaic dispensation. Charis was fascinated that there existed a way of life where correct action had been so carefully laid out.

As the shadows lengthened and the sun began its rapid descent beneath the green hills to the west, Sosipater returned, delighted to see Paul and Charis engaged in continuing conversation. That night, their dinner conversation ranged over topics unrelated to God and the history of Israel. Paul discovered that Charis was well educated, had read the major Greek authors, including Plato, Aristotle, and the great poets. As the night wore on, she summoned one of the servants to fetch a scroll of poems by Sappho, which she read by lamplight. Paul found himself squirming a bit at the explicit expressions of intimacy read unselfconsciously by Charis. Her expression and feeling in reading the poetry were exquisite; Sosipater was dozing off toward the end when Charis laughingly called it a night, and Paul headed for the guest quarters again.

Shortly after sunrise Paul arose and accompanied Sosipater down the mountainside to the center of town, where he reported on his discussions with Charis to Barnabas. The latter received Paul's report with glee, convinced that if Charis would become a follower of The Way, the entire community would have substantially more status and stability among the Antiochenes. It would be a major coup! Barnabas encouraged Paul to make the conversion of Charis his most important priority. Paul agreed.

Several days later, Sosipater appeared and invited Paul for dinner the next night. Paul immediately accepted. At the appointed time, he appeared at Sosipater's door, and was quickly admitted, responding to the heartfelt greetings of both Charis and her husband. Paul was surprised to find two other couples at the house, and within a short period of time, he was engaged in relating essentially the same stories to them as he had to Charis. He received, at best, a polite but disinterested reception from the other couples but Charis could not hear enough. When the guests claimed the lateness of the hour and left, Charis and Sosipater remained awake with Paul, discussing what Paul described as the "New Covenant" brought by Iēsoûs the Anointed One, in fulfillment of the promises made by God to the prophets. This time, he described the communities of Iēsoûs's followers in Capernaum. He described Philip and his four daughters; he included a description of his own change of life brought about by the direct action of Iēsoûs the Lord. He even described Judith and the easy and comfortable relationship that existed between men and women in that community. Charis was both surprised and delighted to hear that women could participate fully in both liturgy and daily life as part of the New Covenant.

Sosipater had dozed off, so Charis gently took his hand and helped him to their bedroom.

"You know the way to the guest quarters, don't you?" she said. "See you in the morning." Paul was asleep in a moment, feeling fulfilled and knowing he was making excellent progress with Charis.

When Paul arose the next morning to return to the docks with Sosipater, Charis insisted that he remain and continue their conversation from the night before. At Sosipater's encouragement, Paul agreed, and he and Charis were soon engaged in more discussions of the Scriptures. The day passed in a flash; and at the time that Sosipater could have been expected, one of his slaves arrived with the news that a caravan had just arrived from Damascus and that Sosipater would remain in town for the night. Paul and Charis continued their discussions through dinner.

After dinner, Paul broached a new topic that he was just then mulling over in his own head. While Charis had been fascinated by the idea of a code of behavior in virtue by which one could evaluate actions, Paul suggested that Iēsoûs had introduced a new kind of code. Instead of a code that itemized as many items as possible and evaluated them individually, so that the number of precepts expanded without limit, he suggested that Iēsoûs had emphasized an old idea, namely, that the ultimate standard of all behavior was whether love was served in each action. Charis could not stop asking questions about this idea. Her eyes lit up with delight, and she continued the conversation until Paul's eyes seemed unable to remain open, long past the time that the Antiochene lamps had blinked out. Darkness covered the city. The servants had long retired.

"Paul, you have been an angel. I have felt my life open up before my eyes. Never before have I felt so…so…alive, so *whole*. You are a remarkable man, clearly sent by God to me."

They had been reclining on separate couches, with a table between them on which the unwashed dishes from supper still lay. She got up, came over to Paul's couch and sat on the edge. Her hand took Paul's, and his heart began to beat wildly.

"You are the first person to describe the world to me as it really is. It is only if we live in love that we can really *be*. And when I am with you, I *exist* so fully. I am filled with life, with hope, with the fullness of God's message. I am ready, Paul, to turn from the shallow gods of my past… yes, from Io and all the rest…and to be baptized as you say I must, into the community of Iēsoûs. I want to be part of your family that lives in love for the rest of my life."

She raised Paul's hand and placed it on her breast. He felt the erect nipple through the thin cloth. He gulped. She bent down and kissed his eyes gently, then his cheek, and then his mouth. He could feel the tautness in his loins amid the confusion in his brain. He wanted her, but he knew that it violated every principle he stood for.

She reached up with her other hand to her shoulder and unclipped a beautifully worked gold *fibula* that held her gown together at the shoulder. It dropped down, exposing the other breast. Paul began to shudder. He didn't want to offend her…indeed, he wanted her with everything in his being. She was his for the taking, inviting, her passion being aroused with each passing second. He could feel her tongue moving at the edges of his mouth.

"Please, please, Charis," he moaned weakly.

"I know, my love, I know," she purred back.

With an inhuman effort, he sprang up from the couch. "Charis, my love, we can't. It is wrong. We can't."

"Oh, Paul, just once. Then never again. Just once," she begged.

"Oh, God, I want to. I hunger for you."

She sat on the couch, the top of her chiton down around her waist, her eyes barely discernable in the dim, yellow lamplight.

"But we can't," he said. "I must go. I can't remain in this house, or I know what I shall do. I can't stand to be near you...I love you, I love you. But you are another man's wife, and my friend at that."

She stood up, and as she did so, the chiton dropped to her ankles. Her arms went around Paul's neck.

"Just once...please, take me. Take me now. Then leave, and I'll never ask again."

She moved her body against Paul's, and Paul felt his resistance melting. His hands dropped to her buttocks.

"NO!" he cried, and he ripped her arms from his neck, threw them down forcefully, and stepped back. "Dress yourself!"

"You bastard!" she cried. "I grovel before you, debase myself in front of you, and you spit on me! How can you! You talk of love, but you aren't a man at all! Toss me aside, will you? Treat me as a piece of garbage!"

"Charis, no. That is not what I meant..." He was astonished at her anger.

"Look at me! LOOK AT ME! Any man in Antioch would die for the chance I gave you! And you send me to the dung heap! Well, let me tell you what you can do with your Iēsoûs and his Rule of Love! You can stick it in your ass!" And with that, she picked up her chiton and tossed it to him. As he caught it, she let out a shriek. She screamed again. Instantly, three servants appeared, wide eyed, astonished that they should see their mistress standing nude, with her chiton in Paul's hand.

"He tried to rape me! He ripped off my clothes! Kick him out! Beat him!"

Two burly men grabbed Paul by the arms, dragged him down the stairs, threw him bodily out the front door and then slammed it. Paul found himself sprawled spread eagle on the dirty street. He could hear Charis's hysterical screaming behind the door. It had all been so quick. He held his head in his hands. What would Sosipater say? My God! What a mess! He dragged himself to his feet and began to trudge down the mountain toward the center of the city. His legs were shaking, his heart beating. How could his success be destroyed so quickly? He couldn't even pray, so miserable did he feel.

CHAPTER 3

Guilty of Stupidity

He pounded on the main door of the familiar home for the third time; someone down the street hurled a curse at him for waking up the entire neighborhood, but there was not a sound from the inside of the well-appointed house. One more time he tried, one more curse came from the second story window; a dog started barking, and he saw the yellow glow of an oil lamp through the crack in the plank door. A muffled inquiry about who was beating down the door brought Paul's *sotto voce* response, and the door swung open, disclosing a half-asleep, tousled major-domo asking, "What in the world…"

"I must see Barnabas. Let me in." He pushed his way into the *impluvium* and into the peristyle-courtyard past the half-asleep man sprinting toward the sleeping quarters in the pitch dark until he came to the familiar door, where he pounded again. This time he heard immediate muffled sounds from within, and Barnabas appeared at last, a small oil lamp in his hand.

"Paul?"

"Something terrible has happened." He tried to blurt everything out at once, wide-eyed, almost incoherent, standing in the open doorway.

"Paul, Paul. Wait. Come in. Calm down," Barnabas urged, clearly alarmed at the wild demeanor of the small man in front of him. He closed the door, lit a larger oil lamp on a lampstand, motioned for Paul to be seated on a cushion, and took his place on another cushion against the far wall of the small antechamber to the master bedroom. Paul could hear the questions the tired children were asking of Deborah in an adjacent room as she tried to assuage their fears.

"I d-d-d don't know where to begin…" Paul stuttered.

"Calmly, calmly, my friend. Everything will be fine…" Barnabas soothed.

After a few moments, Paul related the events of the day, that Charis had been on the very verge of baptism and that she had misunderstood the message that God's love was the prime value of a baptized community. Barnabas listened intently; and when Paul related the last elements, the charge of rape and his being forcibly ejected from Sosipater's house, he put his head in his hands.

"This is very serious. Sosipater has been with us such a short time, but in that time, he has been able to provide employment for many of us. If he believes Charis…" His voice trailed off. Silence. The consequences were obvious.

"But, Barnabas, you must believe me…I never…"

"I believe you, Paul. The question is, will Sosipater?"

"Perhaps we should go down to the warehouse now and give him our story before he hears it from his wife," Paul suggested.

"Paul, if you had time to get here, Sosipater knows. I am sure that one of his men ran down with the charge."

Paul dropped his head, dejected.

"What do you think he will do?" Paul asked quietly.

"He will press charges. There will be a trial. What I am not sure of is whether Sosipater will bring charges within our own Jewish council, since both you and he are Jews, or whether it will be before the Antiochene council, since Charis is a citizen of Antioch and is not a Jew. If the charge is brought in the Gentile council, your Jewishness will count against you."

"But I am a Roman citizen…"

"That will merely change the punishment if you are found guilty. You will be branded an 'infamous person,' will be publicly dishonored, possibly banished from Antioch, and forever forbidden to serve on juries or hold public office."

"But…but I am not guilty! I did nothing…"

"Whatever you did or did not do, you incurred the wrath of the most important woman in the city and, I am afraid, turned our most important patron away from us! How could you let yourself be alone with her at night? Couldn't you see the danger you put yourself in? Dining alone together, drinking wine! Her husband not at home! Paul, that was stupid!"

"But we were…were talking of…of Iēsoûs…"

"It makes no difference what or whom you were talking about. The only things that matter are that she accused you and that your presence in the wrong place at the wrong time will make her charge credible!"

"But…but…it…is…false. She wanted to make love; I couldn't sin in that manner…"

"Maybe you should have!"

"Barnabas…"

"Lie down here, get some sleep. I am going back to bed. I'm sure we will hear more of this in the morning." Barnabas stood up and disappeared into the next room with the small oil lamp, pulling the thin curtain over the open doorway. Paul blew out the larger lamp and lay down on a thin pallet. He couldn't sleep for a long time.

CHAPTER 4

Trial

A WEEK LATER, THE TRIAL began before the *boule,* or council, of the city of Antioch. The *Bouleterion* was a rectangular building with three ranks of stone benches on all four walls. About thirty men were in attendance, and Paul sat in the center of the room, alone, on a wooden stool. The prosecutor rose from the first rank of benches and read the charge: "Sosipater, son of Hyperbus, of the city of Antioch, has pressed charges of Attempted Rapine against one Paul, son of Paulus, of the city of Tarsus. The accused is a Roman citizen.

"The charge is that the accused did, on the third day of last week, attempt to forcibly possess the noble Charis, depriving Sosipater of his rights of exclusivity to his wife, thereby heaping shame upon Sosipater. The noble Charis successfully resisted his advances only by summoning in desperation the servants of the house, who entered into her bedchamber only to behold the accused standing in front of the noble Charis holding her clothing in his hands, and the noble lady quaking in fear, her body being exposed by force to the eyes of the accused. The accused was forcibly ejected from the house, and is hereby charged with attempted rapine. So say the people of Antioch."

The *archon,* or president of the council, addressed Paul: "How do you plead?"

"He pleads not guilty," said a young man in a white toga from a bench directly across from the prosecutor. It was John Mark, the nephew of Barnabas, whose mother, Mary, was from a prominent Jerusalem family.

He had studied rhetoric in Tarsus and had recently returned. Although this was his first defense, his demeanor was confident and easy.

The prosecutor brought Sosipater to the center of the room and invited him to make his charges to the boule. He did so, not looking at Paul. Then the prosecutor had the servants enter the room, and they swore that they had seen Paul holding Charis's gown and Charis standing naked and cowering in the corner, screaming for help. The prosecutor triumphantly proclaimed the obvious guilt of Paul and took his seat.

John Mark arose. "Men of Antioch, in defending the accused, I have asked him many, many questions and have formed my own opinion, which I will share with you. I have every belief that he is, indeed, guilty!"

A gasp arose from the benches; Paul stood up, his mouth open.

John Mark held up his hand to urge quiet. "Guilty of imprudence; guilty of placing himself in a compromising position; but he is clearly not guilty of the charges that have been pressed."

A more normal quiet returned; Paul sat down again.

"I will present my proof in two parts. First, I will acquaint the court with the character of the accused; I will demonstrate that he could not possibly be guilty of this charge because of his nobility of character. I will then prove not only that he *could* not have committed the act of which he is accused, but that he *did not in fact* commit the deed.

"First, you should know who the accused is. He is known as Paul, the son of Aemelius Paulus of Tarsus, a noble and leading man in that city. Their family was brought to Rome by Pompey and was in the service of the Aemelii, one of Rome's most important families. The grandfather of the accused was given his freedom by the Aemelii, and his father was awarded Roman citizenship by the divine Augustus because of the importance of the service he provided the Roman army in the east. Hence, the accused is a Roman citizen.

"He was educated both in Jerusalem and in Tarsus, where he studied with the leading scholars in both locations. Indeed, following the pattern of Socrates, he has given up all interest in matters of money-making or politics and has devoted himself entirely to the professing of a philosophy held by the strictest school of his ancestors. This philosophy seeks blessedness in a life of piety and holiness, doing homage to the god who is worshipped in Jerusalem. Included in that profession is an adherence to a strict code of Law, given by God to his people in the most ancient of times, that commands honor to God and parents and includes prohibitions against murder, greed, theft, falsehoods, and adultery. That a person who spends his entire life practicing the virtues expressed in this Law and bringing others to similar lives of piety should stoop to an act of forcibly depriving his friend Sosipater of that which is rightly his, that he would violate all his professed principles, ingrained in his character by years of instruction, such an act is unthinkable for this honorable man.

"However, I have an additional piece of proof. Recall that Sosipater charged that Paul ripped the clothing from the noble Charis and that Sosipater's menservants found him with that clothing still in his hands."

Nods from the benches.

"Bring the clothing here."

Someone brought a chiton to him.

"Bring the menservants in."

They were.

"Is this your mistress's clothing that you took from the hands of Paul?"

They nodded.

"Now, gentlemen of Antioch, notice that the cloth is not torn or ripped; it is perfectly sound and shows no evidence of having been forcibly removed from the lady's body. Indeed, the accused maintains that the lady attempted to seduce him, that he refused to dishonor his friend Sosipater, and that he rebuffed her advances, even after she removed her clothing to make the invitation more irresistible. She would have carefully undone the fibula that holds the parts together. Now, menservants, did you find a fibula anywhere in the room?"

"Yes."

"Where?"

"On one of the couches."

"What more proof do you need? It is clear that the accused, with the permission thoughtlessly given by Sosipater to spend time in private with the Lady Charis to instruct her in his philosophy, found himself in the unfortunate position of being the object of lust of a woman so taken by his virtue that she wanted him for herself. Further, when she was properly rebuffed, she took advantage of her high position and made a false claim before this honorable court. I feel sure that Sosipater will take the appropriate actions with his wife to restore his own honor, which she has besmirched in making such a false and vile claim. Gentlemen of Antioch, I call for a verdict of acquittal!"

He sat down.

The archon asked the prosecutor if he was ready with a rebuttal. He stood up, shook his head dramatically, his thumb and forefinger cupping his chin, and walked to the center of the room.

"'Philosopher,'" he spat out. "Philosophy? In the inner chamber with a woman? The defence strains our credulity! While the noble wife of Sosipater is respected by everyone in Antioch, is there anyone who believes she has studied grammar, or geometry, or rhetoric? He would next have you believe that someone can read without being able to distinguish an alpha from an omega. Was it Plato or Aristotle that the accused teaches? Nonsense. It was just an excuse to worm his way into the private part of the house when the master was away.

"Further, I have done investigation into the kind of philosophy the accused teaches. First, it is that common to the Judaeans and we all know how they refuse to honor the gods of the city, bringing the risk of bad fortune to everyone! However, we permit them, and only them, to behave in such an impious manner. So, at best, his 'philosophy' is one that attempts to persuade one of the most respected women of our city, the high priestess of Io, to desert the service of a goddess who has protected our city from ancient times."

"Second, and most damning of all, even among his own people, he is known as an innovator, a bringer of hated novelty to piety. Even granting that these Jews have an old heritage, the accused does not respect its age or traditions. Hence, he is not truly a 'philosopher,' molding his life after the pattern of his hero, whom they call *Moses*. No, he has some new prophet, a criminal executed after a proper Roman trial about fifteen years ago. 'Philosopher?' I say 'Charlatan!'

"And the 'proof' of the fibula? A weak woman, when confronted with a man out of his mind with passion, will do what she is told to do under threat of death! Of course he forced her to disrobe; her real virtue was that she risked her life in screaming for help! Her virtue remained intact, despite the shame of having to invite the menservants into the chamber and permit them to feast their eyes on her misfortune!"

"Men of Antioch! The defense has proved nothing but has helped me to demonstrate the depravity of a man who would attempt to steal the virtue of an unsuspecting and defenseless woman under the guise of 'philosophy'."

John Mark quickly arose, not permitting the prosecutor time to leave the floor and retake his seat among the jurors.

"Our learned prosecutor has displayed for you, I fear, the shortcomings of his own education! He supposes that only established principles held by the ancients are 'true.' Had anyone prior to Pythagoras proved the equality of the square of the hypotenuse with the sum of the square of the sides of a right triangle? Does that mean that he was an 'innovator?' Or was he one of the wisest of men? And was not Aristotle the first to analyze syllogisms, identifying the proper structure of arguments, unknown even to the great Plato? Was he an 'innovator?' Of course he was! Anyone who sees truth more deeply than his predecessors must be an 'innovator.' Even Moses, a hero to those Greeks who hear the Word of God in the books written by him, even Moses was an 'innovator.' For God revealed his Law to him, and he wrote down what God said. By characterizing 'truth' as 'anything but innovation,' the learned prosecutor has just offered you the result of a mind impoverished of philosophy. Hence, I am not surprised that he is unable to recognize true philosophy when he sees it.

"As to the veiled suggestion that we who follow Moses are somehow enemies of the state and that we put the city at risk by not worshipping your gods, you know that we offer sacrifice daily in our temple in Jerusalem for the *princeps*; you are all aware of the decree of the prince, sent to Alexandria and to Syria, maintaining both the great friendship of the Jews with the Romans, and to quote the tablet erected not long ago in this very city, 'to permit the Jews to keep their ancient customs without being hindered so to do.' We hold it to be the utmost of piety to conform ourselves to the Law God gave us, which includes the worship of our God only. Just as Socrates could not act against any voice that his *daimon* provided him, so we cannot act contrary to our laws. This is the best of citizenship, since our laws also include the commandments that describe a peaceful, productive, and honest form of citizenship.

"Finally, a man might use force to take what belongs to another man only when the least outcry would not bring worse violence upon himself. Look at this man. Does he look like an athlete? Like a *pancriatist*? Knowing that there were many menservants in the house, any one of whom is stronger than he, do you think that he would use force when the slightest outcry would bring disaster? While I have agreed that he exercised poor judgment in being behind closed doors with another man's wife, he did so with her husband's explicit permission, given because Sosipater trusted him. And Sosipater is a patron of many of the members of the assembly to which the accused belongs. Do you think he would risk offending his friend and patron? While you may not agree with his philosophy, it is clear that a man so well educated, so well born, who has a following of many men from our city, myself included, is not totally *stupid*. And he would have to be if you believe the prosecutor! Force? Impossible! He is paying the price of an honest man who brought about the rage of a woman rejected. Find him not guilty!"

The archon nodded to John Mark as the younger man slowly returned to his place. Paul sat silently, his head erect, his eyes not averting those of his judges.

"Gentlemen, you have heard both sides of the case. Are there any questions from the jurors to either the prosecution or the defense?"

Silence.

"Then, in accordance with the rules of this court, let the vote be taken."

A clay pot was passed from person to person, and each man dropped in either a white or a black pebble. The clinking went on for a few minutes, amid silence. Then the archon received the pot and upended it into a clay tray. The prosecutor and John Mark approached the seat of the archon, and all three watched as a functionary of the court counted the black and white pebbles; there were only four black pebbles, indicating a "guilty" vote. Twenty six were white.

"The accused is judged innocent of the charges by this court," proclaimed the archon. "He may go in peace; his honor is intact."

CHAPTER 5

Consequences of the Not Guilty Verdict

THERE WAS LITTLE JOY IN the crowded room where the assembly usually met. The trial had been over for three days. Though Paul had been found innocent of the charges, Sosipater refused to hire any of the dock-workers in the room. Not only that, but other employers were refusing to hire them, with no reasons given. They were just not hired. The men were angry, standing idly on the docks.

"It is only temporary," Barnabas assured them. "You are the best workers on the docks; everyone knows that. Soon there will be jobs again."

The men grumbled, worried, and after a perfunctory prayer, they left for their homes.

"What can we do?" Paul asked.

"We must bring the announcement of the Good News to others."

"What?"

"We must leave Antioch for a time. You, John Mark, and I must leave. I don't know whether Sosipater will ever learn the truth about his wife; I don't know if he will ever return to our assembly. But with all of us gone, he will have no reason to continue to make our brothers suffer unemployment. We are almost out of money. Brothers from the other assemblies in the city have shared what they have but we have so little. If the brothers can't work, their families will starve. We must show Sosipater the way to an honorable solution, and that means that we leave Antioch."

"And go where?"

"Cyprus. My birthplace. I have a brother in Salamis and many cousins in Paphos. I have not seen any of my family for almost fifteen years. So much has changed in my life since I left Cyprus. I would like to share our discovery of the Good News with all of them. John Mark has never seen his uncle and it will be good for him to be with us for a while. Further, some of my relatives are wealthy, and they may help us by contributing to our costs of announcing the Good News."

"Would John Mark come with us?" asked Paul. "He seems to be moving in the right social circles. His defense impressed many important people."

"That is just why I would like him to accompany us. He was invited to dine with Philebus, the archon, tomorrow night. I have heard that he would like to invite John Mark to become a client, which would open up many opportunities for him, including the possibility of forming an alliance through his daughter."

"Marriage?"

"Possibly. That would make my sister, Alexandra, happy. Her husband, Asher, has become wealthy by manufacturing tiles for mosaic floors, but they have no social status. This will provide that."

"But…"

"Of course, you see the problem. First, John Mark becomes attached to the archon and marries his daughter. And next, he will be in the Temple of Zeus with his father-in-law, sharing a sacrificial meal. My sister and her husband will see this as necessary and excusable…but you and I know what that will ultimately mean."

"But John Mark knows that Zeus does not truly exist and that eating meat sacrificed to Zeus is meaningless."

"But what message does this send to the rest of the brothers?" Barnabas asked. "They see him, one of the most prominent young members of our assembly pouring libations before dining, and you can imagine what they will think. No, he will be lost to us forever…"

"But will he come?"

"He will if you ask him, Paul. He looks up to you, as you know. If you ask him to accompany you, so that you and he can spend time together discussing the Good News, praying, and deepening your friendship, I think he would come. And you, my friend, could help all of us by working to deepen his dedication to our work. He is a shining light, and we must cause him to grow in God's love. Let this be your task, and it will make up for the mess you have created for me here."

Paul winced inside and dropped his head. He had no response.

"When will we come back?"

"I don't know. Probably in the fall. I want things to settle down here. That can happen only if we are gone."

"I...I...could go alone, if you would think that would help."

"No, that will not be enough. In fact, I am sure that the Holy Spirit is behind this entire affair...it is His will that we go to visit my family. There may be many in Salamis who will embrace our Way. Nothing that happens occurs except through the direction of the Holy Spirit. That is why I am sure we have to go."

"When should we leave?"

"Tomorrow. I will visit Lucian and invite him to assume leadership of our assembly; I will explain everything to Deborah, and we can start for Seleucia. We should be able to find a boat within a week."

"Barnabas, I'm sorry that..."

"Paul. Nonsense. This is what the Spirit wants. This is what we must do. Otherwise, we would never have thought about visiting my relatives in Cyprus and bringing the Good News of Iēsoûs to them. Look upon this as the Lord helping us to make the right decision."

Paul closed his eyes, uttered a short prayer under his breath, and with a tear in his eye, embraced Barnabas.

With that, the two men left to look for John Mark.

CHAPTER 6

John Mark

PAUL AND BARNABAS FOUND JOHN Mark with a group of young men in a tavern in the Forum Valentis, located in the center of Antioch. Barnabas and Paul were warmly greeted by the young attorney and the three of them found an isolated table in the back of the tavern.

Barnabas did most of the talking, laying out the need for Paul and him to leave Antioch for a while until the results of the trial settled down. He then pointed out their need of him, John Mark, to accompany them and participate in bringing the Good News to Barnabas's and John Mark's relatives in Cyprus. Initially, John Mark's reaction was negative. He enjoyed the congratulations of his peers, all of whom had heard of his invitation for dinner from the archon that night.

"Uncle Barnabas, how can I leave Antioch now? Everyone is talking about the trial. No one thought I could ever win! Sosipater will have to hire our followers of the Way just because traffic up and down the river is increasing. There's no need for either you or me to leave."

Paul reached over the table and grasped John Mark's hand. Their eyes met.

"John Mark, I understand your position. I was in exactly the same position as you about four years ago. You know of my having been sent to Damascus to warn other Pharisees about the destructive ideas promulgated by the followers of Iēsoûs. That journey was interrupted by Iēsoûs himself, when he appeared to me and redirected my life. He also said that I would recruit others to bring his Good News to the world. In this matter, John Mark, it is not merely me who is calling you, but it is Iēsoûs calling through me. Let this be as a revelation to you. Come with us and invite others to turn from darkness to light, so that they may have life and their sins forgiven."

John Mark didn't move. "When do you plan on leaving?" he asked.

"Tomorrow morning. There is a barge leaving shortly after dawn for Seleucia, where we'll look for a ship for Cyprus."

After a long silence, he said, "Paul, here's what I'll do. I will go home tonight and pray over this matter. If it appears to me that I am being called through you and Uncle Barnabas, I will meet you on the dock where the barge ties up. If I am not there when the barge unties, you will know my decision."

Paul and Barnabas agreed with him, and they parted.

CHAPTER 7

En Route

BEFORE SUNRISE, BARNABAS AND PAUL arrived at the dock where a barge loaded with exports from the city was expected to shove off as soon as the crew arrived. The two men recalled the events of three years ago when they watched the ship on which Barnabas, Paul and Timothy had been passengers leave that very dock without them and how Barnabas recruited Menachem, the *primus pilum* (chief enlisted man) of the Roman legion stationed there. They recalled the breakneck ride down to Seleucia and the remarkable delay the ship had encountered so the three could meet the ship outside the estuary.

The crew began to arrive, chatting amiably with dockworkers and watching the last of the cargo being lashed down. The barge had no sails, but there were three men who would man the oars for the trip back upstream from Seleucia, where they would have received a load of goods from the larger sailing vessels in the harbor. A tall man, barefoot, wearing a sparkling white tunic and a Roman broadsword at his side, ambled up to the dock accompanied by a woman. He stopped at one of the warehouses next to the dock and engaged in a conversation with someone holding a sheaf of papyri documents. Paul concluded that the barefoot man was the captain and that he was finishing up the administrative details regarding the trip.

No John Mark.

Barnabas looked at Paul and raised his hands in anxiety as he walked over to the captain and began discussion on fare to Seleucia. Coins were handed to the captain, and the two passengers stepped onto the barge.

The captain and the woman with him stood a few feet away from the barge, engaged in conversation. *The woman might be the captain's wife,* Paul thought. No one seemed to be eager to begin the three-hour voyage. The crew was lounging on top of crates and bales of cargo.

No John Mark.

Barnabas walked up to one of the crew and asked why they were waiting.

"Some passenger has not yet arrived," he said.

Barnabas thought, *I remember that event when the captain would not wait for two passengers...*

The captain and his supposed wife went into the warehouse and brought out two light chairs and sat in the shade, continuing their domestic conversation.

Then came a square carriage drawn by two huge black horses, and it stopped next to the barge. A corpulent elite man with a broad purple senatorial stripe on his toga struggled out of the carriage door, and immediately after him, John Mark.

"John Mark," exclaimed Paul and Barnabas simultaneously.

"I am Caius Vibius Marsus," announced the senator. "I hereby deliver your colleague, though I hate to do so."

"Why?" asked Paul, dredging up an encounter some eight years ago.

"Because I wanted to employ this man to handle the legal affairs of this province. I heard of his remarkable defense of some Jew who was caught with the wife of Sosipater. Anyone who could do that has to be a first-rate lawyer. Say, haven't we met before?" he asked Paul.

"Yes, about three years ago, on the voyage from Tarsus to Antioch."

"I remember you now...you are the only person who ever refused to accept an *aurius* for doing me a service. In fact, I think you maneuvered me into giving you two aurii for the poor and for your synagogue. Yes, I remember you."

"I am pleased to see you again, sir," Paul said.

John Mark's mouth dropped open in astonishment.

"Well, here is your lawyer. He has decided to accompany you two to Cyprus, which is a waste of a perfectly good lawyer. But he said if we go to the dock and the barge has actually left, he'd accept my offer; but if it were still tied up, he'd go with you two. So there you have him. May your trip be worthwhile." And with that, he got back into the carriage, and John Mark hoisted his traveling bag into the barge.

They cast off and started to float down the river.

Paul asked the captain about how he had known to wait for the senator. He said he had not known, but someone came to the administrator and simply said that they were to wait for the senator. "So we did."

Mysterious things happen on the Orontes River, thought Paul. *Could it have been an angel?* He remembered the passage from Exodus: *Now, go and lead the people where I have told you. See, my angel will go before you.*

Paul uttered a short prayer of thanks.

The voyage turned out to be idyllic. They had had little problem finding a small freighter out of Seleucia bound for Cyprus. The winds from the northeast favored the journey. As the sun was dropping in the west, they departed Seleucia running before a steady breeze. As they settled down for a night on the deck, Paul looked back and caught sight of the gleaming white marble temple to Io on the top of the hill above the city. Their course to the west-southwest offered a spectacular view of the six columns on the western side and thirteen on the southern, long side. *It is a beautiful building,* Paul thought, but his stomach knotted as it brought back memories of his encounter with Charis. He turned his gaze seaward, the dark blue of the sea contrasting with the puffy, flat-bottomed clouds whose tops were beginning to be tinged with the orange-pink of sunset. A raucous flock of gulls wheeled and plunged just off the starboard bow, swooping down to pick off the topmost members of a school of menhaden. Paul enjoyed the rise and fall of the small ship. The deckhands were relaxing in the forecastle, and a single steersman handled a tiller, a horizontal pole lashed to two steering oars on each side of the stern. The grizzled, gray-bearded captain stood next to him. A small deckhouse was constructed halfway between the mast and the stern, but it was used for the captain alone.

The voyage was scheduled for only two days, and since the captain indicated that the weather seemed promising, the three men had not brought any tenting material for protection on deck. Hence, they sat on the starboard side, their backs against the deckhouse. And since they were running before the wind, they felt only a gentle breeze, even though they were speeding across the waves at amazing speed.

The seventy-foot long ship was laden with a combination of luxury goods from Parthia and India, brought to Seleucia via the great land trade route that connected Antioch with the East. Additionally, there was a variety of manufactured goods, mostly glass, from Alexandria, brought north by coastal merchant galleys. The vessel had a great, wide-spreading square-rigged linen mainsail and a smaller square-rigged sail on a bowsprit that rose at about a thirty-degree angle from the horizontal. Both sails were reinforced with a grid of ropes sewn onto the fabric, which transferred the stress of the wind to the structure of the ship.

In the bow of the ship were two massive wood anchors reinforced with iron bands with removable lead stocks that lay next to the anchors. These cross pieces were inserted in the square hole at the top of the anchor so that the hooks would dig into the bottom of the sea. Two similar but smaller anchors were at the stern.

Paul was silent, depressed that the events of a mere ten days had so changed his life. He was amazed at the speed with which the members of the assembly had changed their minds about him. He recalled the palpable relief when Barnabas announced that they would be embarking on a voyage to bring the Good News to the Jews of Salamis and Paphos. It seemed that everyone understood that this threat to their economic life was going to be eliminated. They were almost too anxious to say goodbye and were halfhearted in wishing them a speedy return. John Mark said he expected to be back before shipping ended for the winter, which meant late fall.

Barnabas and John Mark were engaged in a discussion about the family, so Paul got up and walked to the bow of the ship. The gentle rise and fall of the bow as the seas passed beneath the hull was relaxing and exhilarating. As a wave caught up with the ship, its stern would rise, and for a few moments, it would accelerate as it rode down the front side of the swell. Then the bow would dip into the trough, and a great sheet of spume would be thrown on both sides of the bow.

The water was alive, breathing, sparkling in the setting sun. Flying fish skittered away from the bow, sailing above the waves and then disappearing back into the dark-blue abyss. Living water. That is what is used for baptism. Living water. Water that gives life. He had never baptized anyone in salt water. Why not? No reason. Rivers and streams were fine…they were rushing to the sea anyway. Same living water.

Paul had heard of the elaborate water systems that the Essenes had built in their community at Wadi Qumran. They had living water in the middle of the desert. Their water did not run to the Great Sea on which he found himself. It ran to the Salt Sea, where nothing could live. He had been thinking about baptism prior to the Charis disaster. For Barnabas and those with whom he had had discussions, baptism signified repentance, a turning from the world and a choosing to live a new life. It was a ritual that distinguished their assembly from all others. The Essenes used ritual bathing often, and the Pharisees used ablutions of the hands before each meal and regular ritual bathing, especially for women. Hence, the symbolism of cleansing was common to many Jews. Even the Greeks cleansed themselves with water before they entered a holy sanctuary. But the baptism of those who followed Iēsoûs was laden with more powerful symbolism. This had been working itself out in his mind these past few months. Now, seeing the breast of the sea gently breathing, feeling its rhythm, its spirit, on the back of his head—more as they mounted the back of a swell and less as they caromed down the front, he knew that baptism was connected mysteriously to life and death. But exactly how?

It is becoming clear. First, we know two things about Iēsoûs, the Christ. He died a horrible death at his own choosing. But, secondly, he was raised by the Father from the dead. Not only was this a verification of his Messiahship, which everyone in the Way believed, but there is a deeper meaning. Death itself was conquered. For the first time. Others, such as Elijah, had been taken into heaven; but no one had ever been killed, laid in a tomb, and raised by God in glory. This was the most obvious sign of the End Times. Death had been conquered. The Greeks have their Eleusinian Mysteries, whose initiates were provided with secret means to overcome death. But no one who has been initiated into those mysteries has demonstrably proved the conquest of death. The followers of Orpheus and those who participate in the rites of Osiris and Attis, all of them are deeply, passionately concerned about life after death. Everyone, it seems, has at the very core of their being, an inexpressible panic about the possibility that when they breathe their last, their experience will terminate. Blackness, lack of sensation, silence: these are intolerable. That is the way God made us, making us ready for the truth about Iēsoûs, the Messiah. He offers us hope against that which otherwise brings the most soul-gripping fear that it is possible to have.

But there is more. And this insight was never whispered to me by any man. It came directly from the Lord. I know it. The Christ did not leave this world after his resurrection. He chose to remain in it, as his assembly. His Spirit was present in the love that is shared among the small number of families who live a common life, waiting his return to bring a consummation of time. He remains in the world, and this is really the Good News.

Finally, baptism is the means that the Way uses to bring new members into the assembly. Hence, believers are baptized into Christ since the assembly is Christ in the world. But what does this mean? It means that those who enter the assembly join with Christ in his death. He turned his back on the selfishness that rules the world. He chose to be exactly what Adam should have been, obedient to the will of the Father. Unquestioningly. Perfectly. He died because he turned his back on the world of sin, of self-aggrandizement, of focusing on the little isolated world of the individual, shriveled self. Instead, he poured himself out as an example of how a human being ought to behave. And the product of this perfect love was his being raised from the dead and his living with us now until the end of time. Hence, when we are baptized, we turn with him from the world, and we enjoy the same fruits of obedience. We rise with him from the dead; we enjoy the unending life that has conquered death. We have what all the pagans only hope for. We have achieved, through Christ, through the assembly, the conquest of the only true enemy of humanity. In baptism, we join him in his death, but even more so, as we arise from the living water, we join him in his resurrection. We are born anew, from death to life.

Oh, what powerful thoughts! They can't be shared with Barnabas yet. While he is a good man, he just does not see what world-shaking truths the Lord has revealed. And to me! Why? I can't ask. And why would He let me become involved in so sordid and mortifying an episode as with Charis? I must admit that Satan tempted me. He almost won. But the Lord protected me from sin, even though I believe some of the brothers actually believe I did sin. Why did you let that happen? Why did you make me suffer? I was doing your will, and she was almost convinced...she simply misunderstood. I can't believe you did that to me! In fact, I am furious with you! I never coveted her! I never led her on! I spoke only of you, being as convincing as I could. You let Satan twist the meaning of love in her mind, but why didn't you warn me? Can't you see I needed you? You want me to share what you have taught me, but you certainly need to be "my shield and my buckler." Oh well, that means I have to find some women who will be able to enter women's quarters without scandal. But how will they be taught? Maybe I can find one who has a good husband; I can teach both of them, without danger, and then she will be able to teach women. But why did you not just tell me that, instead of putting me thorough the disgrace of a trial? I have never been so furious in my life, and I am unable to show it. I keep it bottled up inside me. But somehow, you know my innermost thoughts, even before they become thoughts! But I still want to say what I feel. If you want me, you must never again bring such a thing upon my head! Never. I won't tolerate it. Please. Please.

The sky had turned from orange pink ruby turquoise to inky black, with a carpet of stars winking en masse. Paul ambled back to the starboard side of the deck house, where Barnabas and John Mark had spread out their blankets on the deck. Both were lying on their backs, staring at the heavens in silence. Paul did likewise, and the three men chatted aimlessly, sharing stories of their childhood and laughing about their respective escapades, close calls, and the various and sundry items that make up the sharing of friends. Paul was grateful for the warmth of both John Mark and Barnabas...he didn't know when he fell asleep.

CHAPTER 8

Bringing the Good News to Salamis

THE ARRIVAL OF THE GLORIOUS ruby-orange orb was announced by a fanfare of color on the high cirrus clouds. Early light had disclosed the first shadow of a headland on the horizon, and each rise of the ship shoved that shadow a fraction higher.

"Cleides Islands," Barnabas announced. "We are directly on course. The captain will keep those islands off our starboard bow; then we will see the Carpasian Islands, where a wonderful harbor exists, and behind them, Mount Olympus, near the headlands of Cyprus. In fact, we should see Mount Olympus very soon…if that is not, in fact, the mountain and not the islands."

"Are we doing well, then?" John Mark asked.

"Indeed. I believe the captain thought we would not make Salamis before dark and that we would have to anchor offshore and make harbor tomorrow morning. But with the favorable winds, we just might make port by nightfall."

"That would suit me just fine," John Mark said. "This hard deck is not much of a mattress. I hardly slept at all."

"You are just too used to soft ways," Barnabas said, laughing. "How about you, Paul? Did you sleep?"

"I don't remember when I fell asleep. And I awoke only with the sunlight. But I agree with John Mark. I ache all over from this deck. Look at those sailors. They seem so comfortable, sprawled everywhere."

The men broke their fast with bread and fruit they had brought on the trip and watched Mount Olympus and the eastern tip of Cyprus slowly glide by them throughout the day. Barnabas described the temple of Aphrodite Acraea, located on Mount Olympus. This temple was unusual in that it could not be entered or even seen by women.

True to Barnabas's prediction about schedule, the small ship dropped its sails just outside the city of Arsinoê, just south of Salamis, which served as the harbor for Salamis , since its harbor had recently silted in. They had been traveling west-southwest along the panhandle of Cyprus, and the coastline turned sharply toward the southeast. Both Salamis and Arsinoê were located on this coast. Arsinoê was a smaller city, but it had a natural cove inserted within rocky cliffs. The citizens of the city had constructed a breakwater on the shallow sea bottom in an Lshape that protected the harbor from the south and east winds.

The crewmen furled the sails and broke out oars on each side. They slowly rowed the ship into the harbor and approached the stone dock with a dozen powerful strokes. Then they shipped their oars, and the steersman deftly pivoted the ship until it slowed to a stop a mere four feet from, and parallel to, the quay. The waiting stevedores threw the crew a couple of handlines, and the ship was made secure.

The three debarked with a wave to the captain and made their way northward along the coast road toward Salamis. After a ferry ride across the Pediaeus river, within an hour, they were inside the spacious house of Barnabas's surprised brother, Phidippides. The latter had married into an old Cyprus family that had managed copper and silver mines for the emperor for many generations, and he had increased the family wealth and that of his imperial patron by opening new shafts and expanding the smelting facilities. The mines were at Tamassos, in the center of the island, nearly a three-day journey upstream by barge by way of the Pediaeus River into the broad plain of the interior. Copper, coppersulfate, and cupricoxide were barged down the river. For centuries, the products were shipped from the harbor at the mouth of the river at Salamis, but the cutting of the forests and conversion of the land to large-scale farming had permitted silt to fill the mouth of the river, so ships could no longer enter. Hence, the products of the mines were loaded on oxcarts and brought to Antinoê for shipment to all parts of the world.

Phidippides and his wife, Drusilla, were the perfect host and hostess. Individual slaves were assigned to each of the guests, and shortly after arrival, the three men, joined by Phidippides, found themselves sweating inside the hot-room of the private baths attached to the house. Then, having been scraped clean by strigils (dull-bladed sickle-shaped instruments), they proceeded to the hot bath, then to the tepid bath, and finally to the cold pool. An hour later, they found themselves anointed with fresh olive oil, dressed in clean garments, and reclining in the large triclinium of their host and hostess. In Roman custom, Drusilla joined the men. She was in her early fifties (as was her husband), and her hair was coiffed in what Paul concluded was the most current style in the court of the princeps. Finely wrought gold jewelry hung from a necklace, draping itself over her bosom. She was dressed modestly in a palla and a himation, held together with jewel-encrusted fibulae. Paul noticed that her sandals contained small jewels on the straps.

After an extended dinner expertly prepared by a large culinary staff, the three travelers were assigned individual guest rooms. They all claimed exhaustion from the trip and were quickly asleep.

The next day was the Sabbath. Barnabas asked where the closest house of prayer (*prosuche*) of Jews was located. Phidippides described the location but indicated that he no longer attended any assembly. Barnabas accepted this information without any indication of surprise, although Paul knew that Barnabas was disappointed.

John Mark took to Phidippides in an instant. Paul and Barnabas could see that the young man was impressed with wealth and easily adopted the lifestyle of the rich. He adopted a tone toward the slave assigned to him that mimicked the impersonal and authoritative tone that their master used. He asked endless questions about mining copper, constantly probing for more and more information. To the delight of, Phidippides John Mark hung on every word, remarking often on his brilliance and skill in managing the mines. He asked if they could visit the mines so he could see not only the raw ore coming out of the ground but also the smelting process, wherein the ore was turned into copper. Phidippides agreed, and he invited Paul and Barnabas to accompany them the following week. Indeed, they would continue from Tamassos over the mountains to Paphos, the capital of the province, where Phidippides would make a periodic report to the proconsul, Lucius Sergius Paulus.

On the Sabbath, the three men visited the house of prayer, located in the large home of a wealthy grain merchant named Joachim. About twenty men and women were present, and the three newcomers were made most welcome. Their custom was to spend about an hour in social conversation prior to any scripture readings or prayer. The first item of business when visitors arrived in the assembly was to inquire about their backgrounds. It was not long until they discovered that Paul had studied under Gamaliel. Naturally, he was invited to select a passage from scripture and to comment on it. Paul was perfectly delighted and chose the First Song of the Servant for his reading.

When the time came, everyone crowded into the peristyle courtyard of the house, the men on one side and the women on the other. Servants had brought stone benches, but some had to stand in the colonnaded porches to each side of the garden. Paul unrolled the scroll on a high table located at one end of the garden, located the passage in the scroll and looked up. Then he began, reciting the verses from memory:

Here is my servant whom I uphold,
My chosen one in whom my soul delights.
I have sent my spirit upon him,
He will bring fair judgment to the nations.
He does not cry out or raise his voice,
His voice is not heard in the street;
He does not break the crushed reed
Or snuff the faltering wick.
Faithfully he presents fair judgment;
He will not grow faint, he will not be crushed,
Until he has established fair judgment on the earth,
And the coasts and islands are waiting for his instruction.

Paul looked at the assembled men and began his explanation. "Men and women of Salamis, I bring you Good News! You have probably not heard before that the words of the prophet that we just heard have been fulfilled in our days!"

People looked up, surprised. Frowns appeared on some of the older men's faces. Paul continued, describing briefly the life of Iēsoûs, the marks of his authenticity expressed in his healings and miracles, and even more, his crucifixion and resurrection. People squirmed uneasily; more frowns appeared on the elders' faces.

Paul concluded enthusiastically: *God raised him from the dead as a final, conclusive sign. This is a sign that death is overcome, not only the physical death that we all face, but the moral death of sin. He came into the world as the prophet foretold. We just heard that he would bring judgment to the islands and restore love to our world. He invites us to participate in his life, through baptism into his death and resurrection. Faith in him will produce a new world and will restore all of Israel to the covenant made with our father, Abraham. I invite you, brothers and sisters, to join Barnabas, John Mark, and me in being part of the New Covenant that God has made with his people.*

He sat down, confident that he had done well.

Joachim rose, led the group in prayers, recited the Sh'ema, and dismissed the assembly. No one came up to Paul afterward to offer congratulations; they seemed to avoid him purposely and treated Barnabas and John Mark the same. Within minutes, the three men were alone with Joachim.

"Thank you…" Paul started, but he was interrupted by a frown and a hand held up by the old man.

"Barnabas, I know your brother is a very prominent Jew, despite the fact that he married a goy. So I don't want to offend you, since I will offend Phidippides. But the strange ideas your friend brought to this house are insulting. I don't know what these young intellectuals are trying to do, but saying that the Messiah has come is very, very dangerous. We live with the Romans in peace; they leave us alone. To even say aloud that there is a Messiah who lives and who is looking for followers is treason!"

"And you, young man!" he said to Paul. "We have the right to assemble here because of the goodness of our prince in granting us the right to pray in our traditional way. We live with our Greek neighbors in peace. When you bring treason into our house of prayer, you put all of us at risk. Your remarks might well get back to Sergius Paulus, and then all of us might be arrested and killed! Have you no sense? How can you..." He shook his head in exasperation, at a loss for words, kneading his hands together.

Barnabas took Paul by the elbow and began to lead him out, but Paul resisted. "No, Barnabas, let me answer the old man."

"Paul, it will only make matters worse. Come. Come."

The frustrated Paul acceded to the advice of his patron and left, scowling. John Mark followed, confused. The door slammed behind them. The three trudged back to the house of Phidippides without conversation. Paul was angry that he had not been permitted to engage the old man in debate. He had been forced to retreat from a challenge and had lost considerable honor in the process. Barnabas was distressed because he did not want Phidippides to hear rumors that he and his friends were anti-Roman. But the understanding of a Messiah as one who would restore the kingship of David was too hard to overcome. Maybe if Paul had been sensitive to that issue and had started with kingship and redefined it, they would not have such a problem.

John Mark could not understand why his uncle would not let Paul argue. Even he could have responded, except that the age differential would have been too extreme. If they were to bring the Good News to the rest of the Jews in the world, they were surely not off to a very good start, he thought.

They returned to the house, and after a particularly quiet dinner with only the four men, Barnabas broached the subject.

"Phidippides, some rumors might reach your ears, and even more importantly, might reach the ears of Sergius Paulus. Please let me give you the benefit of hearing the truth from me."

And with that, Barnabas began, starting with the story of Iēsoûs but couching it in terms that minimized the political element of his life, even glossing over the fact that Iēsoûs was crucified. He pointed out that Iēsoûs had died because of an unjust trial at which witnesses had perjured themselves, but he never mentioned the word "crucified."

After almost two hours, he stopped, ending with that day's altercation in the house of prayer.

"Joseph, my brother, even though you are younger, I have always looked up to you for philosophical guidance. I know you follow the way of our fathers more exactly than I do. I have never denied my heritage, but I don't flaunt it in the face of my employers. If you and your friends are interested in introducing novelty into our ancient ways, I urge you to think carefully about the consequences. There is a large population of Sons of Abraham in Salamis, and we live in peace with our neighbors. I ask you not to sow ferment among the brothers. It will do no good to anyone. I will write a letter to Sergius Paulus, send it by special messenger on horse, and when we see him in a week or so, I will let Paul explain to him why he is not preaching treason!"

The three men looked seriously at Phidippides.

"And, if Sergius Paulus thinks it *is* treason, then you, Paul, may offer your head for the rest of us!"

At first, there was silence. Then Phidippides began to laugh.

"Don't worry! I am too important to Sergius Paulus. I have made him so much money that when he returns to Rome, he will remember this two-year period with pleasure. I buy slaves from him at top prices. You know, they only last five or six months in the mines. Fortunately, there is a large enough supply from the conquests of the Roman army that I always have enough to run the mines. He won't upset things just because of a few rumors. But just to be sure, I will take precautionary steps."

It had grown late, so the men said good night and headed for the bedrooms.

CHAPTER 9

Social Inequality

SEVERAL WEEKS PASSED; THE TRIP to the mines had to be delayed several times due to the press of Phidippides' business in Salamis. In the meantime, Paul sought out the *archisynagogos (Synagogue president)* Joachim, and attempted to smooth over the unpleasantness that had resulted from the first meeting. Joachim, however, was adamant. The mere mention of a "Messiah," or of a "kingdom" was, to him, the preaching of sedition. He visualized their community as being embattled by the Greeks, and it was. They were subject to scornful comments on a regular basis for what many people saw as atheism, as they did not participate in the normal city festivals to Aphrodite, and some were honestly convinced that such an insult to the goddess would bring her disfavor to the city. Hence, any excuse to discredit them would be taken advantage of, especially if it were a suggestion of disloyalty to the prince.

On subsequent Sabbaths, the three travelers visited another synagogue but did not attempt to interpret scripture; instead, after two visits, they decided to speak privately with the *archisynagogos* to discuss the Good News. This man, however, could not accept the idea of a resurrection. He quoted Qoheleth: *Everything goes to the same place, everything comes from the dust, everything returns to the dust.* There was no place in his world for the idea of a resurrected person! The three men decided not to return to that synagogue.

Finally, after they had been in Salamis almost four weeks, they began their trip to Tamassos by barge, towed upriver by two yoke of oxen who plodded along the path on the north side of the river. Six bargemen poled the barge out from the bank, so the travel upstream was at the same rate as a slow walk. The barge, however, was fitted out luxuriously with a large deckhouse enclosed with shutters in the stern half and open with chairs for passengers in the forward half, rich carpets on the deck, and a full galley in the forward part of the boat. The enclosed portion of the deckhouse contained six small staterooms.

The journey upriver was a total of ninety miles, even though the distance as the crow flies was only about seventy miles. However, except for a half-hour stop every four hours to change oxen, the barge plodded upstream continuously, even through the night. Hence, it was possible to traverse the entire distance in about two and a half days in unspeakable luxury.

"I have never imagined anything like this in my entire life," John Mark said, further idolizing Phidippides.

The quiet countryside, with fields and orchards as far as the eye could see, framed with mountainous backdrops on both the north and south horizons, drifted by hour upon hour, and servants brought fresh fruit, wine, and full meals upon demand. After nightfall, a musician entertained them on a *kythara*, singing songs of old. Paul, Barnabas and John Mark looked at one another self-consciously when the bard sang a hymn, written in ancient Epic versification, to Aphrodite:

I sing of Cytherea, Cyprus-born,
Who grants all tender gifts to us;
On her alluring face
Are always smiles;
On her allure the flowers dance.
Greetings, guardian goddess of well-built Salamis
And sea-girt Cyprus! Grant us an alluring song!
For I remember thee…and yet another song.

Phidippides took absolutely no offense and enjoyed the well-known song thoroughly, clapping delightedly at its conclusion. His three companions joined politely, sensing the social necessity and inwardly embarrassed that one of their fellow Hebrews would be so enculturated as to acknowledge a goddess.

To what extent can we even say that Phidippides is a Jew?" Paul asked himself. He knew he could never ask aloud, as it would be a deep insult both to him and to Barnabas. Hence, he held his peace, inwardly torn by his Pharisaic training, which demanded an interior assent to and behavior that was congruent with the principles of Jewish faith. The idea of acknowledging another as divine turned his stomach.

In time, Phidippides indicated that perhaps they should retire, and the party departed to their respective staterooms. Soon, the only sound was the padding of bare feet from the bow to the stern of a crew of three pole-men, each of whom placed his pole on the bank at the bow and walked toward the stern at the same speed that the barge moved forward. By the time he got two-thirds of the way astern, another man had firmly placed his pole on the bank at the bow. Paul listened as feet padded rhythmically outside the stateroom, water lapped at the hull, an ox snorted leather harnesses creaked faintly, and then sleep stole upon Paul's soul.

The morning brought the vista of a narrowing valley, the mountains now descending much closer to the river. To their right were carefully tended vineyards, purple grapes hanging in profusion. The mountains ahead and to the left were rugged and rocky, with forest extending up the slopes but thinning out toward the rocky peaks. One mountain stood out, shaped remarkably like a breast.

"What is the name of that mountain?" John Mark asked his host.

"That is Mount Olympus" was the reply.

"I thought that Mount Olympus was to the east and that we passed to the south of it on our voyage to Salamis," John Mark replied.

"You did, you did." Phidippides laughed. "There is a Mount Olympus on the boundary between Thessaly and Macedonia, but we have two on our island. This way, if the gods choose, they can rest on our mountain."

"Uncle Phidippides," John Mark interjected, "how can you speak of 'the gods,' being a Jew?"

Phidippides paused for a moment and collected his thoughts. "John Mark, to be a Jew is to be born a Jew, to be circumcised on the eighth day, to celebrate Passover, to pay the one-half shekel tax, and to pilgrimage to Jerusalem once in your life. That cannot be taken away. However, we live in a large world dominated by those who believe in many gods. To offend their gods is to offend them. Hence, one becomes used to a certain way of life, giving lip service to beings who don't exist, in order to avoid enmity with those who truly do exist. It is accommodation only; it is what one must do to live. But it makes me not one bit less a Jew, just as you are."

Barnabas placed his hand on John Mark's arm when he sensed that the younger man was about to begin an argument, and he responded instead. "We understand, Phidippides. Your position is important for our entire family. We know that you have chosen the course that is best." And with that, the matter dropped, except in the minds of the other three individuals in the silk-draped deckhouse.

The day passed uneventfully, the current increasing as the river narrowed. Bridges over streams entering the river became more common, and the ox team was increased from four to six. The speed seemed to slow down, as the animals pulled the increasingly resistant load. The drovers used their whips to make sure that every ox was pulling its fair share.

As the sun began to drop beneath the mountains to the west, houses began to appear on the shoreline; Phidippides announced that they were on the outskirts of Tamassos and that within a short time, they would be at the dock. A chariot pulled up on the road, and a tall man in an embroidered tunic dismounted, dismissed the driver, and deftly leaped from the bank onto the deck of the barge.

"Greetings, Lycias," Phidippides called out as he rose to greet the visitor.

"Welcome, Master Phidippides," the man responded "I received word of your imminent arrival only an hour ago; did you send a messenger?"

"No, Lycias. No need to waste the effort. I figured you would hear soon enough." And with that, the two men retired to the bow of the barge to talk privately.

They tied up at a stone dock to which were tied five barges of identical size, but they were freighters and had no deck structures. These were in various stages of loading, mostly with dull copper-colored ingots stacked one atop the other in the center of each barge. Next to the dock were piles of these ingots, from which stevedores loaded wheelbarrow after wheelbarrow and ran them up the gangplanks and onto the barges.

Behind the stockpiles of ingots were three large beehive shaped furnaces spewing out smoke, and an antpile of sweating, cursing men clad only in loincloths, performing what appeared to be a chaotic dance around and before the four-foot-wide arched entrance to the furnace. But out of this apparent chaos regularly appeared a smoking iron kettle withdrawn on a long iron pole, which, as it was being tipped, produced a sparking copper stream as it was poured into a cast-iron mold.

What was most apparent, however, was the odor. Although the wind was from the east, the entire area stank unbelievably. Remarkably, no one seemed to mind it; everyone went about his business apparently unfazed by the rotten egg stench.

"Where does the smell come from?" John Mark asked Phidippides when they had tied up and Lycias had departed.

"From the furnaces," Phidippides explained. "You always have that odor when copper is smelted. It comes from the burning of part of the rock that we don't need."

Phidippides led the three off the barge. They proceeded to walk down the length of the dock and turned right down a narrow street lined with three-story apartment buildings constructed out of grimy, yellow-stained sandstone. The stench was almost intolerable from that which spewed out of the furnaces and that which exuded from the buildings, of unwashed bodies, and of sewage in the street.

"It is a little unpleasant until we get outside the slave quarters," Phidippides said. "Of course, almost everyone in this town is a slave. Everyone at this end of the town works in the smelter. Over there," he pointed to several massive holes in the side of a hill ahead "are the mines. The miners live next to the entrances in those apartments."

When they trudged up the hill, the stench began to lessen. The higher they got, the more they could see the yellow swath of smoke wafting westward over the town below. After passing another block of apartments, from which the same people-stench exuded, they arrived at a walled enclosure, the door of which opened without Phidippides having to announce himself. They entered a spacious garden, and a set of shallow-riser, broad-treaded marble steps led to a colonnaded entrance to the main house. As they reached the top of the steps, which were manned by servants eager to greet the master, Paul turned and looked over his shoulder. There, a thousand feet away, gaped four huge holes in the side of the opposite hill, into which and out of which streamed ranks of sweaty men in loincloths pushing or pulling wheeled carts, and dumping the blue rocks into a brick sluice that ran down the side of the hill toward the town. There was a never-ending stream of rocks being poured down the hill, and a never-ending stream of men trudging in and out of the black maws.

At dinner, taken in a large, high-ceilinged triclinium with colonnaded arches, at one end open to a vista down the river and at the other end open to a peristyle garden, Paul asked about the lives of the slaves.

"Well, the mine-slaves don't last too long. They work from daylight to dark, and we are always losing some to cave-ins and rock-falls. I have the overseers rotate their jobs so that on one day a man will be at the face of the mine ripping out the ore with a pick and for the next three days loading and wheeling the ore out. That gives them a little sun. If they don't get sun, they tend to die quicker."

"What about food?"

"Oh, we have quite a few female slaves who cook for everyone. They get one hot meal a day, after work, and some bread and fruit in the morning. We have three miners' apartment buildings, with about two hundred miners in each. There is a central kitchen, a dining room, and about fifty sleeping rooms in each."

"Where do they come from?"

"Most of them from across the Rhine and along the Danube. The army is always skirmishing there, and that gives us a steady supply. We lose about six men a day and have to replace them, or we won't be able to ship our quota of finished copper."

"It seems like a difficult life."

"But at least it is 'life.' The alternative is to be killed on the spot on the battlefield. *Better the slave of a poor man than a rich man in Hades,* Phidippides said, quoting roughly from the store of commonly known wisdom.

"And they have death, and only death, to look forward to," Paul said aloud, to no one in particular. "Constant, backbreaking labor, then death."

"Well, what else can a slave expect?" Phidippides asked, mildly surprised at the course of questioning.

"One of the things we expect, as followers of the Way, is that after death we will be united with the Lord Iēsoûs and that we will then be perfectly happy and fulfilled. This offers us, though we be slaves of Iēsoûs Christ, a life of hope and eager expectation."

"I thought your Iēsoûs Christ was going to return and bring his kingdom."

"He will, but at the end of time, which we believe to be soon. In the meantime, if one is baptized into his body, then when one dies, one is united with him at death. That is a message that would give hope to those miners."

"Perhaps," Phidippides said after a moment's hesitation. "But perhaps not. Maybe they would just begin to kill themselves to achieve this happy state in advance of their natural death. And what would I do for workmen then? No, slaves should not be part of your 'Way.'"

Barnabas looked at Paul, a slight frown on his face, and Paul knew to drop the subject.

Later that night, Paul lay in his room, a window open to the east, with a cool breeze wafting in and not a hint of odor from the furnaces roaring below and to the west. He thought of the slaves, utterly without hope, utterly lost in a miserable life of drudgery without letup. Paul wanted to visit them, to tell them of the Lord Iēsoûs, who died for them as well as for the people of Israel. They needed to hear; they would grasp the hope offered in a second. They would not be afraid, like those in the synagogues of Salamis. Those to whom he had been presenting the remarkable message of Iēsoûs the Christ seemed to be unaware of their need for the message. So they ignored it. They chose to be blind, not to open their eyes. But those poor people down the hill, who were cramped together in squalor, unable ever to bathe or have a day of rest, who were worked until they dropped and then had no hope for what awaited them after death; they would grasp this offer of succor in a second! They had a desperate need for hope, those poor, benighted German and Dacian slaves. Of course, they probably didn't speak much Greek, only enough to receive instructions about mining. Maybe, just maybe, it was people like those slaves who needed the Good News even more than those in the synagogues. Perhaps...perhaps. Then sleep.

CHAPTER 10

Iēsoûs bar Elymas

AFTER A WEEK, PHIDIPPIDES ANNOUNCED that his business was complete and that they would now travel to Paphos, to report to Sergius Paulus. The next morning, they would walk with pack animals to the town of Lemnia, which they would reach before nightfall. There they would board a barge and float down the Aiela River northbound to the port city of Soli, which had an excellent harbor. There they would find a coastal merchant vessel for the trip west along the north coast and then go around Acamas Promontory and south-southeast to Paphos. Phidippides indicated that if winds remained out of the east, they would have a good chance of making Paphos in one full day. Captains would often leave in late afternoon; round Acamas Promontory at night, since it had an excellent lighthouse; and arrive at Paphos before the next nightfall.

As it occurred, they got to Soli on the first day, but the weather changed, and the winds blew strongly from the southwest. So they remained in Soli, having found a vessel waiting to sail when the weather changed. In the meantime, they wandered around the town, noticing the two large temples in the agora, one to Aphrodite and one to Isis.

Paul asked Phidippides how prevalent worship of Isis was in Cyprus, and he indicated that this was the largest temple on the island dedicated to this goddess, but there were many more that were erected about one hundred fifty years ago, when the Ptolemies of Egypt controlled the island. And while the trade of Cypriot merchants was more oriented toward Cilicia and Syria, they still had a large number of ships that plied the sea lanes to Alexandria, which was only three days distant from Paphos with favorable winds.

"What is it that attracts people to the worship of Isis?"

"I think it is primarily the ancient connection of Isis with the afterlife. While she is a protectress of those who sail the seas, she also protects those who cross the river Styx and promises her initiates their souls will not suffer eternal death."

"Interesting," said Paul.

They remained in Soli for four more days, and finally the wind shifted back to the northeast, and their ship left. The next day, they arrived in the large harbor of Paphos, which was crowded with ships of all kinds, including a Roman trireme of ninety oars. The harbor was crowded since many of the ships had been loaded and were ready for departure for points west but were stranded by the ill winds of the past week. Only now were they finally getting underway, and the outbound traffic was very heavy.

The next day, the four men found themselves in the triclinium of Lucius Sergius Paulus, the proconsul of the island. A luscious meal had been set for nine diners, one of whom was the captain of the trireme and another a Jewish sophist from Alexandria who was on the staff of the proconsul.

During the dinner, this sophist, whose name was Iēsoûs bar Elymas, entertained the guests with remarkable feats of making coins appear and disappear before their very eyes. Sometimes he could make a coin duplicate itself and then each of the duplicates duplicate itself. He claimed that he could do that just as easily with a million denarii as he did with two! However, he was not interested in money, only truth and healing; hence, he said he would never stoop to duplicating a fortune in a split second.

In addition, he took a perfectly empty black bag; turned it inside out, demonstrating its emptiness and, before everyone's eyes, first pulled out a single colored silk scarf. Then he replaced it, made it disappear, and next pulled out one of another color. Then one of a still different color... and he did the same thing four more times! He then replaced them, caused them to disappear into thin air, turned the bag inside out again to prove that it was empty, and proceeded to pull the same number of scarves out of the bag, but this time they were all knotted together!

Paul was absolutely astonished, as was everyone else. Bar Iēsoûs claimed the power came from the ancient Egyptian gods, under whose tutelage he learned this remarkable magic.

Paul asked what his primary duties were for the proconsul.

"I prophesy harvests, primarily. I am able to see into the future, so I tell the proconsul how much grain and oil and wine he will be able to export three to six months in advance. Further, I drive out demons from those possessed, provide love potions or amulets for those desiring a particular woman, and create phylacteries to protect people from any and all demons, sickness and suffering. Among other things…"

"Indeed, I myself wear one," said Sergius Paulus, overhearing the question and response. "Here it is." And with that he reached inside his tunic and brought out what appeared to be a necklace of silver but which upon closer examination proved to be an image of a snake with its tail in its mouth, with a large number of inscriptions on its body.

"Before bar Iēsoûs made this for me and placed it on me with the proper prayers, I could not sleep at night. Demons bothered me and made me restless. Now I sleep like a baby. No demon has bothered me since he placed this around my neck."

"By whose power do you perform such feats?" Paul asked.

"There, my new friend, is what it took me twenty years to learn. First, the world is populated by many, many *daimones*, some of whom work for the good of good people and some of whom are bent on their destruction. This world is a battlefield in which the evil *daimones* are forever on the prowl to bring a good person to destruction. However, if one knows the correct formula and the correct *daimon* to address, it is possible to thwart these evil ones and permit the good *daimones* to triumph. My training, twenty years of it, lets me design just the correct formula, write it perfectly, chant it without error, and hence bring the correct good *daimon* to achieve the desired results."

"And you can influence the evil *daimones* as well?"

"Of course I have the power. I know their names, how to summon them, and how to cause them to perform their evil work in the world. Hence, for instance, I can strike a man blind in mere seconds, and I can determine just how long he will be blind."

"No!" exclaimed Paul. "Can you really?"

"Of course; but I am far too good a person to actually do that. I might do it to one of our proconsul's enemies, but never except in the direst of necessity."

"It must take a very long time to conjure up the evil *daimon* who causes blindness," Paul continued. "Must it come from Alexandria?"

Bar Iēsoûs looked at Paul, and a scowl developed on his face. "I know you are a guest of the proconsul, my patron, so I will not consider your questions to be affront to my skill," he said.

"Please, please do not take offense," Paul said with apparent contrition. "I was amazed at your power to duplicate money. But I have faith in a God that I believe to be more powerful than your *daimon* who brings blindness. In fact, I do not believe that your *daimon* of blindness can touch me, so well am I protected!"

"What? You challenge me? You put me to the test?" he shouted.

"Yes," Paul said quietly. "I have been sent to the world by Iēsoûs the Christ; and his Father, who created the world, protects me in every matter. He will protect me from your *daimon*. If you have any power, then strike me blind now. This instant. Do it! DO IT!" Paul shouted.

"This would be an improper use of my vast power, to strike blind a helpless and ignorant traveler."

"Then you can't strike me blind?"

"I can, but I choose not to. It is too severe a punishment for one who has probably been drinking too much wine, far from home, and who has challenged one whom he really does not know sufficiently well." Beads of sweat appeared on the man's forehead.

"Before the proconsul himself," Paul said, standing up and walking to the center of the room, "and before all these men, I release you from any guilt should your *daimon* be successful in striking me blind. I accept what you call a 'severe punishment,' if you can do it. Now, I challenge you one last time. STRIKE ME BLIND! NOW!" He stood there defiantly.

Bar Iēsoûs quickly jumped to his feet, grasped a glass of wine, and threw it in Paul's face. Paul wiped the liquid from his face and continued staring at the man, now quivering with anger.

"You fraud. You impostor. The God of your fathers, whom you have abandoned, protects me from all your puny *daimones*. He has sent his Son, Iēsoûs the Christ, whom I announce, and he has protected me from all the evil that you can conjure up."

"You have not heard the last from me! You have made the wrong man your enemy! You will pay for this!" And with that, bar Iēsoûs stormed out of the dining room.

"Sergius, I…I…I apologize," stuttered Phidippides. "I had no idea that this friend of my brother, whom I hardly know, would behave in such…"

"Phidippides, nonsense! It was wonderful! Your young friend is the first person I have ever seen stand up to that blowhard! It took courage and enormous confidence in his god. I would never have chanced it! To risk so much for such a small victory! Why, why would you take such a chance?" he asked Paul. "Come, recline next to me and tell me."

"You, Sergius Paulus, being a man of power, are impressed by power. I could see that. By challenging bar Iēsoûs, I could demonstrate to you that the God of Israel, who sent his Son to announce victory over death, is vastly more powerful. This is the God to whom you and your family ought to turn."

So for the rest of the evening, the proconsul and Paul spoke of Adam, of Abraham, of Moses and the prophets, and of the fulfillment of the prophecies in Iēsoûs. He emphasized his death and resurrection and his promised return; he carefully distinguished between political kingship and the Kingdom of God, which would be made manifest after the End Time. He used exquisite care to avoid the problem he had run into in Salamis.

For two days after the dinner, Paul and Sergius Paulus spent the most of their time together. Paul remained in the proconsul's house. One night the proconsul summoned him because he had certain questions. Paul visited him, but then the proconsul complained that having cast off the amulet made by bar Iēsoûs, he was having trouble sleeping again. Paul laughed and said that it was no problem at all. And with that, he laid his hands upon the proconsul's head, lifted his eyes to heaven, prayed for a few moments, and then traced the sign of the cross on the man's forehead.

"That will permit you to sleep with ease, my friend, for the rest of your life. You need no amulet. The angels of the Father will descend and protect you from all evil *daimones*. Good night."

The proconsul quickly fell into a deep sleep.

CHAPTER 11

Baptism as Politics

THREE DAYS LATER, PAUL SHOWED up at the inn where Phidippides had rented the entire second floor for himself and his three guests. Phidippides' work was almost complete, and he had sent a messenger to Paul advising that they must soon leave. Barnabas, on the second floor, was completing the packing of his traveling bag. He greeted Paul warmly.

"We have not talked since before the dinner. I must confess that you frightened me out of my wits! I had no idea how that confrontation would work out! I must say, I thought you were out of your mind. But you were successful!"

"God was successful," Paul said, not enthusiastically.

"I agree," said Barnabas. "Now, what is happening? Phidippides said that the proconsul canceled all his appointments for three days, and his staff said that he spent every minute with you! Has he received the Word of God?"

"That is what I came here to discuss with you, Barnabas. He desires baptism."

"Wonderful! Have you made plans to baptize him?"

"No. That is why I am here."

"I don't understand…"

"You see, he told me that he has been initiated into the Eleusinian Mysteries, into the Rites of Isis, and has reached the fifth level, that of Persian in the cult of Mithras. He sees baptism as just one more initiation into another mystery cult, one in which at the End Time he will be protected from the evils that befall the rest of mankind."

"That is all true."

"But don't you see, he looks upon this as an *individual* action. There is no assembly. There is no community. And he has no interest in forming a community around him. He simply wants baptism. He will acknowledge Iēsoûs as Lord, and then both we and he move on…he having been initiated into one more mystery, and we going to other places. But that won't work! There must be an assembly of those who will protect one another from the sin that roams the world. It is not right to baptize one person, no matter how much he desires it! We must baptize him into Christ and for that, there must be a community into which he is to be baptized!"

At that point, John Mark entered the room. He reiterated everything that Barnabas had said, how he had been deathly afraid of the consequences when Paul had stood up to the magus and equally elated when Paul had driven him from the field. Then Paul repeated exactly what he had told Barnabas.

"I understand your concern, Paul, but you must baptize Sergius Paulus. After all you have done, you can't refuse to baptize him! That would be an enormous insult. It would make him an eternal enemy of the Way! Here you demonstrate the power of God before him, instruct him in the Way of the Lord, and then refuse to baptize him? Impossible!"

"I just can't. It is wrong. I can't."

"Then I will," Barnabas said. "It is clear that as the leader of this group of 'apostles' sent from Antioch, it is both my decision and my right to perform the baptism. How do you start an assembly without baptizing someone first?"

"But that 'first' must be willing to bring others into the assembly; his entire household must be baptized, as a minimum. Since he is unwilling to do that, claiming he hasn't the time to wait for everyone else to hear about and accept Iēsoûs as the Messiah, his faith will wither and die. No one can survive without a community. I grieve for him, one chosen, and with such promise, but doomed to destruction!"

"Let the Lord decide if he is destroyed! The Lord has placed him in our hands, thanks to the grace he gave you to say what you did. We must not lose the chance to have the proconsul of the island as a member of the Way!"

And with that, the three men returned to the home of the proconsul, were admitted without any hesitation, and within the hour, Sergius Paulus was baptized in the shallow reflecting pool in the center of his peristyle garden. Immediately after the ceremony, he thanked the three, embraced them, and told them that he now had to return to the business of governing the island. Anything they needed in Cyprus was theirs for the asking. And anytime they needed to see him, they could simply announce themselves at the door…but for now, he was very busy, thank you, and must take his leave. And with that he disappeared into his private quarters, and two servants ushered the three men out into the street.

"Now what?" John Mark asked aloud as the door closed behind them.

"Phidippides is going back to Salamis tomorrow," Barnabas said. "He said we could return with him if we wanted."

"There is nothing for us in Salamis," Paul said.

At that moment, Phidippides entered, and his greetings to Paul were effusive. "I understand that Sergius Paulus has become a Jew! Congratulations, Paul! But he said that we could meet this evening to conclude our business; how can he engage in business if you have just circumcised him?"

"He wasn't circumcised; he was baptized," Barnabas said.

"But that does not make him a Jew," Phidippides responded in a noncombative tone.

"It is too difficult to explain in the time we have, brother," said Barnabas. "But believe me, he is now a follower of the Way, part of the New Covenant."

"Well, that pleases me, since I am indirectly responsible for his good fortune. He will not forget that."

"Would you like to hear more about Iēsoûs, Uncle Phidippides?" John Mark asked. "Then, whenever you see Sergius Paulus, you could point out that you, too, are part of the Way."

"Don't joke like that," Paul said harshly.

"What do you mean, 'joke'?" said John Mark.

"One does not follow Iēsoûs in order to do more business."

"Of course not, but it would not hurt things…"

"Barnabas, I owe a great deal to your nephew; indeed, my honor is intact because of him. And I don't forget that. But this kind of discussion should never be occurring! You must correct him, since I am too much in his debt to do so!" And with that, Paul stalked out the door.

"He'll cool off," Barnabas said. "And while your heart was certainly in the right place, and while there is no one who would like to see my own brother as part of the Way more than I would, he and I have already decided that I would not attempt to change his way of life. I did not mention it to you or to Paul, but it is agreed. Thank you, John Mark, for doing what you felt was correct."

"Will you return to Salamis with me?" Phidippides asked Barnabas.

"No, but I am not sure where we should go. It is too early to return to Antioch. Perhaps we could visit Cilicia or Pamphylia. There might be some there who would be open to hearing the Good News that we bring."

"I have a good friend in Perga," said Phidippides. "He has purchased many shiploads of copper from me; he is a Jew, but he is more like you than like me, if you know what I mean. His name is Tychicus, and he knows the scriptures well. He has a large family, at least five sons and four or five daughters; I will give you a letter of recommendation, and he will show you hospitality.

"Further, I need to have someone make contact with the person near Iconium who handles copper mining and smelting there. Sergius Paulus has instructed me to attempt to have the Iconium copper price increased by one or two tenths. In addition to the letter of introduction, I will provide you with an authorization to negotiate on my behalf.

Barnabas frowned and dropped his eyes. "I don't know if we can pursue both business and spreading the Good News."

"Barnabas, you must recognize that it costs something to engage in this activity of yours. Someone has to provide cash for it. I can assure you that I will provide a goodwill donation to you equal to one-tenth of the increase in copper prices from Galatia and Lycaonia. I will advance you twelve aurii, which should provide for both of you for up to a year. Further, you are Paul's patron. I suggest you simply advise Paul of our arrangement. Traveling costs money. And if you provide for his support, he should shout your praises from the rooftops, not object in any way. In fact, I believe there are some mines close to Iconium where Paul and you may be able to provide the miners your 'Good News,' which I know Paul wanted to do when we were at our mines. And while I don't give a fig for your new lifestyle, I can't do anything for my little brother except try to help you do what you want to do."

"That will be fine. We will go to Perga."

"Let's go down to the harbor and ask about a ship. You will have to wait for a south wind. It is a good two days' sail across open water if you have favorable winds. And we should be getting more south winds now that it is getting close to summer."

Three men headed for the harbor; Paul, sitting in a small tavern down the street and sipping a cup of well-watered wine, saw them leave. He had regretted his remark as soon as he made it, but John Mark was getting under his skin. Instead of becoming more deeply dedicated to the Way, he seemed to be more impressed with the luxurious life that they had led while in the company of Phidippides, and the very idea of using the Way as a part of business simply enraged him.

Oh well, he is young…and I owe him. I must control myself. I must show my love for him and not be tempted by Satan to treat him as the world does. I must see him as a brother, as a member of Christ. Perhaps God is reminding me that while I had extreme confidence in him before the magus, I must not become conceited. Ah, what weakness I have within myself! Left to my own designs, I fall apart! Jumping on the poor young man! Lord, help me!

He got up and ran to catch up. They seemed to be heading for the harbor, and he was ready for anything now.

Part II

CHAPTER 1

South of Attalia

The Storm

FOR A DAY AND A half, they had run before a stiff south wind from Paphos; but it had shifted gradually to the west, and now with lowering clouds and approaching rain squalls, the captain lowered the sails and put out a large sea-anchor from the stern. It was an X-shaped device with heavy leather stretched over the frame. It had large wooden floats at the top of the X and weights at the bottom. It rode just beneath the now-frothy surface, and by dragging it, the boat would drift less before the offshore wind. The sea had become gray and rough with spume being blown off the tops of the whitecaps.

"Another two hours and we probably would have made the harbor," Paul commented, the hills behind Attalia disappearing in the rain squalls. "But we are in for a blow now!"

The crew was battening down everything on the ship; they knew what was coming.

"If you want to go below into the hold, you may do so," the captain said to the three men. "You won't get as wet as up here, and you won't get blown overboard." He handed them a small clay pot with four small circles of isinglass inset in the sides and an open top with a wire hanger. A small candle was lit inside.

"Let's go," John Mark said.

The others agreed, and the three men navigated unsteadily across the heaving deck to the small hatch. They dropped down among the casks below, and immediately the hatch was shut. Paul heard a bolt slide through a hasp, and he pushed up on the hatch. It wouldn't budge. He found a hook in the deck above and hung the clay lantern, which gave off a dim, yellow glow.

"Well, we won't get wet…unless this ship sinks…in which case we go with it to the bottom," John Mark said.

"Have no fear," Paul said firmly. "We are not bouncing to and fro, from Antioch to Salamis to Paphos and now to Perga, because of our desires. Our course is being guided by God. It is he who desires that we accomplish the work assigned us. And until that work is complete, he will not let us perish."

"What do you think is the work that is assigned us?" John Mark asked.

"Clearly, it is to proclaim that Iēsoûs is Lord," Paul said without hesitation.

"To whom?"

"To our brothers and sisters in the Diaspora."

"And what if they don't listen, like in Salamis?" John Mark asked.

"Then we proclaim Him to the Gentiles."

"Like Sergius Paulus?"

"Exactly, except we would have insisted on a community, not a single individual."

"And when they accept Iēsoûs, as we have, as the Anointed One of God, then we invite them to circumcision?"

Paul hesitated.

"John Mark, maybe we can discuss this later," Barnabas said, putting his hand on the younger man's shoulder.

"Uncle Barnabas," the youth said, shaking off the older man's hand, "you know how I feel about this. I have been holding my anger in check for a week now. I would like to have Paul answer my question."

"We invite him or her to baptism," Paul said firmly.

"And then circumcision?"

"No. Not necessarily. There may be times when it will be proper to ask for circumcision, but not every time."

"Why? How else can someone become part of the people of Israel? God gave us laws about this! He did not *suggest* it and leave it to our discretion." John Mark's voice was dripping in sarcasm. "Clearly you remember, Paul, what is written: *If an alien who resides with you wants to celebrate the Passover of the Lord, all his males shall be circumcised; then he may draw near to celebrate it; he shall be regarded as a native of the land. But no uncircumcised person shall eat of it; there shall be one law for the native and for the alien who resides among you.* Paul said, "What about the circumcised person who does not care a whit for the Law, or for God? What about the majority of our people, the peasants and people of the land who do nothing to draw near to the Law? Are they, because they are circumcised, part of the 'People of God'?"

"They are just the people Iēsoûs came to save!" Mark said heatedly. "They are the people to whom we must proclaim the Good News! Then we don't have the problem of circumcision!"

"But it is also written, *Circumcise the foreskin of your heart!* And again, *'God will circumcise your heart and the heart of your descendants, so that you will love the Lord your God with all your heart and all your soul, in order that you may live.* God is telling us that it is not a physical operation that brings one into the People of God; it is the love of God. This is what Iēsoûs the Christ taught. And if we proclaim that He is Lord, that He will return, that He is the means to our salvation, then the physical operation means nothing!"

"Then you think that baptism makes a Gentile a Jew?"

"I don't care whether he or she is Gentile or Jew! I only care if he or she believes that Iēsoûs is Lord."

"Then you would have these baptized people celebrate Passover with us? You reject the Law of Moses!"

"No, I don't reject the Law of Moses! I believe the Law of Moses has been expanded, has had certain limits removed by the death and resurrection of Iēsoûs. We have a New Covenant, a new way of looking at the Law. It no longer restrains, it enables us to…"

"NONSENSE!" John Mark shouted.

"Peace, peace," Barnabas said, placing his hands on the shoulders of the two men, who were by now swaying, braced, almost nose to nose. "This storm is getting worse; I am beginning to feel sick. I am not sure that we will survive, and you two are arguing! Is that any way for two brothers of Iēsoûs to behave? Both of you, both of you, calm down. Beg God for forgiveness for the harshness in your hearts!"

"I...I'm sorry," John Mark said.

Paul waved it off, not responding. He made his way over a few amphorae to a place where he could lie down. Water was dripping through the deck, and the ship was creaking and groaning from the storm above. Barnabas tried to sit on the amphorae but could not get comfortable; John Mark just stood there in the small open area beneath the hatch, near the lantern. The human silence was broken only by the coughing and gagging of Barnabas as the sea got the better of him.

CHAPTER 2
No Reconciliation

Two days later, the seas had subsided, the wind shifted to a gentle south-east breeze, and the captain brought in the sea anchor and raised the sails. He headed northwest, taking a bearing from the sun, unsure where he was, and after another half day, hills appeared on the horizon. The ship made for the coast, and when it was within a couple miles, it began to run to the northwest, parallel to the coast.

"I know where we are," the captain announced loudly after about an hour's run. "We will see the city of Side in a couple hours. The temple to Athena will be visible. We will pull into the Melas River for the night, just this side of Side, where there is a mooring place, and will secure fresh water. Then it will be only a day's run to Attalia. Then it's about ten miles to Perga."

Everyone was relieved. The problem with a multiday storm was that it was impossible to tell where one was after the blow. There was no telling how far one had been blown, despite the drag of the sea anchor. However, that which distinguished good captains from others was their ability to guess their location. Then, when a favorable wind returned, to pick a course that would bring them to the original destination. They also knew the shape and direction of each segment of coast on the Mediterranean, so within a short time of catching sight of the shore, the captain would know exactly where he was, based on the direction of the shoreline and the shape of the hills.

John Mark and Paul had hardly spoken since their argument; Barnabas attempted to mediate the rift that had grown up between them, but without success. In fact, the older man saw that they had become intractable. John Mark had insisted that any Gentile who was to be baptized also had to be circumcised. Paul insisted that circumcision was optional and inessential. He did not deny that in some cases it might be important. But he denied that it was a condition for becoming part of the People of God.

Hence, when the ship pulled into the harbor just east of the city of Side, Barnabas was not surprised when John Mark said that he would be leaving the ship either here, in Attalia, or wherever he could book passage back to Antioch. John Mark spent the day in Side and returned sullen in the late afternoon.

Barnabas initially asked Paul to speak to the young man and urge him to remain. But Paul would have nothing of that. "If he wants to leave, let him," Paul responded.

Hence, since there was no ship that was leaving that anchorage anytime soon for the area near Antioch, John Mark's departure was delayed while the ship made excellent time to the Attalia harbor and the captain looked for a mooring spot along the warehouse-lined wharf. John Mark isolated himself above the prow of the ship and avoided contact with Paul.

In the meantime, Barnabas spent a couple hours with the captain inquiring about the geography between the harbor at Attalia and the city of Perga. After the conference Barnabas reported what he had learned.

"That is the Catarrhactes River on the left," Barnabas announced. And it's not navigable except for small boats. However, a road follows the river up through the mountains to Perga; that is the way Alexander the Great marched into the interior."

Paul, however, was in no mood for a travelogue. He worried that his intractability regarding John Mark was shortsighted. Maybe it would be best to attempt a reconciliation. After all, the Lord insisted that his disciples love one another, not that they necessarily agree on all issues. What harm could come? For the many years that Jews had been living in the Gentile world, here in Asia, in Parthia, in Egypt, and in Babylonia, those who desired to convert to Judaism were required to be circumcised. Maybe, just maybe, he had been too liberal with Sergius Paulus…

At that very point in his thoughts, John Mark came up to him. Before Paul could say anything, the young man said, "I regret that Satan has made you so obstinate. It may have been better for us if you had remained our persecutor, for you will be the downfall of many."

Paul was stunned, and for a moment had no response.

"I leave you now, Paul," John Mark said, "with sadness and regret. I shall return to Antioch to continue to spread the Good News of Iēsoûs the Messiah to all the Jews and to invite the Gentiles to join us in the worship of the One God."

"Suit yourself," was all that Paul could think of saying.

Within an hour the ship was made fast to the wharf a gangplank thrown down, and John Mark was off the ship, his bag slung over his shoulder, without a glance back.

Paul stood by the rail and watched the young man disappear until Barnabas came up to him and clapped him on the shoulder.

That night Paul and Barnabas found a tavern on the wharf where they could purchase food for the trip to Perge, slept on the ship, and at first light both were awakened by the dockworkers swarming over the ship to unload the cargo.

Within minutes, Barnabas greeted Paul with an embrace and a smile. "Let's go, my friend. Let us find Tychicus in Perge. Hopefully he can at least provide us with a soft mattress and a bed that is not moving."

"May the Spirit of our Lord guide us," prayed Paul as he slung his bag over his shoulder.

CHAPTER 3

Lucky Tychicus

THAT EVENING, THEY ENTERED PERGA through a magnificent fortified gate
flanked by two massive round towers that communicated an unmistakable impregnability. They found themselves on a wide paved street
crowded with merchants, citizens, children, and pack animals. They
passed a new colonnaded gymnasium, dedicated to the Emperor
Claudius, with a greater-than-life-size statue of him clothed as the god
Heracles, a massive club resting on the ground and grasped by his left
hand, his right hand extended upward in a gesture of peace. The skyline
was dominated by a spectacular classic temple to Artemis at the top of
a central hill at the end of the main street. Adjacent to the temple they
soon entered the agora and, after a series of questions, were directed
to the area next to the marketplace that housed the offices of various
exporters and importers. There was a wide courtyard, surrounded
on three sides by a colonnade, with a shaded walkway onto which the
offices of various shipping businesses opened. Each business had its
name or symbol in mosaic on the floor of the stoa in front of the open
double doors that gave access to that business. Barnabas was told to
look for the word, *Kuprothen* on the floor, indicating the business of one
who imported goods *From Cyprus*. The fifth shop had that inscription,
beneath a ship's form blown by a depiction of the *South Wind*. Barnabas
and Paul walked inside. A young man was sitting in the corner, writing
on a papyrus scroll. He looked up and offered a cheery greeting.

"Is this the business of Tychicus?" Barnabas asked.

"It is, sir. May I help you?"

"My name is Barnabas, and I am sent by my brother, Phidippides of Salamis." He proffered a small sealed scroll, which the youth took and disappeared through a door in the rear of the room. In a few moments, a rotund, balding man in a dirty tunic smiled into the room. The broad grin displayed a gap where his long-lost two front teeth had once been.

"Greetings, greetings, to the brother of my distinguished friend Phidippides! You are welcome, you are welcome indeed. Come in, come in." And with that he dragged Barnabas through the door into the small atrium of a house with a tiny peristyle garden and three rooms opening off the garden.

"What news do you bring from Cyprus? And who is this?" he asked.

"My brother is well and sends his best," Barnabas said. "And this is my companion, Paul of Tarsus."

Tychicus nodded his welcome warmly. Paul was struck by the remarkably outgoing character of this roly-poly individual, who ushered them graciously toward the garden and clapped loudly for a slave. A young woman appeared and, recognizing guests, disappeared immediately into one of the doorways, only to reappear moments later with a large bowl, a decorated ewer of water, and two linen towels. Paul appreciated the Jewish formality of being offered the opportunity of cleansing one's hands and face. After that was complete, the woman knelt down and used the balance of the water to wash their feet.

The three then sat in the garden, and their host inquired about their trip, knowing that they had experienced a rough trip from the weather he had noticed during the past week. "The man two doors down had a ship from Caesarea that he had been expecting; it appears that it went down in the same storm. Two survivors from the crew arrived only hours before you did! You were fortunate."

"Thanks be to God," Paul said.

"Amen," said Tychicus.

The young woman returned with goblets of wine and some small, hot, sweet cakes that she offered to the guests. Paul thought it remarkable that she could have produced such cakes without notice, although it must not be uncommon for this household to have unannounced guests.

For the next half hour or so, the three men chatted amiably.

"Now, may I ask, are you also in the copper business, like your brother?" Tychicus asked.

"No, Tychicus. We visit your city prompted by God to bring everyone the Good News that the Anointed One, foretold by the prophets, has indeed visited us. We need to share this…"

"You mean *Iēsoûs*, the Christ?" Tychicus asked, wide eyed.

Now it was Paul's and Barnabas's turn to be shocked.

"The same!" Paul blurted out.

"I was baptized in his name a year ago."

"By whom?" Barnabas asked.

"By Sylvanus, from Jerusalem," Tychicus responded.

Barnabas erupted in laughter. "Sylvanus! I know him well! How does he look?"

"He looks wonderful! Big and blustery, but he's getting quite a bit of gray in his beard!"

"And why in the world would a dealer in Arabian incense come to Perga?" Barnabas asked.

"He came to purchase a quantity of aromatic compounds from Selge, a city north and east of here in the Taurus Mountains. These are produced from some trees in their area and are used exactly as frankincense is used in Jerusalem, but their cost is a mere fraction of the Arabian."

"And…"

"Well, I handle copper shipments to Selge and a number of other cities in the mountains, even to Pisidian Antioch. In fact, I have a caravan returning once a month. I have to bring back to Perga whatever each city produces, and Selge produces crystals from the dried seeds that smell great when they burn."

"Amazing!" Barnabas was all grins. "You've never met Sylvanus, have you, Paul?"

Paul shook his head.

"A wonderful disciple. His father is Chrysippus bar Timaeus, a freedman of Herod the Great King. He developed the frankincense business in Jericho but quite mysteriously went blind! Within a year he was reduced to begging at the side of the road. It was he who was cured by Jesus in Jericho. His entire family became followers, and Sylvanus took over the business when his father died. The frankincense route is entirely through Nabataean territory, and since travel in that area is so dangerous, Sylvanus was exploring other alternatives for the incense business."

"It is so clear that we are being guided by the hand of God," Paul said. "Of the thousands of people in Perga, of the millions in Asia, why is it that we happen to be directed to one who is a brother in Christ?"

Both of the other men acknowledged the impossibility of anything except divine direction.

"But you are a Greek, are you not?" Barnabas asked gently.

"I *was* a Greek. Sylvanus had me circumcised before he baptized me. I am, like you, a Jew."

"Where did he find a *mo'el*?" Barnabas asked, referring to the man skilled in the correct performance of the circumcision operation, without whose services one ran a high risk of sickness and even death.

"Another remarkable coincidence," Tychicus answered. "There was a *mo'el* from Pisidian Antioch whom I know well, and who happened to visit me on business on his way to Cyprus just after I had decided that I would become part of the People of God. I don't see that man once a year! But he arrived the day *after* I decided to become a Jew. He was clearly sent by God."

The two others nodded confidently.

"Are there many Jews in Perga?" Paul asked.

Tychicus shook his head. "Not enough to form a *minyan*," he said, referring to the minimum of ten men required by Pharisaic law to constitute a synagogue.

"It must be difficult for you…" Paul began, but he realized that he might embarrass his host.

"Not really," Tychicus said, smiling amiably. "I was a God fearer for more than ten years, having learned of the Torah when I visited Pisidian Antioch. I have had my heart circumcised and live among the pagans. This means I must often eat food that has been offered to idols when my wife and I visit our friends; that can't be helped. If I lived in Jerusalem, I could live the way I would like to live, observing all the commandments. But here it is impossible. Here I must work on the Sabbath. I cannot *act* like a Jew as I would like, but Sylvanus taught me that the Father of Iēsoûs our Messiah, is a loving father who understands the kind of life I live and that he knows the innermost workings of my heart. Hence, he knows that I do not desire to live outside the practice of the Law. He knows that I nearly gag on meat that I know was bought in the market behind the Temple of Artemis."

"More than anything, you need others who can share the life you have been given in Christ Iēsoûs ," Paul said softly. "A community of brothers and sisters would provide you with the protection you need from the world of sin. We have come to found such communities."

"You will be wasting your time here in Perga," Tychicus said. "But there are Jews in Pisidian Antioch who might listen to you."

"What about the Gentiles here?" Barnabas asked.

"First, most of them hate Jews. My patron, Marcus Plancius Varus, will not do business with any Jews."

"Why?"

"His aunt was named Fulvia Portius. She had a Roman senator for a husband, Saturninus Lanuvius Portius. She converted to Judaism, and four of her teachers persuaded her to send a large donation of gold and purple to the Temple in Jerusalem. She secured permission from the emperor, Tiberius, since exporting gold was then, as it is now, illegal. When she entrusted her gifts to the four men, they took them and promptly disappeared! None of it got to Jerusalem. Her husband, my patron's maternal uncle, was mortified! He was the laughingstock of all Rome! He convinced Tiberius to expel all the Jews from the city in punishment. Well, some did have to leave, and many laid low for several years. That happened when my patron was a young man, but he has never forgotten."

"What about you?"

"He doesn't know!" Tychicus said *sotto voce.*

"Which means that you, of all people, can hardly be the basis of a community of worshippers here!"

"Right! But remember: of all men alive, I am the one most favored! My mother did not name me for the goddess of luck for nothing! I know the goddess has no reality, but my mother knew that I was favored by the God who is praised in the highest heavens! God will keep my secret from my patron, who, by the way, is an excellent man and whom I willingly serve as freedman despite his hatred of what I hold most dear!"

"Then what do we do?" Barnabas asked.

"Don't waste your time here. But accompany me through the mountains next week to Pisidian Antioch. I have a shipment of fish that I must transport, after which I need to go to Klaudiconium."

"Tychicus, you bring more benefits. I had not mentioned it before, but I have a document that authorizes us to attempt to negotiate an increase in price for copper mined and smelted in Klaudiconium. This authorization comes from my brother, Phidippides, and includes a one-tenth commission on the increase in price. He has specifically included you to receive half the commission."

"That will be a difficult negotiation," Tychicus said. But I know an influential man in Klaudiconium whom I can contact and gain access to the person who can make the decision."

"There is no particular rush, so we can spend as much time in Antioch as you need to establish a community of followers of Iēsoûs," said Tychicus. " We will find a community of Galatian Jews who love the Lord and whose hearts are likely to be opened by God when they hear the Good News of Iēsoûs the Christ."

"But that is pretty far into the back country," Paul said tentatively.

"Right. But I speak their language, and many of the men speak Greek. Don't worry. God will provide! Now, let's eat!"

CHAPTER 4

On the Road toward Antioch in Pisidia

A WEEK LATER, BARNABAS, PAUL, and Tychicus mounted horses at the head of a caravan of twenty pack mules laden with stout woven baskets, each of which contained one hundred pounds of smoked tuna fish caught by the fishing fleet at Attalia. Six muleteers coaxed, whipped, and whistled the complaining animals into a line, and at Tychicus's shout, the long line began its walk out the north city gate and past the monumental statue of Kestros, the god whose name the river bore, and toward whom the muleteers nodded a slight obeisance. They certainly did not want to ignore the proprieties, since they would follow this river through the high mountains to the north to Lake Limne, thence around the east side of the lake and through the Anthios Valley to Antioch. It would take about six days, assuming they could make twenty-five miles per day.

Neither Paul nor Barnabas was used to riding a horse, but Tychicus assured them that because of the rough country, they would never move at a pace faster than a walk. Nevertheless, the two men had difficulty controlling their horses, as they communicated their inexperience to the animals and the latter took advantage to do what they wanted, such as stopping to graze. Tychicus shouted instructions to the neophytes, to little avail. Finally, Tychicus cantered over, snatched the reins from both riders and, with two expert tugs, had the horses promptly in tow, as docile as lambs. Paul and Barnabas just laughed uncontrollably, each holding on to the wooden saddle pommel to keep upright.

With the sun low in the western sky, the caravan arrived at a small village with a corral at one end. A teenage boy saw the approaching group and shouted out the news to the other villagers, who came out to help the muleteers unload the animals, groom and feed them, and make the caravan ready for the night. Paul and Barnabas dismounted stiffly and followed Tychicus down the unpaved sandy street. Mud-brick courtyard walls topped with red clay barrel-tile extended the walls of the red-roofed houses. Children ran up to the strangers, laughing and begging for small gifts. Tychicus was ready with a handful of tiny sweet cakes he had stuffed in his shoulder-bag. Paul and Barnabas were embarrassed that they had nothing to give the barefoot children. Tychicus stopped at the last house on the street, knocked, and strode in through the quickly opened door, waving his two friends on. They were greeted in the courtyard by a plump and smiling woman with flaming red hair peeking out from beneath her white head-scarf. Tychicus was clearly at ease in this house, and the only men appeared to be servants. As the three men entered the living area, piping hot soup was ladled out into three bowls, and fresh bread was being cut by the redheaded woman.

Their language sounded harsh and was without the cadence of Greek. But laughter abounded throughout the village, and either the village had prepared for their arrival, or their spontaneous hospitality was more than Paul had ever encountered.

After dinner, Tychicus explained that they would normally have a storyteller come in to entertain the guests, but considering that two of the three did not understand their language, they brought two young men into the room, one with a flute. After a moment of introductions, one began to play and the other to sing a slow and plaintive melody with a tonal structure different from any Paul had heard. For quite a while, the two continued, until the landlady recognized that Paul had fallen fast asleep. She motioned to the two musicians, and they exited with a smile and a nod to Tychicus. He had flipped them a coin.

The awakened Paul and Barnabas were shown a small room next to the fireplace, just big enough for two beds with straw mattresses. Within moments, both were fast asleep, not having given a single thought to where Tychicus would spend the night.

CHAPTER 5

A Surprise

AT FIRST LIGHT, THE SOUNDS of bustling preparation for breakfast aroused Paul and Barnabas from their sleep, and as they entered the main room of the house, they saw Tychicus already seated at the table. The cheerful redheaded hostess greeted the two and ladled out two more bowls of steaming porridge like that in front of Tychicus. The door opened, and a tall, muscular man with hair the same color as the landlady strode in and greeted everyone in a cheerful voice, though Paul and Barnabas could not understand the specific words. He carried a Roman-style helmet slung by the chin strap from his arm and wore a military cuirass and a broadsword. He sat at the table, received a bowl of porridge with a nod of thanks, and began to talk with Tychicus, ignoring the other two men. They remained in conversation until both bowls were empty, and then, with a perfunctory nod to Paul and Barnabas, the tall man rose and strode out the door.

"What was that all about?" Barnabas asked.

"His name is Urfel, and he is Isrid's brother." Tychicus nodded toward the landlady. "He is in charge of our escort through the mountains."

"Escort? Why?" Paul stopped; he had forgotten that the caravan had a valuable cargo and that it was not safe to travel through the mountains off the Roman road. Robbers plied their trade there, as their ancestors had plied the same trade as pirates three generations ago on the Mediterranean. When Pompey had cleared the Middle Sea of these pirates, the latter simply moved inland into their mountain lairs.

"How many men will we have?" Paul asked.

"Fifteen, plus Urfel, who counts for at least five," Tychicus said with a smile.

"I would certainly not like to be on the receiving end of anything he offers in anger," Barnabas said in the same lighthearted manner.

"I have never been west before," Paul said. "Do all his people look like him? Big? Such fair skin, blue eyes?"

"No, not all," Tychicus said. "Urfel is of the Trocmi tribe. For the most part, his people came from northeast of Ancyra. But his grandfather moved here just as Pompey was making the Middle Sea safe for travel. The tribe that lives in the mountains is the Tolistobogi. And these two tribes have absolutely no use for each other. That is why Urfel is such an excellent escort. He would like nothing more than to have the opportunity of a Tolistobogi attack, so he could bash in a few skulls. And the Tolistobogi know that. So in the eight years that I have been using Urfel to escort me along this road, there has never once been any trouble," Tychicus said with a sweeping gesture that expressed his absolute confidence.

"And were we in danger of being robbed all day yesterday?" Paul asked, the frown on his face indicating that he felt uneasy about the entire arrangement.

"Not really," Tychicus said. "Yesterday, we were still in the province of Pamphylia. There is a force of auxiliaries in Perga that would quickly move on any bandits within the province. But today we cross into Galatia. And while it, too, is subject to Rome, the capital is Ancyra, and that is nearly two weeks' journey from here. What goes on in the mountains is handled by those who pass through the mountains."

"Could we have gotten to Antioch another way?" Paul asked.

"Yes, we could have," said Tychicus, slightly vexed. "But it would have added nearly a week to our trip, through Selge. And while there is a Roman road, it is really no safer than this route. We must pass through the Tolistobogi land."

"But I never thought about bandits."

"Paul, if you and Barnabas want to return to Perge, you can do so now. There is no danger. You can leave the horses at my place, and you can go to Antioch any way you want," Tychicus said with some ice in his voice.

"No, no," Barnabas said. "We appreciate what you are doing. Truly, we know that you know your business."

Paul nodded, reacting to the look he was getting from Barnabas.

"All right. Then let's go," said Tychicus, assuming his easygoing way. He ushered the two men out the door, where he tarried for a moment with Isrid, the redhead.

Paul's eyes popped when he saw the escort. Urfel was moving toward the self-developing front of the column, mounted on a gigantic horse. He had a massive broadsword at his side, along with a battle-ax and a shorter dagger. His circular bronze-and-leather shield was slung on his saddle. And while the fifteen other men were slightly smaller, they were similarly armed. They had four pack mules, one of which carried two bundles of ten-foot-long lances slung on each side. It was a veritable army and in excellent humor, with lots of guffawing and apparently irreverent joking, though Paul could not make out the actual words being used. Before too long, order began to emerge, and Urfel waved his right arm. The column struggled into motion. Urfel and three soldiers led the way, with eight more interspersed, two by two, among the pack animals, and four men bringing up the rear. Paul, Barnabas, and Tychicus rode just behind the lead group.

As the day wore on, the river became more and more narrow. The road hugged the river, and periodic wooden bridges spanned the creeks and small rivers that flowed down the steep and wooded mountainside into the Kestros. It was shortly before noon when they reached the first rapids, which required them to leave the edge of the river on a steep and narrow path up the side of the mountain, through dense forest. The sweating animals reached the top of a ridge, and the party suddenly found itself next to a high vertical cliff, nearly a thousand feet above the roaring cascade below. Urfel motioned for everyone to dismount to let the animals rest. Paul and Barnabas stood at the edge of the rocky road and peered down at the magnificent cataract and then northward, where ridge upon ridge of green mountains greeted them.

"Somewhere, up there, is Antioch," Tychicus said. "And this is just the beginning."

The magnificence of the scenery moved Paul deeply. He realized that most of his life had been spent in the lowlands. The hills of Judea were nothing like these mountains. He thought of the psalmist, who prayed, *Glorious are you, more than the everlasting mountains.* Now he knew what the psalmist meant. He had seen Mount Hermon, north of Galilee, but to be up so high on the mountainside, with much more above, filled him with an awe that he had never felt before.

The next two days were more of the same, except that the river continued to shrink and the rapids became more frequent. Each night they camped at a well-established campsite. It was clear that the caravan moved a specific number of miles per day, arriving at the campsite well before sundown. This was the best site of all so far, Paul thought. Nice and flat. Previous sites had been on hills, so one couldn't sleep easily. There were lots of fir trees to get boughs for a soft bed. And over there, on the rock, was thick, green moss to go on top of the boughs. It was up about fifty feet from the river, with sheer walls on three sides, offering protection from the wind. It seemed ideal.

Urfel, however, seemed restless. He was seen climbing up on the rocks above the campsite, nervously examining the perimeter of the site.

"What's the matter with Urfel?" Paul asked Tychicus.

"Oh, he's always like that in this campsite," Tychicus said.

"Why?"

"No real reason. He's always like that."

"Hmmmm," Paul said, but he decided not to press the matter.

Urfel returned, sweating from the exertion of climbing, and huddled with his three chief lieutenants. They nodded, and Urfel disappeared down the road they would be taking tomorrow. Dinner was served, and the sun fell behind the mountains, leaving a rich magenta-and-pink strewn sky as a reminder. The entire party reveled in the changing colors. Pink turned to ruby red streaked with yellow, all beneath a background that gradually transformed itself from baby blue to azure to indigo...then to spangled black as the clouds seemed to evaporate, to be replaced by a nearly tangible Milky Way. And as the campfire turned to embers, a rich yellow glow appeared above the mountains to the east, and a golden orb rose majestically into the blackness.

Just then, Urfel returned to the campsite and immediately huddled with his lieutenants. There were nods of agreement, and four sentries were posted, armed with their long lances and wearing leather body armor and helmets. Paul did not notice that this was double the norm.

Quiet stole upon the group. A few soldiers and muleteers were playing knucklebones. One soldier played a mournful song on a small flute. Urfel and Tychicus spoke quietly together in that awful, non-melodious tongue.

Ugh, thought Paul, *it sounds so ugly! But that is the product of our ancestors' overweening pride, of their hubris, as they tried to build the Tower of Babel.*

Paul stretched out on his luxurious bower topped with moss. *Ahhhh,* he thought. *This is wonderful! I thank you, Father, for your gifts...for...*

Sleep overtook him before he could end.

Screams! Chaos...shouts...curses. Paul sat upright, shocked out of his sleep. Shadows were all over the campsite, barbarian shouts and suddenly Paul saw Urfel dash directly by him, without his broadsword, bareheaded, running out of camp. Tychicus saw the same.

"Urfel...help...Urfel," Tychicus shouted.

They were being attacked! Sounds of sword upon shield...shouts,... agonizing cries that must have been for help.

Suddenly, a mountain of a shadow appeared in front of Paul, a club in one hand.

"Chrusia,...Chrusia," the shadow shouted, gripping Paul with one massive hand and raising him so that the only the tips of his toes reached the ground. Paul was petrified, unable to speak.

"Chrusia, Chrusia," the beast shouted, his putrid breath flooding over the smaller man's face

"I…I…have no gold, no gold, no gold," Paul stammered.

"Chrusia!" the man repeated, clearly his only Greek, as if shouting louder would produce the coins he was looking for.

"NO GOLD!" Paul shouted, his knees knocking.

The man sneered, held Paul at arm's length, raised his club above his head and brought it down. Paul staggered backward, slipped over a rock, and raised his arm defensively. This eased the blow, but the club hit his left upper arm and then smashed into the side of his head. Down he went to the ground.

"CHRUSIA," the ape shouted again, and he raised the club menacingly over the now-helpless Paul.

"CHRUSIA…CHRUSIA" came the shout from Barnabas as he shook some gold coins in a leather sack. "Here…here…gold!"

The ape-man turned and snatched the bag, and as he felt it, weighing its heft, he pulled out a coin. It gleamed in the moonlight.

In the meantime, the campsite was pure chaos. Several men were lying on the ground, groaning, and virtually everyone was fighting with someone, but no Urfel.

Paul was unable to move. He watched the shapes around him, unable to make out who was who. He could not even make out Barnabas or Tychicus.

Suddenly there was a piercing cry from the edge of the camp. The attackers instantly drew back, swords at the ready, but pausing in their efforts. From the shadows of the rocks emerged two men, Urfel at the rear, his left hand grasping the hair of the man in front, his right hand holding a knife to his throat!

"It's BuraghBsarugh," Tychicus shouted aloud. "Urfel's captured BuraghBsarugh!"

Paul sat up. There was silence in the campsite as the attackers silently withdrew, unwilling to be the cause of death of their leader.

Urfel screamed an order in their language, the helpless BuraghBsarugh seemed to confirm it, and the attackers dropped their swords. One of the escort, blood streaming from his side, quickly thrust his erstwhile assailant through with his sword, and that act was met with a savage scream from Urfel, justice was instantly accomplished by one of the lieutenants, who cut his own man down with a single blow.

"He said no more bloodshed," Tychicus whispered to Paul and Barnabas. "Buragh and four others will be our hostages until we get to Antioch. Then they will then be sent to Ancyra—unless there is another attack, in which case they will be killed instantly."

Buragh shouted out what seemed to be four barbaric names, and the four men approached Urfel's lieutenants, who quickly bound their hands and placed ropes around their necks. Urfel shouted out another order, to which the attackers howled in protest but to which the escort cheered. At the protest, Urfel slid his knife along the side of Buragh's neck and drew blood. BuraghBaragh screamed an order, and the attackers sheepishly began to remove their clothes and their shoes. The white of their skin showed up in the bright moonlight, and with laughter, Urfel's men picked up branches, ropes, and anything nonlethal, and chased the men barefoot and naked from the campsite.

In a few moments, the men of the escort returned and began attending to the three of their men who had fallen in the fray. One was dead, by the hand of his commander. One had an ugly face wound, and the other had a stomach wound, his blood flowing freely. Two attackers were dead. The man with the face wound was bandaged, but the man with the stomach wound was taken gently to the edge of the camp and propped up against a tree. Two companions sat with him, offering him wine and comfort. The man wept bitterly and screamed in pain but could not move. Urfel walked over to him, having had Buragh bound and chained to an armed soldier. He sat down next to him and cradled him in his massive arms, crooning to him like a nursemaid to a baby. It was not too long before it was over, and the sound of picks and shovels digging in the rocky soil could be heard throughout the campsite.

No one slept the rest of the night except Urfel, whose loud snoring provided a sense of security for everyone. Paul thought, *If Urfel sleeps, there can be no danger.*

Barnabas told Tychicus about the money that had been stolen. It was all he and Paul had, though he could probably arrange a loan from his brother in Cyprus. But that would take months and months. Tychicus was sympathetic, but apparently the man who had stolen the coins had slipped away just as Urfel was bringing Buragh into the campsite.

"How much did you have?" Tychicus asked.

"Ten gold aurii," Barnabas said. "But, he grinned, "I had another twenty lead discs the same size as aurii in a separate pocket inside the pouch, so it felt like at least thirty aurii. I thought someday that would come in handy."

Tychicus laughed.

"He still got two and a half year's wages for someone in the city," Barnabas said. "And that would last someone in these mountains for almost the rest of his life!"

"I can lend you what you need when we get to Antioch," Tychicus said. "You can give me a note, and we can send it for repayment to your brother. He will certainly honor it, and I won't charge you interest!"

"Done," said Barnabas, and they shook hands.

Paul tried to sleep, but couldn't. His knees quaked each time he thought of that upraised club, poised and aimed at his head, delayed only by the tinkle of Barnabas's gold coins. The foul-breathed monster would have killed him just for spite!

Lord, you clearly have taken care of me, for which I thank you. And as you order everything in this world to your will, you knew exactly what would happen. But, Lord, must you, must you bring me to the very brink of death before I have completed my mission? Oh, Lord, please don't do that again!

The eastern sky began to lighten in response.

CHAPTER 6

Antioch in Pisidia

Two UNEVENTFUL DAYS LATER, AS the party plodded slightly uphill in the Anthios Valley, in an area where the rugged Taurus Mountains had gentled themselves into rolling hills, the fortifying walls of Antioch became visible. For the past day and a half, the party had traveled through cultivated land, with small villages of a dozen or so homes every couple of miles. Olive groves, grain fields, fruit orchards, and vegetable farms were interspersed with rich grazing land. Unlike the untamed and rugged Taurus Mountains to the southeast, this gently rolling land had been appropriated and placed under the firm control of capable husbandmen.

The road into Antioch was reasonably crowded with farm wagons and pack animals. The procession, which included five men with their hands bound behind their backs and ropes around their necks, attracted attention from passersby and those working in the fields. Curly-headed young boys ran up to the caravan and anxiously pled for information from Urfel, proudly at the head of the caravan and personally leading his conquered enemy.

"Robbers, mister?" they asked.

"Ugh," Urfel grunted, nodding his head.

"Will they be killed, mister?"

"Ugh," Urfel responded, staring straight ahead.

The boys fell in with the caravan, inviting others to join them to witness the event when the group reached the magistrate in the city.

It could be seen from outside the walls that the city lay on a series of hills, with a four-columned temple rising on the highest ground, at the eastern end of the city. The theater could also be seen rising on the adjacent hillside, slightly to the southwest. A jumble of other buildings, red-tile roofed, rose and fell with the seven hills inside the city walls. When the now-enlarged group entered through the rather narrow south gate, Paul noticed that the inscriptions above the gate were in Latin, not in Greek. This was clearly a Roman colony, a city that had a large number of retired Roman soldiers as a population base. The dress of the soldiers at the gate imitated that of a Roman soldier, though the soldiers hailed Urfel and ordered him to stop for questioning in Greek.

After an hour of questions, discussions, sending for higher authorities, waiting for the under magistrate, more questions and discussions, and a final decision to take possession of the prisoners and charge them with murder and piracy, the group was permitted to enter the city. The prisoners were hauled off to the jail to await trial, the location of which would be determined by the governor in Ancyra, four days away by military messenger.

"Let me show you the sights," Tychicus said to Paul and Barnabas after he had finished giving instructions to the chief of his muleteers and had dismissed Urfel with effusive praise of his ability as a soldier.

The city was laid out in the manner of a Roman camp, with the street on which they found themselves being the *Decumanus Maximus*, which ran east-west, straight as a die. The street was paved and sloped to the center, where periodic three-to-four-inch holes permitted both rainwater and the slops poured into the street to run into a hidden sewer. Shops lined both sides of the street, displaying food and merchandise; interspersed were taverns, a couple of inns, and a few brothels.

After a short while, they reached a wide cross-street running north-south. "This is the *Cardo Maximus*, the main street of the city," Tychicus announced. "We'll turn here to get to the bath." In less than a hundred yards, the street became colonnaded, with wide covered porticos extending about fifteen feet on each side. The capitals of the columns were of the Ionic order, and the architrave above the capitals was decorated with deeply incised, twisted vines. As they came to the end of the colonnade, Tychicus said, "Now, just ahead to the right is the Square of Tiberius." And in a few moments, they encountered an exceptionally wide paved area that led eastward. Several hundred yards down the forum was a magnificent three-arched gate laden with statues and high reliefs. Tychicus indicated that they had to dismount and walk in the square, as animals were prohibited. On each side of the forum were multistory houses with overlooking balconies. As they approached the gateway, which Tychicus called the *propylon*, they noticed that the reliefs were of the emperor Augustus's various land and sea victories. All the inscriptions were in Latin.

They mounted the steps of the propylon, passed through the arch, and entered the Square of Augustus, with its four simple but soaring Corinthian columns at the front of the *pronaos* and two others set behind the outermost columns, halfway to the main body of the temple, called a *cella*. The top of the gable roof was nearly forty feet high. But the most impressive element was that the entire hillside behind the temple had been carved out in a semicircle the width of the square, and a two-story portico had been constructed around the entire temple area. The ground floor had columns in the Doric order, and the second had Ionic. The overall impression was of an understated elegance, order, proportion, and simplicity. This new temple glowed, its white marble appearing rose-colored from the sun beginning to sink in the west.

Their sightseeing completed, the men returned to their mounts and proceeded northward up the Cardo Maximus, nearly to the northern gate, where a large ornamented fountain announced the proximity of the baths. Sure enough, to the left was a large bath, and the men spent the next hour there, enjoying the most common luxury of their world.

Refreshed, and with the sun providing a rich afterglow, they proceeded south, retracing their steps to the *Decumanus Maximus*, where Tychicus indicated they turn right. To their surprise, as they approached the theater, the street turned into a tunnel and passed directly beneath the southern portion of the building. As they clip-clopped through, every noise echoed loudly, and the men shouted and whistled, taking delight in the unusual experience. Once they were through the tunnel, the agora appeared on their right. Tychicus pointed out the magistrate's residence and the barracks for the municipal guard. Next to the magistrate's residence was a large basilica, on the main floor of which business was being transacted, contracts entered into, the final sales of the day being made, and the commercial life of the area being concluded under the watchful eye of the ruling class on the balcony above.

On two other sides of the agora were shops and offices occupied by artisans and businessmen. Tychicus pointed down a narrow street just off the agora and led his compatriots down the dirt road to a small house Tychicus's employer owned, where they would stay while in the city. Tychicus knocked, a servant quickly opened the door, another young man darted out to take the horses to the stables, and the three tired men shared a quick meal before plunging into the delicious, clean beds in the tiny bedrooms of the house.

CHAPTER 7

A Response to a Homily

Two days later was the Sabbath. Tychicus led Paul and Barnabas to a house near the baths, in the northwest part of the city. It was larger than most, with a small atrium, to the left of which was a small anteroom, and then a larger one with a relatively high ceiling. Two small windows were glazed in translucent stone. There were about fifteen men in this room, plus five women who were all clustered in the back. It was immediately clear that Tychicus was both well-known and welcome, and he introduced both his guests to all the men. Some, it appeared, were not Jews by birth but were God-fearers, or Greeks who accepted Torah as God's Word, who followed the ethical precepts found in the Law, but who were not circumcised. One of the men had heard of Tychicus's adventure on the trip into town, and he was asked to recount the attack, which he did briefly and with color. At the conclusion, he was roundly clapped on the back for having survived, and with that, the men took their places on the benches that lined the walls.

The women sat at the rear.

One of the men, perhaps the oldest of the group, walked to a niche in the wall and produced a scroll, which he took to a table in the front-center and unrolled. Then, prior to reading, he began to pray, blessing God, thanking Him for having created the world, for having brought them His holy word, and for remembering always His covenant, even with those Jews far from Jerusalem, far from His Holy Mountain. After remembering some of the needs of the small group around him, he picked up a pointer and began to read from the book of Isaiah:

Jacob is my servant whom I uphold
Israel my chosen one in whom my soul delights.
I have set my spirit upon him,
He will bring fair judgment to the nations.
He does not cry out or raise his voice,
His voice is not heard in the street;
He does not break the crushed reed
Or snuff the faltering wick.
Faithfully he presents fair judgment:
He will not grow faint, he will not be crushed
Until he has established fair judgment on earth,
And the coasts and islands are waiting for his instruction.
Thus says Adonai,
Who created heavens and spread them out,
Who hammered into shape the earth and what comes from it
Who gave breath to the people on it,
And spirit to the people who walk on it.
I, Adonai, have called you in saving justice,
I have grasped you by the hand and shaped you;
I have made you a covenant of the people
And a light to the nations,
To open the eyes of the blind,
To free captives from prison
And those who live in darkness from the dungeon.

The man stopped and rolled up the scroll.

He then began explaining the text, pointing out that it referred to Cyrus, the Median prince who had defeated Nebuchadnezzar of Babylon and had permitted the Jews to return to Jerusalem. He pointed out how the strength of God was showered upon Cyrus and that his acts permitted the ultimate rebuilding of the Temple, and the re-centering of all Jews in both Temple worship and the Word of God. It was this that made them, the Jewish community in Antioch, the children of Israel, a light to all the *goyim*, the pagans all around.

"The Lord then changed who He was talking to. He suddenly began to talk to us, His People. He said to us, *I have called you in saving justice; I have grasped you by the hand and shaped you.* Who else could He be talking to? He grasped us by the hand in Egypt. He shaped us in the wilderness, where we still find ourselves. Yes, my brothers," He said, ignoring the ladies, "we find ourselves still in the wilderness, far from the place where God's presence dwells. But it is only here that we can be a 'light to the nations, to open the eyes of the blind' who are in every part of this city. For they are blind who offer sacrifice to Artemis and who travel out to the sanctuary of Mên. They are in a prison of ignorance, and it is we who free them from the darkness of their dungeon. For this reason, brothers, in everything that we do, we must be careful to live God's Law, to care for one another, and to deal with the pagans with honesty and uprightness. Then will all men, like you, brothers" he nodded at the three God-fearers "find their way to Torah and to the prophets and to the Lord."

He sat down, and there was a time of silence so that the words of the elder might sink in.

Then he arose.

"Would one of our guests like to exhort the brothers?" he asked.

Paul's eyes were shut; he was rocking ever so gently back and forth on the bench, his hands clasped together in his lap. For a moment, no one moved. Then Paul opened his eyes and stood up.

"Brothers and sisters," the women were startled, "we have heard a wonderful exposition of God's Word. But the mystery of His Word is to understand that there are many layers of meaning that speak to us. Let me show you a different layer, one that our learned speaker could not have known."

There was a slight buzz in the room as people looked at one another. The elder remained impassive, a slight smile on his lips. He nodded encouragement to Paul.

"While Cyrus was, indeed, important in bringing us back from Babylon, and while he was God's favored instrument at that time, there is one whom God chose who fits the scripture even better than Cyrus.

He is one who walked this earth only a few years ago, who was so marked with God's favor that I am convinced, as are many, many others, that he was the true Anointed One of God, the true *Moshiach*."

Another buzz. *Moshiach* was a powerful word, well recognized even among those who knew no Hebrew. The men looked at one another, not sure what was now to come. Paul plowed on.

"This man, whose name was Iēsoûs, was the *Christos*," he said, using the Greek equivalent of *Moshiach*, the one upon whom God sent His Spirit, as the prophet foretold. For in his life he did many mighty deeds: he subjected demons to his will, cured the sick, opened the eyes of the blind, and freed captives from the prison of their ignorance. He proclaimed that the Kingdom of God is upon us, that the End Times and judgment, fair judgment, are at hand.

"Recall what was just read: 'I have made you a covenant of the people.' Was the Lord referring to Israel as the 'covenant?' How can this be? The covenant is the Law that we have received from Moses. Was the Lord peaking of Jacob, known as Israel, or of all the sons of Israel? Can a *person* be the Law? Or can a *people* be the Law?" Paul tried to make the point powerfully, but his voice cracked, and the phrase dribbled out weakly.

While there was some expression of discomfort, the eyes of his listeners were intently upon him, unsure of where this would take them.

"Listen, my brothers and sisters, let me tell you about the perfect Son of Israel, Son of Abraham, the only one who could be spoken of as 'the covenant.' His name is Iēsoûs, and he is the person the Lord is referring to.

"We also heard that the Lord sent his spirit on him. This man, Iēsoûs, is exactly the person the Lord filled with his Holy Spirit, making him the true 'Jacob,' the true 'Israel.' It was he who opened the eyes of the blind, both through acts of his own power and by opening the minds of those with whom he spoke while he walked this earth. It was he who liberated us from the prison of darkness of understanding. For he offered us the baptism of repentance, wherein we turn from the things of this world to the things of God. And it is he who offers us, those of the 'coasts and islands,' the 'nations,' true instruction. *He* can be said to be the covenant because he incorporated in his very life, even to dying for us, the faithfulness that can come only from God. And God demonstrated this for all of us when He raised him from the dead on the third day! This is absolute proof that He 'grasped him by the hand.' He is the true Israel, the true 'chosen one of God' in whom the Lord delights. It is He that we preach and whom we invite you to accept."

"But there is one additional point. While the Father took him to himself after having raised him, he remains with us in the communities that are founded in his Spirit. He remains with us as the true Israel, the New People of God. It is in his assemblies that he continues to live. He is present with those who profess his name, as the Israel of God."

Paul sat down. The president of the synagogue led the congregation in a prayer, and the atmosphere within the room changed. The prayer service was ended, and the room reverted to a community center, conversations sprouting up regarding the normal concerns and affairs of the small group. No one said anything about Paul's comments, much to Paul's surprise. There was no hostility, but no enthusiasm either. The three men shared some bread and a malt drink with the other men, served by one of the younger women. They spoke about the uncertainty of the reaction of the community and left when the group seemed to disperse of its own momentum.

CHAPTER 8

First Fruits

LATER THAT EVENING, THE THREESOME was surprised by a knock on the door. A young man with the beginnings of a wispy blond beard stood in the fading light of sunset and asked for the man who had spoken at the synagogue. The servant ushered him into the small dining room where dinner was being served.

Tychicus arose from the couch and greeted the young man and, when he realized that the man was looking for Paul, invited him into the dining room with a request to bring another couch for the guest.

"I am Epaenetus," the man announced. "I heard you this evening when you expounded on the Law. I follow the God of Israel as a God-fearer and am intrigued by the idea of a New Israel. I have come to learn more."

For several hours, the three engaged the young man in conversation, this time bringing up the reality of Iēsoûs's cruel form of death and describing how the scandal of the cross became the crowning symbol of glory.

As the hour grew late, Epaenetus took his leave, and Barnabas and Paul discussed the good fortune of his visit. This was precisely what Paul had hoped for, just one person to begin with. They retired that evening full of the joy that comes with a successful venture.

Two days later, Epaenetus returned with his wife, Diana, and the five of them spent a good part of the day discussing scripture and the message Paul and Barnabas brought regarding Iēsoûs. She was not a God-fearer and had virtually no knowledge of the Greek translation of the Hebrew scriptures, but she was infected with the excitement that

Epaenetus had brought home. She was most interested in the idea of God's having raised someone from the dead. She told Paul that she had been initiated into the rites of Orpheus and that for her, the most important task in a person's life was preparation for the afterlife. Paul encouraged her to discuss her beliefs.

"We appear to be flesh, but that is really an illusion," she said. "In reality, we are spirits that are, for a time, consigned to a body as if it were a tomb. What we call 'life' is really the process of purifying ourselves so that when we are released from this tomb by death, we will be escorted to the Isles of the Blest, where we will live with the gods in perfect harmony. There will be no toil, no pain; those who have persevered three times through this life will be brought to the Tower of Chronos, where flowers of gold are blazing and the populace make wreaths and garlands of flowers and enjoy true music, of which what we hear today is a mere image. The gods perform this true music on golden lyres. There will be in that life perfect happiness."

"How is one selected to share in this wonderful state?" Paul asked.

"The determination is made based upon whether one has lived a righteous life. If one is consumed with greed, with violence, with despoiling the poor, one will certainly be judged below the earth and will be sentenced to unbearable toil in the afterlife. But those men who have lived a virtuous life, who have controlled their passions, have honored contracts, and have been courageous both in battle and in civic life, and those women who have lived virtuously, not meddling in public affairs, being careful and moderate in managing the household, and being chaste and modest, avoiding contact with men other than their husbands,those men and women, upon death, appear before the goddess justice, who sits at the right hand of the throne of Zeus and oversees the works of those on earth. She welcomes the just to eternal bliss and condemns the unjust to everlasting toil."

"What of those who are neither totally just or utterly depraved? Most men and women are really neither, but act justly some of the time and evilly other times?" Paul asked.

"Those spirits must undergo a period of purgation after death. Then, partially purified, they return to this life in another body, once again given the opportunity to live a just life."

"And are there ways that a person is assisted in living such a life?"

"Of course. We have the mystic rites, the most ancient and the holiest of rites, given to us by Orpheus himself and practiced for centuries."

"Are these the unholy orgies of Dionysus?" Paul asked.

"Ours are the *original* Dionysiac rites," she said. "Those adherents of Dionysus have been corrupted with excesses of drunkenness and unbridled sexuality and violence. What you are probably familiar with is totally foreign to us. Our music is not the wildly sexual music of the pipes and flutes that one hears in the countryside. No, ours is that of the lyre, born of Apollo, and is gentle and harmonious. We use this music at our initiations, where we are urged to live a life of virtue. And before we die, we are given gold leaves that have written on them sacred words that will bring us to a higher place in the Isles of the Blest. To be initiated into the mysteries is the key to life itself; it is the way we overcome death. That is why, when Epaenetus told me he was considering being baptized by you, it felt so comfortable to me, and that is why I want to learn of your rites of initiation."

Paul sat for a few moments, reflecting on what she had said. He knew this would have to be done delicately, for if he simply told her the truth, that her Orpheus was a fraud and did not exist, then she would likely be alienated. Later, she would understand. But how to broach the subject now?

"First," he began, "we Jews have an ancient tradition, written in our holy books, which began when God spoke directly with our father, Abraham. This is the same God that created the heavens and the earth, the Lord of the Universe. He spoke to Abraham and made a covenant with him; He promised that if we were faithful to the One, True God, we would be His people. One of His conditions was that we worship Him alone.

"We know that God often uses angels as mediators between Him and the human race. And it is possible that Orpheus might be confused with one of these. But the Christ we celebrate is vastly above all angels. His conquest of death, known by the fact that God raised him on the third day, both announces the End Times for those who belong to Christ and gives us hope that we, too, will be raised with Him. In baptism, we become one with Christ; we die with him and rise with him. And in the very near future, he will return in glory, on clouds, and we will join him. When the end comes, and it will be soon, we will be joined with him in glory."

"When you say 'rise with him,' do you suggest that the body, too, becomes immortal?"

"Absolutely. For us, the body is not merely a 'tomb' that is left behind, though for a while we leave the body when we die. But at the end, we are rejoined to a glorified body, a body that has become perfect and will not be subject to corruption."

"And where will the body live?"

"Where God sees fit. It will be a place of perfect beauty, and it will be with the Lord Iēsoûs Christ. I can't say exactly 'where,' but God will provide."

"I would like you to tell me more about Iēsoûs, about your holy books, and about rising with him at the end."

And so, for the next several days, Paul and Barnabas met regularly with Epaenetus and Diana. Paul started with the first book of scripture, called "When God began to create..." from its first words, and progressively worked his way, by memory, through important parts of the Torah and the prophets. While Diana originally had no concept of the Hebrew scriptures, she had a good grasp of the Greek poems, of Homer and Hesiod and the poems attributed to Orpheus, which celebrated the various Greek gods. She had the ability to make connections, much to Paul's chagrin, between the myths of the Greeks and the content of the scriptures. Paul constantly corrected her, saying that the poems of Hesiod were nothing more than pure fantasy, having no relation to reality, while the scripture contained the truth about the world.

"Apollodorus of Athens described the flood that occurred and explained that Deucalion and his wife, Pyrrha, were saved because he created an ark and brought two of every animal into that ark. And every other man and woman was drowned in the flood. After the flood, the ark landed on Mount Parnassus, where Deucalion offered sacrifice. And a pleased Zeus asked what he would like, and he replied, 'To make men.' Hence, Deucalion and Pyrrha threw stones over their shoulders, and the race of men and women began again. In fact, our name *laos* comes from the ancient word for stones, *lass*. This myth says that Deucalion and Pyrrha are my ancestors. The story of Noah simply says that Noah and his wife are my ancestors. What is the difference?"

Paul responded that, "The main difference is that the Greek myths are stories made up by poets. Scripture not only tells a story, but it embeds in that story the means of our salvation. There is a deeper level to scripture than just the words you hear; when you hear that all generations sprang from Noah, the Lord is saying, through Moses, that since Noah 'walked with God,' the children that he would produce would not be children of evil tendencies but children filled with grace from God. Further, the story is not merely of a flood, but what happened after the flood: God made a covenant with Noah and placed his bow in the heavens as a sign of that covenant. That covenant meant that God forever will be with us, the Children of Noah. Yes, even with the Gentiles, those who do not yet know the mysteries of God. The truth of our scriptures lies in the fact that God uses them as a means of communicating the true depths of our world to us."

"Then your baptism is different from our initiations into the mysteries?" She asked."By all means. Your initiations are merely human magic. You are misled into believing that because you undergo a ritual, you are so changed that your everlasting happiness is assured in the next life. Baptism does not do that for you. In baptism, you undertake a life of faith in Iēsoûs the Christ. But this means that you change your way of living, incorporating the Law that was given to Moses into every part of your being. You no longer behave the same; you adopt a life in Christ Iēsoûs, one of love, one of living in virtue. You are not 'saved' by being baptized. You begin the life in Christ that, if you persevere, will lead to your salvation. We are not 'saved,' but merely on the way to being 'saved.'"

By the time the Sabbath came around, Epaenetus and Diana joined Paul, Barnabas, and Tychicus in the house of prayer in the city. Diana was introduced to the few females at the rear of the room, and Epaenetus joined the other God-fearers, slightly separated from the other male worshippers. There was a little problem, since about half the Jewish men who had been there last Sabbath were nowhere to be found; hence, they had only nine Jews, plus the three God-fearers. Ten Jews were required for a synagogue. Paul and Barnabas spoke with the president of the assembly and suggested that they include the God-fearers to achieve a minyan, or minimum number. The president thought that was absurd and was not pleased with the idea.

"If we include them, why can't we just go out into the street and bring any Greek inside to secure a minyan?"

"The God fearers follow the Law," Barnabas said.

"They are not truly members of our community," the president said. "You know our tradition well: one does not say the Sh'mah or read Torah unless there are ten Jews, and if one is not circumcised, one is not a Jew."

"But what is better: to say the Sh'mah or read Torah with fewer than ten or not to pray or read at all?" Paul asked.

"That is not the question. The question is what the Law states."

"The question of ten is never mentioned in Torah," Paul responded.

"But the Oral Torah includes it," the president said. "And the discussion is over. We have an insufficient number, and everyone will go to his house and keep the Sabbath. During the week, I shall speak with those who are not here and find out why they prevented us from praising the Lord together." With that, he waved his hand in dismissal, and everyone left the room, murmuring in confusion and disappointment.

CHAPTER 9

Epaenetus and Diana

THE NEXT WEEK FLEW BY. Epaenetus and Diana spent every day with Paul and Barnabas. In this time, friendship among the four of them deepened. Epaenetus had inherited a farm from his father, who had been a Roman soldier and who had been given a tract of land just outside the city. The farm had originally had almost one hundred sixty acres, which was large for that area. But he was one of four brothers, each of whom received forty acres. This was still a fairly large piece of land, and he had four slaves who lived with him and Diana in the city and who went out to the fields each day at dawn and returned at dusk. He had put thirty acres into fruit and nut trees years ago, and they were now producing substantial fruit, which he sold in the city. He leased forty acres from his youngest brother, who had no interest in farming, and he put that in grains and legumes. In the final ten acres, he grew vegetables for the family and sold the excess in the city. By most standards, he was a prosperous peasant. His wife, Diana, came from a family of textile merchants in the city. And with the dowry she brought, they remodeled their city house to permit retail shops to operate opening onto the main street where they lived. Diana assumed the added responsibility for dealing with their seven tenants, for finding new ones when the old ones left, and collecting rent on the ides of each month. This gave them the luxury of spending hours and hours with Barnabas and Paul.

The next week, they appeared at the house of prayer but could feel an emotional difference in the air. The men were not as friendly to Paul and Barnabas and were decidedly cool to Epaenetus. Even the few ladies seemed to snub Diana.

The president commenced the service, all recited the Sh'mah, and one of the men who had been absent the last Sabbath opened the roll of Torah and began to read. Paul instantly recognized Leviticus:

> *You shall keep all my statutes and all my ordinances, and observe them, so that the land to which I bring you to settle in may not vomit you out. You shall not follow the practices of the nation that I am driving out before you. Because they did all these things, I abhorred them. But I have said to you: You shall inherit their land, and I will give it to you to possess, a land flowing with milk and honey. I am the LORD your God; I have separated you from the peoples. You shall therefore make a distinction between the clean animal and the unclean, and between the unclean bird and the clean; you shall not bring abomination on yourselves by animal or by bird or by anything with which the ground teems, which I have set apart for you to hold unclean. You shall be holy to me; for I the LORD am holy, and I have separated you from the other peoples to be mine.*

The man rerolled the scroll and cleared his throat.

"Brothers, you all noticed that several of us did not return to celebrate Shabbat with you last week. It was not because we were ill or were away from the city on business. No, we did not come because of the apparent acceptance of the new ideas of these men who recently arrived in our city. One of them, Paul, spoke of a 'New People of God' and a 'New Covenant.' This is what is objectionable to us. There was one covenant, that made between God and our father, Abraham. To propose another is to attempt to change the Law, which can never be changed. These newcomers must recant their error, now, before all the brothers, or they must leave."

Paul and Barnabas were wide eyed in surprise. They looked at the president of the synagogue, but he kept his eyes directed on the speaker. Clearly, it had been agreed beforehand that this would occur.

Paul rose. "May I speak?"

"Only if you recant what you spoke two weeks ago," the president said.

"I…we…uh, no, I can't do that," Paul responded, looking at Barnabas and Tychicus, who nodded assent. "The Lord has revealed to me exactly what I am to say."

At that the president held up his hand. "Silence. You now ask us to believe that the Lord, the Holy One blessed be He, who created the earth and the heavens *spoke* with you?" the president shouted, wide eyed and clearly angry.

"The Lord Iēsoûs revealed to me what I was to bring to all the brothers," Paul responded.

"'Lord Iēsoûs,' you say! There is but one Lord, the Blessed One! You cannot speak in this house and apply that term to any but the Holy One. Tell us that you erred, or leave."

Paul stammered, unable to respond quickly. Tychicus stood up and took Paul by the arm, nodded to Barnabas, and gave an unspoken direction to follow him. The three men headed for the door. Epaenetus rose also, as did Diana, and the five left the house.

Paul was shaking, angry, not only at the suddenness of the attack but at himself for having failed to respond promptly and effectively. The group returned to the small house where they were staying, and they tried to sort out this unexpected turn of events. And to Paul's dismay, Epaenetus announced that he had decided to become circumcised and baptized, to join the People of God and become a follower of the Christ. Their expulsion was a complicating factor, for it would be impossible for Epaenetus to become a Jew and to be excluded from the assembly. For while the community was small, the essence of being a Jew was its community. While they could not maintain social separation from the Greeks, their mutual support and identity provided them with enough spiritual sustenance that they could transmit their identity to their children despite the large proportion of Antioch Jews who married Greeks and were never again seen in the house of prayer.

After a couple hours of discussion, Tychicus suggested that he had business in Iconium, another Roman colonial city to the southeast, about a three-day journey, in that part of Greater Galatia known as Lycaonia, and that Paul and Barnabas ought to accompany him there. He would be able to secure some horses and felt that some of the Jews in that city might be more receptive to the Good News about Iēsoûs Christ than those in Antioch.

"But will we be able to be baptized?" Epaenetus asked, concerned.

"Yes," Paul said, looking at Barnabas for a reaction. "We will baptize you into Christ Iēsoûs, and then you can return to the synagogue and be circumcised there after we leave. You need say nothing for a while, since they know we are friends. But if you simply ask to be admitted to the community by circumcision, I'm sure they will do so. We will return here soon."

"And what about Diana?"

"The same. We will baptize her, and she can then ask to be admitted to the assembly.

"They will baptize her again in a ritual bath, but it is a different baptism. It is not of the spirit, but of water alone. But she will then be a Jew, just as you will be," Barnabas said. Clearly, he and Paul saw eye to eye on this. No prior discussion, but full agreement. Paul felt relieved.

"Come to our home," Diana said. "It is Shabbat, and we can read the scriptures and pray in our own home. I will have our servants prepare a wonderful meal for us, and we can enjoy the balance of the evening."

Paul and Barnabas looked at Tychicus as if looking for direction. He smiled and nodded his head. All five arose at once and left for the home of Epaenetus and Diana.

CHAPTER 10

Baptism

THE NEXT MORNING, AT THE first sign of light, Epaenetus, Diana, Paul, and Barnabas met at the monumental fountain at the north end of the Cardo Maximus, just next to the baths. The fountain received a torrent of water from the main aqueduct that served the city, and from this place a series of smaller aqueducts wound through the city providing water to four other main fountains and even directly inside the larger homes of the elite. The city had not yet begun to stir, as the nights were still short. Barnabas asked Epaenetus and Diana whether they believed that Iēsoûs Christ was the Messiah, the one foretold by the prophets; whether they believed that his death and resurrection was a sign from God that he had conquered death for all time and for all who believe in him; and whether they would lead that kind of exemplary life of virtue and love that Iēsoûs demanded of his followers. Receiving affirmative and enthusiastically positive answers, Paul and Barnabas prayed over them, asking the Spirit to descend upon them, to make them one with the rest of all the believers, and to strengthen them for their ordeals in a hostile environment. Paul then nodded to the two, and seeing that the area was deserted, they took off their tunics and entered the fountain naked. Paul and Barnabas both joined them and immersed them together beneath the water. As they did so, Paul said, "In entering the water, you enter death with Christ." After a second, they lifted both of them out of the water. "In arising from the water, you arise with Christ. And in so doing, you become one with Him and his assembly. Blessed be God forever."

And with that, they laughingly, happily stepped out of the fountain, and Epaenetus and Diana put on their clothes. Each person embraced the others, sharing a joy that is impossible to describe. Tears were in Diana's eyes, and the four walked down the empty main street back to the side street that took them to Epaenetus's home.

"When you return," Diana said, "we will have you speak with the rest of our household. Epaenetus has been speaking of Iēsoûs to his brother. He said he would like to meet you when you return."

This pleased Paul to no end. He saw this couple as the seed, the means of contacting others in the city. If he could get enough, they could create their own synagogue, their own assembly. Ten should not be too difficult to get, especially if five or six of Epaenetus's slaves might be interested. That would solve the problem of the hostility of the existing synagogue leaders. They could create their own! Simple. Clean. And Epaenetus had a house big enough to use for the assemblies.

As the sun rose, they reclined at table, prayed, and Paul blessed and broke bread using the traditional words of Iēsoûs, "This is my body given for you." He did so with the wine, and after all had partaken, Barnabas prayed a psalm and breakfast was served.

About an hour later, a servant announced that Tychicus was at the door, and Paul and Barnabas arose, embraced both Epaenetus and Diana, and joined Tychicus, who had two riding horses and four pack animals led by two native Lycaonians. They mounted, this time a little more surely than they had a little over a month ago when they left Perga. They joined the traffic in the Cardo Maximus heading for the south gate. As they came close to the gate, they saw the president of the synagogue walking the opposite way on the street. He saw them clearly but did not give a sign of recognition, and the three followers of the Christ, after seeing him, kept their eyes riveted on the gate ahead.

CHAPTER 11

To Iconium

THE ROAD TO ICONIUM RAN through a valley at the foot of barren mountains to the northeast. Their route was to the southeast, and they made good time on a road that was little more than a cleared ribbon where the boulders had been moved to one side or the other. The surface was almost gravel, and travel was easy. There was no agriculture in the area, as it seemed it was almost a desert. The stubble foliage that dotted the area was gray-green and about waist-high throughout. There were no trees at all. For hours upon hours, they trudged along, seeing no signs of life, no rivers, only the dreary landscape.

"I feel the way this area looks," Paul said to Barnabas.

"What?"

"God called me to His service, to bring the Good News of Iēsoûs Christ to the world. For over eight years, I have been doing this. And what do I have to show for it? Almost nothing. Everywhere I have preached Christ Iēsoûs, I have failed. I failed in my hometown, rejected by my own parents and my poor, unfortunate wife. I nearly destroyed the assembly of brothers and sisters in Antioch in Syria. I failed in Cyprus. I failed this month in Antioch."

"You can take credit for Epaenetus," Barnabas said.

"*We* can take credit for Epaenetus. But I was the one who alienated the president of the synagogue. Why is it so hard?"

"Was it 'hard' for Epaenetus and Diana?"

"No. But they were Gentiles."

"But they will soon be Jews."

"Why can't our brothers see what we see? What makes them so blind? They read the same scriptures. They should see exactly what we see."

"Paul, you were given a kind of gift that few people will ever have. You received a revelation from the Lord that I have not had. What is easy for you is difficult for others. You gave up a way of life only because the Lord spoke to you."

"I feel like I am still in that storm at sea south of Attalia. We have no home, no place to stay, tossed one way then the other. Why can't some assembly see the light and invite us to settle down with them forever?"

"Do you know where Iēsoûs stayed during his ministry?" Barnabas asked.

"Capernaum?"

"Not really. He would stay a few weeks in one place and then move on to another. He really never did settle down, and often he would leave under pressure from the elders of a village. Everyone wanted to be healed, but when Iēsoûs would challenge them in a parable, many felt uncomfortable and often asked him to move on. Are we any different? Aren't we called to announce the Kingdom of God that is upon us? It is not visible, so it is not easy to see. We must develop a different kind of 'sight,' and that takes a sense of the Spirit. Not everyone has the ability to see, but Iēsoûs knew this, and he just kept moving on. Remember, after his death, there was only a handful of his followers left. Most went back to what they were doing before they took up with him. Changed, yes. But not undertaking the work of announcing the kingdom. We are doing just what he did. And since you received the revelation from him, you should be telling me these things, not me telling you!" He ended with a good-hearted laugh. "Cheer up, Paul. What did you expect? At least no one has threatened to crucify us...yet!"

They trudged on, silent. Before nightfall, their guides found small villages next to which they could camp and from whom they could purchase water from the extraordinarily deep wells. Paul and Barnabas were astounded at the idea of buying water, but there was no other source.

On one day, they saw not another human being but did see thousands of wild asses running through the scrub. On the third day, the terrain began to change, with signs of agriculture, then trees, then richer and more lush foliage. Small rivers passed under the road, and the transformation wrought by water was astonishing. They passed through small agricultural villages often, now, and irrigation canals laced the countryside. Men and children were spread throughout the fields, tending every imaginable kind of crop.

About midmorning on the third day, Tychicus pointed to a pair of conical peaks on the horizon to the east. "Below those peaks lies the city of Klaudiconium."

"Which city is that?" Paul asked.

Tychicus laughed. "Everyone still calls it Iconium, but the prince, Claudius, has taken an interest in several of the cities in this part of Galatia. A couple years ago, he approved a new name, using his as the first part. We also have Claudio-Laodicia and Claudio-Derbe. It is really quite popular."

"Are there any financial benefits?" Barnabas asked.

"I'm afraid not," Tychicus answered. "Iconium wants to be a *colonia* in which case the taxes will be reduced. But so far, there are not enough Roman veterans to press the case successfully. Who knows? Perhaps in the future…"

The road led inexorably toward the twin peaks, and by late afternoon, they approached the walls of Iconium.

Part III

CHAPTER 1
The Physician

ONESIPHORUS NODDED OFF FROM SHEER exhaustion as he bumped along the road astride his little burro. It was nearly noon, and he had been riding for three hours after spending the night at the bedside of a young farmer in a village ten miles south of Klaudiconium. The sturdy little animal knew the way home, so there was no need for the rider to pay attention. He knew he would get no sleep until nightfall. Patients will have been lining up at his house since sunrise, and they would beg for attention when he arrived. In twenty years of practicing medicine in the city, he had gotten used to sleeping on his faithful little nag. The rider's chin bounced on his chest, shoulders slack, but his body somehow remained upright on the small domesticated version of the ass that populated the surrounding countryside. Onesiphorus had playfully named the animal Bucephalus, after the massive war horse tamed by Alexander the Great.

He popped awake when the animal turned onto the main road to the city, whose walls were visible a few miles away. He noticed a group of travelers ahead by about a hundred yards. They had horses and a couple of pack animals, so they must be merchants. On the other hand, the horses were not heavily laden, so they probably had little merchandise with them. Perhaps they were going to purchase some of the famous rugs that were manufactured in the city, or maybe they were going to attempt to buy some copper from the mines to the northeast. His entire life was spent this way, looking at what everyone else saw but trying to see what was going on beneath the surface. He was always looking for hints, always trying on hypotheses, evaluating, and then either accepting them and acting or rejecting them and proposing another. That was the way he had been trained in Alexandria, following the methods of Hippocrates and the Cnidian physicians. For two years he had studied there, after being trained for two years by his father. And then, sixteen years ago, he returned to his home, when it was still called Iconium. Two years ago, he purchased his freedom from his master, Thamyris, whose household had owned him, his father, and his grandfather, all physicians.

As he dozed and waked and dozed again, his mind wandered aimlessly. He thought of the young farmer whose life he had hoped to save but who would undoubtedly die within a few days. One of the most important lessons he had learned in Alexandria was to recognize his own limitations. If he understood the disease, he could prescribe a cure, but there were some diseases about which no one knew the exact cause. And when confronted with these, he knew better than to try something that would be of no avail. He would always attempt to restore the proper balance of the humors within a person, but he also knew when the proper balance could never be achieved, such as last night. The young man was bleeding internally. Onesiphoris gave him medicine for the pain, made from the poppies he grew in his large herb garden. He would be comfortable for a few more days, maybe a week. But he would die. He reflected:

I spend my life trying to extend life. But I will, ultimately, be defeated. I cannot defeat Death, I can only hold him off for a while, force him back into the shadows. That farmer's young wife, wide eyed, hopeful, walked to the city two days ago to beg me to come to him. She is looking at Death but doesn't recognize him. The old woman in the village had done all she could, had given him amulets and had prayed over him. She had attempted to exorcise the demon, but I know that there was no demon, only imbalance. In this case, a fatal imbalance.

How careful I must be. They all think that purifications and prayer will heal. As though the gods wish us evil, and as though we can perform an incantation and force a god to do our will! How irrational! But everyone, except us few physicians, believes that. If I ever let on that such incantations were idiotic, they would stone me. So, I tolerate them on the part of the village healers, because they have nothing else. And I have so little more...

CHAPTER 2

Preview of Falling Sickness

As THE CITY WALLS NEARED, Paul began to feel flushed; he felt time beginning to slow down.

Oh, no, he thought. *"Not here. Not now. Oh, God, Father, please, not now.*

But that feeling overcame him, that feeling of perfect peace, where everything was perfectly clear and understandable. He had an instantaneous vision of the glorified Christ, triumphant, sitting adjacent to the Throne of the Most High, with a glorious cross streaming golden rays. This was unmistakable in its reality as the center of all being. And this Christ was connected to thousands, Jews and Gentiles, all of whom recognized him as the means of conquering death, the darkness below that shrank from the light of his cross. As a result of this connection, he saw those countless Jews and Gentiles living lives of virtue, thereby overcoming the dark rays that attempted to enfold them from below. For them, virtue flowed almost necessarily from their connection with the Conqueror of Death. For while they were capable of self-absorption, of giving themselves over to debauchery and promiscuity, these activities simply had no attraction compared to the benefits of life. He looked carefully, and all the humans were naked. Their passions were so controlled that lust was unthinkable. Sexuality, the bane of the flesh, was transformed by the action of Spirit. They existed on a higher plane. It was clear. The fleshly desire to couple with another was merely an analogy. It was shadow reality. The desire to become one flesh was an analogy of the true desire to become one Spirit. That is the reality. To become one, through the Spirit, through Christ.

Paul knew it was coming. He stopped his horse abruptly and dismounted. He looked at Barnabas but could say nothing. He knew that as soon as the vision ended, he would be humiliated. But he could say nothing. It had already started. He fell to the ground, rigid.

Reaction

Bucephalus kept plodding onward, carrying its burden whose feet just barely missed the rocks in the road, chin on chest, drifting in and out of a semi-sleep. The physician became instantly alive, aroused by the shouts just ahead among the merchants. He saw one man dismount, stand stiffly at the side of the horse for a moment, and then keel over like a felled tree. No hand outstretched to break the fall. Like a tree—crash, onto the side of the road. He recognized it at once: the divine sickness, it was called. But he called it the falling sickness because Hippocrates had demonstrated that it was not related in any way to the divine. However, the common perception was that a demon had entered into the poor fellow on the ground. The doctor kicked his mount in the ribs and slapped him on the rump to get him moving toward the figure. He was all business now.

As he rode up, two of the men were busy spitting on the figure; one was stooped over him, trying to talk with him.

"Don't bother. He doesn't hear you. I'm a doctor."

The men pulled back.

"A demon has entered him," one man screamed.

"Let me at him. Stand back," Onesiphorus said. "He will begin to convulse in a moment. Don't worry; he is all right. Just stand back."

The doctor knelt down next to Paul and produced a foot-long round stick that he forced between Paul's teeth. As if on cue, Paul's legs and arms began to shake uncontrollably. His eyes were rolled back in his head, and foam dribbled from the corners of his mouth. No sound came out, just an incredible, overall twitching of every element of his body. A nasty sound came from Paul's bowels, and flecks of brown fecal matter descended on his twitching legs. The doctor simply cradled his head to keep it from being bashed on the rocks at the roadside. He ignored Paul's arms and legs, which were being battered and bruised from their forceful contact with the ground. Everyone except the physician stood back.

After a few minutes, the convulsions seemed to lessen. Paul's body became limp and then it was over. Paul's eyes were closed, his breathing shallow and rapid.

"Give me some water," the doctor ordered, and a canteen filled the day before yesterday at great expense was brought to him. He laid Paul's head gently on the ground and walked to his saddlebag and brought out a piece of clean, soft cloth. He soaked it in water and began to clean the shit from Paul's legs.

Tychicus looked at Barnabas, amazed at the care that the stranger was exhibiting in this disgusting task.

"We can learn from this man," Barnabas whispered. "That is, in practice, what the message we proclaim is all about."

Tychicus nodded. He also looked at the two hired-hands who accompanied them. They were ridiculing the doctor in their barbaric tongue, which Tychicus understood perfectly, and which the doctor clearly overheard but ignored.

Paul opened his eyes. Blinked. Looked around. For him, there had been no passage of time. He was amazed to find himself on the ground, arms and legs sore from the battering of the rocky ground. His shoulder ached as though it had been struck by a battering ram.

"Where am I?" Paul asked. "Who are you?" he asked, looking directly at Barnabas. He closed his eyes and shook his head. For several minutes he closed his eyes and then opened them again, clearly confused.

"He will be all right in a few minutes," the doctor said to Barnabas.

"It happened again, didn't it?" Paul asked Barnabas thickly. Blood flowed from his mouth where he had bitten his tongue before the doctor inserted the stick.

"You will be fine," the doctor said.

"Who are you?"

"Onesiphorus, of Klaudiconium. I am a physician who happened to be traveling just behind you. I saw you when you dismounted—"

"I dismounted?"

"Yes. You have had an episode of the falling sickness. I want you to come to my house and stay there overnight. If it should come again, I want to be close to you."

"It usually doesn't come a second time," Paul said with difficulty.

"Well, I just want to be sure. Let me help you back up on your horse."

As they rode the couple miles to the city, Barnabas and Tychicus introduced themselves, and the former explained that he had a letter of introduction to the person who controls the copper trade in Iconium, that is, Klaudiconium."

"That would be Eupator, and I not only know one of his clients, Thamyris, but he is my patron. I purchased my freedom from his household only two years ago. I would be pleased to introduce you to him. Through Thamyris, I'm sure you will be able to meet Eupator."

Barnabas offered a silent prayer, recognizing the hand of the Lord in this fortuitous meeting, as the essence of both business and proclaiming the Good News was based on the system of patrons and clients, personal relationships that arose and declined. Without the personal connections, both business and preaching would be impossible.

As they approached the west gate to the city, they noticed the monumental statue of Perseus situated in the center of the road before the gate. It was at least four times life-size, with his left hand holding the *harpe*, a sword typical of him with a vicious-looking reverse sickle on the dull side, and with the gorgon-head grasped in his right hand, holding it out at knee-level. His attention was to his left, reminding everyone that he conquered the Medusa by making sure he did not look at her.

"Our founder," Onesiphorus said casually as they passed toward the gate. "Ours is an ancient city, with a long and illustrious history. Perseus reminds us that our culture conquered the ugliness of the barbarian way of life. He reminds us to look away from the kind of ugliness that will easily turn men's souls to stone, except they don't know it. So, they wallow in filth and think that they are leading a full and complete life."

Paul looked up, still woozy, not really comprehending what was going on around him. The vision that he had just before the attack did not permit him to see anything else. He remembered it. He remembered the all-consuming peace he felt when he saw what the world really looked like. He felt as if he had been dragged to the top of the mountain, out of the cave, into the sunlight. He had a chance to glimpse reality for a moment. But he was forced back down into the darkness, into the shadow world. How sad to have to return. But he knew so much more than he had known before. Another revelation. Another sharing. And why now? Was it because he was so discouraged? He couldn't focus on anything. The world drifted by meaninglessly. He saw the statue. He heard the doctor's comment. How shallow. How empty. He could say nothing. His soul was drawn back to the vision. Nothing else mattered.

CHAPTER 4

Aftermath

THE MORNING SUN PEEKED OVER the tip of the conical mountain and streamed full upon Paul's sleeping, upturned face. He opened his eyes and squinted against the brightness. Hand shielding his face, he looked around, puzzled. He lay in a clean bed in a room just larger than the bed itself. The end of the room at the foot of the bed had floor-to-ceiling shutters that had been thrown open, apparently last night. At the side of his bed was a small table with a vase of white chrysanthemums.

He looked out into a peristyle garden overgrown with flowers and herbs and vines, most of which he could not identify. At the center of the garden was a fountain that extended halfway across the garden, water flowing from three different levels. "Where am I?" he asked. He felt totally rested. He propped himself up on one elbow and looked around for a chamber pot. Naturally, it was right where it should have been, under the bed on the floor. He could hear no stirring in the garden, so he threw off the clean, soft blanket and looked for something to wear. Beneath the table he found a white tunic of some kind of soft material and a pair of sandals, which he put on. He walked into the garden and tried to recall where he might be. Looking around, he saw other doors opening onto the garden and other people still asleep in their beds. *There must be twenty rooms like mine*, he thought. *What a strange place.*

He walked to the end of the garden and heard a woman softly singing on the other side of a door. Concerned that the door might be to women's quarters, he turned away and started to walk back toward the room where he had awakened. He was startled as the door suddenly opened, and a woman carrying a basket with figs and dates and pieces of bread came through. She was as startled as he, and she laughed heartily at her surprise.

"Good morning, Paul," she chirped. "How do you feel?"

"G…g…good morning," Paul stammered. "I…I feel…I feel just wonderful! Who are you?"

"I am Lectra, Onesiphorus's wife. I help him with his patients."

"Forgive me," Paul said. "My memory is a bit blurry. The last thing I remember is riding toward the walls of Klaudiconium," he fibbed. He recalled the vision with absolute clarity, but she would not understand.

"Onesiphorus said you had a bout of the falling sickness, and he brought you here. You have slept for one and one-half days and two full nights! He said he had never seen anything like that, but since you seemed to be recovering, he did not wake you."

"He is a physician, then," Paul said, "and he cared for me?"

"Yes, and yes," the smiling lady said. She was in her mid-forties, and wisps of jet-black hair peeked out from the hair covering. Her long tunic was cinched at the waist and was of the same soft material he wore. Her complexion was pale, but with a ruddiness around her cheeks. She was on the stocky side, obviously strong, and had a smile that never left her face. Her eyes were the color of sapphires, deep, clear blue, a striking combination with her dark hair.

"We call this place a *paionios,* a place for healing."

"This is not an *Aesculapium?*" Paul asked in a horrified voice, concerned that he might be in a temple dedicated to the god Asculapius, where Greeks often went to be healed.

"No, no. Onesiphorus studied medicine in Alexandria, and he believes healing comes from the one, great, unknown God. He believes that health is a gift of that God and that his job is to assist God in bringing about a rebalancing of those natural forces with which God imbued the universe and thereby cure disease to the best of his ability. He does not believe that gods give or take away sickness. Hence, he does not use incantations or purifications."

"I am anxious to meet the man who has treated me so well."

"You will. He is seeing patients now, but you can come into the dining room if you like for breakfast. Barnabas and Tychicus are not yet stirring, though I expect that they will be up soon. They seem to be early risers. I will get you something to eat and then bring food to those patients who can't leave their beds."

She led Paul through the door she had come out of, across a small courtyard and into a large dining area set with long tables and benches, but no couches.

"I know this looks strange to you, but we often have so many people here that reclining on couches does not permit us to fit enough people in for a meal. So we use this method. I hope you don't find it too uncomfortable. After a while, you will get used to it."

She quickly swung a clay plate and a small knife onto the table, swished some figs, dates, and bread from her basket onto the plate, and provided a clay cup and a small flagon of liquid next to the plate.

"Onesiphorus has prescribed this liquid for you. It is called *kykeon*, and it is made from barley. You will have to get used to the taste, but you must drink all of it. I will return soon."

And with that, she was gone.

As Paul sat down, Barnabas and Tychicus entered the room. They cried out in unison, and all three embraced.

"Paul…"

"Barnabas…"

"Tychicus…"

"You gave us a scare," Barnabas said.

"The Lord provided Onesiphorus exactly when he was needed," Tychicus said. "You can't imagine our relief when you fell down and he was there. I never cease to be amazed at how the Lord is with us every moment, watching, caring, even bringing a doctor at the instant he was needed."

"I am anxious to meet him," Paul said.

The two newcomers knew just where to look in a cabinet just inside the door, and they produced their own plates, fruit, and bread. They poured a liquid into their cups.

"Are you going to drink this *kykeon*, too?" Paul asked. "It's horrible!"

"No. It is the juice of a *persikos*, made by our host. He removes the pit and puts the fruit into a tiny wine press, and out this juice comes. It is marvelous!"

Barnabas and Tychicus described their experiences for the past couple of days. The latter described his visit with Thamyris, a wealthy freedman of Titus Statilius Taurus. This Taurus was currently a consul and the son of another Statilius Taurus, who was the celebrated general of the great Augustus and who built the first stone amphitheater in the Campus Martius in Rome. Thamyris operated a fabulously successful carpet business for his patron.

He would engage weavers both in Klaudiconium and in the outlying villages; purchase exquisitely woven wool carpets from them; and ship them to Rome, Alexandria and Antioch in Syria, where they would sell at more than ten times the purchase price. Sixty percent of the profits would return to the patron, and forty percent would be retained by Thamyris. He was one of the wealthiest individuals in the city.

Tychicus had told Onesiphorus that Barnabas needed an introduction to the individual who operated the copper mines to the northeast of Klaudiconium. Tychicus disclosed that copper prices in Paphos had dropped, due to additional supply coming from these mines. Phidippides had asked his brother, Barnabas, to discuss the matter with the individual (most likely a freedman). The goal was to have the Klaudiconium producer raise his prices so as not to compete with copper from Cyprus. Competition was viewed as ungentlemanly, and a shared monopoly with agreed-upon prices was felt to be the proper way to do business. Profit margins should never be cut!

Tychicus reported that they had had an excellent meeting with Thamyris, and the latter had invited Barnabas along with Tychicus and

Paul (assuming he was well) for a dinner at his home, where Barnabas would meet with Eupator, the freedman of Marcus Castelios, the governor of Lycaonia. The latter had rights to all minerals mined in the province, and Eupator was in charge of the copper mines for the governor. Since Tychicus seemed to want his two protégés to accompany him (after all, his loan was paying for their entire support) Paul feigned excitement and agreed to accompany his two companions the next evening.

The friends chatted awhile longer and were mildly startled when the lanky doctor popped his head into the room. "I heard you were awake. You look fine," he said to Paul as he walked in.

"I feel great!"

Onesiphorus poured himself some peach juice and sat down.

Addressing Tychicus, he said, "I have sent a messenger to Thamyris, thanking him for the kind invitation to dine with him and with his betrothed, Thecla, but I have far too many people in the *paionios* to permit an evening of revelry."

Tychicus raised his eyebrows, which was noticed by Onesiphorus, who responded with a laugh. "I know. Most patrons would be highly insulted if their client refused an offer of hospitality. But about a year before I secured my freedom, Thamyris became gravely ill. We all expected him to die, as his heartbeat was irregular, and he had pain in the arms and shortness of breath. I had been experimenting with a potion created from the elixir of foxglove, and I discussed the fact that we might try this in small quantities. I explained that in general, the extract of this plant is lethal, but I had seen some patients with irregular heartbeats improve with small doses. He agreed, and I tried the mixture. Within a week, he had improved, and within a month, with regular dosage, he was back to normal health. He was convinced that I had saved his life. And in fact, the medicine did save him. But there is now a sense in which he is *my* client and I am his patron. So strangely do things work in life! So I have no concern about refusing his invitation. However, you, Paul, look healthy enough to go, so I give you permission. But take care to limit your intake of wine, and make sure it is well watered. Finally, you are to eat no beans.

Otherwise, you may enjoy the evening. For today, I want you to rest, but you may plan to accompany your friends tomorrow."

And with that, he tossed off the balance of the peach juice and strode out the door, nodding to Tychicus and Barnabas. "Feel free to stay here in my home until tomorrow; then you can find an inn within a few minutes' walk of Thamyris's home. The synagogue usually has a few guest rooms available, so go there first." He bounced out, smiling at the three men. "Lectra will give you a bill for my services, along with the cost of hospitality while you reside here. Fortunately, I don't have too many patients. Otherwise, you could not remain here."

The three men nodded; Paul rose and extended his arms to embrace Onesiphorus. He responded with a soft chuckle and went across the garden, where another patient waited.

CHAPTER 5

A Productive Dinner

THE HOME OF THAMYRIS WAS sumptuous. It opened just off the agora of the city, with a wide staircase of a dozen steps leading to a pillared portico that sheltered the high double door. Servants were stationed outside the door, and one opened the door when Tychicus announced his name to him. The three men entered into a massive atrium with a ten-foot-square mosaic-tiled impluvium to catch rainwater in the center, and with statues of maenads at the four corners. A statue of the Divine Claudius, outfitted as Heracles, was on the left wall, and one of the Great Mother was on the right, seated on a wheeled throne with two lions as armrests. Directly behind the atrium was a peristyle garden festooned with sculpture and with a massive fountain at the center. The party was escorted down the left portico flanking the garden to the largest private dining room that Paul had ever seen. There was room for twelve couches, although only eight were prepared.

As they entered, Tychicus threw his arms out toward a man engaged in conversation with two women and another man. "Tychicus," the younger of the two men exclaimed happily. "Welcome, welcome."

"Thank you, Thamyris," Tychicus responded, striding toward the smiling host, who was overweight and probably in his late thirties. He wore a togawithout a stripe but which sported exquisite embroidery at the edges. His thin salt-and-pepper hair was combed straight down over his broad forehead. Small black eyes were almost hidden behind the perpetual squint of someone with bad eyesight. His fleshy cheeks were clean shaven.

"Meet two of my colleagues, Paul" (Paul nodded politely) "and Barnabas." He also nodded. "These are friends from Antioch in Syria, visiting our city for a while."

"You are welcome in my home," said Thamyris. "Let me present my betrothed, Thecla, and her mother, Theoclia. And this is my business associate, Lentulus, from Lystra, and Eupator, who is responsible for the copper mines to the northeast."

Barnabas and Paul shook hands with Lentulus and Eupator in the Roman fashion, with each party grasping the wrist of the other. They merely nodded to the women. After a short time in conversation, Thamyris assigned guests to the couches as serving men and women entered with the first course. Thecla was given the place of honor, sharing a couch with her betrothed. Her mother, Theoclia had the next most honorable place, with Lentulus, Eupator, Tychicus, Barnabas, and Paul filling out the remaining prepared couches. Tychicus and Thamyris dominated the conversation, discussing the economy of Iconium and the benefits of being a colonial city, with many retired Roman legionnaires living in the area.

Lentulus, gray-haired and seeming somewhere around fifty, was particularly quiet, but at a pause in the conversation, he looked at Paul and said, "Haven't we met before?"

Paul seemed to think for a moment and then reddened. "I think we met when you were taking your son (was his name Timothy?) to the harbor in Tarsus. That was almost three years ago. My father and I were shamed by the behavior of my wife."

"Paul, I apologize. I had completely forgotten about that. I hardly had a few minutes with you after we got to the harbor. I remember a terrible rainstorm just prior to the ship's shoving off."

"I was very impressed with your son, Timothy," Paul added. "How is he? Is he back from Alexandria?"

"Yes, he returned several months ago and is participating in my business, which was financed through a loan from Alexander the Alabarch in Egypt. It has been a very successful venture."

Barnabas chimed in: "Did Timothy tell you about our wild ride from Antioch to the port of Seleucia?"

"It has become a legend in our town, and he loves to tell it. We all end up laughing as we visualize you, Barnabas, racing down the Orontes River. Sometimes he embellishes it by claiming that it was really no race since they stopped for an hour of pleasure in Daphne on their way to the coast!"

"I can tell you," Paul said with a smile in his voice, "There were no stops!"

"I can laugh about it now," Lentulus said, "but if Timothy had missed the ship and had lost the contract on the cultivation of *kannabis* it would have been a disaster for me and my family."

"Is that some kind of plant?" Barnabas asked.

"Yes. It is a remarkable plant out of which we manufacture the highest-quality rope and nautical cable. Further, we have discovered how to use the stalk of the plant and to make thread that can be woven. The end material is three times stronger than linen, weighs about the same, and lasts twice as long. Much of our weaving operation occurs here in Iconium, using the skilled weavers employed by Thamyris. We then ship the fabric to Tarsus, to the Paulus who must be your father."

"Indeed, it is my father. I have had no news of the family since I left Tarsus about two years ago. And I had never heard of this new material. Our family business used skins of cattle to make tent material. I know how important is the balance between lightness of weight and strength of the material, especially when the end product is a tent," Paul added.

"My son, Timothy, spent almost two years in Alexandria, and when he returned, he reported the conversations you and he had on the ship to Antioch in Syria and Caesarea. He thought the philosophy you present is attractive. Since Timothy has been under the tutelage of a philosopher since he was a child, I found his comments of some interest."

"I certainly don't want to impose myself on this lovely gathering," Paul responded.

Thecla perked up and said to Paul, "I'd love to hear what you offer. Are you a Cynic?"

"No. While I am currently traveling, I consider that I have a home, and I do not plan to lecture uninvited in the agora. I merely bring a certain Good News to those who invite me to speak."

"Now you have me interested," Thecla said. "Tell us what this Good News is."

"That question cannot really be addressed quickly, especially at a wonderful dinner party."

"I'd like to hear it as well," said Lentulus, "though we don't want to turn this into a symposium."

"I'd like to propose a compromise," said Paul." Is there a synagogue near? If so, I will contact the president and ask if I can address the community next Sabbath. I know that any or all of you would be welcome."

"I know the synagogue president," Thamyris added, "and I'll be happy to speak with him. And we can all attend and hear this Good News."

Lentulus nodded, with a smile.

"I shall beg to be excused," Eupator said. "The only 'Good News' I am interested in would be that my slaves are happily clawing more green ore out of the mines." He laughed.

"And I hope that you and I might discuss some matters regarding copper at your convenience," Barnabas said.

"Yes, indeed," said Eupator. "Call on me tomorrow midmorning."

Barnabas caught Tychicus's eye, and saw a "yes" in his nod.

"I look forward to our discussion," Barnabas said.

At that, serving slaves began to bring in the first course of the meal. A woman in a white, flowing tunic entered with a cithara. She walked to the opposite side of the room, continued standing, and began to play and sing well-known poems by Sappho. The seven-stringed instrument was held up by a strap around her left wrist, and she played with her right hand. Paul focused on both the singer and the words of the song. The words were descriptive of a gentle and sensitive love, and the accompaniment created a gentle atmosphere within the room. Thecla leaned back onto Thamyris' breast and looked up smiling, lovingly to his down-turned face.

A beautiful love, Paul thought. *How sad that I never had that experience. The opportunity was there, but my short-sightedness made it impossible. I must reflect on this within the framework of the glory of the cross. His actions were the result of his unconditional love for us. What I see here can be best understood as a reflection of his love. This indeed is the essence of the Good News.*

As the dinner ended and everyone arose from the couches and began to sidle toward the door, Lentulus approached Paul, saying, "I have been married for twenty-one years to a Jewish woman, whose name is Eunice. Her mother, Lois, came to live with us five years ago because she was being snubbed for the departure of her daughter with me many years ago."

"What do you mean 'departure of her daughter'?"

"It's a long story that I'll share with you at a better time. I'll be at the synagogue to hear what you have to say, though I worship Mithras, as do almost all the Roman legionnaires."

"I'll look forward to seeing you next Sabbath," Paul said, extending his arm in a Roman handshake as the guests filed out the door and walked to their lodgings.

CHAPTER 6

Love and Sabbath

IT HAD TO BE HALFWAY through the night. Paul could not sleep. *After sundown I will address the synagogue in Klaudiconium, including Thamyris, Thecla, Theoclea, her mother and Lentulus. I have a better opportunity to found a community here than ever before. Cyprus and Antioch in Pisidia were disasters. Now I have a real chance. Thamyris has the financial strength to provide the support of the community. I think that if I can convince him, Thecla and Theoclia will follow, and then we will have some women who can share in the mission. The movement needs women to spread the Good News among women. I can never again get myself in a situation like that in Antioch. I recall how, two nights ago, Thecla looked at Thamyris. Her love for him is palpable, and he seems to return it. I shall make the centerpiece of my teaching the model of that love that was expressed by Iēsoûs the Christ. The ultimate act of love is giving up what is most precious, one's very life. Christ expressed God's love for us when he willingly gave up his life so that we might live. That is what exists for Thecla and Thamyris. They can participate in this love of God as expressed by Christ by loving each other. They must understand that we do not deny the Torah. I think I have to remind everyone of the Torah, which instructs us that* "you shall not commit adultery; you shall not kill; you shall not steal; you shall not covet." *And whatever other commandments there may be are summed up in this saying:* "You shall love your neighbor as yourself." *Love does no evil to the neighbor; hence, love is the fulfillment of the Law.*

Yet, within this framework, it is crucial that as we live among Gentiles, we must not fall into their excesses, especially sexual excesses. I won't bring it up in my first sermon, but hopefully in a second, follow-up sermon. I will remind everyone that those who belong to Christ have crucified their flesh with its passions and desires. In Christ, one lives in the spirit through whom our sexual desires are controlled. I wish I could speak of the kind of intimacy that seems to exist between Thecla and Thamyris. I could never look at Ruth the way Thamyris looks at Thecla. If they can see their love as being modeled by Christ, then they will certainly have the kind of marriage I wish I had. That's what I will emphasize...

He dropped off to sleep.

CHAPTER 7

Business

THE NEXT MORNING, THAMYRIS ACCOMPANIED Barnabas and Tychicus to meet with Eupator. The latter greeted them warmly, praising Thamyris for the food and entertainment and congratulating him on the beauty of his betrothed wife. Responding to Eupator's inquiry, Thamyris said that the wedding would take place in four weeks.

Then they got down to business. Eupator invited two men, Demas and Hermogenes, to participate in the meeting. Hermogenes operated a smelter that produced copper ingots from the copper ore. Demas manufactured a broad array of copper pots, pans, trays, and bowls and shipped them to Attalia for distribution around the Mediterranean. Both wore copper bracelets with Eupator incised, indicating their status as slaves of Eupator. Nevertheless, they were accorded the same cordiality as Eupator showed toward Thamyris and Tychicus.

After a few minutes of polite conversation, Eupator led off. "Gentlemen, a close associate of Tychicus here has indicated that it is in everyone's best interest to raise the price on our copper. I'd like to hear what you think."

"How much an increase?" asked Demas. "And who is proposing this price change?"

"Phidippides, an agent of Sergius Paulus in Cyprus, has authorized his brother, Barnabas, to represent him regarding an increase in our selling price of between one-tenth and two-tenths."

"A two-tenths increase is impossible," said Demas. "I pay twenty denarii per standard ingot; that ingot will produce thirty high-quality household trays that sell for three denarii. An increase in my cost of ingots will put my products out of reach for many people and will decrease my income. I'm opposed to this idea."

"I'm also opposed," Hermogenes said. "If the price of household trays goes up, there will be fewer sold. And with a reduction in sales, Demas is not going to buy as much copper from me. My profits will drop as well as your income, Eupator."

"I fail to see what benefit would accrue to us if we increased our price," Eupator said. "I listen carefully to my partners; we have worked in the copper trade for over twenty years. We have a good source of slaves from the Romans to work the mines. No, I don't think we'll raise our price," Eupator said authoritatively. "And forgive my curiosity, Tychicus, but what is the relationship between you, Barnabas, and Paul?"

"Sir, Paul might be initially understood as being like a Cynic philosopher, in that he has no interest in generating wealth and power. He brings to the world what he and I call the 'Good News of Iēsoûs Christos,' regarding a holy man from Palestine who was sent by God to forgive sins and to fulfill the Law of the Jews, bringing all people to eternal life."

"Why am I negotiating with people who are not in business?" Eupator asked.

"Let me suggest, sir, that I bring a written authorization from my brother, Phidippides, to engage in this matter. I have a business in Antioch in Syria that is being operated by my family. I am not ignorant of business matters because for a time I travel with Paul, my client and friend." There was a bit of sharpness in Barnabas's voice, and Eupator's face reddened a bit.

"I don't mean to offend you," Eupator quickly responded. "However, I must see a significant benefit to my patron before I change my pricing. And I have not seen that. Thank you for your effort." Thus Eupator quickly closed the meeting.

And with that, Thamyris, Barnabas and Tychicus bade goodbye to Eupator, Demas, and Hermogenes and headed back to their respective abodes. They discovered that Paul had found a synagogue through Thecla that had several guest-rooms and had taken them for a period of four weeks. The synagogue was adjacent to the home of Thecla and Theoclea.

CHAPTER 8

The Sermon

PAUL, BARNABAS, AND TYCHICUS ENTERED the synagogue as soon as the doors were opened. Sabbath would begin in about two hours, at sundown. They found the synagogue leader without trouble, a tall man about sixty years old with Semitic facial features and a ready smile.

"My name is Jonah. Welcome."

Barnabas introduced Paul with lavish praise, mentioning that he had studied the Torah in Jerusalem under Gamaliel. Jonah asked if Paul might do both the scripture reading and provide a sermon after the reading. Paul respond instantly, with a broad smile.

"Wonderful. It so happens that my only student, a man by the name of Titus, had planned both to proclaim the reading and deliver the homily. He will welcome your approach to the Word of God. He is a God fearer and has been with me for almost three years. I want him to succeed me, since there are so few Jews who want to study the Torah here in the province of Lycaonia."

"What is delaying his appointment?" Paul asked.

"He is a Greek and has not been circumcised. He keeps putting it off."

"Is this a problem in other synagogues here in Klaudiconium?" Paul asked.

"Indeed it is. Women often join us, but their husbands in general refuse to submit to circumcision. In fact, there is only one *mo'el* in the city who specializes in adult circumcision."

Paul nodded and added, "Circumcision can be such a barrier. How many Gentiles love the Torah but choose to stay separate from the People of God.

"As to scripture, I propose to read the fourth description by Isaiah of the Suffering Servant. Would that be acceptable? I can deliver both without prior preparation."

"Of course," Jonah responded.

For about an hour the men discussed the Jewish community in the city, especially the issue of Gentiles' participation in Sabbath services, along with their general lack of keeping food laws. Celebrating Jewish holidays was also a problem.

"Well, gentlemen, it is almost time for Queen Sabbath to be greeted. Are you ready, Paul?"

Paul nodded with a smile. Jonah directed Paul and Barnabas to the front of the meeting room, which was divided longitudinally into two parts, the larger of which was for men, the smaller for women. Before long, people began to filter in, engage in small-talk, and take their seats. Thecla and Theoclia took seats in the first women's row, smiling greetings to Paul and Barnabas. There was some commotion on the men's side when Thamyris arrived and slowly took his seat, chatting with acquaintances. Lentulus entered alone and quietly took a seat in the back row. Thamyris caught his eye with a nod. Soon, both parts of the synagogue were filled, and some stood along the back wall. Jonah strode down the center aisle of the men's portion, along with a handsome young man with blond, curly hair. Both wore blue-edged prayer shawls, their forearms wrapped in thin leather strips and a small leather box attached by leather strips to their foreheads. As they came to the front, they intoned loudly: "Hear, O Israel!"

The community responded:

The LORD is our God, the LORD alone!
Therefore, you shall love the LORD, your God, with your whole heart,
and with your whole being, and with your whole strength.

Take to heart these words which I command you today.
Keep repeating them to your children.
Recite them when you are at home
and when you are away, when you lie down and when you get up.
Bind them on your arm as a sign and let them be as a pendant on your
forehead.
Write them on the doorposts of your houses and on your gates.

By the time this was complete, the young man, square-built with smiling eyes, had reached the front of the room, had opened a rectangular box in the wall containing several scrolls, and removed one reverently. He laid it on a table at the center of the front portion, unrolled it for a short time, and then laid a pointer with a miniature hand on the end at one verse.

Jonah arose.

"Thank you, Titus. We are honored to have a scholar who studied under the famous Gamaliel in Jerusalem. He is visiting us for a little while and would like to share his insights into God's holy word."

He gestured to Paul, who picked up the pointer and began to read:

See, my servant shall prosper, he shall be raised high and greatly exalted.
Even as many were amazed at him so marred were his features, beyond
that of mortals his appearance, beyond that of human beings,
So shall he startle many nations, kings shall stand speechless;
For those who have not been told shall see, those who have not heard shall
ponder it.
Who would believe what we have heard?
To whom has the arm of the LORD been revealed?
He grew up like a sapling before him, like a shoot from the parched earth;
He had no majestic bearing to catch our eye, no beauty to draw us to him.
He was spurned and avoided by men, a man of suffering, knowing pain,
Like one from whom you turn your turn your face, spurned.
And we held him in no esteem.

Yet it was our pain that he bore, our sufferings he endured.
We thought of him as stricken, struck down by God and afflicted,
But he was pierced for our sins, crushed for our iniquity.
He bore the punishment that makes us whole, by his wounds we were
healed.

When Paul had completed the reading, he took a deep breath.

"I'm sure you have heard this part of the prophet Isaiah before. When I tried to understand it, I asked myself, 'Who is the prophet referring to?' Initially, it seems easy, but it is complex. Who, I ask, is the first speaker? It is the Lord; the 'servant' is the servant of the Lord. Next, we have a sudden shift in who is speaking. It is the prophet himself who will tell us about the Lord's servant. 'He shall be raised high and greatly exalted.' 'Raised' from what? How is he 'exalted?' I would offer a first suggestion: The Lord's servant was raised from the dead and exalted by God, seated at the Lord's right hand.

"We read that 'many were amazed at him.' Why? Because during his life, he performed many powerful works, curing illnesses, expelling unclean spirits, even raising the dead. Further, he taught the meaning of Torah with authority.

"But what comes next? Listen:

So marred were his features, beyond that of mortals his appearance,
beyond that of human beings
So shall he startle many nations, kings shall stand speechless;
For those who have not been told shall see, those who have not heard shall
ponder it.

"His features were marred because he was beaten like a criminal; his body was bloodied and broken by the lash. All who hear of this cannot explain it, how a servant of the Lord should have been treated. But the word is going forth through all those who share this remarkable reality.

"We next hear what is truly remarkable: he grew up like any of us. He could have lived in our neighborhood or village. He did not have a regal bearing or anything by which we could reason to who he really was. In fact, he was spurned by men and bore pain and suffering. We don't know why he bore such pain yet, but we know he was not held in any esteem. We have to listen more to the prophet to understand why.

"We next read: *Yet it was our pain that he bore, our sufferings he endured.* This is remarkable and unheard of elsewhere in scripture, that one person should through his pain and suffering substitute himself for us. We thought that the Lord was punishing him for his own sin; but he suffered the ultimate penalty of crucifixion for us. He bore the punishment for our sins, *crushed for our iniquity.* We were made whole by his suffering on the cross. Why? Because of his love for us. This was not an emotional attachment that one person has for another. It not only the sacrifice of his life, but the lifting of the just punishment that is due to all of our failures.

"By now, you must be asking whom the prophet is referring to. I'll tell you. It is Iēsoûs the Christ, crucified under Pontius Pilate. But his death did not complete his task. We read in the beginning of the discussion of Isaiah that *he shall be raised high and greatly exalted.* What does this mean? It means that God raised him from the dead and by that act exalted him above all other men and angels.

"You note that I identified him as *Iesoûs,* the Greek translation of Jeshua; but I also called him *Christos,* the Anointed One. This is the one that we Jews have been waiting for, the one who will bring forth justice on the earth, who will judge all nations and establish peace. He has actually revealed himself to me, and I know that he will return soon. The End Times, as described by many prophets, are upon us. It is through faith in Iēsoûs Christos that we shall receive his spirit and shall live our lives in peace and harmony."

"He is the fulfillment of the Torah, the prophets, and the writings. Everything written in our scriptures points to him. I urge you, I challenge you: believe in him. It is through him that we have recovered the relationship with God that in Hebrew we call *Tzadik*, or *Justice*. Adam introduced sin and death in the world. Iēsoûs bore our sins and reestablished the life of love in God, and by so doing overcame death. We are talking of matters of 'life' and 'death.' Choose the former through Iēsoûs the Christ."

"'Life' occurs within our souls when we see the love that Iēsoûs the Christ expressed for us is the model for our life. When we love another, when we look into our beloved's face and smile deeply, we are doing precisely what Christ did for us. Our love for others is an expression of the model we see in Iēsoûs the Christ's willingness to die for us. This is where true life occurs. It is in sharing that life that we become whole."

Paul returned to his seat. Jonah arose and invited the congregation to stand as he intoned a psalm in Hebrew *Odeh Adonai b'cal-libbi*, "I will praise you, Lord, with all my heart." The congregation immediately chimed in for the next twenty verses. There was no text, but everyone seemed to know the words and the melody. At the end, several men came forward to Paul and congratulated him. Paul had noticed Lentulus, but he silently left with the other men. The last of these was Titus, who had removed the phylacteries from his arm and head.

"Rav, I am Titus. I study Torah under Rav Jonah. I am moved by how you interpret Isaiah. Do you think we could spend some more time together?"

"Yes, Titus, we can. Please call me Paul.. That is sufficient."

The two men pulled up chairs next to a window that had wood louvers inset that could be adjusted to let in outside air or to keep out rain. The window was directly across from a window in the adjacent house, the width of a walkway between them. Unknown to both Paul and Titus, Thecla was sitting next to her window and could hear their conversation clearly.

"As Jonah told you, I am a God-fearer in this synagogue. This Christ that you proclaim has paid the price for our sins. But what does this mean? What kind of sins?"

"Having studied Torah, you certainly know the basics. First, the worship of false gods is perhaps the most grievous sin, as it is an offense against the Lord. Second, we have those things that Iēsoûs taught. He said, *You shall not kill; you shall not commit adultery; you shall not steal; you shall not bear false witness; you shall not defraud; honor your father and your mother.* These are important, but the greatest challenge is the next level of rectitude, which is to sell everything that one has and follow him. There were many of his followers who listened to this and left him. To live in poverty is something that can be found in scripture, but is not often recognized as an obligation if one chooses to follow him."

Paul and Titus continued talking for several hours in the light of a single candle. Thecla remained at her window and absorbed the questions and answers. Finally, Titus bade Paul good night by extending his arms and enfolding the Paul's slight frame in a strong embrace.

"'Till morning," Titus said as he walked out the door.

Paul nodded in the darkness.

CHAPTER 9

Consequences of the Sermon

THE SUN HAD HARDLY RISEN when Paul heard Tychicus and Barnabas talking in the common room adjacent to the synagogue's guest rooms.

"I heard Titus and Paul talking well into the night; Titus is very bright and a candidate for someone who would be a leader in a community that proclaims Iēsoûs," Barnabas said. "His family are both native Lycaonians and extraordinary farmers. Jonah told me last night that they have an arrangement where they provide all the food for the slaves who work in the copper mines."

Paul walked into the room and greeted his friends with a broad smile. He also noted a low table with fresh figs, a bowl of yogurt, and a large loaf of thick brown bread baked yesterday. He happily helped himself and took his seat on a cushion next to the table.

"I expect Titus to arrive sometime this morning. He is full of questions and is completely open to the message we bear," Paul said.

"You know that he is closely connected to Eupator, providing food to the slaves that mine the copper," Barnabas said.

"No, I didn't know that," Paul said. "I wonder if I could convince him to let me speak with some of the miners. I so wanted to speak with them when we were in Tamassos, but I knew I could not pursue the matter with your brother."

"Yes, Paul," Barnabas responded. "We were constrained there. You must make sure Titus knows that Iēsoûs came to slaves as well as to the free. Perhaps he can approach Eupator and be permitted to speak with at least a few of the workers after they leave the mine for the day."

"Agreed." Paul nodded.

It was after noon before Paul heard Titus knocking on the synagogue door. Delighted, Paul rushed to the door and met the broad smile of the blond man. They took their places as before next to the window, not aware that Thecla had also heard the knock and had taken her place so that she could hear the conversation only a few feet away.

"Paul, I was unable to sleep last night, so many new ideas were bubbling up in my mind. I have never heard such a remarkable story. How can I understand Iēsoûs within the framework of my study of Torah?"

"Let me try to explain this. You recall in the first book of Torah, we read that the Lord God created everything. Quote for me the words of the creation of *the Man,* or in Hebrew, *ha Adam.*"

Titus responded quickly, *The LORD God formed the Man out of the dust of the ground and blew into his nostrils the breath of life, and the man became a living being.*

"Right. And what happened to him?"

The LORD God planted a garden in Eden, in the east, and placed there the man whom he had formed.

"Good. Now what can we conclude about *the Man* as he related to the Lord God?"

"First, *the Man* had to be perfect in every detail, having been not only created by the Lord God but placed in a garden that also had to be perfect. There had to be a supreme bond of love that bound *the Man* to the Lord God."

"Excellent. We have an example here of what the human being should be like, loving the Lord God and being loved by the Lord God because of his perfection. Then what do we read?"

"First, *knowing that it was not good for the Man to be alone, the Lord God created all the animals of the world and gave him dominion over them.*"

"Yes, and then: H*e took out one of the Man's ribs and closed up its place with flesh. He then built the rib that he had taken from the man into a woman. When he brought her to the Man, the Man said: "This one, at last, is bone of my bones and flesh of my flesh; this one shall be called 'woman,' for out of man this one has been taken. That is why a man leaves his father and mother and clings to his wife, and the two of them become one body.* "Well done," Paul exclaimed. "I know you can recite the next line, that they were naked but were not even aware of it. This means that they were not corrupted by passion but loved each other in the Spirit. *The Man* had been given one single commandment, which was not to eat of the fruit of the Tree of Knowledge of Good and Evil. During that period when *the Man* (in Hebrew, *ha ish)* and *the Woman* (in Hebrew, *ha ishah*) lived together sinlessly. The Lord God and they were bound together in perfect love.

"Then we all know that they disobeyed the one simple commandment given by the Lord God, and as a result they first knew passion, since otherwise they would not have sewn garments or hidden from the Lord God. Further, and most significantly, death was introduced into the world. *By the sweat of your brow you shall eat bread, Until you return to the ground, from which you were taken; For you are dust, and to dust you shall return.*

"Does this mean that passion is evil? If so, how could *the Man* and *the Woman* have begun the human race?"

"No, Titus, passion is part of the Lord God's plan for the world. However, if one can avoid passion, it is better. Marriage itself is good, as we see that all men cling to their wives, but passion has a tendency to distort the love that one must have for others."

"Are you married?" Titus asked.

"No, I am not." Paul said. "And I shall never marry, since I know that would interfere with my proclamation of the Good News of Iēsoûs Christos."

Thecla was sitting on the edge of her chair at the window. Her heart beat faster at hearing that Paul was unmarried. She resolved that she would ask Paul tomorrow if he would advise her in the same way that he was counseling Titus. Everything Paul had said to Titus resonated in her soul; how incredible if he could get to know her. She might be able to fill the void in her heart that she had felt upon first meeting him. While Thamyris was a good man and would give her a comfortable life, he had no sense of the Good News she had been hearing these past several days. Tomorrow, she would walk next door and ask Paul about deepening her understanding of this man who was the model for all love in the world.

CHAPTER 10

Slaves

THE NEXT DAY, PAUL WENT into the meeting room expecting to find Titus at their usual location. He was surprised to see Thecla sitting where Titus usually sat.

"Good day," he offered, smiling. He saw a woman of medium height and weight whose white skin was dominated by a raging head of red hair. Paul recalled seeing the same physical features when they entered into Galatia several weeks ago. She could have been the younger sister of Urfel, the giant escort on the trip to Antioch in Pisidia. She had the same blue eyes and broad shoulders and the same even white teeth. Paul looked around and saw no one else in the area.

"Sir, I come here because I have heard you speak about Iēsoûs the Christ. I myself worship the Great Mother, but the god you preach may be more powerful than her."

"I remember you from three nights ago, when we dined at the home of Eupator. You were with your betrothed, Thamyris, who has been most kind to us. I would like to suggest that we walk to his home, and with his consent, we can discuss Iēsoûs with him."

"I don't believe that he is interested in a new god."

"Thecla, I do not proclaim a 'new god,' but the one and only true God and his Son. The Lord God of Israel existed before this world, created it and everything in it. All other gods are not truly existent."

"Well, I am anxious to learn about this Lord God. You can begin now."

"I want to teach you, but I suggest that I visit your home and teach your mother as well."

"Neither is she interested." She smiled.

"Thecla, I must have at least another woman or a family member from Thamyris in order to begin. And I need you to leave this place now and return to your home."

"Why? Is this Iēsoûs opposed to having women as followers? Is this like the religion of Mithras, so popular among soldiers?"

"By no means," Paul responded. "Women are welcome, but there are some who would improperly interpret our being alone together. I know you are pure of heart, but you are, in fact, betrothed to another. I'm concerned for what others might conclude if we are not cautious."

"I still want to learn about Iēsoûs" she said as she stood up and stalked from the room.

Paul sat down at the table, put his head in his hands, and exhaled slowly.

How can this be? Our best chance to found a community and suddenly it becomes impossible. A married couple is what we need, so that I can teach both without the repetition of the disaster in Antioch. Titus might be able to interest his wife, if he has one Amazing that I don't know his marital state.

Just then, Titus arrived, and unbeknown to Paul, Thecla was at her place next to the window, where she heard every sound.

"Why so glum?" Titus asked, noticing the distress on Paul's face and his lack of a normal greeting.

"Thecla just left here. She wanted to learn about the Lord Iēsoûs, but I refused because I could not teach her alone."

"Why?"

At that point, Paul recited the entire episode in Antioch with Sosipater and Charis. "Except for Barnabas, you are the only person in the world who knows of my shame and the need to leave Antioch for Cyprus under those conditions. I don't know what I would have done without Barnabas. But I must never put myself in such a position again. Thus, I appeared to reject a person who might easily have formed a community of followers around her. That is what grieves me so."

"You must remain patient," Titus counselled. "The Spirit of the Lord Iēsoûs will be with you, and we together will be able to proclaim the Good News."

Paul was stunned. This was the first time Titus had indicated that he might be willing to participate in Paul's assigned task. He silently said: *Lord, you pick me up when I fail. How could I not have had faith in your presence?*

"Paul, I'd like to know exactly who the Good News is directed to. Since the Lord was a Jew, I know he would want his own people to proclaim him. But why are you spending your time with Jews outside the land of Israel? You have been teaching me the Word of God that we find in scripture, which seems to indicate that we non-Jews must become Jews through circumcision first. Jonah has been urging me to become a Jew for over a year. But the barbaric mutilation makes no sense to me. I understand that a baby eight days old hardly feels it. We'll never know that, but I'm sure that if someone cuts off my foreskin, I'm going to be in agony for who knows how long? Is the Good News directed only to Jews?"

"No, Titus. I hold that the Good News is proclaimed to women and men, Jew or Greek. In fact, it is directed to slaves as well as to those who are free. And that applies even to the slaves who work in the mines to the north of the city."

"I don't know how, since most of the slaves were bought from Vespasian, the commander of II Augusta Legion. These came from a place called *Britannia* somewhere near the western end of the world. Almost none of them speak Greek. But, remarkably, their language sounds very similar to that of the Galatian people called *Trocmi.* They are strong and excellent workers, for which Eupator paid a hefty price."

"Do you have any slaves like these?" asked Paul.

"Yes, I have a foreman whom I purchased from Eupator so that we could coordinate the provision of food for the miners. He speaks some Greek, but not much. I could bring him here tomorrow if you think it is not a waste of time to attempt to speak to them," Titus said.

"I need you to understand that the Lord Iēsoûs taught two great commandments, the first of which we affirm every time we say the Shema.

That is, we shall love God with our whole being, and our neighbor as ourselves. The Lord taught that anyone around us who has some need in order to live life fully is our "neighbor." In this case, the slaves working the mines are our neighbors and our task is to respond to their needs."

"I don't know how we can help the miners," Titus said.

"Let me propose something. What is the greatest need for a miner?"

"To be freed, I guess," Titus said.

"And how could this happen without inciting a slave revolt?"

"I have no idea."

"Well, listen to this. Let's find out what Eupator paid per slave. I would guess it is in the area of three hundred denarii. If a slave could accumulate fifteen denarii per year, in twenty years he would have enough to buy his freedom."

"And how would a slave accumulate that much money?"

"Let Barnabas and Tychicus recommend an increase in the price of copper, with that increase going to the slaves to be used for their manumission. If the increase could be calculated to amount to one-tenth, Eupator would have no increase in his cost, and the slaves would see the possibility of freedom. Sergius Paulus in Cyprus would have his increase in price. Everyone wins."

"It will take a genius to calculate the proper values; do you know who could do this?"

"The Lord has already provided him: Barnabas. If anyone can do this, it is my friend. Let me go now and find him. This will be a different, but consistent, proclamation of the Good News." And with that, Paul jumped up and without ceremony rushed out the door, shouting over his shoulder, "Come back here at sunset, and I'll tell you what Barnabas says."

CHAPTER 11

Manumission

PAUL FOUND BARNABAS TALKING WITH Jonah in his rooms attached to the synagogue.

"Barnabas, Titus and I have an idea that I'd like to explore with you. It has to do with two items. First, your meeting with Eupator on raising the price of copper. Thesecond deals with my desire to address the slaves in the mines. We think we have a solution to both situations. Here it is.

"I speak of the love of Christ for all people, both slave and free. We assure them that by professing a belief in Iēsoûs they will achieve everlasting life, especially since Christ will soon return.

"Next, we appeal to Eupator to do two things: First, raise the price he charges for copper by one-tenth. With your brother Phidippides raising his price, increased income will result to Eupator. But the third thing is that the added one-tenth of income be allocated to the slaves so that they might put this money aside to buy their manumission. Your task will be to figure out how much must be put aside each year so that at the end of, say, twenty years, there will be enough for each slave to buy his freedom. It means that the increased price generated by Eupator will come from the Cyprus market. What do you think?"

"First, Paul, I don't think Eupator will consent to your interfering with the slave population. Second, don't you also expect the End Time to occur in less than twenty years? And, third, you will be dealing with people whom you won't even be able to talk with, as they speak that barbarian tongue."

"Titus will get us an interpreter, I don't know when the Lord will re-appear, and I would simply ask Eupator if we could address his slaves. No demand; just a request."

"Well, I think you are moving in the wrong direction. Our goal is to found a community of faith, professing belief in the Lord. To do that, the right people must be attracted, such as Jonah and Titus, Thecla, Theoclia, and, of course, Thamyris. How would a community of slaves come together to pray and read the Word? No, Paul, I cannot support this misdirected effort."

"Barnabas, you must see these slaves as examples of the people the Lord died for. He did not offer eternal life to the 'right' people, but to everyone, slaves as well as free. In fact, you and I might not be examples of the 'right' people."

"All right, Paul, here's a compromise. You and Titus meet with Eupator and present the outline of your manumission proposal. It must be disclosed to no one else. If Eupator likes the idea, I will relent. But the idea must not be shared with anyone but Eupator."

"Agreed," Paul said, and he got up and went to the synagogue to wait for sunset and Titus.

While the world was bathed in the golden-rose spectacle of the sunset, Titus walked into their usual meeting room, offering a subdued greeting.

"What's wrong?" Paul asked, sensing a problem.

"Well, I thought the details of how a manumission program would work would be less important than whether the idea would be acceptable to Eupator. So I decided to go to Eupator and find out how much he paid for the last shipment of slaves from Britannia and how much he would accept to free a typical slave. I didn't disclose the relationship between our plan and increasing the price of copper. I'm sorry to report that Eupator was not only uninterested in the issue. He was angry that anyone was even discussing the matter."

Paul's shoulders slumped.

"You have not heard the worst," Titus continued. "He called in Demas and Hermogenes to ask their opinions, as he usually does. They too were aghast at what they saw as interfering with the essential relationship between business and slaves. I was not prepared for such an outburst. They accused you and Barnabas of introducing new and dangerous ideas through our proclamation of the Good News."

"I must tell Barnabas about this," Paul said. "We had agreed to appeal to Eupator alone, but now it appears that we will have no access to slaves. Once again, those who are in such need of the Good News will be deprived of it. It was an error for you to act on your own, Titus. An error that will hinder us in our proclamation."

"Rely on Tychicus," Titus offered weakly. "Let him go to Thamyris; he may be able in turn to speak with Eupator."

"What about Thecla?" Titus asked.

"I fear that I have shut the door there," Paul responded.

Thecla's heart beat a touch faster as she overheard this comment. *I will find some way to help Paul,* she thought.

Titus continued. "Then focus on another sermon next Sabbath. Point out that our religion is recognized as legitimate by our emperor, Claudius. Point out that our moral code is the best in the world, that our Torah leads people to lives of virtue and recognition of the social structure within which we live. We are not revolutionaries, nor do we attempt to change the legal system under which we thrive."

"I will speak with Barnabas," Paul said. "That may be the best solution."

CHAPTER 12

An Appeal to the Jews

"In the name of all that's holy, how could Titus do that?" Barnabas exclaimed, red-faced. "Now we have not only lost what you wanted, but may have alienated those people central to our mission."

"Titus recommends another sermon," Paul offered. "Maybe if we point out that we are not introducers of novelty, we might be at least able to convince the few Jews of this city to open themselves to the word of our Lord."

"All right. Here's what you do: Go immediately to Jonah and describe the problem. Take Titus with you, as Jonah will certainly be responsive to him. Point out that your topic will be, 'The Wisdom of the Jews.'"

It took the balance of the day for Paul to find Titus and the two of them were unable to locate Jonah as he was in a village several hours away from the synagogue. Titus headed to his home and agreed to return the next morning to their special spot.

Paul heard him arrive several hours after sunset while he was rehearsing the discussion they would have the next morning.

It was not until afternoon that Jonah had been able to meet with Paul and Titus. And when they greeted Jonah, Paul could recognize a little less enthusiasm in Jonah's greeting. It didn't take Jonah very long to broach the issue of addressing the mining slaves.

Titus was about to respond, but Paul didn't give him the chance.

"As you and I are sons of Abraham, you can be assured that we had no intention of altering the relationship between slaves and their masters. After all, we were ourselves slaves in Egypt."

"Yes," Jonah said. "And God gave us Moses so that we could be freed. And the first act of our freedom was the destruction of our ex-masters, the Egyptian army. I never emphasize that part of our history. You can preach that in Jerusalem, but it is dangerous to do so here."

Chastened, Paul reached out his hand toward Jonah. "Thank you for helping me understand how to preach to those in the Gentile world," he said. "However, may I speak on the issue of the virtues we have within our tradition?"

"What text would you use?"

"I would use a text from Sirach dealing with the passions. In the land of the Gentiles, it is clearly where we distinguish our behavior."

"I am not familiar with this text," Jonah said.

"It has to do with the control of the passions," Paul said. "I read this text while I served in the Synagogue of the Alexandrians with Simeon bar Gamaliel. Most of the members were Greek. This text was well known."

"Fine. Choose the text you think best." Jonah nodded and left.

Paul noted that he did not offer him any sign of peace on departure. *Maybe he's too busy*, Paul thought.

During the next several days, Paul remained in the synagogue, both praying and collecting his thoughts. First, he had to dredge up the text he wanted to use. The text of Sirach that he proposed to use went like this:

Every wise person teaches wisdom,
and those who know her declare her praise;
Do not fall into the grip of your passion,
lest like fire it consume your strength.
It will eat your leaves and destroy your fruits,
and you will be left like a dry tree.
For fierce passion destroys its owner
and makes him the sport of his enemies.
Do not let your passions be your guide,
but keep your desires in check.

If you allow yourself to satisfy your passions,
they will make you the laughingstock of your enemies.
Take no pleasure in too much luxury
which brings on poverty redoubled.

Paul wrote out the text for Tituswho would undoubtedly would be the lector; he elected not to write out his commentary, as he wanted to leave the possibility for the Spirit to enlighten him while he was speaking. During those days, he missed the company of Titus, who felt bad about the crisis he had been responsible for. Meantime, Thecla maintained her position next to the window, hoping to hear the conversation between Paul and Titus. Her mother urged her to leave her position and reintegrate herself within the family, as she was not fulfilling the normal duties of a daughter. But she insisted that when Titus returned, she would overhear Paul's marvelous insights. She yearned for his return and would not respond to her mother.

Sabbath finally came, and about an hour before the proclamation of the Sh'mah at sunset, Thecla was in the first row of the women's section of the synagogue. Jonah politely greeted her and expressed his pleasure at her presence. Jonah saw Thecla as a means to interest Thamyris in joining the synagogue community, so he was exceptionally polite to her, complimenting her on her appearance and asking for Theoclia, her mother.

Thamyris was notably absent from the assembly. Tychicus and Barnabas sat in the first row of the men's portion, which included only eight other men. Most interestingly, Paul noticed Lentulus in the back row. There were six other women, about half the number who had attended the week before. Thecla turned around and greeted them politely, asking herself where the other women might be.

"At least we have a minyan," Tychicus whispered to Barnabas, who merely nodded.

Then one of the women lit the candles, the Sh'mah was intoned, and the service began. Titus read the text, and Paul rose and walked to a chair normally used by Jonah but which Jonah insisted that Paul use, consistent with the posture of a teacher when he is teaching. He recited the text from memory, paused for a short time, then began to preach.

"Many of you might not be familiar with the text I have chosen; it was written in Jerusalem about two hundred years ago and is often read in the synagogues of Alexandria. I was part of the Synagogue of the Alexandrians in Jerusalem, where I first had the good fortune of reading it.

"The first question I'm sure you have is, What does *wisdom* mean? We have an entire book, the book of Proverbs, in which the Lord God of creation offers us examples. We read, *The beginning of wisdom is fear of the Lord.* We all know that the 'fear' we speak of does not mean 'being afraid,' but, rather, being dependent upon God's Word in how we act. The one who follows the Torah in his or her daily life is given Wisdom.

"But sometimes it is necessary to have more guidance in following the Torah, and that is where today's text is important. This focuses on passion. What *is* passion? It has two faces. First, it is that emotion that permits one to excel at something. For example, if one is a singer, the emotional state of practicing with a mastersinger and being driven to excel is one use of 'passion.' And this leads us to the second use. Passion is always a state of one's soul; its emotion is self-driven. We have all read that God told our ancestors, *Thou shalt not covet thy neighbor's wife, goods, or animals.* This means that we should not hunger for the possession of these, such that such possession becomes the condition of our happiness. Passion is the overweening desire for possession, whether for a person, for wealth, for power, or for honor. Passion is the willingness to use things or people to our will, such that the possession of them determines our happiness.

"Passion is a substitute for the love that is modeled in the Christ. He was exalted by God because his love for us, in suffering and dying for our sins, provides us with an example of true Wisdom. But this is not human wisdom, since most people would not understand this kind of love. He exhibited a kind of passion that no one else in the world could.

His Passion was our salvation, our being given eternal life despite our not deserving such a gift.

"We distinguish his passion from that which I read a few moments ago. We are urged to avoid self-serving passion, keeping it in check, lest it destroy us. The opposite of passion is love, whether this is love of a man for a woman or a parent for a child. The opposite of a passion for honor is self-service to benefit a community or to relieve the poverty of others. The opposite of passion is living in chastity with a wife or husband in order to be able to serve God in a loving manner. While passion in a marriage to bring about the next generation is not condemned, if one is to resist passion for a time to pray, this is better than having no restraint.

"This is our wisdom; this is our virtue, distinct from the Gentiles, and found in Torah as fulfilled by the Lord Iēsoûs Christos. We emulate his passion expressed by unbounded love for us, who are not deserving of such love. It is incumbent upon us to resist the passion that is the opposite of love and to live in passion that arises out of the virtue that permits us to spend our lives to benefit others. To this end, the Lord charged me to go among the Jews first but also among the Gentiles to create communities that would permit that passion to thrive and to change the world through their love of one another. Perhaps the deepest mystery is that Iēsoûs remains in the world in these communities. His love binds everyone to one another and to him. This is the mystery that is proclaimed in your midst. You join the community by affirming your belief in him and by being baptized into him. Let us bring Iēsoûs the Christ into this community."

"Amen."

"Amen," responded part of the community. Paul noted that some simply rose and walked out of the building silently.

What happened? Paul ruminated silently. *Last week there were positive signs that the community was open to the Lord. I don't sense the same this time. Why did Titus leave so quickly?*

Before he could answer himself, he felt a tap on his shoulder. It was Lentulus.

"What a pleasure," Paul said. "I'm delighted that you could join us."

"As my son, Timothy, was impressed with you, so also am I. My personal slave, who is Timothy's teacher, has many of the same ideas that you have. I'm not sure I'm ready to agree with your next philosophical step that sexual passion outside marriage is an evil. I agree that one's partner should not necessarily be treated as an object, but in a household with female slaves who are desirous of making her master happy, I see no reason to resist passion. One never truly knows the true feelings of a sexual partner, but one can perceive what is expressed by that partner and conclude that she is not merely an object but is improving her position by providing pleasure to whomever she is assigned to."

"Perhaps we can meet again and discuss this further," Paul mumbled, having caught out of the corner of his eye that Thecla was talking with Jonah. He felt the need to insert himself there and softly bade Lentulus goodbye, which was received with a touch of disappointment.

Jonah, seeing Lentulus leave, waved Paul over to where he and Thecla were standing.

"Thecla is very complimentary of your sermon, Paul." He smiled. "She has expressed a desire to join our community of Jews and perhaps even become a follower of Iēsoûs. I think that would be excellent, don't you?"

"I can think of nothing better, except that Thamyris would join her, and even her mother."

Thecla sweetly added, "Jonah has pursued Thamyris for years, but my espoused has no interest in being circumcised. And my mother is too devoted to the Great Mother to abandon her belief," she said, her red hair framing a smiling, white face.

"Perhaps, Jonah, you could help Thecla; I'm not sure how long Barnabas and I are going to be here, maybe forever; maybe we leave next week," Paul said, smiling at Jonah.

"Well, I would happily instruct Thecla in our religion, but I don't know enough about your Iēsoûs. I think both would be better handled by you, Paul. I know you have spent time with Titus. perhaps you could find your way clear to include Thecla in your discussions."

"I will look into it," Paul weakly. "I can never tell when Titus is available, but we may be able to work something out."

Thecla gave Paul a heartfelt smile that communicated more to Paul than receiving instruction about Iēsoûs. For the first time, Paul noticed the cleavage apparent due to a loosening of the outer tunic at its top. He felt a tightening in his chest. He could not imagine how she would appear on her wedding night with Thamyris, but he tried for a moment.

"Since we live so close, I'll find out when Titus could meet with us, and I'll let you know. If you are available, you can join us."

Thecla nodded, reached out her hand, and touched Paul's forearm. With that she swished out the door.

Jonah bade Paul good night, slightly less convivial than in the past, which brought the question again to Paul's consciousness. *First, did I fail tonight? And, second, what, precisely, is Thecla's interest? Is it joining the Jewish community headed by Jonah? Or was she truly interested in Iēsoûs ? Or is she for some strange reason interested in me? Danger! Be careful.* Paul returned to his room. He did not hear Barnabas return to his room for some time, but by then, Paul was almost asleep.

CHAPTER 13
Kala

Morning brought the normal sounds of a city at work, with tradesmen taking up their tasks and animals being driven from place to place. Conversations of all kinds flowed underneath the guest -quarters of the synagogue. But inside those walls, all was quiet. Jonah had not appeared in the dining room. Probably still asleep. Bread baked yesterday was on the table along with whole peaches and a cold herbal tea. Paul helped himself.

Before he could finish a peach, Titus walked in.

"Good Shabbat," Titus said with a smile.

"Shabbat shalom," Paul responded.

"I have not slept a wink, Paul. I need to discuss two major items with you that you brought up last night but left hanging in midair."

"Let's go to our special spot," Paul said, getting up from the table. "Want to bring a peach?"

"No, I'm not hungry. Maybe after we talk."

They sat down next to the window, unaware of Thecla's unseen presence a couple feet away.

"You spoke of passion last night. This disturbed me immensely. You never asked, but I was married for three years. We were both born in the same communal farm halfway between here and the mines. She was a slave among the women who prepared food for the miners. She was born with a facial deformity where her upper-lip never closed in on itself. Her upper lip formed a delta from the edges of her mouth to a point under her nose, exposing her front teeth. As soon as the mother saw this, she threw her on the dung-heap, expecting her to die in a day or so. But my mother, having just given birth to me, picked her up and nursed her, recognizing her as a free slave, and named her Euphraina, Joy.

"So we grew up together. She was shunned by almost everyone because of her ugliness. But I never saw her as anything except someone whose only pleasure in life was making me happy. As she grew, she became a highly competent cook, constantly creating new and delicious meals for the fifty or so slaves working the mines. When all the girls of the village were seeking to entrap a young man, she was singularly unsuccessful. The boys laughed at her and called her Kaka. My name for her was Kala, or Beautiful.

"We discovered sex when we were about eight years old. My parents put a thin mattress filled with straw next to my bed, and there came a time when mutual curiosity began to produce a pleasure that both of us enjoyed. As we moved toward maturity, so did our sexual life. She created novel ways of expressing her love for me that made our life together full of happiness. When I was expected to engage in the village traditions regarding finding wives, I participated woodenly, not interested in anyone except Kala, who, being a slave, was ineligible for me. But when I would return home after one of the village festivals, her tears of fear that I would find a village girl for my wife turned into tears of joy at my return and, generally, a new form of sexual passion that her instincts had created. At such times, I discovered ways to bring her to peaks of passionate love, which caused me as much joy as she gave me."

"When we were sixteen, I made the decision that I would never seek another woman to be my wife. And while Kala and I could never marry while she was a slave, I negotiated a price for her with my parents. It was a total of three hundred denarii, payable at thirty five denarii per year. At the end of ten years, she would be freed, and we could marry. They thought it ridiculous that I would not simply marry a free woman and bring Kala into our household. They even offered Kala as a wedding gift if they could strike a good marriage for me with a village woman. When

I told Kala that I had rejected everyone except her as a wife, she brought me to such heights of passion that I felt I was about to give up my soul."

"Within a year, she became pregnant. Her pregnancy was difficult, and she was in pain almost constantly from the third month. Sex was out of the question, and I experienced a joy in our abstinence. The village had several midwives, all of whom shook their heads when I asked them for help. In the sixth month one courageous midwife told her to remain in bed until the birth. Birth came after her seventh month, with a stillborn girl who had a beautiful face. But Kala bled after the stillbirth, and by morning she was dead."

As Titus finished, he was wracked with sobs, tears streaming down his cheeks. Paul reached over the table and grasped his hand. He bowed his head, searching for the right thing to say to his friend. Neither heard the sobs that emanated a few feet away.

"*Passion* is exactly what the Word of God refers to where it is written that a man cleaves to his wife. This is what happened to you. I would ask you to visualize your feelings as being an example of the overwhelming love that Christ has for those who believe in him. Your love for Kala is an example for everyone. Passion was a vital tool for deepening and expressing your mutual love and is not condemned. But as deep and perfect as that love was, if one were to forgo that expression for another, higher spiritual love in order to proclaim Christ, one would be able to understand more fully the character of that calling."

"I will try to understand that," Titus said, wiping his tears. "How does this relate to the baptism you spoke of?"

"Baptism as we understand it was initially practiced by a prophet by the name of John, who retired to the wilderness in the Jordan Valley. He preached a repentance of sin and conversion to living the precepts of Torah, expressed by immersing oneself in the Jordan River. Our Lord followed him for a time but then initiated his own ministry in Galilee."

"The Spirit revealed to his followers that baptism has a deeply spiritual meaning, in that we enter into the water of baptism and in so doing enter into the Lord's death. As we come out of the water, we participate in his resurrection into eternal life. We are spiritually born from above and become part of his body, which thrives as it awaits his second coming. This is the gateway to his love, surpassing passion as you surpassed passion with Kala."

"Is the ceremony extensive?" Titus asked.

"No, it is the ultimate in simplicity. A baptized person immerses one into living water, which could be a stream or river, or a ritual bath; asks them if they believe that Iēsoûs is Lord; and recites the words, *I baptize you in the name of the Father and of the Son and of the Holy Spirit.* Those being baptized remove their clothes prior to immersion, symbolizing the leaving of an old life, enter naked, and as they arise out of the water, they put on a new, clean white robe, symbolizing their new life. Then the entire community welcomes them with a kiss of peace."

"Paul, I want to be baptized. I want to spend my life with you and Barnabas and proclaim the Good News of Jesus Christ."

"The best way is to start this proclamation with your family. Remember, you are becoming part of a body, which means we do not believe alone but as a family. This is not an initiation like one into the cult of Mithras or the Great Mother. There is one God and one Son whom he raised from the dead. We believe as brothers and sisters, not as individuals. If you want, I will help in this matter. But...but I am not willing to baptize you as a single individual."

"I don't know if I can do that," Titus said. "I'll do my best. Perhaps you could join me at my farm tomorrow, where I will assemble my brother, sister-in-law, and several cousins. They all worship the Great Mother, so it will be a surprise to them that I am choosing a new way of life."

"No, Titus. I believe this new way of life was chosen for you. You will bring many into our family."

CHAPTER 14

Problems

Titus left, having embraced Paul.

No sooner was he out the door than Thecla entered, wearing a light tunic normally worn in the women's quarters and too revealing for wear outside. Paul caught his breath as she approached him, her long red hair only partially covering her feminine features, which were visible through the material.

"Thecla…" he stammered, flustered.

"Yes, Paul. I came to you because I want to be baptized into the assembly of Iēsoûs the Christ."

"Thecla, how can you make such a statement? You have heard about the Good News only twice; you can't possibly desire such a dramatic change in your life."

"But I know more than you know. I have listened to your conversations with Titus and know as much as he does. I want to experience the boundless love that the Lord offers me. I am willing to give up all passion and substitute a spiritual love apart from that of the body. I want to experience a love more satisfying than that of Titus for Kala. I want to belong to the body of Christ and to live his Good News."

As she spoke, her voice quivering with emotion, she slowly walked toward Paul, her breasts and pubic hair becoming apparent through the sheer embroidered cloth.

Paul sensed danger. *Not again! No. If Jonah should walk in, it will look horrible! I have to avoid the situation in Antioch…I won't confront he but just get her out of here with me alone. If only Ruth had looked like that, our marriage might have survived. God, she is beautiful. No, don't even think that. Out, out, quickly.*

"Thecla, if you return to your home right away, I will follow you in a few minutes, and we can speak of this matter there. We cannot remain here, and you know that. I will not let you down. I will come to you."

"All right, Paul," she said, her smile and flashing eyes speaking more than what could be considered 'spiritual.'

Paul gently took her elbow and retraced her steps to the synagogue door.

Please, Lord. May no one see her as she walks from the synagogue door to her house. Such a scandal that would create. Miraculously, no one happened to be on the street at that moment. *I praise you, Lord. You are my shield and buckler.*

Paul guided Thecla, making sure that she was in her home.

Moments later, Paul walked over the same short route, and the street was packed with the normal traffic of business in a large city.

Having returned to the synagogue, Paul suddenly recognized that he ought to enlist Thecla's family in a totally ironic task of doing the opposite of preaching the Good News. But he realized the entire mission would be destroyed if the mere appearance of anything inappropriate should occur. He decided first to request help from Theoclia. A few steps brought him to her door.

He knocked loudly and asked for Theoclia when a slave opened the door.

A stately woman in her late thirties, dressed in an expensive brocade tunic appeared in the entranceway of the house. Paul greeted her formally, expressed his pleasure in seeing her again, and asked if she could summon Thecla.

"As long as you are here in this house, she will come away from that window that otherwise she won't leave. I think she is in love with you," she said.

"Impossible," Paul blurted out. "I have only seen her three times, I think, plus one time a few minutes ago."

"Do you know that she has sat at that window and listened to you since first we met? She refused to leave the window, even when ordered by me. I summoned Thamyris, since she must obey her betrothed. But she refused. She ignored even him, and he is quite angry, not only at her, but at you and your associates."

Paul's shoulders slumped. "Could you summon her?" he asked.

"Of course." She nodded to the slave. "Come into the garden." They walked in and sat in the colonnaded stoa. Within moments Thecla appeared, but in a tunic very similar to that of Theoclia and completely appropriate.

"Thank you, Paul, for visiting me. I want you to know that I will break off my engagement with Thamyris. I want to pursue the kind of spiritual passion that you spoke of with Titus. I want to be baptized and become part of the family of Iēsoûs ."

"Thecla, that is absurd," Theoclia spat out. "Your marriage to him will provide this entire family with security. Not only is he enormously rich he is a good man. He will provide for all of us in a way I have counted on. Don't do this."

"Thecla, listen to your mother. She is right. Marry Thamyris, and perhaps you can save his soul. I will baptize you and him together, as well as any others you can bring to the Lord," Paul pleaded. He realized that if Thamyris were shamed by the breaking of the engagement, not only would Thecla be outcast, but the entire mission in Klaudiconium would be put at risk. He had to avoid another failure.

"I've made up my mind," she said. "Paul, do not separate me from Iēsoûs. Baptize me now."

"I can't, Thecla. It is not the way. A community is critical. If you can invite others to baptism, I will cooperate. But I am opposed to baptizing people so that they might think that they are being initiated into a pagan cult. That's what you're asking."

And with that, Paul nodded to Theoclia turned his back on Thecla, and left.

"Go find Thamyris," Thecla commanded the slave, still standing behind Theoclia.

"You aren't going to break it off right now, are you?"

"I am. And if Paul won't baptize me, I will baptize myself. I will do so in the ritual bath in the synagogue. I will join that assembly, following Torah. Everyone will know that I am also a follower of Iēsoûs the Christ. I shall spend the balance of my life seeking to experience the spiritual love he has for all people. I shall return to Rav Jonah now and let him know of my decisions."

"Thecla, won't you at least wait awhile? You are only sixteen, and as you age, you may see things differently. Don't ruin your life with this novel experience," Theoclia pleaded.

"I'm going immediately to Jonah. When Thamyris arrives, send for me. It is I who must inform him of my decision."

An hour later, Jonah knocked on Paul's door. Opening it, Paul could see from the expression on the synagogue leader's face that trouble was brewing.

"Paul, get Barnabas and meet me in my quarters," Jonah said curtly.

"I don't know where he is, but we will come to you as soon as possible."

Jonah nodded and left.

Maybe I can talk with Onesiphoris. He understands everything about the key people in the city. He may have some advice, Paul thought.

He quickly left, and within a few minutes, he had found Lectra, Onesiphoris' wife, hustling among the open doors around the peristyle garden.

"Paul, it's good to see you, are you ill?"

"Not physically, but I need some spiritual healing."

"He's around here somewhere caring for some patient. Give me a moment, and I'll find him. Go into the dining room, you remember where that is." She thought, finger to forehead, and then lit off to one of the open doors.

It was not long before the tall, smiling man greeted Paul with enthusiasm. "To what do I owe this visit?" he said.

"I need you to use your Alexandrian training to provide a cure for my soul," Paul started. "Barnabas and I came to this city to found a community of people who recognize a particular person exalted by God and belief in whom will provide everlasting life. Somehow, we have been unsuccessful."

"How do you know? In my business, it often takes time for a cure to work. It doesn't produce health immediately, but sometimes it takes days. Have you waited long enough for your cure to work?"

"Let me tell you what these three weeks have produced: First, Thecla affirms belief in the one we preach, but she wants to break her engagement with Thamyris. He will certainly blame us. Second, we proposed to Eupator a scheme to raise prices of copper and use the increase for manumission of slaves. This was not well received. Third, we are Jews, but it appears that our own people are rejecting what we call the Good News. I may have one person who has come to belief, but without a community we sow our seed on a highway. Perhaps with your knowledge of the city, you might have a spiritual draught you could prescribe."

"I don't have something readily available, Paul. In fact, I have heard of what many people consider problems. Your proposal to manumit slaves has caused the operators of the mines and smelters to feel that you would create tension among the workers. And your Jewish friends accuse you of not being faithful to tradition, of introducing novelty. I don't know what this means, but several of my patients have said they would attempt to block you from speaking in the synagogue. Finally, I've known Thecla for all of her sixteen years, and if she affirms belief in your Iēsoûs, there are ten or a hundred who will reject him. I regret providing you with this potion, but I only treat what I understand. I recommend that you leave our city and start elsewhere, being careful to avoid the mistakes you have made here."

"Where do you recommend?"

"I know just the place. It is about twenty miles south, called 'Lystra.' My friend Lentulus, who deals in a new fabric, lives there with his son, Timothy. I urge you to seek Lentulus out and see when he plans to return home. Accompany him, and avoid angering the society that you enter into. Exercise care in what you say and do; offend no one, but offer your belief quietly and without challenge. Drink this draught three times a day."

"I praise our Lord for your wisdom. I shall speak with Barnabas today. And what is your fee for this?"

"My fee is that you tell me one story about this Iēsoûs on the basis of which I might gain eternal life."

So Paul sat and told one of the stories kept alive by Philip the apostle, about Iēsoûs speaking on a hill near Capernaum about the ten statements starting, *Blessed are you poor, for yours is the kingdom of heaven.* Then, embracing the lanky doctor, he left to look for Barnabas. Time to plan, to look for Lentulus and perhaps Titus.

CHAPTER 15

Problems Mount

As Paul returned to the synagogue, he overheard a commotion next door. It was Thamyris.

"How could you have let that Paul fellow fill your head with nonsense?" he shouted. "Who in the world would give up marriage with a person who has loved you for over a year in order to express some sexless love for a man you've never seen or even heard of until the last few weeks? How can you love a figment of your imagination?"

"You don't understand, Thamyris. He gave his life for me out of love. It is this love I need to reciprocate. I will give up sex for a short time but will gain eternal life when he returns, which will be soon. I give up something that is good for something that is better. I invite you to join me in this new life."

"Join you? You think anyone would join you?"

"Yes. I know that Paul has made the same choice, and I believe that his friend Titus has also chosen eternal life. Since the Lord will be returning soon, it will soon be apparent that my way of life will be everyone's."

Paul took a deep breath and knocked loudly on the door. A slave quickly opened it, and Paul strode toward the voices. He entered the peristyle garden and Thamyris immediately confronted him.

"Paul, what have you done to Thecla? What nonsense have you put into her young head?"

Instead of answering Thamyris, Paul looked intently at Thecla and said, "Thecla, Thecla, don't make a mistake. Do not break your betrothal

177

to this fine man. Instead, marry him and then we can talk about the Christ. I believe that being married with the kind of love you desire, but focused on Thamyris, you will experience the kind of love that leads to eternal life. This is what the Lord wants of you."

Suddenly, Theoclia appeared, her face red and distorted. "Thecla, I command you to stop this ridiculous conversation. Paul, I want you to leave. Thamyris, remain here, and we can calmly discuss this." Paul began to leave but hesitated.

"NO." Thecla stomped. "I want to love the Lord Iēsoûs for the rest of my life. Paul, baptize me now, in this fountain," she said, referring to the one in the center of the peristyle garden adjacent.

"I cannot do that, Thecla. We baptize into an assembly as the body of Christ, and we don't have that here."

"Then I'll solve the problem myself," she shouted. She disappeared into her bedroom area and quickly emerged holding a white robe. Her chin thrust out, she marched over to the fountain, quickly stripped off her tunic, and stepped naked into the fountain. Picking up a copper cup lying on the edge, she scooped up water and poured it over her head. "I baptize myself in the name of Iēsoûs the Christ." She stood there for a moment, smiling at each observer in turn, until Theoclia shouted, "Thecla, in the name of the Great Mother, cover yourself."

Thecla picked up the white tunic, put it on, and said, "I have been baptized into eternal life. This robe is a symbol of my vow of sexual purity for the rest of my life, exactly as you told Titus, Paul. It is done and cannot be undone. I will gather women around me, and in a short time, I will baptize many so that we will have your assembly, Paul." With that, she stepped out of the fountain and reentered her bedroom area.

"Paul, you are not welcome here," Theoclia said. "Thamyris, you have my best wishes. I don't know what new ideas have come into our city recently, but I hope you, Thamyris, can rid us of such destruction. An assembly of women breaking their betrothal vows! The very thought of it… he spun around and Paul did not have the time to say anything.

Thamyris clenched his fists at his side. "Paul, you have brought only harm to our city. What kind of a god is there that would work to the destruction of the family, urging the violation of legal contracts? If it were not for Tychicus, you would be beaten in the agora for the evil you have brought."

Thamyris stomped out, not giving Paul a chance to reply. Standing dumbly, he entered the guest room area of the synagogue. There he saw Barnabas speaking with Jonah, but with some tension evident.

"Paul, Jonah is telling us that a group of men from his assembly have objected to your interpretation of scripture. First, attempted to stray the relationship between masters and slaves. Having a system of slaves buying their freedom undercuts the economy in this area. Secondly as the result of your sermon on passion, the wives seem to have picked this up and are refusing sex to their husbands. Jonah has informed me that you can no longer speak in his synagogue."

"I hope you can see that these complaints have no basis," Paul said, attempting to defend himself.

"They have basis, Paul. As much as I am honored to have a scholar like you in my assembly, we are a simple people and accept the Torah and the prophets as they are, not interpreted differently than we are used to. Further, it appears that Titus will be leaving our assembly because of your new teachings. I personally regret that as you knew how important he is to me. Please plan on leaving your guest rooms as soon as you can. There will be no charge for the length of time you have occupied them." And with that, Jonah turned away and headed to his quarters.

Recognizing Paul's dejected look and slumped shoulders, Barnabas put his arms around Paul's shoulders. "Don't be too distressed. We'll find other quarters," Barnabas cheerfully asserted.

"Wait until you hear about Thecla and Thamyris," Paul said, and he commenced to describe what had just occurred next door. No sooner had he concluded with the self-baptism than Tychicus came in. He had been working for several days on a business proposition with Tamyris and announced that his proposition was rejected not because of any business reason but because he was identified with Paul and Thecla's baptism.

"I have no reason to remain here," Tychicus said. "Thamyris has closed all the doors in Klaudiconium to me. I must return to Perga. I know that his interpretation of what happened with Thecla is not consistent with our Lord's teachings. But that does not change the attitude of the business community here. It is amazing that a sixteen-year old girl can affect my business dealings with Eupator, with whom I have dealt for over twenty years." And with that, he walked to his sleeping room.

"We need to discuss all this with Titus," Paul said. "He indicated that he would like to join us in announcing the Good News, but doors seem to be closing on us. I spoke with Onesiphorus earlier today, and he was not encouraging. He feels we should leave instead of being cursed with continuing failure."

Now it was Barnabas's turn to put his head in his hands and slump his shoulders.

"I know Titus will return soon," Paul said. "He is exactly what we need, but it's probably too late for him to turn things around. We'll just have to wait until we find out what the Spirit wants from us." With that, Paul separated from Barnabas went into his sleeping room. He tried to pray, but nothing came out. He lay down and in the shortest time was sound asleep.

CHAPTER 16

Exit Strategy

PAUL WAS AWAKENED BY AN insistent knock on his door. It was early evening. *Maybe it's Titus,* he thought as he dashed to the door.

"Paul, good evening," Titus said, beaming.

"It's not really very good," Paul said. "Wait until you hear of our problems."

"Don't worry; nothing is so bad that the Spirit of Christ does not have a solution!"

"What do you mean?"

"I've heard the whole story. Barnabas and I have spoken with Lentulus. You recall him from our dinner with Thamyris. He is actually from Lystra, a town about twenty miles south of here. He has concluded his business here, having executed a contract to deliver his cloth woven here from the *kannabis* plant to Tarsus, where it will be fabricated into tents for the Roman legions. He has invited you and Barnabas to travel with him to Lystra to meet his son, Timothy. I will accompany you, if you'll have me, so that I can learn more about the Lord from you."

"Is Lystra large enough to have a population of Jews that we can preach to?" Paul asked.

"I don't know," Titus responded. "We know that Lentulus's wife is Jewish, and he has an inquisitive son, Timothy, who has an excellent education."

"I'm not sure…" Paul ruminated aloud.

"Paul, you know you can't stay here. Thamyris is telling everyone that you are a threat to the city, urging young women to break their betrothal vows, and you are right now urging worship of a new God surely and worship a new god. There is a risk that some of the younger men might become violent. This has put Tychicus in a terrible position as a client. He will leave soon for Perga, and his business here is ruined unless he condemns you, which he won't do. You really must accept Lentulus's offer. You don't really have an alternative. Talk to Barnabas. But do so before Lentulus leaves, and with his departure, I don't know where else you can travel to."

"Thank you, Titus, for your concern and love. I shall indeed speak with Barnabas tonight. Can we speak of this with Lentulus?"

"I can arrange that," Titus answered.

"Let me find Barnabas; we will pray that the Spirit of the Lord guide us. Further, you had expressed a desire to participate in our ministry; if so, I'm willing to baptize you as soon as you like. We could be your family."

"Would I have to be circumcised?"

"No. Circumcision for one not born a Jew is unimportant. What is critically important is your faith in Iēsoûs as Lord, as the one whom God raised from the dead and exalted to sit at his right hand. That is what makes Gentiles part of the true People of God."

Titus reached out and embraced Paul, who felt a tear coursing down his cheek.

"I must find Barnabas," Paul said. "There is no way Jonah would let us use his ritual bath for a baptism, but Onesiphorus might let us use his fountain. I am going to ask him if he would be so kind."

With that, he rushed out. Titus left for his home, rehearsing in his mind what he would tell his family about his plans to leave Klaudiconiium with Barnabas and Paul. He would ask to be given a portion of his ownership estate in the farms his family owned. He would then not be a financial burden but would provide added support for the future. The Good News does not get proclaimed without cost.

On his way, he saw Barnabas and Lentulus walking toward the synagogue.

"Greetings in the Lord," Titus said. "I trust you are looking for Paul." They nodded.

"I think he's at Onesiphorus' *paionios*, asking to use his fountain to baptize me."

"Blessed be the Lord," Barnabas uttered as he embraced him.

"I presume that's an initiation ceremony," Lentulus said.

"Yes and no," said Barnabas. "Paul and I will have a full day to give you a good answer on our way to Lystra."

Titus's face lit up with a broad smile. "When do you leave?"

"At first light," said Lentulus. "There is more unrest here than I've seen in the three years I've been doing business here. We must leave before something really bad happens."

"I need to stay here for a week or so to handle the financial consequences of my desire to proclaim the Lord with you and Paul," Titus said. "But I will follow you to Lystra when that is done."

"We must get to Paul," Barnabas said nervously.

"I'll see you soon," Titus said as he resumed his walk to the family compound.

Shortly thereafter, Lentulus, Barnabas, and Paul met in the synagogue guest quarters. They agreed that they would baptize Titus at first light. Paul was distressed that there was insufficient time to have a celebratory meal, but Lentulus insisted on an early departure.

"Barnabas," I have been praying over how the Holy Spirit can utilize Titus best. I know that he is desirous of participating in our mission by traveling with us. If we do take him with us, then we cannot hope for any positive result of our time spent here. Thus, I propose that after Titus is baptized he remain here preaching primarily to Gentiles. He has a large family and a large number of people who work with him. By leaving Titus here, the Holy Spirit has a chance of forming an assembly of Gentiles that would be open to incorporating Jews as well."

"I agree, Paul," Barnabas said. "I'm sure Titus will be disappointed not to travel with us. But he has a better chance of forming a community of Gentiles than we have. Let us go immediately to his family compound and invite him to be the key to an assembly here."

Paul and Barnabas immediately went in search of Titus, who was celebrating with his family. They laid out their plan to permit Titus to remain behind and to preach the Lord Iēsoûs. While his face expressed disappointment, he enthusiastically responded affirmatively, to the relief of Barnabas and Paul. Titus then introduced his extended family, who were clearly prospectively individuals who could easily constitute a *minyan*. Paul and Barnabas were introduced to each family member, and after almost an hour of responding to questions dealing with Iēsoûs, Paul and Barnabas departed, leaving an atmosphere of warmth and openness.

"Barnabas, we made the right decision. I think Titus will be successful," said Paul.

As the first slice of purple appeared in the east, Paul, Barnabas, and Titus entered Onesiphorus' garden. He and Lecla were there offering a greeting. It did not take long for Paul to utter some prayers and quote that part of the Fourth Song of Isaiah, "Suffering Servant," where the servant bore the punishment that makes us whole. Then, with no further ado, Paul assisted Titus to strip and stand in the flowing fountain. Paul also entered and recited the formula. "I baptize you, Titus, in the name of the Lord Iēsoûs, into his assembly. May you always live in the love he has for us until he comes again."

With that, Titus donned a white garment he had brought with him and said, "I pledge myself to a life of witness to the Lord, spreading the Good News to the extent that my efforts permit me. Amen."

The parties embraced; Paul thanked Onesiphoris and Barnabas sneaked a coin into the hand of the physician, who smiled a reluctant acceptance. Lentulus was outside the walls with two armed men and two extra saddle horses. No conversation; a wave, and the party exited the city by the south gate. The road led straight to Lystra. Paul slumped down, dejected at the most recent failure in his life, but hopeful for Titus 'success.

Part IV

CHAPTER 1
Storm

Five hours after the party's departure from Klaudiconium, the wind picked up and low lying clouds scudded close to the ridges of the hillocks rising to each side of the Royal Road. Lentulus had described that this was a section of road that stretched from the city of Susa in Persia to Ephesus on the coast of the Roman province of Asia. It took ninety days to travel the entire road by foot, but because of a series of way stations, it was possible for a cadre of post riders to traverse the seventeen hundred mile distance in nine days. Lentulus quoted Herodotus's comments on the system, made almost five hundred years ago: *There is nothing in the world that travels faster than these Persian couriers. Neither snow nor rain nor heat nor gloom of night stays these couriers from the swift completion of their appointed rounds.*

"Looks like we're in for some weather," commented Lentulus. "This could cause some problems for us. The engineers for Darius I built this section during the dry season, constructing it right in an ancient riverbed, which lowered the cost. But during our rare winter storms, it is necessary to search out high ground, since the resultant river swamps the road."

The party had followed a dry riverbed from Klaudiconium southwest and had just entered an unusual configuration of black rock outcroppings exposed on both sides of the road. Caves existed from the base of the rugged rocks up to the highest pinnacles, ranging in size from six to eight feet up to twenty to thirty feet. Several of the caves had thresholds slightly above the roadway. To the left, the outcroppings had no soil at their tops, but on the right side, the tops were covered with what appeared to be a grassy plain.

There was a crack of lightning and an immediate clap of thunder. The wind freshened, and the temperature drop was palpable.

"Let's go," Lentulus commanded, and he kicked his mount in the flanks, to which the horse bolted into a gallop. The two armed guards did the same, but when Paul and Barnabas tried to emulate their companions, it had no effect on the horses, who were clearly aware of the inexperience of their riders. Paul thought of their experience a few months ago on their way to Antioch in Pisidia. More lightning and thunder brought a hard rain. Almost immediately, it became obvious that what they considered a road would quickly become a riverbed. The horses lowered their heads and wanted to stop. The two riders resorted to kicking the beasts and whipping them on their rumps with the ends of the reins, to no effect. It was raining so hard that Lentulus and the two other riders were lost to sight. Within minutes, the water on the road had risen to almost two feet; brush and tree limbs were floating down what was becoming a cascade.

"What shall we do, Barnabas?" Paul shouted.

Barnabas did not hear. He was intent on getting his mount to move. The water level continued to rise, a muddy torrent now halfway up the legs of the horses, who were beginning to demonstrate their fear by violently shaking their heads, as if to beg their riders to take command. The force of the rushing water now began to push the horses downstream, as it was up to their bellies. Paul uttered a prayer, begging for help. He could barely see Barnabas, whose horse was almost swimming. Paul took the reins, on which he had been pulling back, and threw them over the horse's head and grasped the animal around the neck, communicating his faith in the horse's wisdom. Quickly, it responded and caught up with Barnabas, who imitated Paul's release of reins. As though the horses could speak with each other, they both turned crosswise to the current and headed toward the rocky outcroppings. Within a few minutes, the depth of the water decreased, and as they neared a gaping cave in the rock, the horses struggled up the slope in front of the cave and entered it, which provided shelter from the rain. Paul had been insensitive to the continuing rumble of thunder, so centered was he on the flash flood in which they were trapped.

The cave floor sloped upward, but the ceiling was flat, with the net result of a declining height of the cave. Both Barnabas and Paul dismounted, patted the necks of the horses in gratitude, and removed their saddlebags and horse-blankets. Peering out from the entrance of the cave, they saw what had been a dusty road transform itself into a roaring torrent festooned with branches and other flotsam. The problem was that the water continued to rise. In fact, water was beginning to lap at the entrance. Paul paced off the distance to the rear of the cave, where the ceiling was a mere four feet from the upslope floor. He looked across the river and saw that the water was entering similar caves. He was unable to estimate the relative elevation of those caves but noticed that water was beginning to enter their own cave. Both men and horses backed toward the rear.

The roar of thunder continued, with flashes of lightning momentarily illumining the cave. The men sat down, both trying to calculate how long the river would continue to rise; neither shared his thoughts. The horses stood nervously, water rising above their fetlocks. It started to darken without any relenting of the storm. The back of the cave was wrapped in a black mantle. Both men were seated on the cold, hard stone floor. Hours passed. Paul and Barnabas invited each other to pray for deliverance, which was repeated as often as each party felt appropriate.

Paul spread out the smelly horse-blanket he had removed from his mount and attempted to sleep. After tossing uncomfortably, he fell into a fitful sleep. Sometime later he was awakened by the lower level of thunder, with lightning illuminating the sky at a distance. The rain had also decreased in intensity. Barnabas slept on his horse's blanket, and Paul was careful not to wake him. Most importantly, Paul could barely make out that the water at the entrance to the cave had declined, with the horses' forefeet standing on soggy ground several feet outside the cave. Paul retreated to the back of the cave and was quickly asleep.

A beam of sunlight startled Paul. He looked over at Barnabas, who was still fast asleep. He heard birds chirping amid the continued sound of water rushing below the cave. In an instant he realized that there were no horses. Paul called out Barnabas's name, and he quickly sat up.

"No horses!" Paul bawled out.

"Look how the water has dropped!" Barnabas shouted. "It is still rushing in the center, but the edges are beginning to become exposed. They must know the way home. Too bad we weren't awake. We could have followed them."

"We'll have to stay here and wait for the road to reappear. There will have to be traffic, and someone will know where Lystra is located, assuming it wasn't washed away in the storm."

"Too bad we don't have any food in the saddlebags," Barnabas said, and Paul immediately agreed.

"Look at that stubby tree at the edge of the water," Paul said. "It looks like clusters of grapes hanging there."

"Paul, we can't take a chance on eating something that might be poisonous," Barnabas counseled.

"We'll just have to wait until the road opens again."

For the rest of the day, the muddy water flowed past the cave, but it was noticeably dropping. Still, there was no traffic on the road beneath the flow, so the two men continued to sit at the edge of the cave, hoping to see some travelers, but no one appeared.

The sun was about to set when a lone figure on a horse rode on the edge of the river-bank, his gaze sweeping left to right, clearly searching for something. Barnabas was the first to recognize him.

"Timothy," he shouted, standing up and waving.

In moments, the young man was at the edge of the cave, dismounted. He was tall, with a thin face and a broad smile. His large ears sprouted out from beneath a full head of sandy hair.

"Paul! Joseph! Praise be to our Lord, God of Abraham, that you are still alive. When the horses returned to their stable, we were sure you had been swept downstream and killed."

"The hand of the Lord preserved us," Paul responded, extending his arms to embrace the lanky young man. Barnabas followed suit.

"Joseph, it is so good to see you!"

"We now call him Barnabas, Son of Consolation," Paul offered.

Timothy responded, "My father was sure that you were just behind him, and when he discovered that you weren't, he thought you had fallen from the horses and were swept downstream. He's been frantically searching with several men from the town, fearing that all he would find would be your bodies. There were three other travelers who drowned during the flood. This was the worst storm we've seen in countless years."

"Do you have any food?" Paul asked.

"No, I don't, but those stubby trees that have the clusters of berries over there are edible. They're bitter, and we rarely eat them except with honey. But if you haven't eaten in a couple days, we can pluck off enough to ward off starvation," Timothy suggested.

Barnabas set out immediately for the tree, a mere fifty feet from the cave entrance, pulled off several of the grape-like berries, and popped one in his mouth.

"Aaaaagh!" he cried out, expelling the remains of the fruit on the ground.

Paul laughed, and Timothy ran over, carrying a small skin filled with water, which Barnabas immediately grasped and squeezed out a stream.

"We can wait until we find either Lystra or some honey," Barnabas proposed through a smile.

"We're less than an hour's walk," Timothy announced. "We can load your travel bags onto my horse, and that will make it easy."

The threesome loaded up the baggage and started walking close to the rocky walls, generally able to keep their feet dry but periodically wading through the remains of the flood.

"You were lucky," Timothy affirmed. "Many of these caves are death traps, with water rising to the ceiling, drowning those seeking shelter from the rain. You selected one of the good caves."

"No, Timothy, we did not choose the cave. The Lord did by inspiring the horses to find just the cave we needed. We are always guided by him, always. We prayed, with the psalmist, *In you, O Lord, I take refuge…be my stronghold, give me safety*, and the Lord gave us what we needed, horses who were directed to the right place."

"I have heard that psalm," Timothy responded.

"I noticed that when we first met, you praised the God Barnabas and I worship. This is a change since last we met on your way to Alexandria."

"Indeed it is a change. While I was in Alexandria, for almost two years, I was given the opportunity to live in the household of Alexander Lysimachus, known as the Alabarch, who was the agent of the empress Antonia in growing, harvesting and shipping Egyptian grain to Rome. Life in his household was like life with the Emperor, so rich was he. As you recall, my father borrowed three hundred thousand denarii from him to support his business with the new fiber that our Scythian slaves call 'kef,' which we call *Kannabis*. It is like linen in that it grows, but is much stronger. I was a bond slave during that period when there was an outstanding balance on the loan above fifty thousand denarii. That took about two years.

"But Alexander permitted me to study philosophy with his older brother, Philo. It was with Philo that I realized how deep and old my mother's religion is. When we get to Lystra and have hours uninterrupted, I'll share some of the most important aspects of Philo's work. Most important is what he calls the allegorical method of interpreting scripture. That means that the text does not contain the whole truth being revealed but that there is a deeper level of understanding that is available to scholars."

"What can that possibly mean?" Paul responded.

"Let me give you an example," Timothy proposed. "We read that *God planted a Paradise in Eden toward the sun-rising, and he placed there the man whom he had formed.* Now, Philo points out that God did not physically till the earth to make a garden like we would. So there must be another meaning. He affirms that since there are many causes for the soul to become diseased there has to be some sort of excellence available. This is called *virtue*, which looks toward the paradise as its archetype. This is clarified when the paradise is oriented toward the sunrise, which provides light and clarity in making moral judgments."

"I like that thought," Paul responded. "But such interpretation must occur within the scope of the scriptural text. We can't have a text depart dramatically from the plain meaning of the words."

"I agree," Timothy added. "That is the first task of what Philo calls 'allegorical interpretation.' He has several scrolls that deal with this sort of analysis on the entire Torah."

At that time, they came to the top of a rise above the caves, and Timothy shouted out, "There it is. We're almost home."

"Is that a real cluster of buildings or an allegory?" Paul teased.

"When you taste my mother's cooking, you will be able to judge for yourself."

As the threesome approached the village, people came out to greet them.

"Where is my father?" Timothy asked.

"He has not returned," a stable boy said, taking control of Timothy's horse.

As they arrived in the village, there was one building that stood out from the others, built of gleaming white stone, with a four-foot wall surrounding it. As the stable boy led the horse through the gate, several women came out of the house, crying out their greetings to the party.

"Timothy, we're so glad you're back, with our guests. Have you seen your father?" asked a smiling woman of about forty who wore a scarf over her hair, but not a full veil. The first signs of gray hair were peeping out at her forehead.

Timothy said, "They took refuge in one of the safe caves, luckily."

"Welcome," she exclaimed genuinely, extending her arms. "I've heard so much about each of you. Lentulus must be beside himself with concern. I hope he returns home before nightfall. I know he was searching downstream. He actually said he would be looking for two bodies, so fierce was that storm. In the meantime, Timothy will show you your rooms so that you can bathe and change clothes."

Night had just fallen when the household was aroused by the arrival of Lentulus into the courtyard, riding one horse and leading two others. Eunice was the first person out, directing the household slaves in welcoming her husband. Timothy followed immediately, along with Paul and Barnabas.

"Lentulus, they are here. They arrived in midafternoon. Timothy found them."

"Where?" Lentulus asked everyone in general.

"Upstream. They found a cave that happened to be safe," Timothy responded, taking the reins so that his father could dismount.

"Praise to the Lord God worshipped by you, Timothy. I prayed to your God and he answered me, delivering my friends from the storm."

"Amen," responded Eunice.

Lentulus approached each man and embraced him, clearly relieved that they had survived. Amid that shared gratitude, they all entered the house.

CHAPTER 2

Ideas

Due to the emotional strain on seemingly everyone, the entire household retired early. Paul and Barnabas had been given clean clothes, since everything in their saddlebags had been soaked in the storm. Hence, they slept well and did not arise until the sun was high in the sky. They found Timothy engaged in discussion with an almost-emaciated man who had thin, unkempt hair and was dressed in a patched but clean tunic. Paul guessed that he was at least seventy years of age. Additionally, there were two men, one middle-aged and one in his twenties, both of whom were wearing prayer shawls.

"Good morning," Timothy sang out. "Come, meet my tutor, Photius, and two of my best friends from our synagogue, Ezekiel and Ezra."

These two stood and bowed to Paul. Ezekiel, the older of the two, had a full gray beard that flowed down his tunic. His yellow teeth showed through the hair and was the only hint that a smile was in place. The younger had a carefully trimmed jet-black beard and was prematurely almost bald. He was dressed in an expensive tunic with embroidered trim. He too welcomed Paul with a broad smile.

Barnabas and Paul introduced themselves with a bow and Photius remained seated on a small stool. Timothy and his two synagogue friends sat on cushions at Photius's feet. The philosopher motioned Paul and Barnabas toward two other stools. Paul accepted and sat facing Photius, but Barnabas excused himself and headed toward the dining room.

"So this is the Paul whom my young charge has been talking about almost incessantly. He contends that you teach the philosophy he brought home from Alexandria, taught by Philo."

"I know very little about Philo, but I teach a way of life exemplified by Iēsoûs of Nazareth."

"What school is in that place, Nazareth?" Photius asked in a polite voice.

"No school, but the birthplace of man whom God filled with wisdom, giving his life for all people as the means to achieve eternal life."

"Is the 'god' you speak of the same as that of the Jews who is worshipped by Eunice?"

"That is a difficult question," Paul responded carefully. "In one sense, there is only one

God, who created the world and everything in it. He produced a number of prophets, who were filled with a certain kind of wisdom, to some of whom he gave the Law that is the basis of our lives. Following the Law brings about righteousness in this life and happiness in the next. All of this comes about through Iēsoûs whom I preach. I hope to establish a community of followers here in Lystra, with Timothy's help."

"I've never heard him speak of this Iēsoûs so how will he help?"

"He doesn't know it yet, but he is almost ready to proclaim him," Paul said, looking directly at Timothy.

Timothy spoke up. "We spoke of him years ago on that ship between Tarsus and Caesarea Maritima, but since that memorable journey, I have studied under Philo, who makes no mention of this Iēsoûs. I consider myself a Jew who worships one God alone, who tolerates no other source of holiness."

"You are correct," Paul responded. "But one who was exalted by our God revealed himself to me, and it is he whom I preach. Let me show you why, based on the Holy Scriptures." And with that, Paul began to make a case for Iēsoûs starting with quotations from the prophets, especially Isaiah, and culminating with the description of the Son of Man as found in the Book of Daniel. Most importantly, he described the crucifixion of Iēsoûs as a sign of glory, not a scandal or act of foolishness."

The discussion took the entire day, and Photius listened care-fully, not interrupting. Eunice noted the intensity of Paul's speech and ignored announcing meals, which the balance of the family consumed at their normal hours. It was almost nightfall before Paul finished, and Timothy suggested that they end their discussion for the day, to which Paul quickly and enthusiastically agreed. Ezekiel and Ezra were invited to remain, and they agreed as well. Paul was interested in the fact that these two synagogue leaders would eat with Gentiles, even though Eunice kept a home that conformed to Torah.

As they entered the dining area, Lentulus took a position on one of the couches and gestured for the six to recline while Eunice motioned to a serving girl to bring food.

"Photius, you have spent almost thirty years in my service. What in the world kept you enthralled for a full day? You haven't shown that much interest in a philosophical discussion for more years than I can remember," Lentulus said, smiling.

"Well, I haven't heard such remarkable ideas since I was a youngster. But I have a proposition to make." Pause...glances exchanged. "I propose that we lead a garlanded ox to the center of town and sacrifice it in honor of the two gods we have among us, Zeus and Hermes."

"Are you joking with us?" Timothy asked, eyes wide, hands clasped.

"No, I'm not. Paul has described exactly what we have in our story of Baucis and Philemon. Paul spoke of a man who was sent by God to bring about holiness and righteousness. In this case, Zeus joined Hermes to announce the Good News of gods coming into the world. They were not immediately recognized. Are you familiar with that example of Good News, Paul or Barnabas?"

"No." Both shook their heads.

"Let me begin the story," Photius said, settling into his couch. "You can eat while I talk.

"The power of the gods is great and knows no limit, and whatever heaven decrees comes to pass. To help convince you, in the hills of Phrygia, an oak and a lime tree stand side by side, surrounded by a low wall. I have seen the place, since the King of Troezen sent his wise men into that country, where his father, Pelops, once ruled."

There is a swamp not far from there, once habitable land but now the haunt of diving birds and marsh-loving coots. Zeus went there, disguised as a mortal; and Hermes, setting aside his wings, went with his father, carrying the caduceus. A thousand houses they approached, looking for a place to rest. A thousand houses were locked and bolted. But one received them. It was humble, it is true, roofed with reeds and stems from the marsh, but godly Baucis and the equally aged Philemon had been wedded in that cottage in their younger years and there had grown old together. They made light of poverty by acknowledging it and bearing it without discontent of mind. It was no matter if you asked for owner or servant there. Those two were the whole household; they gave orders and carried them out equally.

"So when the gods from heaven met the humble household gods, and stooping down, passed the low doorway, the old man pulled out a bench, and requested them to rest their limbs, while over the bench Baucis threw a rough blanket. Then she raked over the warm ashes in the hearth and brought yesterday's fire to life, feeding it with leaves and dried bark and nursed the flames with her aged breath. She pulled down finely divided twigs and dry stems from the roof and, breaking them further, pushed them under a small bronze pot. Next she stripped the leaves from vegetables that her husband had gathered from his well-watered garden. He used a two-pronged stick to lift a wretched-looking chine of meat hanging from a blackened beam, cut a meager piece from the carefully saved chine and put what had been cut to seethe in boiling water. In the meantime they made conversation to pass the time and to prevent their guests from being conscious of the delay."

"There was a beechwood tub suspended by its handle from a crude peg. This had been filled with warm water, and it allowed their visitors to refresh their limbs. In the middle of the floor, there was a mattress of soft sedges. Placed on a frame and legs of willow, it made a couch. They covered it with cloths that they only brought out for the times of sacred festivals, but even these were old and worn, not unworthy of the couch."

"The gods were seated. The old woman, her skirts tucked up, her hands trembling, placed a table there, but a table with one of the three legs unequal: a piece of broken pot made them equal. Pushed underneath, it countered the slope, and she wiped the level surface with fresh mint. On it she put the black and green olives, which belonged to pure Minerva; the cornelian cherries of autumn, preserved in wine lees; radishes and endives; a lump of cheese; and lightly roasted eggs, untouched by the hot ashes all in clay dishes. After this she set out a carved mixing bowl for wine, just as costly, with cups made of beechwood, hollowed out and lined with yellow beeswax. There was little delay before the fire provided its hot food and the wine, of no great age, circulated, and then, removed, made a little room for the second course. There were nuts, a mix of dried figs and wrinkled dates; plums and sweet-smelling apples in open wicker baskets; and grapes gathered from the purple vines. In the center was a gleaming honeycomb. Above all, there was the additional presence of well-meaning faces, and no unwillingness, or poverty of spirit.

"Meanwhile, the old couple noticed that as the mixing bowl was emptied, it refilled itself, unaided, and the wine appeared of its own accord. They were fearful at this strange and astonishing sight, and timidly Baucis and Philemon murmured a prayer, their palms upward, and begged the gods' forgiveness for the meal and their unpreparedness. They had a goose, the guard for their tiny cottage. As hosts they prepared to sacrifice it for their divine guests. But, quick-winged, it wore the old people out and, for a long time, escaped them, at last appearing to take refuge with the gods themselves."

"Then the heaven-born ones told them not to kill it. 'We are gods,' they said, 'and this neighborhood will receive just punishment for its impiety. But to you we grant exemption from that evil. Just leave your house and accompany our steps as we climb that steep mountainside together.'"

"They both obeyed, and leaning on their sticks to ease their climb, they set foot on the long slope. When they were as far from the summit as a bowshot might carry, they looked back and saw that everywhere else had vanished in the swamp. Only their own roof was visible. And while they stood amazed at this, mourning their neighbors' fate, their old cottage, tiny even for the two of them, turned into a temple. Wooden poles became pillars, and the reed thatch grew yellow until a golden roof appeared, along with richly carved doors, and marble pavement covered the ground. Then Zeus spoke calmly, to them: 'Ask of us, virtuous old man, and you, wife, worthy of a virtuous husband, what you wish.'"

"When he had spoken briefly with Baucis, Philemon revealed their joint request to the gods. 'We ask to be priests and watch over your temple, and since we have lived out harmonious years together, let the same hour take the two of us, so that I never have to see my wife's grave, nor she have to bury me.' The gods' assurance followed the prayer. They had charge of the temple while they lived. And when they were released by old age and by the years as they chanced to be standing by the sacred steps, discussing the subject of their death, Baucis saw Philemon put out leaves, and old Philemon saw Baucis put out leaves, and as the tops of the trees grew over their two faces, they exchanged words while they still could, saying, in the same breath: 'Farewell, O dear companion,' as, in the same breath, the bark covered them, concealing their mouths."

"The people of Lycaonia still show the neighboring trees that sprang from their two bodies. Trustworthy old men related these things to me, there was no reason why they should wish to lie. For my part, I saw garlands hanging from the branches, and placing fresh ones there, I said, 'Let those who love the gods become gods. Let those who have honored them be honored.'"

"That was a lovely story," Paul said with great feeling. "There is much truth that we share, including the requirement of hospitality to anyone who is hungry, despite the level of wealth or poverty."

"How can you say that?" pronounced Ezekiel, the elder synagogue leader. "You are proposing that we take seriously that false gods appear to people. Torah teaches that we acknowledge one and only one God, who led us out of Egypt. I was ready to tear my garments."

"Peace," Paul said softly. "Many of my friends recognize Zeus as another name for YHWH, whom we worship. And we have another name, Iēsoûs, as standing for the Son of God, whom I profess as the one exalted at the right hand of God, who brought the Word of the Lord to all people, Jews first, but also Greeks as well."

"But the story that you approve," said Ezekiel," has one of the visitors proclaim that 'We are gods.' Does that not suggest that there are multiple gods, and does this not invalidate one of our most important scriptural affirmations: 'Hear, O Israel! The LORD is our God, the LORD alone!'"

"We must understand," Paul responded softly, "that the story was written many years ago, before the *Moschiach* was sent by our Lord. Our ancestors knew that angels were sent to bring a message to someone. Recall that the Lord's angel visited Hagar and asked her where she was going. Divine messengers are part of our tradition, not only of the Greeks. So, for our story, Zeus could easily represent an angel who brings Good News. We must understand what these names represent, not assuming that they refer to real entities. The essence of the story is the divine action of two poor people when confronted with unknown people who are hungry and exhausted from a journey. This is much of the message of Iēsoûs that I preach."

Ezra, the younger of the men from the synagogue, smiled broadly. "Well said, Rav. Many of the younger people in our community can relate to that explanation. There are many, many stories like that of Baucis and Philemon. It might be worthwhile to examine these stories and see if they correspond to our holy truth."

"No," shouted Ezekiel. "We must focus on educating our young people in the Torah and the writings. Once we appear to accept Zeus speaking to men, we will have lost the battle. And you, Paul, by giving credence to Greek falsity, are sowing the seed of our destruction. We live among Gentiles, and they would welcome young men such as Timothy here if they would first speak favorably of Zeus and then participate in festivals and sacrifices. Then they marry goyim, and it's all over. Our holy truth is lost for all time. No, we cannot accept Zeus and Hermes even as representing someone else." And with that, he stood up, looked at Ezra expectantly, and headed for the door.

"Rav Ezekiel, do not leave in the middle of our discussion," Ezra pleaded. "Paul has studied in Jerusalem among Pharisees of great repute. Give him some time."

"No, Ezra, and you should come with me. I was promised a wonderful day of scholarship on Torah, but instead I am forced to listen to falsity and no Torah. If you stay, 'I'm not sure what the rest of the men of our synagogue will say' at least they won't think that I pay attention to that drivel." With that, he stormed out of the room."

As he left, Timothy arose and seemed desirous of catching the older man, but Photius also rose and reached out toward his student. "Let him go," he commanded. "I agree with your guest, Paul, in this matter. We must be always aware of how the divine is present in our lives. And in many cases, acts of loving-kindness are encouraged by those people whom you would never expect, poor people who are blessed with the gift of generosity."

Paul stood up and raised both hands toward heaven. "In my most private discussions with my beloved teacher Gamaliel, the Hebrew phrase *gemilut chasidim* was used as the criterion for holiness before the Lord. It is translated as 'acts of loving kindness.' This idea is incorporated in the revelation that was given me when Iēsoûs called me to be the apostle to both Jews and Gentiles. This is what Baucis and Philemon did. They were rewarded by never having to see the beloved consumed by death. This story is valid, despite the fact that different names for the divine are used. The essential idea, that the Lord urges all of us to such acts, is characteristic of ancient Greek and ancient and modern Hebrew thought. The exact phrase *gemilut chasidim* does not exist in Torah, but we read in the Prophet Zecharia, *Thus says the LORD of hosts: Judge with true justice, and show kindness and compassion toward each other.* Further, it appears in the Oral Torah of those superb sages who mediate night and day on God's Word. Finally, I would teach as follows: *Put on then, as God's chosen ones, holy and beloved, heartfelt compassion, kindness, humility, gentleness, and patience.* And this teaching is not inconsistent with the story my new friend, Photius, has shared with us." With that, Paul was seated, and Timothy resumed his place on the floor.

"Paul, your teaching is parallel with what I have taught both Lentulus and Timothy," Photius said. "I am pleased that you met. But is there anything more that you have to say about your Iēsoûs?"

"Indeed there is," Paul responded. "But let us postpone further discussion for now and resume tomorrow. This will give the Holy Spirit time to become present in our hearts."

CHAPTER 3

Becoming Part of the People of God

DURING THE ENSUING MONTH, PAUL spent as much time as he could with several men in the small synagogue. They owned only partial scrolls of Torah, part of Isaiah and a scroll containing about fifty psalms. Ezekiel claimed to have been educated in Antioch in Syria, but he could not name anyone whom Paul had known. It became clear that there was discomfort between Ezra and Ezekiel that was more than intergenerational. Ezekiel read scripture in Hebrew, but since there were few scrolls in the library of the synagogue, his knowledge was quite truncated. Ezra, on the other hand, claimed to have been educated in Ephesus, under teachers who did not know Hebrew but had extensive scrolls in Greek. Some of these scrolls, such as those named for the Maccabees that Ezra had brought with him, were not given the honor of being scripture by Ezekiel. Timothy felt quite close to Ezra, and while his training under Philo had given him tools to interpret scripture, Ezra had not learned Hebrew and had done limited reading of Scripture even in Greek.

Barnabas, on the other hand, spent as much time with Lentulus as possible, discussing the business of manufacturing products from hemp. Lentulus enjoyed Barnabas's insights, even to experimenting with a cloth that was half hemp and half wool. Then they tried half hemp and half linen. The latter was particularly successful—with the longitudinal, warp threads of linen and the cross, weft threads of hemp, a lighter and more flexible cloth resulted. As they experimented, they consulted with Paul, who had learned working with leather in Jerusalem and who advised on the size of the fabrics and with reinforcing added so that the fabric could be used for tents for the legions.

One evening four weeks from their arrival, Barnabas asked Lentulus if they could talk for a while.

"You have been a most gracious host, my friend. Being with your family has been a wonderful experience. But I must bring up two issues. First, Paul has made progress in introducing Timothy to the Lord Iēsoûs. He confided in me that Timothy is likely to ask for baptism in a few days. But Timothy is his only success. The men at the synagogue have taken the side of Ezekiel and are not pleased with what Paul is teaching. Even Ezra has been convinced that Paul is introducing innovation into their religion."

"I'm surprised," Lentulus said. "Eunice and her mother, Lois, are perfectly happy with the Good News Paul is preaching. I generally don't discuss religion with them, since I'm perfectly happy with my devotion to Mithras, but the women seem to have others who feel the same."

"Here's our problem, Lentulus. There are not enough Jews in Lystra to constitute an assembly here. And there is a need of a minimum number for an assembly, say twenty, which would be ten men and their wives. Except for Timothy, we can't point to more than five people who might undergo baptism and make an act of faith in our Lord. This means we're going to have to leave. We've heard about Derbe as being the very size to give us a better chance of having enough Jews for an assembly. We could then invite Gentiles to join our group, which would attract others."

"While I will hate to see you leave, especially with the affection that has grown up with you and Paul, I understand the problem."

"Now for our second problem: Timothy."

"Timothy?" Lentulus jumped.

"Yes, my friend. He has indicated that not only will he embrace baptism, he wants to travel with us. This solves one problem, which is that we don't baptize people in the same way as other religions have initiations, as you experienced in your Mithras devotion. It is critical to have a family that gathers, not isolated individuals. If Timothy comes with us, we will be his family, and we can baptize him."

"But I have planned on Timothy's working with me, side by side, in our business. It will be an enormous loss if he should leave with you."

"This is what you and he must discuss, Lentulus. I can't help there. I would be happy to treat Timothy as a brother and do what I can to help him grow. But he is a man of faith, desiring to spend his life with us as we build up our communities."

"Which *communities*?" Lentulus asked, a touch of sharpness in his tone.

"It is our goal that we create communities dedicated to Iēsoûs who gave his life freely for our benefit and who will return to judge everyone in the world. The bond of our communities is love for one another in imitation. I truly believe they will come about. The Holy Spirit will not abandon us. As it is, your wife, Eunice, and her mother, Lois, have attracted six women and three men who meet on the Sabbath. Of course, Timothy meets with them."

"I will talk with Timothy about his leaving Lystra," Lentulus said. "Does his mother know of this?"

"I don't know," Barnabas responded.

"It will break her heart."

"I hope not. She has been faithful to our God all her life. This is just one more way she can demonstrate her love."

The two men walked inside, each filled with a different kind of apprehension.

CHAPTER 4

Circumcision

DURING THE NEXT WEEK, PAUL redoubled his efforts to apply the formula with the younger men in the synagogue that was on the verge of bringing Timothy to baptism. But while Ezra seemed open to accepting Iēsoûs as the Son of God, his unwillingness to conflict with Ezekiel kept him from discussion of his own baptism. When he heard that Timothy would be baptized he refused to discuss it. "Let him do what he feels best," he said. "As for myself, I cannot accept the Son of Man as described by Daniel to have been shamefully executed on a Roman cross. The Son of Man was given authority and power and was to be worshipped by the Gentiles, not crucified scandalously."

A few days later, during the evening meal, Timothy expressed his desire for baptism. Paul wiped tears from his eyes and went over to him, arms out to embrace him. Lentulus grasped Eunice's hand, knowing that this meant that Timothy would leave with Paul and Barnabas at some time in the future.

Photius clapped his hands and smiled broadly. "The rule of life that Paul is presenting has excellent philosophical grounding," he said. "The idea of founding communities bound together by love of God and of neighbor is perfectly solid. I have watched Eunice and Lois in their devotion to the Jewish God, and the household they have created has afforded me a marvelous life. Except for the claim that the Torah, Prophets and Writings are from God, including some extreme food laws and regulations on ritual uncleanness, I could live with either Eunice's or Paul's rules of life…and so can my student, Timothy."

"I asked Ezekiel if we could use his *mikvah* for the baptism," Barnabas said, "so that others can witness the baptism and enjoy a meal afterward, but he declined. Hence, we will use the small, private ritual bath here in the house. But this means only Barnabas and I will be able to witness the ritual."

"That is fine," Lentulus said. "We can enjoy a banquet afterward, and whoever joins us will be welcome. I hope some of the members of the assembly attend, especially Ezra. Eunice has provided more than half the support of the group. It would be a scandal if they should not come."

Several days passed, and Eunice had invited all the members of the synagogue for a banquet after Timothy's baptism. She had received the acceptance of Ezra and his wife, plus the women and men who constituted her community.

Paul explained to Lentulus that people were simply unaware of what this event was all about. Ezra explained that the majority of members thought a baptism was identical with an initiation ceremony to a pagan cult. The use of a *mikvah* was common within the Jewish community, as prescribed in the holy book *Leviticus*. Not only was it used by women at the end of their menstrual period, it was used by men after nocturnal emissions. It was also used by one who was a non-Jew (known as a *proselyte*) who chose to convert to Judaism. Hence, immersion in a ritual bath was common and accepted, but the utilization of the *mikveh* to become an adherent to a separate aspect of their religion was resisted in the name of conservatism.

The day of Timothy's baptism arrived. In addition to Paul and Barnabas, a small party consisting of Lentulus, Eunice, her mother, Lois, Ezra and his wife, Photius and Timothy's sister, Rebecca, had gathered outside the *mikveh* area, intending to congratulate Timothy when he emerged. Timothy, Paul, and Barnabas, after greeting the family and friends, entered the small room that contained the recessed pool, accessible by one set of five steps to go down into the bath and a separate set of steps up.

As Timothy removed his tunic and took his place on the first step down, Paul and Barnabas both exclaimed, "Do not go down." They both saw that Timothy had never been circumcised. "Put your tunic back on," said Barnabas. "We must discuss the fact that you are not part of the People of God."

"But Paul, you have always said that circumcision or non-circumcision is immaterial," Timothy blurted out.

"That is true of Gentiles. But you were born of a Jewish woman and fell under the requirement of Torah for descendants of Abraham, where he was commanded to circumcise the men of his people as a sign of the covenant. Hence, you must be circumcised, and then you can be baptized."

When the three men emerged, with Timothy in the same tunic, Eunice guessed at the reason that baptism had not taken place. She defended Timothy immediately.

"You must understand, Paul, that when Lentulus brought me to this place as his wife, I was the only Jew in town. Every Jew here can trace his or her residence here from me or my mother. When Timothy was born, there was no synagogue, and hence no one who could perform *bris* on my child. Indeed, it was not until he was ten that Ezekiel came, who was trained in our traditions. But he was trained only for babies eight days old, not for adult men. So Timothy never had the chance to be circumcised."

"But what about his two years in Alexandria?" Paul asked.

"No one thought of it then. No one ever asked, and since he never participated in a Greek gymnasium, the issue never arose. Recall, he was just learning about our tradition. And when we heard your opinion that circumcision and uncircumcision did not matter, but only faith in Iēsoûs, the matter seemed as though it had been laid to rest."

"What I mean by that is there is no distinction between Jew or Greek in the body of Christ. But where a male child is born of a Jewish mother, he must follow Torah before baptism."

"Where can I be circumcised?" asked a bewildered Timothy.

"Ezra, do you know someone we call *mo'el* in Hebrew, especially one who ministers to adult men as opposed to babies?" Paul asked.

"Yes, I do. His name is Joshua, and he has a small school teaching the thought of Hillel. He presides at a synagogue located in Derbe. He will greet you warmly, Paul, unlike Ezekiel."

"Why does Derbe have anything to do with my circumcision?" Timothy asked.

"Because that is where we are going as soon as it is convenient," Barnabas answered.

"We have been unsuccessful here in establishing a sizable community, and that is because there are so few Jews living here. In Derbe, I understand that there is a vibrant Jewish population that is likely to be open to the Good News that we bring about Iēsoûs the Lord. That is where we need to go to do what the Christ has assigned to us," Paul elaborated.

"And, Timothy, we would be happy if you would join us in our efforts. We will solve the issue of your circumcision in Derbe, then you will be baptized," Barnabas added. "It normally takes four to six weeks for a man to recover from the operation. And while you are recovering, we shall attempt to create a community dedicated to the Lord Iēsoûs."

Timothy looked at his father, an inquisitive look on his face.

"While I had hopes of your working with me in my business," Lentulus said, "I have consulted with Photius and am convinced that I should not block your plans. In fact, within the next week, I shall have a caravan carrying kef thread to Tarsus. Derbe is almost on the way, so you can travel with that caravan in complete security."

"Wonderful," exclaimed Barnabas.

"Now," continued Lentulus, since we have a feast ready, let us not waste the food and effort gone into it." And with that he led the party into the dining area, where wine was already mixed and the odor of freshly cooked lamb wafted over the area.

Suddenly, someone was pounding on the door at the main entrance to the house. Someone was shouting, "Paul of Tarsus, come forth and stand before your God! Come forth! Come, come forth!"

Paul and Lentulus strode to the entrance and swung the door open. Standing there was a crowd of men standing behind Ezekiel. The crowd stood there holding rocks in their hands. Ezekiel cried out, "Thus says the Lord: *If your brother, your son or daughter, your beloved spouse or your intimate friend entices you by saying "come let us serve other gods," do not yield or listen to any such person, nor show pity or compassion, but you shall kill that person. You shall stone that person to death for seeking to lead you astray from the Lord your God who brought you out of* the *land of Egypt in the house of slavery.* Paul of Tarsus, you have been tried and found guilty of enticing the Jews of Lystra to abandon the faith of our fathers and to worship a new god."

Before Lentulus could drag Paul back into the house, a fist-sized rock flew from the crowd and found its mark just above Paul's ear. Paul's knees buckled, and Lentulus caught Paul's body before it hit the floor. Ezra ran to the front of the crowd. and screamed at Ezekiel and the group:

"Drop those rocks," he shouted. "You have killed him! How could you possibly commit such a crime!"

With that Ezra helped Lentulus drag Paul inside the entrance-way and slammed the door. Blood was flowing from Paul's head, and Lentulus searched for a pulse at the side of Paul's neck. By this time Eunice had grasped the situation and quickly brought some clean cloths to bind Paul's head.

"He is not dead," Lentulus shouted. "He will be all right. He will be all right!"

As Eunice bound Paul's head, he opened his eyes, blinked a couple of times, and asked nobody in particular, "What...what happened?"

"Nothing serious," Lentulus said with a smile. "Merely a theological disagreement taken to its logical conclusion."

"That is a theological argument that is offensive to me," Ezra said through clenched teeth. "I shall no longer participate in the assembly of Ezekiel. In fact, Paul, would you be kind enough to baptize me and my wife into the Lord?"

"My partner Barnabas will baptize you and anyone else from your assembly who will proclaim Iēsoûs as Lord. I thank the Lord that I am able to suffer with him in order to bring one more person into the Body of Christ. Further, after you have been baptized, we shall ask you to baptize your wife, and then she will be able to baptize any other women who desire to become part of His Body."

"Let us then return to the feast that Eunice has prepared, in recognition of the presence of the Holy Spirit, who will lead us to unforeseen goals," suggested Barnabas.

Blessed are you, oh Lord our God, King of the Universe who brings forth new members of Christ, Paul prayed loudly and strongly.

The party returned to the small mikvah, where Barnabas baptized Ezra, Ezra baptized his wife, and she baptized Eunice, Lois, and two female household slaves. The party returned to the dining area and enjoyed the love that was characteristic of the assembly of Christ.

CHAPTER 5
A Codex

THE NEXT DAY, LENTULUS SUMMONED Paul, Barnabas and Timothy into his library, into which he rarely invited anyone. The back wall included shelves on which were about twenty scrolls and three objects about sixteen inches long and twelve inches wide.

"What are those?" Paul asked.

"We call them codices," said Lentulus. "The wooden covers enclose about fifty sheets that we call *pugillares membrani.* Timothy, bring one over to Paul so he can look at it."

When Paul got one in his hand, he opened it and saw the writing on both sides of the sheets of papyrus. "This is astonishing," he blurted out.

Barnabas came across the room and shared Paul's amazement. The first page had a large Latin title: *Strabonis Rerum* Geographicarum, which stressed Paul's knowledge of that language.

Paul turned to the next page and saw that the author began the work by describing the insights that had been recorded about the locations of the various parts of the world by previous philosophers.

"This is a remarkable way to write something," Paul remarked.

"If you have the time, you will see that the author, Strabo, describes the location of many cities, the relationship of one city to another, and in many cases the distances between the cities."

"What a treasure," Paul said as he randomly turned the pages.

"Timothy purchased this codex while he was in Alexandria. This particular volume includes information on our part of the world. Let me show you," said Lentulus, and he carefully turned the pages toward the last part of the book. "Look here: here is a description of Klaudiconium, and it points out that the city is located on the Royal Road from Susa to Sardis, which is close to Ephesus. Let's see...look here. 'The road is sixteen hundred miles long, and an army messenger could travel the entire length in nine days. If one were walking, it would take three months.'"

"We can relate to that," Barnabas said with a smile.

"Well, there's something else," Lentulus said with a smile. "Look at what Timothy has done." Lentulus turned to the very end of the codex and unfolded a large sheet of papyrus such that it was four times the dimension of the codex. On the lower center part of the sheet of papyrus was a series of squares and the word *Lystra* written beneath them. From this were two lines, one going upward toward another series of squares with the word *Klaudiconium* written beneath that set of squares. The other line from *Lystra* came upward to the left, intersecting with a line from *Klaudiconium* to the left and marked *hodos sebaste* or "Royal Way." Another line came from the right side of the sheet, passing through this second set of squares and connecting with a small set of squares marked *Laranda* and then continuing upward to the left to a larger set of squares marked *Derbe*. "Look carefully," said Lentulus. "You will see some numbers along these lines. Each number represents the number of Roman miles between the locations of the cities. So if you were to leave Lystra on the road downward to the right, you would come upon *Laranda* in seventy-eight miles. Then, turning upward, you can see the number twelve, indicating the number of miles from *Laranda* to *Derbe*, with the word *Fortified* next to it.

"What Timothy has done is to draw a picture of the way the gods see our area from heaven. We call this picture a *kartēs*, and hopefully anyone possessing one of these will not get lost if he is a traveler. It will guide you at least to *Derbe*, which is described by Strabo as constructed by Antipater the Robber. Notice that Antipater is a Jewish name, and when Pompey cleared our coastline of pirates a little over a hundred years ago, a sizable number of Jews abandoned their ships on our coast and made their way up across the Taurus Mountains to *Derbe*. So great was their fear of Pompey that they founded the city and enclosed it with walls, despite the fact that the overall population would not normally justify the building of such walls."

Timothy then spoke up. "When I was in Alexandria, I studied the geography of Eratosthenes. He was able to calculate both the diameter of the world and the distance from the Earth to the Moon. However, he was interested in broad philosophical principles and not with the practical problems of having something that one could rely upon in traveling. So as we travel to Derbe and perhaps beyond, I intend to keep track of the distances and directions of the various roads that we travel on. I will keep large sheets of papyrus available for my cartography. I will send my work to a friend in Alexandria named Apollos, who sat with me at the feet of Philo."

Paul stepped back and looked intently at Timothy and said, "The Holy Spirit has come upon you, Timothy, in creating just what we need in order to preach the Gospel of Iēsoûs the Christ to the ends of the earth. The ability to understand exactly where each assembly that we originate is located with relation to each of the other assemblies makes it possible to visualize the unity that exists among all assemblies in Christ Iēsoûs."

"There is another practical benefit from my son's work," Lentulus said to both Paul and Barnabas, "and that is that in your travels to Derbe, you will be passing through areas infested with pirates, especially around Laranda. I have two retired legionnaires who always make the trip to Tarsus with me. I will lend them to you for your protection. Once you turn upward toward Derbe, you won't need them, and they will return to me. You should be able to arrive at Laranda in two days."

"That implies that we travel by horse," Timothy responded.

"I will lend you the horses," Lentulus said with feigned exasperation. "I won't have my heir to my considerable fortune walking through Asia like a lost Cynic. I have caravans to Tarsus often, so if you decide to remain for any length of time in Derbe, someone will pick up the horses and return them to me."

"Which legionnaires will be our bodyguard, Father?" asked Timothy.

"Demas and Gaius," Lentulus said. "Demas was my right hand in Alexandria and came with me when I retired. He's worth any five men in a fight, but he is gentle as a lamb. Gaius was with the Fourth Scythia, which was billeted in Adana ad Taurus, about a hundred miles from your birthplace, Paul. He was born in Derbe. He is very important to me because he speaks Trocmi, the language of the sworn enemies of the tribes south of Laranda. As such, he's worth another five men in case of a pirate attack. So I've given you a ten-man bodyguard," he said with a laugh.

"Lentulus, you are indeed an angel in disguise and have treated us as would have Baucis and Philemon," Paul said with great feeling. "As a matter of principle, it is difficult for me to accept benefits from patrons because of the necessity to ultimately pay back the benefits received. I however have committed myself to a life of poverty and care of the poor. But since it is clear that you are lending support for us and your son Timothy, I accept your gifts with humility and an assurance that your son will become my son and that we will spend our lives together preaching the Gospel from Jerusalem to the ends of the earth." And with that Paul walked over to Lentulus, opened his arms, and embraced the surprised centurion.

The balance of the day was spent in preparation for departure the next morning. Prior to dinnertime the two bodyguards appeared and were welcomed warmly by Lentulus and Timothy. Demas was over six feet tall and had closely cropped gray hair that set off the scarred remains of his left ear. His tanned face was wrinkled with lines augmented by his good-natured attitude. He greeted Paul and Barnabas with a typical Roman mutual grasping of forearms. Gaius was just the opposite, being slightly above five feet tall and rectangular in build, with massive shoulders and forearms. His bald head sat on a short neck encased in muscles. His mouth was set in a downward curl, as though the world had treated him badly. He barely smiled as he greeted Timothy and was introduced to Paul and Barnabas.

Dinner was minimal, as their plan was to depart at sunup. Timothy took his mother into a room at the back of the garden and assured her that leaving with Paul and Barnabas was the most important thing he could do and assured her that he would be much closer than Alexandria. After he wiped away her tears, he searched out Photius and spent an hour in conversation, mainly focusing on the fact that he now had a purpose in life.

CHAPTER 6

Departure from Lystra

THE FIRST GLOW IN THE eastern sky illuminated the entire household, which was actively engaged in the preparation for imminent departure. In addition to five horses, there were six of the native small donkeys being loaded with strong, colorful bags containing *kannabis* thread destined for Tarsus. Additionally, one donkey was loaded with two large waterproof skins containing water, since the shallow wells on the road to Laranda did not always flow. Plus, one of the small donkeys was laden with one tent in one of the colorful bags on one side and miscellaneous equipment required for camping by the roadside, including bags of cereal and dried fruit. It would take three days to arrive at Laranda and an additional four days to reach Tarsus. The party would split at Laranda, with Gaius and Demas leading the donkeys to Tarsus, and Timothy, Paul, and Barnabas heading north for about six miles to Derbe.

Paul and Barnabas carried their traveling bags and greeted Timothy and Lentulus, who directed them just inside the house to a table on which were stacked sweet cakes, figs, grapes, and apples.

"Eat your fill," Timothy said with a smile, taking charge of their bags. "We won't have a good meal until we get to Laranda."

Neither Paul nor Barnabas needed any encouragement. As they sat on stools, Eunice brought two cups of hot tea, along with generous slices of an apple tart.

"I pray to our Lord Iēsoûs that you are received graciously in Derbe, quickly establish an assembly in their midst, and return here when your

218

work is done. And I pray that when you return, you're able to leave my son Timothy as leader of our community in the Lord."

"Do not fear, Eunice. The Lord is with us and will protect us on our journey. I'm hoping that within a few months, we will be able to return here," Paul said as he took her hand.

"There is the sun," shouted Timothy. "And there is not a cloud in the sky. It will be a beautiful day."

"I hope you have given me a horse that knows more than I know," said Paul with a smile. "Whatever disaster threatens us, I plan to rely upon this horse's good sense."

The donkeys were harnessed two abreast, and the first two were secured to Demas's horse.

Gaius, Demas, and Timothy easily mounted their horses. One of the household slaves placed a triangular device shaped like two H figures tied together at the top and opening to create a step about two feet high adjacent to Paul's horse, making it easy for him to mount the animal. There was a rope tied to it so that Paul was able to pull it up after he was on the horse and hook it onto one of the horns on the saddle.

Gaius explained, "One of the most difficult skills to be learned in riding a horse is how to mount the animal without help. We hope you will always have a companion who can help you when needed, but just in case either you or Barnabas need to mount when you are alone, these should help you considerably."

With the entire party was mounted, the caravan of five horses and eight donkeys began to move, returning the waves offered by Lentulus, Eunice, and the household slaves. As the caravan made its way through the town toward the road to Laranda, children emerged and ran toward the caravan, waving and merrily shouting, "Take me with you, take me with you." Each house in the town had an open porch where five or six women were actively engaged in transforming the fibers from the kef into thread that could be used to weave fabric. This thread was then packed into bags, and the bags were loaded onto the small donkeys and transported to Tarsus, where the fabric was created. The kef took about four months to grow, so the women of Lystra could plan on spending thread for about a month, every four months.

As the caravan reached the south end of the town, it joined what was called a road but what in reality was an area where the thin grass was trampled down in the brown earth. In addition, as far as one could see, there were intermittent bushes, and rarely interspersed in the thin grass one could see an oak tree. After about a half hour, the beaten path came quite close to a full and bushy oak; Paul noticed that on the lower branches there were many scraps of fabric sewn onto the lower branches. He nudged his horse forward to be directly next to Timothy and asked him about this.

"That is a 'wishing tree,'" he said. "Passersby sew small pieces of fabric onto the tree and simultaneously utter a prayer for some need that they have. You will note that when we get up to the tree, Gaius will attach a piece of fabric as a prayer for an uneventful journey."

Paul motioned to Barnabas to come up to his side, and he described the fabric on the oak tree ahead. "Do we object?" Paul asked.

"No. We should not create problems so early in our journey. Instead, why don't you make an effort to talk with Gaius and Demas about Iēsoûs, and invite them to see that these scraps of fabric are meaningless."

Paul nodded his head and resolved as soon as possible to evangelize both Gaius and Demas.

While there were no villages or towns located on this poor excuse for a road, flocks of sheep and goats were very common. The road was oriented primarily to the south; to the right were shallow mountains several miles away. The landscape before them was dominated by thin grasses sprinkled with low bushes sprouting gray-green leaves. The combination of grasses and bushes gave one the impression that life was barely present. If one looked carefully, one could see the evidence of rivulets descending from the mountains and crossing the road, but there was no evidence of lakes or standing water at the end of the dried-out spring skeletons.

Several hours into the trip, the caravan came upon a massive flock of sheep that seemed to be feeding on both sides the road. Paul urged his horse forward and asked Gaius whether he planned to wait for the flock to finish their feeding or to have the caravan go around the flock.

"I generally avoid an extended excursion off the road, mainly because with the periodicity of water flows, there are many invisible miniature caves beneath the surface such that the weight of a horse could easily puncture the roof of the cave and result in a broken leg. But don't be concerned, Paul, about having to wait for the flock to move. Just wait here."

Gaius raised his hand, and the caravan stopped. He then walked his horse forward toward the flock. Suddenly, like a flash, a huge beige colored dog with a black muzzle came barking and snarling from the opposite side of the flock and stopped between Gaius and the flock. A shepherd started walking toward Gaius, calling quietly to the dog. The animal had a longer body than most dogs of his size and must have weighed one hundred forty pounds. He focused his attention on Gaius until the shepherd arrived. A short conversation with Gaius ensued, and Gaius flipped a small coin to the shepherd A whistle came from the shepherd along with a hand signal, and the dog immediately made its way to the perimeter of the flock, sheep jumping out of the way. When it reached the perimeter, he rolled up his tail like a pinwheel and changed the character of his bark while running back and forth along the side of the flock, nipping the flanks of any sheep not moving in the direction that would cross the road. The sheep at the perimeter pushed the sheep directly in front of them, and within moments the entire flock began to move slowly across the road. The dog joyfully kept the pressure on the perimeter of the flock, periodically stopping and looking at its master, and with no new signals, it continued its successful movement of the flock until the road was clear. The dog then returned to its master, sat at his master's feet, and received a congratulatory petting of its head along with a morsel of food as a reward.

Gaius resumed progress of the caravan, and as he passed the shepherd, he shouted out to him, "I wish I had a cute little lapdog like yours."

The shepherd laughed and waved.

CHAPTER 7

Arrival in Derbe

BY MIDAFTERNOON, THE HORSES AND riders were soaked in sweat, and Gaius announced that they would soon be at a tiny village where they could water the horses and let them graze. Very shortly, the grass became a rich green color, a grove of oak trees surrounded a small lake, and a young boy emerged from one of the houses with the same kind of dog that they had encountered earlier in the day. Gaius quickly negotiated the price to permit the party to spend the night in a small shelter next to the lake. Under Timothy's supervision, Paul and Barnabas removed the bits and bridles from their horses, who quickly began to devour the rich green grass.

After Gaius had broken out some flatbread and a rich chickpea spread, which he prepared and handed out to each of his partners seated in the middle of the shelter, Paul raised his hands and proclaimed, *Blessed are you, Lord our God, King of the Universe, who brings forth bread from the earth.*

"Amen," responded Barnabas and Timothy.

As everyone settled down, Gaius said. "Paul, Demas and I would like to hear more about God whom you proclaim. It appears that our mistress, Eunice, offers praise to the same God. But it seems that you have a different God who is somehow related to the one she prays to. And we are not sure who Timothy prays to, especially since he is apparently traveling to Derbe to become initiated to this God through what appears to us to be a barbaric and inhuman procedure. Please enlighten us."

"My friends, there is nothing that I would rather do than speak with you about the God of Israel and his Son, Iēsoûs." And with that, Paul began to recite the earliest passages from a book called *Bereshit,* or *When God began to create...*It was in a close, personal environment that Paul was at his best. He was able to sense the questions that arose in the minds of his hearers, and he was able to develop a running commentary along with the texts themselves. Barnabas and Timothy followed every word and periodically added their own questions to those of Gaius and Demas. Timothy had lighted a small lantern when the sun set, and when the candle in the lantern guttered out, Demas declared that he could no longer stay awake, and everyone agreed to continue tomorrow.

The five men slept deeply until daybreak.

The next day followed the same pattern, with Paul quoting lengthy sections from the five books he referred to as "Torah," focusing mainly on those sections that described God's love for his people. They rode until sunset, at which time they came upon a square stone monument about three feet tall, engraved with the words: "Leandra XX miles."

"We will camp here tonight," announced Gaius. "We will then arrive in Leandra in the early afternoon, which will give me time to negotiate a contract with the barbarians who will take Lentulus's thread down the Kalykadmus River to Seleucia on the coast. There it will be loaded onto a coastal ship for Tarsus, where it will be woven. The contractor, then, will find a load for our empty pack mules and should arrive back in Leandra in about two weeks. Assuming I can negotiate a contract tomorrow, we should be in Derbe by late morning. You and Timothy, Paul, should be able to find Joshua, the synagogue leader, before sunset the day after tomorrow.

Consistent with Gaius's forecast, at about the middle of the second day, the party of five men passed under the gate of Derbe, on which was inscribed COLJULIAAUGUSTADERBE. There was a modest amount of traffic coming and going on the main north-south street, which was identified by an engraving on each of the side columns, CARDMAX. Just inside the gate on both sides were two sizable stables over which were signs engraved EQ PROHIB. Directly adjacent to the stables were two large warehouses and numerous two wheeled pushcarts offered competitively to anyone bringing freight on pack animals.

Gaius waved to a man seated on a high stool behind a large desk, dismounted, and engaged this man in conversation. In a few moments he shouted instructions and several workers emerged from the warehouse and took possession of both pack animals and horses.

Gaius strode back and waved the men to dismount. "Let's go, men. Bring whatever you need when we find the Jewish house of prayer."

"There seems to be a lot of business undertaken here. I had not expected that," said Paul.

"This is probably the smallest city in the Roman Empire that has colonial status," said Gaius, "meaning that retirees from the Roman legions are given varying amounts of land in and around Derbe, depending on their rank when they retire."

"How many retired legionaries do you think live here?"

"I think there are about three hundred, but I can't be sure," Gaius responded.

"And what about the natives? I can hear conversations around us that are not in Greek."

"There is a small community of Trocmi that live outside the Decumanus gate. King Amyntas conquered this area about a hundred years ago and subjected the natives almost to a state of slavery. While they are no longer slaves, they constitute an underclass, completely subordinate to Greek speakers. The remaining majority generally speak Greek. Of course, there is a small group that you want to deal with, the Israelites. They had lived in the coastal area south of the Taurus mountains and had been practicing piracy with great success until Pompey defeated them and forced them to relocate this side of the Taurus Mountains. They speak Greek but have their own traditions independently of their neighbors. Joshua, their leader, has an enormous amount of influence on the *boule*, or city council. I am sure you will enjoy making his acquaintance. Let's see if we can find him."

It took about fifteen minutes for the party to reach the agora, which was located at the intersection with the main east-west street, known as the Decumanus Maximus. Turning left and then continuing for about five minutes, they reached an area surrounded by a stone wall, accessible by a double gate, on the top center of which was engraved a menorah.

When Gaius was about to lead the party through the gate, Barnabas asked whether Gentiles would be permitted to enter.

"The Jews in this part of the country generally do not segregate themselves from the rest of the population. The entire system of walls in the city was created a hundred years ago, when the Romans forced the Jewish pirates away from the coastline. Leaders of the community at that time were fearful that the Romans would attack the city and enslave the Jews. Fortunately, this never happened, but the walls constitute a symbol of the freedom of the city."

Dominating the end of the street was a two-story stone building with a menorah engraved above the center of the entrance.

"Joshua's house is directly adjacent to the assembly building.

As the party walked down the street, they became aware of a great deal of activity, with linen awnings keeping the sun off piles of vegetables, displays of cloth, sewing equipment, and almost everything needed for a simple and secure life.

Arriving at Joshua's house, Gaius knocked on the plank door and was quickly greeted by a woman who had seen the age of sixty well in the past but whose craggy face displayed an invitation to peace and tranquility.

"Gaius, my dear Gaius. How pleased I am to see you!"

"Esther, Esther! How wonderful to see you!"

An enthusiastic embrace ensued, after which the lady extended a similar greeting to Demas.

Gaius then introduced Paul and Barnabas as scholars of the Jewish law, and Timothy as the son of his patron, Lentulus. In short order Esther ushered everyone into the main room of the house, summoned a young servant, ordered some refreshment, and spread cushions for her guests.

After describing their journey from Lystra, Gaius inquired about Joshua, the synagogue leader and husband of Esther.

"He is not here," she responded. "He and Hipparchus, the magistrate, left yesterday for Tyana, ninety miles from here."

To the question on everyone's mind, she continued: "Our city secures its water supply from a lake in the Taurus Mountains about three miles from here. For many generations, the aqueduct from that lake brought a constant supply of water to our three major fountains. However, many of the older generation-my husband, Joshua, included, have noticed that the volume of water coming to our fountains has undergone a significant decrease. Tyana is configured like us on the backside of the mountains and has an aqueduct to a lake like we do. So last month our city council voted to send my Joshua and Hipparchus to visit Tyana and examine how that city maintains its constant flow of water."

"How long do you think it will take them?" Paul asked.

"We think about a month," Esther said.

"Has anyone been appointed to be the leader of the assembly?"

"Well, there is one man, whose name is Isaac, appointed by Joshua to lead us in our traditional prayers for the Sabbath. He is unable to read but can recite much of our Scripture. I believe that if you were to take his place until Joshua returned, everyone would be happy."

"Nothing could give me more happiness than to be your temporary leader," Paul said. "Tell me about your community."

"Having come from Tarsus, I'm sure you are familiar with the history of this part of the world," Esther said. "Most people forget that the main business was piracy and that the coastline between Tarsus and Seleucia Trachea offered a huge opportunity for pirates to stop a merchant ship close to shore, steal its cargo and either sink the ship or recruit the captain of the ship to throw in his lot with the pirates and become one himself. The noble Pompey brought a Roman fleet to this neighborhood sank fifteen hundred pirate ships, many of which had Jewish crews. He negotiated an agreement with King Amyntas, who had recently achieved control of Derbe, that he would accept ex-pirates to live in the city and become shepherds caring for the supposed three hundred flocks of sheep owned by the king. Most of the Jews followed the Kalycadmus River from the coast up here on the other side of the Taurus Mountains. There might be two hundred families that identify themselves as Jews, most of whom observe the major festivals, but only about twenty families observe the weekly Sabbath."

"How many contribute the annual one-half shekel to Jerusalem?"

"I would say...about half," Esther answered tentatively.

"Is that half of two hundred or half of twenty?" Paul asked with a smile.

"Only Joshua can answer that question; after all, a man does not discuss finances with his wife."

Paul chuckled. "Have you not heard what was written to King Lemuel?"

Who can find a woman of worth? Far beyond jewels is her value.

Her husband trusts her judgment; he does not lack income.

She brings him profit, not loss, all the days of her life.

Esther visibly blushed and said, "With a scholar from Jerusalem presiding, I would expect to see many more than twenty people next Shabbat."

"I'm sure the entire Jewish community will benefit from the preaching of my friend here," said Barnabas. "But could you suggest a place for us to stay while we are here?"

"Timothy and Demas are welcome to stay with my wife and me," said Gaius.

"And our house of prayer has a guest room where you both can reside as long as you need," Esther added.

"We are deeply grateful to these offers of hospitality, but there is one question that I need to address to you. Timothy's mother is Jewish and his father is a Gentile. As I'm sure you know to become part of the People of God, it is necessary that all males be circumcised. At the time of Timothy's birth, there was no-one who could circumcise him. As I'm sure you are aware, very few assembly leaders have the skill to perform the operation. We understand that Joshua is one of the few people who can circumcise an adult. Could you tell us whether he can do so?"

"Periodically, a Gentile, normally married to a Jewish woman, desires to join us, and Joshua accommodates him by circumcision. There has never been a problem, and the man is generally cured in three weeks."

"That is excellent," said Timothy. "While we are here, we can share the Good News of all the gifts that the Lord has given us."

"Also, Demas and I will probably be ready for baptism in a few weeks," offered Gaius.

"Indeed," Barnabas added.

"Come, gentlemen, let me show you our house of prayer and our guest rooms where you can stay until Joshua returns. Esther gestured toward Paul and Barnabas.

Gaius made a similar gesture toward Timothy, and in a matter of moments each person felt Esther's and Gaius's expression of hospitality.

CHAPTER 8

Paul's First Homily in Derbe

IT WAS ABOUT MID-DAY WHEN Barnabas politely knocked on the door jamb of Paul's sleeping room, simultaneously whispering "Paul." The response inviting Barnabas into the room was immediate.

"What will your theme be in your homily tonight at the Sabbath service?"

"My friend, I recognize the spectacular gift the Lord gave us to bring the risen Lord to this community. I plan on starting with the first sin in the world, that is the sin of our first parents who disobeyed the creator God. Next I will point out that within nine generations the whole world was drenched in sinfulness. The Lord God commanded Noah to construct an ark and to save humankind and introduce the idea of Atonement.

Next, God gave Moses the Torah and described exactly how Atonement was to continue through the Temple. Finally I shall show that perfect Atonement has come into history through Iēsoûs Christos. What do you think?

Paul and Barnabas discussed each of these topics for the balance of the afternoon, and as sunset approached, men and women began to arrive, excited by the opportunity of having a scholar participate in Sabbath service. More than the usual number of twenty men and women appeared so that some of the men disappeared for a few moments and reappeared carrying additional stools.

229

The worship space had bilevel benches on both sides and the back wall. On the front wall, the finger-pulls on the ark were exposed, ready for the ceremonial opening later in the service. There were ten men on the side benches, six of whom were wearing prayer shawls. Those without prayer shawls were recognized as Gentiles, called *God-fearers* who were not circumcised but who embraced the Jewish religion. Twelve women sat on the rear benches. Esther sat in the center. At the beginning of the service, it was she who lit two candles that were standing on a table in the center of the worship space.

When the candles were lit, Barnabas arose and in a strong voice intoned, *Shemah Israel* and the congregation responded, standing: *Adonai elohenu Adonai echad*. Not knowing whether the community knew the full text of the *Shemah*, Paul nodded to Esther, who transferred a flame from an oil lamp on the wall to two candles on a table in front of the worship space, saying, *Blessed are You, LORD, our God, King of the universe, who has sanctified us with His commandments and commanded us to light Shabbat candles*.

The entire congregation responded: "Amen!"

Paul stood up and began talking in a conversational style, without a scroll being opened.

Then he began: ***Part One: The Sin of Our First Parents.*** *Lord God, who created the world in seven days, brought forth our first parents and gave them a single commandment in the Garden of Eden, namely, to eat of anything that God had provided except the fruit of the Tree of Knowledge of Good and Evil. Our first parents were created with the gift of freedom, and they disobeyed the Lord God. The consequence of the first sin was that all women would henceforth bear children in pain. Further all men shall till a hostile ground and by the sweat of their brow earn their bread, after which he shall return to the ground for: "You are dust into dust you shall return."*

The consequence of the sin of our first parents was quickly addressed in history when Cain murdered his brother Abel. Within nine generations, the entire population of the earth had become "corrupt in the view of God and full of lawlessness."

Part Two: Universal Sinfulness and Atonement of Noah. *As a consequence, God commanded Noah to construct a massive ark and bring into it one pair of* *every living thing. He did so, and after forty days and forty nights of rain, the earth was completely inundated. Three weeks later, after the ark had come to rest on dry ground, the animals and Noah's family left the ark. There is a text called "Jubilees" that says the following: And on the new moon of the third month (Noah) went forth from the ark and built an altar on that mountain. He made atonement for the earth, and took a kid and made atonement by its blood for all the guilt of the earth; for everything that had been on it had been destroyed, save those that were in the ark with Noah.*

Part Three: Atonement in the Temple *The important idea that we learn from this text is that a sacrifice of a clean animal under the right conditions can produce an atonement or expiation for sins. Let me expand on this idea by examining three critical ideas that deal with sacrifice.* ***First****, we recall that Moses climbed to the top of Mount Sinai and received tablets of the Law from the hand of God. This Law distinguishes us from every other people on the earth and sets the criteria for what is and is not sinful.* ***Second****, God gave to Moses an outline of how the tablets are to be preserved for all time, that is, by providing a Temple, initially something portable but later a fixed house. The Temple would have a most sacred part, which is called the "Holy of Holies," into which only the high priest could enter on the day of atonement.* ***Third****, God instructed Moses to place the tablets in an ark of gopher wood with a cover made of pure gold and two cherubim whose wings spread across the ark. God called this cover a* kapporet *and He said: "There I will meet you and there, from above the cover, between the two cherubim on the ark of the covenant, I will tell you all that I command you regarding the Israelites."*

God's covenant with his people included the provision that seven days after the first day of the year, the high priest shall enter the Holy of Holies carrying the blood of a bull sacrificed outside the temple. He shall sprinkle it with his finger on the front of the ark's cover and likewise sprinkle some of the blood with his finger seven times in front of the cover. Thus he shall purge the inner sanctuary of all the Israelites' impurities and trespasses, including all their sins." It is important to understand what this means. The "Ten Words" that God wrote on the tablets he gave to Moses set the minimal condition for a life that is holy. For example, one of God's commands is, You shall not steal. *If one does steal, he or she has committed a sin against the person from whom something was stolen. One has also committed a sin against God. If restitution is made by the thief including an additional penalty, the sin against the victim can be forgiven; but the sin against God is expiated by the smearing of blood by the high priest on the* kapporet *The key understanding of* **atonement** *is that sacrificial blood shed by the Servant brings about forgiveness of sin. We will explore this as*

Part Four: Atonement by the Servant..

I will describe a person that the prophet Isaiah wrote about. There are three elements that constitute this section: First, this person will be raised high and greatly exalted to the extent that kings and nations will stand speechless. He grew up like an ordinary sapling, he had no majestic bearing that would catch our eye. He was spurned and avoided, like one easily overlooked.

Second, he bore our pain and endured our suffering. He was pierced for our sins, crushed for our iniquity. By his wounds we were healed. The Lord laid upon him all of our guilt. He submitted to punishments and like a lamb led to slaughter without opening his mouth, he was taken away and killed for the sins of his people; he was given a grave among the wicked. Third, making his life a reparation offering his days are lengthened and the Lord's will shall be accomplished through him. Because of his anguish he shall see the light; because of his knowledge he shall be content; he is the Lord's servant, the just one who justifies many since he bears their iniquity. The name of this man will be disclosed soon. It is he who appeared to me and commanded me to spend my life bringing his name to Jews and Gentiles throughout the world. God greatly exalted him and bestowed on him the name that is above every name, that at his name every knee should bend, of those in heaven and on earth and under the earth, and every tongue confess that he is Lord, to the glory of God the Father.

While we are here, Barnabas and I will present to you the life-giving change that results from incorporating him into every relationship that you have. When you are ready, we shall offer you baptism that will incorporate you into the very Body of Christ, which means "The Anointed One." You will never again be the same, but the love of Christ, which is a product of his Atonement, will transform all of your relationships, whether they are familial or economic. We invite you to begin the process of becoming a new person, rooted in Christ.

Paul sat down on one of the stools next to the table, bowed his head and closed his eyes. Barnabas said nothing but motioned with his hand that the participants could leave. They did so in silence, clearly moved by Paul's homily.

After several minutes, after the last person had left, Paul asked Barnabas how he thought the homily went.

"It was excellent, Paul. I could feel the Spirit of Christ in the room. I think we will have great success in this town."

Paul nodded, clearly exhausted, and retired to his sleeping quarters.

CHAPTER 9

Meet Isaac

THE NEXT MORNING, PAUL WAS awakened by the sound of a familiar text being recited in the adjacent room: *Jacob is my servant: I will help him: Israel is my chosen: my soul has accepted him. I have put my spirit upon him; he shall bring forth judgment to the Gentiles.*

He was astonished to hear the text being recited in the Greek language, in the form known as the Septuagint. Interestingly, the text being recited was not a literal translation of the Hebrew text. *Here is my servant whom I uphold, my chosen one with whom I am pleased. Upon him I have put my spirit; he shall bring forth justice to the nations.*

When Paul quoted Scripture to a Greek assembly, he translated the Hebrew text literally into Greek. As a consequence, the mention of *Jacob* and *Israel* indicated that the person reciting the text was not simultaneously translating but was apparently reading the Septuagint.

The guest quarters were separated from the main assembly room by a simple cloth. Paul remained behind the cloth and listened to the recitation of a text from the prophet Isaiah known intimately. After several additional verses, there was silence. Paul took advantage of this to enter the room, where there were four men and five women seated on benches and a man, about thirty, wearing a prayer shawl and seated on a chair facing the small community.

"Good morning, Paul," Esther said through a broad smile. "If I had known that you were awake, I certainly would have invited you to join us. Meet my son, Isaac."

Paul was dumbfounded! The seated man arose and extended his two stubby hands, at the ends of short, malformed arms toward Paul. "I am so glad to meet you, Rav. I heard that you had arrived yesterday and regret that I could not be here to greet you."

Paul could not speak! There was no scroll from which he read. Esther and the others left the room.

"Where is the text from which you are reading?" Paul asked.

"Forgive me. I am unable to read Greek or Hebrew, but Joshua, our synagogue leader, is kind enough to read God's word to me, and I am able to remember the texts and recite them for my friends here in Derbe. I hope that I did not make too many mistakes in this wonderful reading of the prophetic work of Isaiah."

"Not only was your rendering of the text superb. I could not speak the text of the Septuagint but I am limited to being able to translate the literal Hebrew into Greek. How much of the Lord's word have you memorized?"

"I can remember Torah, most of the prophets, and some of the writings. Our synagogue leader, Joshua, reads to me every day. As I understand that you will be taking his place until he returns from Tyana, I am hoping that you would be able to read to me whatever texts we have or the texts that you remember, so that I might increase my knowledge to take the place of Joshua when he dies."

"Joshua has clearly read a significant body of our texts; where does he get them?"

"The leaders of various houses of prayer in this area are constantly sharing texts with each other. While Joshua went to Tyana to discuss the issue of water, he took several of our texts with him, which he will exchange with the leader of that assembly. It will be exciting to hear their texts."

"Come with me, you two," Ester said as she reentered the room. "Your colleagues are waiting for you in the dining room." And with that she ushered Paul and Isaac into a room that included Barnabas and Timothy, seated on cushions and dipping pita bread into a large bowl of hummus. They exchanged greetings and smiles as Paul took his seat on an empty cushion.

"Gentlemen, this is my son Isaac, who lives with us."

"Good morning, gentlemen."

Isaac sat on a small stool, as did Esther, who scooped up some hummus and fed it to Isaac.

"As you can see," Esther said, "God didn't give him arms long enough to feed himself, so I have the pleasure of nourishing his body as my husband, Joshua, nourishes his soul."

To the slightly puzzled expressions on Timothy's and Barnabas's faces, Paul quickly explained that Isaac had committed an enormous quantity of sacred writings to memory, faultlessly using the Septuagint translation of the Hebrew texts.

"Perhaps after breakfast, you can show us the scrolls that you have. I am particularly interested in the Septuagint scrolls," Paul said.

"Why wait?" Isaac said as he gently smiled at his mother and got up from his stool. "I will need some help in removing the scrolls from the ark, but I can show you how to do it."

It was only a few steps to the worship space, which was dominated by a stone slab having attached to it a beautifully crafted gold-leaf menorah Paul walked up to the slab expecting to be able to open some sort of door.

Isaac chuckled. "Forgive my pride, but you could spend a year trying to open the ark and never be able to do it." And with that he walked over to the left wall of the worship space and pushed in on a piece of stone identical to all the others around it. As he pushed it in, other stones slid out adjacent to the slab, which itself rotated slightly, showing a finger space on the left edge. Isaac nodded to Paul, who, using the finger space, rotated the slab cover so that the interior of the ark, covered in purple silk, was completely exposed. There appeared to be seven or eight scrolls.

"May I remove one scroll for study?" Paul asked.

"Of course."

Paul selected the smallest of the scrolls and carefully removed it. He handed it to Timothy.

"That scroll is called 'Esdras,' which I think is the Greek version of what is called 'Ezra' in Hebrew," Isaac said. "It is important to us because it tells the story of Gentile kings who authorized and paid for the rebuilding of the Temple. This text is unusual because it includes the names of all the hundreds of families returning from Babylon."

"Again, you astonish me!"

"Let us close the ark. Simply repeat in reverse order the steps used to open."

Paul did so and commented, "I notice that you have a gold-plated menorah attached to the outside of the ark. Could you explain why so much money was spent on the exterior of the ark?"

"That is a deception for that day when Gentiles rise up against us. In their passion, they will think that the only item of value is the gold menorah, not recognizing that the true value lay inside the ark. It is unlikely that they would ever be able to open the ark as I did a few minutes ago. Pray that we will never have to use this deception."

"You continue to astound me, Isaac," Paul said as he clapped him on the back.

"The credit is actually due to my paternal grandfather, who welcomed Jewish pirates fleeing from Pompey. As a consequence, we Jews have lived in harmony with our Gentile neighbors. Now, let us return to our breakfast."

"Later that afternoon, Gaius went to the assembly's guest quarters and called out Paul's name.

"Come in, Gaius."

Paul was sitting on a stool with a scroll open on a table in front of him. He gestured toward two cushions on the floor, and both were quickly seated.

"I heard about your discussion with Isaac today," said Gaius. "I probably should have told you about him before we arrived here. Everyone in Derbe knows of his remarkable skill in remembering stories. Not only does he remember sacred Jewish texts, but he can recite the plays of Sophocles, Aristophanes, and Euripides. Every month or so, he recites a play from one of the great Greek authors. We are too small to build a theater, but you'll notice on the east side of town there is a hill where the whole population of Derbe assembles to hear him."

"I have never come across someone as remarkable as Isaac," Paul said.

"Wait till you hear the conditions of his birth. The women of our town all know who is pregnant and the probable dates that they are due to give birth. If a woman has too many children, when she gives birth, she takes the infant and brings it to the dung heap, where she wraps it in a blanket and leaves it. If one of the other women in the town has a need for a slave, she will pick up the infant, find a nursemaid, and bring the child into her family as a slave. If there is no need for an additional slave, or if the child is defective, the child is left to die, generally in a couple of days. When Isaac was born, he was left on the dung heap, and all the women were aware of his lack of normal arms. The child cried for six days, but no one picked him up, until Esther, who was of child-bearing age, concluded that the child was crying for her specifically. So she found a needy nursemaid who had previously refused to pick up the child and agreed to pay her double the normal fee. Esther named him Isaac, and Joshua accepted him as a son."

"When Isaac was between three and four years old, when most children are learning the elements of family conversation, Isaac would repeat a conversation that he had heard with absolute precision. This created some social problems when Isaac repeated conversations he had overheard in neighbors' houses that were intended to be private. By the age of eight years he was capable of reciting some of the homilies that Joshua offered on Sabbath. The difficulty, however, was that he had no concept of the meaning of many words. This also produced surprise on the part of the family, since Isaac was totally incapable of reading. Joshua could read a text, to which Isaac listened, inquiring as to the meanings of words he did not understand. He could recite the text he listened to with precision. Further, he could remember the text seemingly without limit."

"I can see Isaac has a wonderful gift to the Jewish community of Derbe. But the gift has a cost. This scroll that I'm reading fixes the text beyond the life of any one individual. While Isaac can recite a large number of texts, when he dies, the text dies with him. A sacred text exists only in the sense that it is written in a scroll and preserved carefully by the community. While we wait in this town for Joshua to return so that Timothy might be circumcised, I think we must attempt to teach Isaac to read and to write."

"This might be an excellent exercise for Timothy," Gaius said.

"I agree. In fact, after he is circumcised, we might leave Timothy here until Isaac is able to read so that he is not burdened with the necessity of having texts read to him."

In the early afternoon, Paul invited Timothy into the guest quarters and described the conversation with Gaius about Isaac. Timothy agreed wholeheartedly with the idea of teaching Isaac to read. So the two of them found Isaac and Esther in the residence and made their proposal to the two of them. They were surprised when Esther rejected it. She leaned over and gently took Isaac's stubby hand.

"First, you should be aware that my husband, Joshua, attempted to teach him how to read," Esther said. "Each year from the time Isaac was six years old, Joshua would take his wax writing tablet and attempt to teach Isaac the basic rules. Joshua told me that the letters are formed differently on the *deltos* than on a papyrus or parchment text, and when he had mastered the *alpha-beta* on the wax tablet, he was unable to identify the letters on a parchment scroll.

"Second, Joshua purchased papyrus sheets so that there would be no transition from the *alpha-beta* from the wax tablet to the papyrus, but the transition from letters to words just never occurred."

Isaac bathed his mother in a broad smile, and then turned to Timothy and Paul.

"Gentlemen, wait just a minute. You have no sense of gratitude to the Holy Spirit. I have been given the gift of memory. I do not deserve it, nor did I ask for it. The price that I pay for the gift of memory is my lack of arms along with my inability to read. I have no intention at this stage of my life to challenge the Holy Spirit by suggesting that the gift of memory is not enough. Hence, you can be assured that I will never attempt to learn how to read. Paul, I will recite for you any text that I have learned, and you may comment on that text for the benefit of our assembly. And when my father returns with new texts, you or he may read them aloud and I shall remember them. I hope you'll find this acceptable." And with that, Isaac retired to his bedroom.

"Esther, Timothy and I beg your pardon for our inability to understand the dynamic of the Holy Spirit's gift not only to Isaac but to the entirety of the community of Derbe."

CHAPTER 10

Another Voice

THE NEXT MORNING, PAUL ENTERED the dining area, where Esther was feeding Isaac. He greeted both and immediately apologized profusely to Isaac.

"I have already begged the Holy Spirit to forgive me for my obtuseness, and hope that your soul will be open to recite some texts in for the next Shabbat."

"Of course," Isaac responded. "Why else have I been given this gift?"

At that point Esther invited Paul to be seated on one of the cushions and brought him some fruit and pita bread. Paul then discussed with Isaac the fact that he would spend several days in the process of comparing the homily for the next Shabbat. "Would you be kind enough to work with me?"

Isaac's face was transformed by a broad smile. "Of course, of course!" he responded.

"Let's try it out," Paul suggested. Isaac nodded, and Paul gestured toward Isaac, who said from memory, *The LORD God formed the man out of the dust of the ground and blew into his nostrils the breath of life, and the man became a living being.* Paul nodded, and Isaac responded:

The LORD God planted a garden in Eden, in the east, and placed there the man whom he had formed. Out of the ground the LORD God made grow every tree that was delightful to look at and good for food, with the tree of life in the middle of the garden and the tree of the knowledge of good and evil.

Paul smiled. "Well done! It will be a pleasure to work together."

However, when Paul made reference to the Book of Daniel, Isaac's brow furrowed, and he confessed that he did not know that text.

"Don't worry, Isaac, I will simply recite it aloud for your benefit and concentrate on several sections on the basis of which we can understand much more about who Iēsoûs is.

It is only partially known among the Pharisees, to whom I belonged, in Jerusalem. I shall recite section that exists in the Aramaic tongue, and I shall translate it into Greek. "

Paul then began to describe the visions that Daniel had of the world in great disorganization. The great sea was stirred up, and four beasts arose out of this chaos. Paul described the lion with the wings of an eagle, the second was the great Bear with tusks in its mouth. It was commanded to devour much flesh. The third beast was a winged leopard, which was given dominion. The fourth beast consumed what the other three beasts had left. It had ten horns plus a little horn in its midst. The picture was one of total arrogance and chaos.

Paul then said, "Here is part of the text itself: *As I watched, Thrones were set up and the Ancient of Days took his throne. His clothing was white as snow, the hair on his head like pure wool; His throne was flames of fire, with wheels of burning fire. A river of fire surged forth, flowing from where he sat; Thousands upon thousands were ministering to him, and myriads upon myriads stood before him. The court was convened, and the books were opened. I watched, then, from the first of the arrogant words which the horn spoke, until the beast was slain and its body destroyed and thrown into the burning fire. As the visions during the night continued, I saw coming with the clouds of heaven One like a son of man. When he reached the Ancient of Days and was presented before him, He received dominion, splendor, and kingship; all nations, peoples and tongues will serve him. His dominion is an everlasting dominion that shall not pass away, his kingship, one that shall not be destroyed.*

Paul concluded and said to Isaac, "this text is a mystery that must be interpreted. I'm sure you recognized the *Ancient of Days* as the Lord God whom we adore. He is depicted as the judge of the world, who brings about justice and righteousness. Most important for us is the one like a son of man who comes on the clouds and to whom was given dominion, splendor, and kingship. This is whom we call Iēsoûs, who revealed himself to me years ago and authorized me to proclaim him. He will be the one who executes judgment as he returns to earth on a cloud. I will see if in my travels I should come across the text above known as *Daniel* that Joshua can read and you can remember.

Paul and Isaac worked together every day in preparation for the next Shabbat service. Paul continue to be astounded at the grasp that Isaac had of the Septuagint

CHAPTER 11

Hope

THE WEEK FLEW BY AND Paul and Isaac worked together on a homily emphasizing that Iēsoûs was a perfect example of the love that he had for the Father. He was surprised when Esther and several other women from the community arrived and chatted with each other, expressing a considerable closeness that existed among the Jewish women. When the men had arrived, Esther took a taper and using the traditional prayer, lit the two candles on the table.

When the candles were lit, Isaac arose and in a strong voice intoned, "*Shemah Israel*" and the congregation responded, standing: *Adonai elohenu Adonai echad.*

Isaac continued, in Greek: *You shall love the LORD, your God, with your whole heart, and with your whole being, and with your whole strength. Take to heart these words which I command you today. Keep repeating them to your children. Recite them when you are at home and when you are away, when you lie down and when you get up. Bind them on your arm as a sign and let them be as a pendant on your forehead. Write them on the doorposts of your houses and on your gates.*

The congregation sat down, and Isaac continued with a series of blessings, some of which were familiar to Paul, but some were new to his ears.

When he finished, he said, "Listen to our visitor, Paul, who will explain the Word of God for our ears."

Paul stood. "I will talk today about how sin came into the world and the consequences for us. When I need to quote Holy Scripture, I shall ask Isaac to do so. Since there are many quotations, we shall permit Isaac to quote without standing up."

The congregation chuckled.

Paul delivered the homily pretty much as he had prepared it several days previously. Having concluded, Isaac stood and invited people to pray for individuals in the town who were ill or had any other need that could be perceived by the community. Then Esther brought forth a fresh loaf of leavened bread and a small pitcher of wine, both of which was shared by all. They wished one another peace and filed out of the worship space.

When Paul and Barnabas were alone, Paul asked Barnabas how he thought the service had been received. "I thought it was too academic. You were not talking to scholars of the law in Jerusalem, but simple people who can neither read nor write and who eke out a living with their sheep. Plus (and this is my opinion only) who really cares if there has to be an expiation for sins? Isaac did a masterful job of being able to recall sacred text where you needed it. Let us see how many return next week."

"Let me tell you, Barnabas, where I am going. You noticed, I'm sure, that I did not use the name Iēsoûs. I do not plan to introduce him until the end of one more homily. I feel the need to carefully prepare the soil before I plant his name, so that the community as a whole will recognize our most important truth: he revealed himself to me in a spectacular manner, but I want to show an equivalent revelation here in Derbe through listening to the prophets. Next Sabbath I will rely upon an important text from Jeremiah. The final homily would return to the Suffering Servant theme with which I started, and at the end of the homily identify Iēsoûs as the Servant being referred to by the prophet Isaiah. That way, I hope to create a rational basis for an act of faith. I will invite the entire community to be baptized into Christ. I hope especially that Isaac will be our first member. I plan to expose him privately to other texts so that he can publicly proclaim him as Lord."

Paul and Barnabas continued the conversation for another hour until Paul's eyes invited sleep, and both men succumbed.

CHAPTER 12

Listen to the Prophets

PAUL AWOKE SUDDENLY. THE MOON was still high in the sky, indicating that night was far from over.

Let me recall exactly what texts I will use next Sabbath from the prophet Jeremiah. I must avoid making my reflection on God's Word into a classroom exercise. Let me try with using a Jeremiah text:

Woe to the shepherds who destroy and scatter the flock of my pasture.

With so many sheep in this area, the reference to shepherds who scatters the flock will easily draw attention to the Lord as being one who restores the flock. I'm sure they will recall that David was a shepherd and a king and that he shall bring justice to the land. *David was king over all Israel; he dispensed justice and right to all his people.* This however is likely to introduce a new question: What is the measure of justice? I suggest we look again to the prophet Jeremiah. Here is what he says: *See, days are coming says the Lord, when I will make a New Covenant with the house of Israel. It will not be like the covenant I made with their ancestors the day I took them by the hand to lead them out of the land of Egypt. They broke my covenant. But this is the covenant I will make with the house of Israel I will place my law within them, and write it upon their hearts; I will be their God, and they shall be my people.*

"I will point out that the members of this assembly are identical with the house of Israel. As a consequence, they have an obligation to live in accordance with God's law given to Moses on Mount Sinai, along with the keeping of the feast days that Jews normally observe."

"I will spend the balance of the time in the homily carefully applying what it means to have the Law inscribed on one's heart. I will be careful to make it a personal experience as opposed to an academic lecture."

After another hour or so of reflection, Paul emerged from the guest quarters and entered the residence portion of the building, where he found Esther and several other ladies engaged in the preparation of dinner.

"Good day, Esther. Do you know where I can find Isaac?"

Before she could respond, Isaac appeared smiling from behind a fabric doorway.

"Isaac! I need your help on the homily I am preparing for next Sabbath. Could we walk together for a while, and permit me to share some ideas."

"I should like nothing better, Paul. Let's go."

They started down the road that led back to Lystra, and Paul began by quoting accurately the section of Jeremiah. Isaac nodded his agreement with the text, but when Paul modified the text, Isaac objected.

"Joshua drilled into my head the fact that God's Word must be kept inviolate, as God inspired the prophets' writing."

The two men argued their positions, Paul contending that his changes kept the essence of the reading intact. Isaac did not budge.

After continued discussion, Paul asked Isaac what he made of the phrase, *I will place my Law within them, and write it upon their hearts.*

"I don't understand this at all," Isaac said. "First, I do not understand how Torah can be placed within a group of people; and second, I do not understand how anything can be written on a person's heart. Does this mean a person's body must be opened up to write on someone's heart?"

Paul instantly recognized the problem: Isaac had astonishing abilities to remember texts, but he had no sense of figurative language. He attempted to introduce Isaac to the rich world of metaphor, simile, and hyperbole, but Isaac was incapable of understanding how one word could have two meanings. In a fairly short period of time, Paul recognized that Isaac had a kind of intellectual sickness, in some ways similar to his own falling sickness. Isaac could not be condemned because of his intellectual shortcomings, which had occurred only because of the enormous gift of a faultless memory.

"I must learn how to love this man as the Lord loved the unknown people whom he cured during his lifetime."

At the next Sabbath service, Paul included the language about the New Covenant being offered to the Israelites in whose hearts God would inscribe the Law. There were several people of the village well known to Esther and Isaac who participated in the service. Paul welcomed them warmly and invited them to bring neighbors on the next Sabbath.

The next week passed quickly, and Paul prepared a lengthy reading from the prophet Isaiah dealing with what Paul called the Suffering Servant. He introduced several texts, one of which identified the Suffering Servant as Israel. However, the key text was that which was introduced in the first homily:

> *it was our pain that he bore, our sufferings he endured. We thought of him as stricken, struck down by God and afflicted, But he was pierced for our sins, crushed for our iniquity. He bore the punishment that makes us whole, by his wounds we were healed.*

Paul then reminded the assembly of the topic brought up in his first homily, namely that when the people of Israel sinned, there was a need for expiation for those sins. The punishment that the Servant bore was precisely the expiation that was required. Further, once the Servant had reestablished the intimacy between the Lord and his people, the prophet Jeremiah provided the context within which the community would avoid sin because they would open their hearts to the Law inscribed therein. Paul continued to show the mutual connectedness of the past three homilies.

"The only major question that you should have is the identity of the Suffering Servant. This may be the most important issue that you will confront in your lives. I will announce his name next Sabbath. In the meantime, Barnabas, Timothy, and I will pray that you will be able to make the ultimate act of faith centered about this person."

"Paul," came a voice from the women's seating area.

Paul looked up and realized that the voice was Esther's. "Yes, Esther."

"You know that women never speak in the assembly, so I beg your forgiveness for my impertinence. But I beg you not to dismiss us and force us to wait two full weeks until we discover the name of the Suffering Servant."

"It is I who must beg your forgiveness, Esther. My life is dedicated to making the entire world know Iēsoûs Christos, the Son of God, who lived and died for us. It is he who bore our sins by willingly accepting crucifixion at the hands of the Romans around fifteen years ago in Jerusalem. He is the one whom the prophets foretold, and whom I invite you to recognize, in the same sense that Abraham made the earliest act of faith that we know of. Isaac, recite for us the passage about the stars in the sky."

Isaac quickly said, "God took Abram outside and said: *Look up at the sky and count the stars, if you can. Just so will your descendants be. Abram put his faith in the LORD, who attributed it to him as an act of righteousness.*

"Thank you, Isaac," Paul said. "Now, Isaac, tell us what we read in the Book Habakkuk about the *rash*

He quickly responded: *See, the rash have no integrity; but the just one who is righteous because of faith shall live.*

"Thank you, Isaac, and thank you, Esther, for your courage. I shall now borrow some of your courage, and I shall describe to you how I have been sent on my journey of faith. I call upon the prophet Isaiah, who proclaimed *How beautiful upon the mountains are the feet of the one bringing Good News, announcing peace.*

With that, Paul began to tell the story of his life, starting with his birth in Tarsus, his being sent to Jerusalem to study at the feet of Gamaliel, and his initial contact with the followers of Iēsoûs. He described his being sent to Damascus with instructions to destroy this dangerous cult. He then described his encounter with Iēsoûs in Capernaum and his radical change from being a persecutor of this cult to one who was committed to announcing the Good News that Iēsoûs the Anointed One had freely given his life in order to bear all the sins of mankind.

"Further, Paul continued, "the Father validated the gift of his life by raising him from the dead. He died for me specifically when I sinned against a woman who was my wife by not offering her the love that was due her. The central criterion is to owe nothing to anyone but to love one another for the one who loves another has fulfilled the Law."

Paul then recounted his journey from Antioch in Syria to Cyprus to Perge, to Antioch in Pisidia, to Iconium, Lystra, and finally coming here in Derbe. He pointed out that the primary reason for coming to Derbe was to have Timothy circumcised by Joshua, since Timothy's mother was Jewish, and Joshua was the only person who had the specialized skill to circumcise an adult. At such time that Timothy was circumcised, he would also be baptized as a follower of Iēsoûs.

The small community did not leave immediately but continued to ask questions of Paul, especially regarding the revelation of Iēsoûs. The most common interest was whether the Lord would be likely to reveal himself here in Derbe. Paul insisted that the Lord would reveal himself specifically in the love that was shared among the members of this community. Questions and discussion continued well into the night, and the community finally drifted off, excited by new ideas and a different way of perceiving the world.

"I am positive my husband, Joshua, will be as excited as I am when he hears the Good News of the Lord revealed by you, Paul," Esther said in parting.

CHAPTER 13

Joshua Returns

Two weeks passed, and Paul's homily generated immense interest throughout the small town. Both Jews and Gentiles posited questions not only to Paul, but also to Barnabas and Timothy. However, Paul recognized a divergence among the answers given by the three of them. So Paul asked Esther if she happened to have a small quantity of papyrus on which he would write some notes that could be used to respond consistently to the excited residents. She quickly presented writing materials, and Paul invited Timothy to serve as an amanuensis.

"Paul, a slave of Christos Iēsoûs called to be an apostle and set apart for the Gospel of God, which he promised previously through his prophets in the Holy Scriptures, the Gospel about his Son, but established as Son of God in power according to the spirit of holiness through resurrection from the dead, Iēsoûs Christos our Lord. Through him we have received the grace of apostleship, to bring about the obedience of faith, for the sake of his name, among Jews and Gentiles, who are called to belong to Iēsoûs Christos."

Paul was very pleased with the result. The only difficulty was that the papyrus was too small to be preserved as a scroll. So he asked Esther for the name of a woodworker and Timothy quickly set out to find him. He showed the papyrus to the woodworker and Timothy described the framework needed to create a codex like he had in Lystra. He would require three small holes drilled near the left side of the panels, through which leather strands could be fastened so that the papyrus could lie flat between the panels that would ultimately be called a "book." The woodworker agreed to try to produce what Timothy was looking for and suggested that he return in two days. Paul was elated at Timothy's report and was eager to share this information with Barnabas and Isaac.

But as he arrived at Joshua's residence, he could hear the excitement about something different. As he walked into the residence, he saw two men who had just arrived, one of whom was slender and more than six feet tall. He was holding a wide-brimmed hat and had distinctive ear locks descending from an extraordinarily large forehead. A broad smile emerged from a full, white beard. Paul concluded that the tall man had to be Joshua, and the other man, probably about forty years old, wearing a traveling hat and a sweat-stained tunic, had to be Hipparchus.

Esther, with an ever-present smile in her voice, quickly organized everyone in the area into a welcoming committee. Some were instructed to prepare food, some to secure water to cleanse their feet, and some to fetch the equipment for camping between Tyana and Derbe from the saddlebags on the small donkey a hundred feet or so from the stables at the east and of the Decumanus Maximus. A small boy was sent to notify Hipparchus's family of his arrival and an invitation to join Joshua's family for a welcoming feast.

After the initial excitement had subsided, Joshua noticed Paul's ear locks and quickly approached Paul, extending his arm in greeting.

"Welcome home, Rav, my name is Paul, originally from Tarsus and perhaps more recently from Antioch in Syria. Your household has extended hospitality to me and my colleagues while you were away. We offer our profound gratitude to God, who inspired such wonderful hospitality."

"What could possibly inspire you to come to our small city?"

"Rav, to answer that simple question will take a considerable amount of time, which I beg you to afford me tomorrow. In the meantime, as the psalmist says: *It is good to give thanks to the LORD, to sing praise to your name Most High, To proclaim your love at daybreak, your faithfulness in the night.*

Esther walked over took Joshua's hand, saying, "Come, husband, we have fresh water prepared for you and Hipparchus. It is not as good as you would get in the public bath, but I am sure you are hungry, and by the time you get the dust of the road off your bodies, we will have food and drink for you."

Joshua and Hipparchus both nodded with smiles and left for the area of the ritual baths in the house of prayer.

And true to her word, in less than an hour, cushions were arranged in circles, and household servants placed hot cubed lamb next to pita bread and eggplant in large circular dishes in the center of the cushions. Joshua and Hipparchus reemerged, cleansed and with clean clothes. At the same time, Hipparchus's family arrived, the women carrying additional food, which was distributed along with Esther's presentation.

Paul noticed the sense of amity that existed between the two families, with much good-natured laughter and cooperation among the women in the preparation of the food. Paul thought, *We have the basis here of a single community baptized into an assembly of Christ. I will broach this issue tomorrow when we meet."*

"Joshua and Hipparchus reappeared, smiling, and took their places with each other's families, reinforcing Paul's insight into the value of this proto-community.

When the servants removed the empty circular dishes and the wine cups emptied, Hipparchus and Joshua gave a report on their expedition to Tyana. They described their meetings with the magistrate and engineers who were responsible for their water system, and they physically inspected all the elements, ranging from aqueducts to underground pipe systems. They met and spent time with a brilliant young man whose name was Apollonius, who was a Pythagorean philosopher and preached a doctrine of living a simple life, rejecting an acquisitive passion for material goods. Both Joshua and Hipparchus described the excellent quality of life espoused by this thinker.

The next morning Joshua greeted Paul warmly and gestured for him to take a seat on the cushions adjacent. With the exception of Esther, who offered a plate of hot pita bread with a broad smile, the residence was quiet.

"I think something I ate yesterday did not agree with me," Joshua said. "I have been sweating all night and feel nauseated. But I don't want to burden you with the problems of an old man like me. I do want to hear the wondrous precepts that you shared yesterday with our community."

"Have you heard about Iēsoûs the Christos, who gave his life for all men and women in fulfillment of many prophecies that we find in our Scriptures?"

"All I know is what Esther describe to me before I fell asleep last night. She said you described him as 'Son of God,' which initially causes me to be very careful about our language, lest we incorporate paganism into our teachings. She told me that you had studied in Jerusalem at the feet of Gamaliel, and this is the only reason that I would begin to talk about this person."

"I will happily demonstrate to you that Iēsoûs is the fulfillment of Torah if you have the strength today. But there is one small item and I should like to bring to your attention. I have brought a young man from Lystra whose father is a Greek and whose mother is a Jew. He has not been circumcised, mainly because of the lack of a *mo'el* in Lystra who has the skill to circumcise an adult. The Our hope is that you will be able to circumcise him so that he can follow in the footsteps of Abraham."

"Of course, Paul. Let us plan on doing this tomorrow morning. In the meantime, permit me to recover today, and we can talk about your Iēsoûs as long as you like. Please ask Esther to help me to my bed, since I feel an intense tightness in my chest."

Paul quickly jumped up, recognizing the pain in Joshua's face, and shouted for Esther to come quickly. She arrived momentarily with a cup of some potion. "Drink this, Joshua. It will relieve your pain," she said, and Joshua followed her instructions, except that before he could finish the potion, he groaned and dropped the cup.

"Help me lift him up, Paul. We need to get him to his bed."

Each knelt on one knee and wrapped one of Joshua's arms around his or her neck. They stood and because he was so much taller than they were, they effectively dragged Joshua to the next room. In the process, Paul's right hand grasped Joshua's left wrist, and Paul could feel an extremely rapid pulse. They awkwardly maneuvered him so that they could lay him down on the bed. Joshua's breathing reflected his rapid pulse.

Timothy and Barnabas, appeared just outside the bedroom. Two female household servants materialized and looked to Esther for instructions.

"Quickly! Bring me some wet towels," Esther ordered.

They arrived, and Esther began lovingly to swab his broad forehead and neck.

Isaac arrived in the room and caught Esther's eye.

"Isaac, tell us what the Lord says!"

He said, *You shall serve the LORD, your God; then he will bless your food and drink, and will remove sickness from your midst.*

Fear contorted Joshua's face as he reached out and grasped Esther's hand.

His breathing stopped, his eyes remained open and fixed. Esther screamed and fell on his body.

Paul, who had been sitting across the body from Esther, gently laid Joshua's arm by his side, stood up and left the room motioning for Barnabas and Timothy to follow him into the guest quarters, as the women of the household descended upon Esther, joining in the wailing and in the ululation characteristic of Middle Eastern women.

"I grieve because we were never given the opportunity to share with him the Good News that seems to have been accepted by Esther," Paul said. "We must be responsive to Esther and make sure she understands that since Iēsoûs died and was raised from the dead so too will God through Iēsoûs bring to him everyone who has fallen asleep."

"How does this affect our overall plans?" Barnabas asked.

"First, Timothy won't be circumcised in the foreseeable future. Second, I see the makings of an assembly of the Lord Iēsoûs centered around Esther. She is highly respected and she has Isaac who can provide her with access to the Word of God. So I think that we plan on remaining here for another month in order to have Esther and other members of the community here baptized and living a life in Iēsoûs the

Christ. It may be that Timothy has to remain here a little while longer, to make sure the community's faith is well grounded. But I think for us, Barnabas, we should retrace our steps and return to Antioch in Syria to declare how the Holy Spirit has enabled us to spread the Good News throughout Anatolia. I think we should be able to leave for Lystra in about thirty days, and we should be able to reach Antioch in less than six months."

Part V

From the Acts of the Apostles, Ch. 14, 21-28

After they (Paul and Barnabas) had proclaimed the good news to that city (Derbe) and made a considerable number of disciples, they returned to Lystra and to Iconium and to Antioch…(in Pisidia).[24] Then they traveled through Pisidia and reached Pamphylia. [25] After proclaiming the word at Perga they went down to Attalia. [26] From there they sailed to Antioch (in Syria), where they had been commended to the grace of God for the work they had now accomplished.

CHAPTER 1

Price of the Apostolate

Antioch in Syria
48 AD 3844

PAUL LEANED INTO THE BRISK north wind that whipped down the valley of the Orontes River. He wrapped his hooded cloak a little tighter at the neck, to little avail. The glowering overcast over Antioch offered the possibility of snow and the certainty of an early nightfall, for it was the shortest day of the year. The abandoned river surface was whipped to a froth. Ships from Alexandria, shallow-draft river boats that ferried farm merchandise up and down the river, and two military triremes lined the right side of the nearly empty quay down which Paul walked. The left side was lined with warehouses, small manufactories, taverns, brothels, and public baths. Ahead, on the left, arose the forbidding gray stone walls of the Roman camp at which the III Gallica Legion was located. Garlands of holly were draped on the twin stone pillars at the open gates to the camp. Everyone seemed to have run for cover due to the piercing, damp cold. Though Paul had wrapped his feet in woolen strips, his ankles and lower legs felt the sting of the icy blasts.

Adjacent to the camp, with a lower, stucco wall colinear with the Camp wall, was a Roman villa occupied by the Primus Pilus, the highest officer in the legion, who, while nominally subject to the Legate of Syria, effectively commanded the legion. The outer doors to the street were open, and holly garlands and sprigs of pine decorated the entrance. As Paul passed by, he could see that preparations for a large gathering were well underway. Oil lamps were being lit and servants could be seen scurrying throughout under the stern supervision of the Major Domo. Paul continued to the corner of the villa and turned left into the narrow side street created by the side wall of the villa and the wall of a warehouse owned by the Jewish merchant Ya'akov of Caesarea. A group of revelers burst out of a villa side door carrying empty wine flagons, laughing their way toward him on their way to the quayside wine shop for refills.

The laughing men turned the corner. Paul heard a door creak open in the warehouse wall, and three shadows emerged, barely visible in the almost darkness.

"Paul?" the leading and smallest shape inquired.

"Yes, Ya'akov, good evening," Paul replied, having recognized the voice from the single syllable.

"Come in for a moment," the shape offered, lighting the frame of the door with the soft yellow glow of a lantern.

"Ya'akov, I am late to greet Queen Shabbat; the *tsibur* awaits me," he said, using the Hebrew word for the "congregation."

Suddenly, he felt a powerful shove between his shoulders, and he was thrust forward into the dark bowels of the warehouse. He could hear the door slam as he lost his balance and stumbled to the floor in a heap.

He looked up and saw two burly men, one standing on each side of Ya'akov.

"Ya'akov, brother, what is the matter? You know..."

"Shut up, you bastard," Ya'akov hissed.

Paul moved to his hands and knees and while rising pled with the leader. "Ya'akov, Ya'akov, what have I done? How have I angered you?"

He was only part way up when the man to Ya'akov's left swiftly kicked upward, catching Paul just beneath the chin. Paul flew backward into a stack of shipping crates, striking the back of his head and collapsing at their base. Ya'akov's two assistants jumped over to Paul. One dragged him to a standing position, slid behind him, and held him upright with his massive arms around Paul's somewhat sunken chest. The other cocked his arm and smashed his hairy fist into Paul's face. Again. Again. Then a savage punch to the exposed stomach and then one to the solar plexus. A third to the ribs was greeted with a distinct cracking sound and the expulsion of air from the trembling man's mouth.

"Enough," Ya'akov said.

Paul slumped to the dirt floor in the fetal position.

Ya'akov came over to the shuddering mass on the floor, stooped down, grabbed him by the hair, and twisted his head so the flickering yellow lantern shone on Paul's face. Blood flowed from the nose, from a gash under the left eye and corner of the mouth.

"W...w...why? Why?" Paul was trying to get his breath, his arms wrapped around his sides.

"You know why, you son of Beelzebub. You are defiling our holy people by suggesting that Greeks can become Jews without following the Law that our father Abraham laid down. I have told you that they aren't real Jews but you didn't listen."

"Ya'akov..."

"Shut up or I'll cut your tongue out! You have just felt the hand of God in just and righteous anger. You have polluted our people. You are worse than Antiochus Epiphanes, against whom the entire Jewish people rose two hundred years ago. He polluted the Temple with a statue of Zeus. And everyone *knew* that he had sinned against The Holy One, Blessed be He! But you: your sin is worse, but not so blatant. Many don't really understand what you are doing. The ignorance of the people of the land will bring our holy people to ruin."

"Ya'akov, you are a brother. You acknowledge Iēsoûs as Lord!"

"Of course I do. I await him with all the other faithful to return in glory to bring redemption to Israel."

"Then how can you raise your hand against one of His Apostles?"

"Apostle! Bullshit! You are a false prophet. You pollute the holy people of Israel. You would violate the covenant by bringing in filthy Greeks without circumcision. And they think they are Jews just because you dip them in water! You are God's enemy and my enemy. Now, get out!"

The two men slid their ham-like hands beneath Paul's armpits, dragged him across the floor, and flung him like a sack of grain into the black street. The force of the ejection splattered him against the villa wall, only eight feet away. He slid down to the street, a mass of physical and spiritual pain.

His head was spinning. He tasted blood, and he could move one of his incisors with his tongue. And his ribs. The pain was excruciating. Only a couple minutes had passed, but he felt that his eyes had been opened for the second time in his life. The first time had been over fifteen years ago, when the Lord Iēsoûs had revealed Himself. His way had been clear then, as now. This was merely the second step. The problem of Greeks versus Jews could no longer be ignored, no longer be skirted. He, Paul, had had the answer revealed to him by Iēsoûs directly and personally. Hence, there was no question about the right answer. There was only an issue of timing. When to resolve it. Ya'akov's assault had provided the answer. Now. But, ohohh, it hurt so much to move. He tried to get up; his knees were shaking; they would not hold him. He slumped down again. His head began to ache at the back, where he had struck it on the stack of crates.

CHAPTER 2
Recovery

HE FELT A HAND ON his shoulder. His left eye had closed, so he could barely see the features of the man stooping down to him. Another shape, veiled from head to toe, stood at his side.

"Paul? Is that you, Paul?"

"Titus. Thank God, Titus." Tears streamed from his eyes as he focused on the thin, sad face.

Not speaking, Titus tried to scoop the smaller man into his arms, but Paul screamed in pain as Titus's arm pressed against the broken rib.

"Just let me lean on you. I have some broken ribs. Is that Leah with you?"

"Oh, may the Lord help me! Paul, I am here," came the response from beneath the veil.

The two of them gently raised Paul to his feet, placed one of Paul's arms around each of their necks, and walked slowly down the street. Paul's legs did their job because if he did not support himself, the pain on his ribs was unbearable. The trio struggled down the deserted street for what felt to Paul like miles but which was in reality only a couple hundred feet. They came to a door in the left-hand wall, which Titus threw open, and called inside for help.

"Barnabas, Barnabas, help us. Paul has been hurt."

A slightly paunchy man with a round face which was covered from the eyes down in a curly salt-and-pepper beard rushed to the door. His skin was swarthy, almost brown, and his bald head sported three distinct lumps as large as the ends of chicken eggs.

He was followed by a short, square woman veiled head to foot, like Leah.

One look at Paul and he barked out a command. "Deborah. Quickly. Run for Menachem; ask him to bring the surgeon." She bolted quickly through a door on the opposite side of the large room, in which only half the oil lamps had been lit. Barnabas helped Titus and Leah gently deposit Paul on the bare wooden floor. Leah quickly ripped a strip of coarse black cloth from her veil, made a small compress, and applied it to the cut beneath Paul's closed left eye.

"Paul, Paul, what in the world happened!" Barnabas asked.

"Two men…I don't know who they were…thought I had money. They must have thought I was on my way to Ya'akov's to make a purchase…I don't know…oh, my ribs…I heard them break…Oh, Lord, Lord…" His head lolled to the left; blood dripped from the corner of his mouth.

"Where did you find him?" Barnabas asked Titus.

"Only a few feet from the door, just off the quayside road. He was in a heap against the wall."

The door that Deborah used burst open, and a stately, toga-draped, clean-shaven man blasted across the room. His crew-cut gray hair topped a bronzed face, a square jaw, and a scarred, flattened nose. He was followed by a slender woman who was taller than he, wearing a red silk gown, with a golden girdle tied high, just under the full bosom. A white, gauze-like veil flowed over a perfectly arranged mass of henna-colored hair. Three rubies hung as pendants from a gold-chain necklace, and smaller, similarly shaped rubies hung suspended from each ear. The pair rushed to Paul's side.

"What in the name of Zeus…" Menachem exclaimed.

Barnabas cast a reproving glance at the man but decided that this was not the time to discuss theology, so he said nothing.

"He was beaten by a pair of thugs," Titus offered.

"Why?"

"Paul thought they may have wanted to rob him."

"Bullshit."

"What do you mean?"

"No one would rob someone who looks like Paul. That ratty cloak, look at the rags on his feet, his sandals. No one would take the time. There's something else."

"Menachem, will you call the surgeon?" Barnabas asked. "I've sent Deborah, but no surgeon."

"Of course. I hope he's not too drunk already. If the Parthians attacked tonight they could walk all the way to Alexandria without being molested."

"Who do you think beat Paul?" Titus asked.

"I don't know. But it wasn't anyone looking for cash. Sarah, go find Priam and have him kick that Hephaestion in the ass to get here!" Menachem barked as a gurgling moan rose from Paul's throat.

"Hasn't someone already left to find him?" his wife asked.

"Don't ask me questions. Do it. Now."

She spun around and left, her perfect coif beginning to sag.

Paul opened his right eye; seeing Menachem, he smiled.

"Who was it?" Menachem asked.

"I don't kn…"

"Don't give me that shit. You know. Who was it?"

"Menachem…"

"Was it Ya'akov?"

"No."

"I don't believe you."

"No. Oh, my head…"

Once again, the door burst open, and a thin young man in a short tunic, carrying a brown leather bag, rushed into the room, followed by Sarah.

"Hephaestion. It's about time. Quick. Look at this man," Menachem commanded.

The young doctor had a head of black curls, a short, neatly trimmed beard that followed the contours of his sharp jaw, and a pencil-thin mustache that dropped squarely to that beard at the sides of his mouth.

He knelt at Paul's side and pressed his ear to his chest. "Get something under his legs. Raise them up," he commanded.

Deborah reentered the room after the physician, raced over to the corner, and brought back two cushions, which she and Leah placed beneath Paul's feet.

Hephaestion motioned to Leah to raise her hand which had been holding the dressing in place beneath Paul's eye.

"Bring me a light," he said to no one in particular, and Deborah sprinted to the other side of the room and brought back two lamps, which she lowered so that the doctor could see the wound.

The young man grunted and pulled the top of the bag open. He reached inside and pulled out a tiny corked glass phial. He poured some of the dark liquid on a linen pad and swabbed the bleeding cut. Then, from his bag, he pulled out a series of tiny leather herb bags whose tops were secured with fine leather thongs. He selected one, sprinkled some of the contents on a folded square of linen, and placed the pad on the injury. Then he produced a thin rolled bandage and wound it around Paul's head to secure the pad. Having tied off the ends, he nodded with approval at his own work.

"Too tight?"

"No."

"Open your mouth," he said.

Paul complied.

"Lower that light." He peered inside. "Nothing broken here, except one tooth seems loosened. You might lose it. Where else do you hurt?"

"My ribs." Paul whispered.

The doctor picked up the knife and with a single motion slit Paul's garment from the neck to the navel. He parted the garment, and gently began to feel the ribs.

"Ohhhh…" Paul moaned.

"May have one broken. Whoever beat you was strong. You will be bruised for a month. Now, this will be painful, but I have to do it. I have to sit you up."

The men helped Paul to a sitting position.

"Sarah, go get one of my tunics for Paul," Menachem said to his wife, who nodded and disappeared.

In the meantime, other members of the congregation had been arriving, and each new arrival asked, in hushed tones, for details of what had happened. Most stood aside at a respectful distance; a few men huddled around the doctor working on Paul.

Sarah returned in a few minutes with a sleeved gray linen tunic, which she handed to Menachem.

"I know how you Jews are about the human body. Ladies, please go over to the other side of the room. I must remove this man's garment."

The two remaining women left silently and joined the knot of new arrivals, and the doctor slit the back of the robe and slid the remainder off Paul's shoulders. He then proceeded to soak some bandages with a liquid substance and then roll the bandage around Paul's swollen body. Paul grimaced but uttered no sound. The ends of the bandage were neatly tied together.

"A cup of water," the doctor ordered.

Barnabas went through the inside door and quickly returned with a clay cup, into which the doctor sprinkled something from a tiny herb bag, and then he swirled the mixture around with his finger.

"Drink this. It will help the pain."

Paul drank. The men helped Paul into the garment and slipped off the remnants of his original woolen robe and cloak. Sarah then joined the knot of other women, a study in radical contrasts, since all the other women were veiled. As Sarah approached, the other women shrank away into a veiled circle, symbolically and expressively creating distance.

"Look how that little whore prances about in front of our menfolk half naked," came one voice from the circle.

"You would think that having been Menachem's wife for so long she would understand how shameful it is to dress that way."

While the women were fully veiled, each woman could identify the other women by their voices. While Menachem was unable to identify the second speaker, he identified Deborah's voice resounding through the room and targeting Sarah.

I will have to deal with this later, Menachem said to himself.

He turned his attention back to Paul. "Now, you must go home and rest," the doctor said as he put his instruments back in the bag and rose from the floor.

"Thank you, brother," Paul said weakly.

"Thank you, Hephaestion," Menachem said genuinely.

"I am always at your service, Commander." He walked out.

"We will take you home," Barnabas said to Paul. He exuded a great comfort with himself and others. But this apparent sense of ease concealed a powerful sense of authority, and it was Paul alone with whom he would attempt to discuss his feelings on any element that affected the small family of believers that congregated regularly in this room.

CHAPTER 3

The Good News
for Gentiles

"No, Barnabas," Paul replied, his voice somewhat stronger. "The Lord makes his will known to me in various ways; tonight I must preach."

"But…"

"Please, Barnabas, permit the Lord to speak through me. The time has come to share what you and I have talked about, namely, the Scriptures and the People of God. Please permit me," Paul pleaded.

"Paul, I am not sure…"

"The time has come. Please."

"All right, Alright."

"Barnabas, we must begin the Shabbat service now," Menachem said. "I have a house full of guests, all awaiting their hosts. While I am grieved at Paul's misfortune, my wife and I must return to our obligations as quickly as we can."

"Menachem, I should go back to get my veil," Sarah said quietly, so that no one else could hear.

"No time. We have a hundred guests of the legion on the other side of that wall. I won't have them see you walking in here with one of those barbaric things over your head. It is bad enough that you do so each Shabbat; but no one else sees you. No." He spoke quietly, and there was no rancor.

Sarah's eyes were downcast. Her mouth exhibited tension. She looked at Menachem with that little-girl, "Puhleese" look; but Menachem shook his head.

"Deborah, bring our *taleetim*," Barnabas commanded, and Deborah brought two prayer shawls, white and trimmed in blue. She quickly went behind Paul and placed one around his shoulders, and then placed one around Barnabas's shoulders.

"Thank you, Sister," Paul said softly.

The women proceeded to complete the lighting of the lamps, placing the cushions on the floor and generally making the room ready for Shabbat services. Menachem strode to the front of the men's side of the room and Sarah to the front of the women's side. They took their places. Sarah sat with her eyes downcast, embarrassed.

Her physical beauty was legendary. While she was in her late thirties, she had had no children, and her figure was remarkable. The soldiers insisted that the gods had shaped her to match the image of the goddess Diana in the pleasure gardens of Daphne, only five miles downriver. And her silk dress, designed to simulate a toga, exposing the upper chest and left shoulder, attracted the eye of every male in the room.

Barnabas helped Paul to his feet and helped him to the front of the room. There he whispered to Paul so that only Paul could hear, "Paul, you must not say anything that will be offensive to Menachem. I know how you feel, especially with tonight being Saturnalia."

"I will not offend him."

"We owe so much to Menachem," Barnabas continued. "He provides this room for us; he provides alms for the poor of our family, food for our Agape meal whenever we want, and most of all, he protects all of us from the anti-Jewish element in this city. He is God's gift to us, and we must thank God every morning and every evening for him. If his official duties that God has laid upon him require that he seem to participate in a pagan cult, we must understand that his heart does not participate. He knows that there is no other lord than the Lord, the Lord of our Fathers, and he acknowledges the Sonship of our Lord Iēsoûs. God has placed him in a position of honor, keeping order in Syria and protecting the People of God at the same time. He has survived four different legates from Rome, and all have confirmed their confidence in him. Does that not prove that it is God's will that he continue in this high office? And do not the obligations of the office require him to go through the motions of celebrating pagan festivals, such as tonight's beginning of Saturnalia?"

It was he, Barnabas, who baptized those whom Paul had taught about the Lord Iēsoûs when it was determined that they should gain full membership in the family. It was Barnabas who had baptized Menachem when he had been a Centurion in the Auxiliaries in Antioch eight years ago. Barnabas himself had been baptized by Kephas in Jerusalem but had left when Stephen was stoned by an angry mob, angered at what they considered the practice of abominable deviations from proper behavior.

Ironically, it had been on the road to Antioch from Jerusalem that Barnabas had stumbled upon the remains of an attack upon six Roman soldiers, five of whom had been slain. The centurion had a severe head wound, but his leather body armor had blocked the full penetration of his assailant's sword. Barnabas and his wife, Deborah, persuaded the group with whom they were traveling to camp at the site of the massacre for two days, long enough to bury the dead and bind up the wounds of the centurion. They carried him in a litter the remaining twelve miles to Antioch, and after he recovered, Barnabas explained that he had merely been carrying out the injunctions of his Lord, Iēsoûs. Within six months, Menachem was baptized and became a member of the family of Jews in Antioch who looked to Iēsoûs as Lord.

Interestingly, Menachem was himself a Jew, raised with Herod Agrippa in Rome in the home of Antonia, the younger daughter of Marc Antony. But he was a fully Romanized Jew who held both the traditions of his Fathers and participated in the cultic acts characteristic of the Roman elites. It was this latter activity that seemed to rankle Paul more as the years passed. And the celebration of Saturnalia, with the gift-giving in honor of Saturn's wife, Ops, and the excesses of both drink and sex that were in grossest contrast with the rigorous moral demands of the Jewish followers of Iēsoûs.

During the past year, Paul had prayed over and reflected upon what might be the largest problem in the mission to the Gentiles. Cultic acts were required of those in positions of authority and power in society. "Religion" was not a separate category of activity in the Greek world; public recognition of the gods of a city was a means of assuring the peace and tranquility of the populace and of assuring bounteous crops, good weather, and large herds. For the military, an act of impiety, not properly honoring the gods, might bring about a defeat, and no one would risk such a disaster. Paul had recognized that part of the success of his mission rested in being able to convince those in power of the Lordship of Iēsoûs Christos. For they would bring their entire households into the fold, as Menachem had brought many soldiers in the III Gallica.

Hence, while he had not discussed this with Barnabas, he had concluded that a Gentile could perform totally perfunctory cultic acts, provided that they were demanded by the individual's social status. The alternative was to forever preclude the possibility of membership in the community of those who held positions of power and influence. Hence, while it went against the grain of a lifetime of experience, he knew that this would be one of the tradeoffs that must be recognized if the Gentile world were to be part of the New Israel. Soon, he would bring the matter up with Barnabas, but not right now.

Barnabas and Paul wound the leather straps around their forearms in preparation for the service, as well as thin straps around their heads, to which were attached small leather boxes which housed small portions of the Torah.

All was in readiness. Paul started walking slowly, with Barnabas's help, toward the front of the room.

Everyone stood up. There was just a little buzz in the room; the contrast of the fully veiled women filling one side of the room contrasted with the regal, bejeweled, stunningly feminine figure dressed in the latest Roman fashion. It was as if people from separate planets happened to meet in an instant.

"I think it is shameless that she comes here dressed like that," came a sotto voce whisper from one of the shapes.

Menachem turned in the direction of the sound, his brow furrowed, eyes flashing, mouth set. There was no sound.

Paul arrived at the front of the room; Barnabas stood in front of a chair to the side.

Sh'ema Yisrael, Barnabas intoned.

And the men and women continued, *Adonai elohenu, Adonai echad.* "Hear, O Israel, the Lord our God, the Lord is One." The ancient cry, the root of Jewish history, rising in their throats as it had in the throats of their ancestors for countless generations.

They continued in Hebrew:

> *You shall love the Lord, your God, with all your heart,*
> *with all your soul,*
> *with all your might.*
> *And these words, which I command you this day,*
> *shall be upon your heart.*
> *And you shall teach them diligently to your children*
> *and you shall speak of them*
> *when you sit in your house,*
> *when you walk by the way,*
> *when you lie down and when you rise up.*
> *You shall bind them for a sign upon your hand*
> *And they shall be for frontlets between your eyes.*
> *You shall write them upon the doorposts of your house*
> *and upon your gates.*
> "Amen."

Everyone sat down except Paul. The men sat on one side, the women on the other. Menachem's wife kept her eyes downcast. Paul waited until everyone was settled, looking at him expectantly. Paul unrolled the scroll of the Torah in his mind, stopped, and quoted by heart, huskily.

"It happened some time later that the Word of The Lord was spoken to Abram in a vision. *Have no fear, Abram, I am your shield; your reward will be very great.*

My Lord, Abram replied, *what do you intend to give me? I go childless. Then Abram said, 'See, you have given me no descendants; some man of my household will be my heir.* And then this Word of The Lord was spoken to him, *He shall not be your heir; your heir shall be of your own flesh and blood.* Then taking him outside he said, *Look up to heaven and count the stars if you can. Such will be your descendants,* he told him. *Abram put his faith in the Lord, who counted this as making him justified.*

"My brothers and sisters, this is the Word of the Lord."

"Amen."

A pause. One eye was already closed; he closed the other, clasped and unclasped his hands nervously. Was the room getting too hot? He felt the dizziness return. He could feel drops of perspiration at the corners of his mouth. *Calm yourself,* he commanded his mind. He looked at the expectant faces of the men, at the crumpled black blobs on the other side of the room; at the downcast eyes of the shameless woman. He took another breath.

"Let us look upon this man, Abram, our father, at the time he was talking with the Lord. We know he was very ancient, since he was seventy-five years old when the Lord called him from Haran, and many years had to pass, with his sojourn in Egypt, his wandering in the desert, and his battles that took him north of Damascus. The Lord had previously told him that it was to Abram's descendants that He would give the Land of Canaan. All of this Abram accepted in his heart. He did not question; he did not argue. He accepted."

Pause.

"Can you imagine how startled Abram must have been when the Lord said that the line of descent would be by the birth of sons and not by the rule of the law in granting possessions to members of his household? He must then have been well into his eighties, hardly of an age to begin families. But he did not express his surprise to the Lord. He accepted what the Lord said. Without question.

"Remember what Torah said: *Abram put his faith in the Lord, who counted this as making him justified.*' Now, what does *Justified* mean? It means putting oneself in the right relationship with the Lord. It means that Abram became, at that instant, the father of the People of God. For while the Covenant did not occur explicitly until later, the Lord commanded Abraham to circumcise himself and his sons, forever. It was at that instant, when Abram accepted unquestioningly what the Lord said, that he was, we could say, *right-wised*. From then on, he was adopted into the correct relationship with the Lord. The later circumcision was an exterior symbol of this relationship, but the relationship itself was fashioned at the moment that Abram's entire being was flooded with belief."

Pause. Looking around the room. *Yes. Yes. This they must understand.*

"And so it is, my brothers and sisters, that it is belief, faith that brings us into the correct relationship with the Lord, the King of the Universe, the Father. It is by Faith that we become part of the Kingdom of God, part of the People of God, of those chosen by God to be His Very Own. For Faith preceded the circumcision; Abram was justified, made the Father of God's People before he was circumcised. Hence, Faith is first; circumcision is second. And, ultimately, it is circumcision of the heart that really counts. But this occurs only through Faith, through the wholehearted acceptance of the Good News that the Lord brings us that we are part of his Kingdom."

"This is how we embrace our brother Titus and his wife, Leah into our family of the Lord. For while Titus is not circumcised, he believes in the Good News, brought through the Lord Iēsoûs, that the Kingdom is at hand. His faith, given by the Lord in an act of unspeakable mercy, is what permitted him to cross the line that separates us from those who do not see the Light. His faith brought him inside the walls of our assembly, inside the embrace of God's chosen."

Pause. He knew Barnabas agreed with him and could see the slight smile of assent on his face. But only Barnabas really understood the problem. The others in this assembly, called *ekklesia* in Greek, did not really understand the problem or Paul's solution. About half were Hellenized Jews who had been deeply impressed by Barnabas's character when he came to Antioch years ago, and who had affirmed that Iēsoûs was a kind of Messiah that had never before been conceived, but was indeed the one promised by God in Scripture. And the other half were Greeks who had been baptized.

But Paul saw something that none of them even dreamed of: that admittance to the Covenant promised by God, becoming part of His Chosen People, could occur by choice, not by birth; and this choice did not necessarily include the initiatory ritual of circumcision. For many years, Greeks and barbarians had become Jews, but they had become part of God's Chosen People through the ritual of circumcision for men. Baptism was practiced among the Jews in conjunction with their initiation into Judaism, but as a symbol of their having been washed of iniquity and sinfulness that is characteristic of all outsiders. It was Paul who saw that the critical act required to cross the border between "outsider" and "insider" was Faith, the same act that so distinguished Abram. And it was this crossing the border that caused such anger in some of the Jews who had recognized Iēsoûs as the Christ, but who had been brought up in the affirmation of the sacredness of those borders and believed that there was one and only one way that one could properly cross the border: circumcision. All else was desecration.

Paul continued.

"You know that there are two other Greek families who want to join our assembly. One; one family is that of Meno, one of Menachem's slaves. The other is that of Justus, a merchant friend of Titus. They have learned of Iēsoûs, the Christ, and they believe as we do. Barnabas plans to baptize them in the spring, and they will be as brothers and sisters to us. Like Titus, we do not plan to ask the men to be circumcised. We shall let their Faith be their circumcision, as it was for our father, Abram, whom The Lord later named Abraham.

"You also know of the objections to my Gospel that other Jews from other synagogues are making around Antioch. You know that they do not accept Titus as a Jew, and some vegetable sellers in the Jewish market insulted Leah, saying that she was married to a pagan and could not buy from good Jews, and that her children would be *mamzers*. We here know that Titus and Leah are heirs to the covenant God promised. But we must make sure that Meno and Justus and all the other Greeks who seek the Kingdom of God and who await the return of our Lord Iēsoûs in glory will know that we preach the truth."

Still, no sign of unrest. Paul was surprised; Titus was everyone's friend. But Meno was a slave, and few people knew Justus. Paul had expected there to be resistance to bringing in outsiders without the critical ritual, circumcision, that was that which identified them as Jews against all others. But the men sat impassively, and one could not tell anything about the women's reaction. For while the women in the eastern Mediterranean behaved with complete passivity in any sort of public environment, they were not at all passive inside the four walls of their homes. And if they felt threatened, they would tell their husbands privately, and their concern would surface later.

Sarah was looking at him full in the face, attentively, appearing not only to understand but to accept fully Paul's radical proposition. At least there would not be any covert attempt to influence Menachem's generous attitude toward this synagogue assembly. And while Paul was offended at what he considered Sarah's pagan behavior by coming and joining them dressed as a pagan, he was pleased that he could see her face and gauge her attitude to his ideas. For Iēsoûs had come to announce the Kingdom to women, too. And since Iēsoûs invited people to relate to one another as brother and sister, as heirs of a common Father, as a *Family*, perhaps women should be permitted to dress at the assembly as they did inside the walls of their homes, in the bosom of their families, without their veils. While it was another radical thought, Paul put it aside.

All this within an instant, perhaps only a second. For Paul had the ability to see relationships among thoughts in an instant, to arrive at conclusions with lightning speed and with a sense of complete clarity in his own mind. Indeed, that was precisely gift that the Lord Iēsoûs had given him years ago as he travelled toward Damascus from Jerusalem. The sudden, blinding clarity that he had experienced both in Capernaum and outside Klaudiconium as he thrashed about in what was to others the falling sickness was the basis of his absolute certainty. His life had thereafter been the logical unfolding of that unclouded recognition that the Messiah had indeed come and had turned the world upside down. But that in reality, the "upside down" world was really "right side up". Hence, the folly of a crucified criminal was the glory of God. And this apparent folly would bring everlasting life to all men and women, Greeks as well as Jews, slaves as well as free.

Paul looked at Barnabas. Barnabas nodded. Barnabas knew, too, that it had been Ya'akov tonight, but the decision to preach this particular homily tonight, through bandages and in obvious pain, that was a masterpiece.

"My brothers and sisters, Barnabas and I have decided that we must leave again, but this time we shall visit Jerusalem. There we will sit with our brothers Kephas and James and the other brothers in Christ. For we must be sure that while we understand the Good News as Iēsoûs the Christ revealed it directly, this Good News is for Greeks as well as Jews. And while Barnabas and I know that God brought Abram into the right relationship with himself prior to his circumcision, we desire to avoid controversy. Hence, in the springtime, as soon as we can sail, we shall present our convictions to the brothers in Jerusalem, in the full knowledge that they, too, will acknowledge the Good News as Iēsoûs presented it to me, personally, in a revelation. And we will bring back to you the confirmation of the truth of our Gospel by the brothers with whom Iēsoûs, the Christ, walked during his life."

Paul sat down. Quiet.

Barnabas stood, faced the small assembly, and raised his hands in prayer, saying, *Baruch attah, Adonoi…Blessed are You, O Lord,…"*

And the assembly arose and joined in: *Our God, King of the Universe, who has given us the Torah of Truth and has implanted with us eternal life. Blessed are you, Lord, who gives us Torah.*

CHAPTER 4

Dialogue

THIS MARKED THE END OF the Shabbat service, and the men and women gathered in small knots, except that Sarah walked expectantly toward the inner door, separate from the other women. Menachem said a few words to Barnabas, nodded to Paul, and walked quickly toward her. He opened the door for her, and she stomped through the opening, with a swish of silk. The door was quickly closed, but it took but a second to hear the fury of Sarah venting, purportedly in private, in Menachem's direction.

"Never, never have I been so humiliated. Those wretched bitches, those scum, they claim that I have no shame! You should throw the entire gaggle out on their asses! Who are they? You are the Commander of the Legion! I am your wife! How could you let that insult pass? Are you no man? Your honor is stained. You owe it to me to regain the honor of our family! I'll show them who has no shame! Menachem, Menachem! Listen to me!" The sound trailed off as the couple left the proximity of the assembly room.

There was silence in the room. One woman's head was bowed. From the quaking of her shoulders, it was obvious that she was weeping. And while the veils were all the same material, everyone knew who was who. It was Barnabas's wife, Deborah, who was weeping. The other women clustered around her, and Titus's wife, Leah, put her arms around her and stroked her. The men stood looking at each other.

"I will deal with Deborah when we are in our home," Barnabas announced to the men.

All male heads nodded, sagely, understanding that she would be properly beaten. The neighbors would hear her screams as Barnabas laid on the blows, and the gossip grapevine would report the severity of the beating; Menachem's honor would be reestablished, and everything would be back in order.

Other women began to weep with Deborah, aware of the agony that lay in the immediate future for her. Barnabas would use a rod, about a half inch in diameter, and he would probably lay on about thirty strokes to her bare back. It would take a couple weeks for her to recover, but the other women would help her with her cooking, cleaning, and water-carrying chores. The female community would close ranks, supporting one of its members who had caused dishonor to her husband and who had to pay the social and physical price.

The females ushered Deborah out the door and toward her home. The men, except for Paul, bade one another and Barnabas good night and left Barnabas and Paul alone.

"Barnabas, don't beat her," Paul said. "Let her scream, but don't do it."

"No, Paul, I must do my duty. She shamed Sarah in front of the community, and Menachem needs to have his honor restored. Deborah knew what she was doing."

"But she was right, Barnabas. Sarah could have put on a veil, like any woman who has a sense of shame. She could have worn it over her other clothes; she did not have to come into this room displaying her flesh to us men and her jewels to the women. You should have said something to Menachem. In fact, you should say something to him anyway about his pagan practices. You know how I feel about that."

"We will not discuss how Menachem acts. I understand what he must do, and that is enough. As for Sarah, she could not wear a veil and go directly from Shabbat services to greet her guests for Saturnalia. You don't understand women, Paul. That is part of your problem. You should have remarried after your wife died; you would be a much better witness to the Good News. Now you are too old. Well, no matter. I have decided what must be done in my household and in this assembly. But, as always, I welcome your thoughts, my friend."

"Of course, Barnabas. We; we must always be honest with each other and share our views with each other. That is certainly in the tradition of Hillel, Shamiah, and Abtalion, our fathers." Paul was referring to the sages who had lived less than a hundred years before, who had engaged in spirited discussions of the meaning and application of the Oral Torah, that set of rules that helped Jews understand the social topography of the times. The schools of Hillel and Shammai often disagreed as to how the Oral Law was to be applied to everyday life, and disagreements were both common and accepted. And Paul, having been taught by Gamaliel, the son-in-law of Hillel, was completely aware not only of the content of the Oral Law but of the possibilities of disagreements as to the proper application.

"We must ask Menachem for money to travel to Jerusalem in the spring," Barnabas said, "above what he gives us to support ourselves here."

"Barnabas, we have been friends for almost five years," Paul said. "You handed me the traditions about Iēsoûs our Lord. You know how much I love you."

But...what?, Paul."

"You even know when I have a problem. Is the fact that we depend upon Menachem for our support the reason that you will beat Deborah tonight?"

"How could you say that, Paul?"

"Because I think we are too beholden to Menachem. He feeds both of us, he provides roofs over our heads; he provides the meeting room; when we have an Agape, he provides the food. We honor him, but if he sins, we say nothing. Perhaps it would be better if we did not depend upon Menachem."

"How?"

"We could work."

"But then we could not preach the Good News."

"We still could; we could talk to anyone who would listen, in the workshops, on the waterfront, while we worked."

"Paul, we are entitled to our support while we do God's work. *You must not muzzle the ox when it is treading out the corn,* Barnabas said, quoting Deuteronomy in a classical reference to the fact that a laborer is due wages for his work.

"But there is a high price for such wages," Paul retorted. "I am not sure that we can always afford the price."

"Peace, my brother. All will be well. Get a good night's sleep, read Torah tomorrow, and I will speak with Menachem about our trip. Right now, it is extremely important that the issue of whether we are correct in admitting new members to our family without circumcision will be allowed to continue. We both know how important that is."

"Yes, Barnabas, you are right. That is the most important thing. But once we cross that threshold, there will be many more problems we will have to solve. It will not be easier; it will be more difficult."

"We will solve them together, with the help of the Holy Spirit, who lives with us and guides us," Barnabas said. "Now I must help you home. You must rest."

"Yes, you are right, my friend."

"It was Ya'akov, wasn't it?"

"Barnabas, you know that I can say nothing. The Lord will repay whoever it was on the last day. Neither you nor I have any need to do anything but await His coming."

The two men embraced gingerly, Barnabas trying to avoid hurting Paul; and Paul becoming dizzy again with the pain. They held each other for more than a few seconds, each trying to draw strength from the soul of the other. Then Barnabas put one of Paul's arms over his shoulder, and the two men walked slowly to the door and out into the black piercing drizzle.

CHAPTER 5

Spring, 49 CE

Jerusalem

THE UNSEASONAL LATE-AFTERNOON HEAT AND the press of thousands of pilgrims in the narrow streets sapped any sense of joy from the three weary travelers. They had hardly spoken for almost two hours, the time it had taken to walk from the Dung Gate at the southwest corner of Jerusalem to the narrow alley in which they were jammed, soaked with perspiration, only one hundred yards from their destination. Tempers in the crowd were short, as it appeared a recalcitrant, wildly braying, overburdened donkey had refused to move any further, blocking the entire six-foot wide passageway. Its cursing owner was beating it with a stick while two men pulled on its halter. One foolish youth had attempted to push the donkey from behind, only to be rewarded by a sharp kick to the knee, which had the young man screaming on the ground, and his friends huddled around him, examining and trying to swaddle the bloody gash. The stench of sweat-soaked wool mixed with the body odors of those who had not bathed for days exacerbated the unpleasant crush of incoming Passover pilgrims from behind.

Then, as though convinced by the overpowering logic of blows and curses, the animal placidly moved forward, relieving the pressure. Paul, Titus, and Barnabas shuffled with the flow, their traveling bags chafing at their shoulders, sweat dripping into their eyes. They drifted along with the gooey mass until they arrived at a plank door in the right wall. Barnabas reached up and pounded loudly with the flat of his hand. An eye appeared through a crack in the door, and it was quickly thrown open.

"Bar Nabas!" An open-armed welcome from a mid thirty-ish red-beard dressed in a light-wool white tunic, using a colloquial combination of the patronymic.

"John!" The two embraced heartily. And as they broke their greeting, Paul saw a dark wet stain that had been impressed on the previously clean tunic.

"This is Paul, of whom you have heard. And this is Titus, of our family in Antioch."

"Welcome, brothers," John responded, embracing each in turn, further staining his tunic.

The small garden was cooler than the street; a colonnaded peristyle surrounded three sides, with doors and windows opening onto the stoa. The red-tiled roofs had a single slope into the garden; and lead gutters caught the rain and piped it into what must have been a cistern beneath the garden.

"I have never seen such Passover crowds," Paul said. "The whole world is trying to get inside this city."

"Let me take your bags," John said, lifting the cloth device slung across Barnabas's and Paul's bodies. He appropriated each bag and easily slung them on his shoulders. "Come, let me show you your room."

As they entered the shaded stoa, a young man brought a tray with four cups and a flagon of wine.

"This is my son, Joshua," said John, his hand resting lightly on the thirteen year-old's shoulder. Polite nods, and the group entered the dim, cool interior. Cushions were on the floor, and Joshua placed the tray in the center of the floor. The men sat, and Joshua served the watered wine.

"Blessed art Thou, Lord our God, King of the Universe, who creates the fruit of the vine," John said.

"Amen."

"Barnabas, I was hardly a man when last I saw you," John said.

"Yes," Barnabas said. "So much has happened since."

"But this house hasn't changed, has it?" John asked.

"No, it looks just the same."

"We are forever in your debt, Barnabas, for having sold your farm and given us the money so we could buy this place. Our three families have lived here and have shared the Good News about Iēsoûs with many brothers and sisters from this place. We thank God for you every day."

Paul looked at Barnabas and raised his eyebrows slightly. Never in the many years that they had been friends had Barnabas ever mentioned that his money had provided a house for the Jerusalem Apostles.

"Joshua, go tell Kephas and James that Barnabas has returned."

For a few moments, the four relaxed, sipping diluted wine. Small talk about the trip from Antioch the rough sea voyage to Caesarea, the overland trip to Jerusalem and news about Deborah, whom John had known years before in Jerusalem. The same kind of lighthearted conversation rippled along that has characterized the reunion of friends through all time.

The door opened, and the doorposts were filled by a boulder of a man, burly, massive of girth and shoulders. Hams of hands stretched out toward Barnabas, and hairy forearms encircled the risen guest. For a moment, silence as the two men embraced.

"Shalom, Barnabas."

"Peace, Kephas, my friend."

The rock walked over toward Paul, who had risen to greet his host.

"The peace of the Lord Iēsoûs," said Paul.

A reticent, formal embrace from the larger man, who held Paul's shoulders and touched his cheek with his own heavy grey beard, murmuring "Peace."

"This is Titus, from Antioch," Barnabas announced, just a bit nervously.

Another formal embrace by Kephas, with "You are welcome here, brother."

Titus nodded and looked at Paul, surprised at the difference between the enthusiasm for Barnabas and the mere tolerance of the other two. Paul's eyes were downcast.

Kephas directed his attention to Barnabas again, and in a matter of moments, the two were mutually engaged, as though no one else were in the room. John poured more wine for the guests, plus a cup for Kephas. Joshua brought some grapes, which were passed around, but Barnabas and Kephas continued their conversation for a good half hour, everyone else being totally ignored. Paul watched Kephas with interest. He had spent two weeks with him and James and John six years ago in this same house, where he had learned much about the life of Iēsoûs and his disciples, of their travels in Galilee, living generally in the open, accepting food and sometimes shelter from charitable farmers and villagers.

Joshua returned and announced that dinner was served, and Kephas struggled his mass into an upright position, with a little self-deprecating comment about age and weight, and led the way out the door, across the courtyard, and into a larger, high-ceilinged room in which a low table was set with a large bowl in the center and ringed with six cushions. A small, gaunt man with closely cropped, thin gray hair and a similarly closely cropped beard sat directly across the table from the entrance door. He did not rise.

"Peace, James," Barnabas said with significant respect. He walked around the edge of the room, knelt on one knee, and grasped the gnarled outstretched hand, deformed by arthritis. Barnabas kissed the hand but did not embrace the still seated figure.

Paul silently followed suit, after which Barnabas introduced Titus, who also engaged in the same silent ritual.

"Sit, brothers." The voice was somewhat raspy and had the same Galilean twang that Kephas had. But the tone was firm, and the eyes were quick, catching Paul's eye, and with a single gesture with an outstretched finger, directed Paul to the cushion to his left. Kephas had already taken the position to his right.

"Blessed art Thou, O Lord, our God, King of the Universe who brings forth bread from the earth," the shrunken man prayed.

"Amen."

"It has been many years, James, since we spoke of your brother, our Lord," Paul said. "Our conversations have lived with me ever since."

"I have heard remarkable things about you, Paul, especially about your trip with Barnabas to Asia, where you founded communities of brethren of the Way."

"The Lord has seen fit to use me as his instrument to the nations."

"But so few Jews, Paul." James picked up a piece of flat pita bread from the edge of the bowl and scooped up some rich lentil paste at the center. Others followed suit.

"But I always start to preach in the Jewish assembly. I always try to show the Jews of any city the Scriptures that identify Jeshua (using the Hebrew pronunciation) as our Lord, as the one for whom we wait. Some have come to believe, but not many."

"You have seen the book of the Lord's sayings?" James asked.

"I have seen three or four, each of which is slightly different."

"Of course, since none of the disciples could write. And while my brother could both read and write, he didn't care to have his words recorded. 'Let them be recorded on my brothers' hearts,' he said, according to Kephas here."

"That's right. 'On your hearts,' he used to say," Kephas chimed in.

"I am learning to read and write," John said, "so that I could study the Torah and the Prophets and the Writings. I have also read part of one of the sayings books, and Jeshua did say things very close to what I read in the book."

"But the sayings book did not speak of his death," Paul said.

"No, it did not," Kephas said. "But I dictated my memory of the last days in Jerusalem just this winter."

"Would you let me read it?" Paul asked excitedly.

"You won't have to. The entire book will be read when the brothers and sisters have our Seder together in two days. For it was just before Pesach that they killed him."

"We remember that Seder each time we share his body and blood," Paul said.

"So I have heard," James said coldly.

"There was no Seder when they killed Jeshua," Kephas said. "We had come to Jerusalem to celebrate Pesach, but we never had the chance. Pesach was on the Sabbath, and they killed him the day before."

"But the Lord revealed to me, directly, that he broke bread and said, 'This is my body' and blessed the wine, saying, 'This is my blood'..."

James turned to Paul. "I know you celebrate an Agape meal in Asia and in Antioch, where you celebrate the love that God showed to us in bringing us Jeshua. But you are introducing blatantly pagan elements into our memory of Jeshua. The nations have their ceremonial meals in temples, in front of their abominable idols. Some of your gentile members of the assemblies are keeping these practices but calling them part of our Way."

"But we do it at his command."

"When did he say it?"

"He said it to me. Directly. Years ago. It was as if he were sitting here where you sit now. He commanded me to remember him through our Agape meal. It is our good offering of thanks. It binds us together, with him as Lord."

"Paul, you did not learn this from us. This is not the Good News."

Silence. Barnabas and Titus had stopped eating. Now Paul looked intently at the bowl of food, as though searching for the answer in the lentil mixture before him.

"James, my friend, it has been the custom of our assembly to remember Our Lord at a meal since I first arrived in Antioch over fifteen years ago," Barnabas said softly. "Those communities of the Way that Paul and I founded in Asia find our custom as important as we do and we know that the meal was celebrated in the assembly of the Alexandrians among the earliest of those Jews in Jerusalem, who brought the knowledge of Jeshua to Antioch. Remember, I was one of them. And I recall that you, Kephas, attended more than one of our meals while I lived in Jerusalem, before Stephen's death."

"Yes, I did attend," Kephas said stolidly. "And it was partly because of those practices that our beloved Stephen was killed by the purists. And that is why we in Jerusalem do not have your Agape meal, though we do gather for Seder, and we do read the sayings book at Seder as well as on each Sabbath."

Paul's eyes misted slightly at the mention of Stephen, and he dropped his head.

James put his hand on Paul's arm. "I'm sorry that our brother Kephas brought up Stephen. Our community forgave your involvement in his death years ago, as you know. We know that you suffer still at the mention of his name."

Paul nodded, a tear squeezing itself out beneath his eyelid and coursing its way down his cheek. He remembered Stephen's youthful zeal for the Torah and Paul felt nausea, just as he did on that fateful day.

A flood of images cascaded from his memory in a torrent. How rich was that year in which friendship had arisen rooted in a common love of God. He could hear Simeon, the son of Gamaliel, share his fear that dangerous ideas existed within the House of Prayer of the Alexandrians, most significant of which was that the proclamation by Jeshua of the proximity of the Kingdom of God could be understood by Romans to be seditious. Then he remembered the willingness of Stephen to violate the maximum of a Sabbath walk in order to provide food for a poor widow. Simeon focused a homily on the necessity of following the entire Law, despite a good intention. Then came the image of Stephen and Abraham of Cyrene after the Shabbat service had ended, standing toe to toe shouting their positions at each other. Instead of love being shared among the members of the community, Paul remembered his sense of astonishment at this exhibition of the opposite of the teachings of their Lord. He also remembered his sense of shame at his failure to separate the parties in the name of God's love. But more than any other image that haunted him was that he clearly saw a fist-sized rock that flew from somewhere over Abraham's shoulder and struck Stephen squarely on the left temple. He staggered to the right, exhaling loudly. His knees locked, and he fell stiffly, like a tree. His head struck the stone step with a sickening crack. Blood gushed from both the wound on the temple and the broken skull. His legs twitched and were still. Maria, Stephen's wife, screamed dumbfounded, and collapsed on the suddenly lifeless body. The final image that shot from his memory was that of the subsequent trial of Cyrus of Ephesus, the thrower of the rock, where he was found not guilty. This memory was made more sensitive because he, Paul, had been in charge of caring for the cloaks of the members of the jury.

His sense of revulsion attached itself illogically to Kephas, who had brought up what was the most unpleasant subject in Paul's life. And he felt humiliated before Titus. Everyone in Antioch knew that Paul had been a Pharisee, had studied under the renowned sage Gamaliel, and had in his youth attempted to punish those who would deviate from the dictates of the Torah, handed down from God as a guide for life. For change was evil; the tradition must be passed on intact. Novelty was not to be tolerated. *Ironic,* Paul thought. *Now it is I who am the most ardent proponent of a radical change, the New Covenant. I won't bring that up now,* he thought. *Maybe later, but not now.* For James and Kephas still stood four-square within the Law; they interpreted what Jeshua had said as being merely a change in emphasis, not a change in essence of God's communication to mankind. Paul could feel the difference in viewpoints between himself and Kephas and James, and even possibly between himself and their friend Barnabas. But Barnabas was his patron. It was he who had promoted him in the Antioch assembly. He must not dishonor him by disagreeing with him. It was highly unseemly for the protégé to challenge his patron publicly, for that might bring loss of face, loss of honor to the latter. Hence, the custom of the time forced Paul to keep silent, lest Barnabas be dishonored in front of James and Kephas.

Titus changed the subject by asking about what Antiocheans had only recently heard of, a group called the *Sicarii* or Jews so highly zealous for the Law such that they assassinated those Jews who were seen to be collaborators with the Roman authorities. There had been a number of deaths in the past year, in public places, where someone had stuck short, sharp daggers into the backs of mid-level officials, such as customs collectors, suppliers of materièl for the Roman garrison, and even a Jewish scribe who translated Roman edicts from Greek into Aramaic. The murders would be done in broad daylight, but the assassin would quickly replace his dagger beneath his (or her) robe and melt into the crowd in the street. But the message was clear: collaboration with the Roman infidels would not be tolerated by zealous Jews. Paul remained silent through the conversation, with Kephas and James condemning the use of violence and reminding everyone that one of Jeshua's key messages was one where one turns the other cheek, and if a person desires one's cloak, give him your shirt as well.

"Look at the idiocy of violence," James was saying. "We ourselves have the scandal that our own Jeshua was humiliated on a Roman cross. How ignominious an end for a messenger of God."

Kephas nodded.

Paul remained silent. *What bumpkins*, he thought. *They look upon the cross as ignominy. Those thick-headed Galileans don't understand the absolute glory of the Cross. Maybe Kephas was too close to see what really happened. After all, rumor has it that he ran for his life when they took Jeshua, and even denied ever knowing him. Some day I'll throw that in his thick peasant face. At least I was consistent with my beliefs. Why did Jeshua choose such ignorant peasants for his followers? Why didn't they come to Gamaliel and talk to him? Or why not listen to Hanina ben Dosa, who had heard him preach? James is a good, though misguided, man, and as Jeshua's brother, deserves all the respect that he receives. But Kephas? That dolt? How did he fool James into giving him such a position of power?*

But I can't bring up the Glory of the Cross now; even Barnabas does not quite understand. Oh, silence is such a burden, especially since the same Jeshua who walked in Galilee with Kephas and the others enlightened me so that I see what they can have not been given the light to see. Silence. Silence. Maybe John will understand; but he might be too young. He is bright, but he has not studied Torah. He can barely read, but there is hope, since he seems to have a good mind. Too bad he was not educated.

All those thoughts went through Paul's mind as the conversation swirled around him. A couple times, Barnabas glanced at Paul, but he knew that Kephas's comment had struck home and that Paul was bleeding inside. His eyes extended sympathy, but the rules of good behavior prohibited him from saying more than James had said.

The meal ended, and Kephas rose, as a sign for the others to leave. James remained in place as the party left the dining room. Kephas bade the party good night, embracing Barnabas and nodding to Paul and Titus, disappeared through a door on the opposite side of the courtyard. The three men continued to their room alone through the gathering shadows cast by the setting sun.

CHAPTER 6

Conflict

PASSOVER CAME AND WENT, CELEBRATED in the house crammed with about forty participants, with James presiding. He read portions of the sayings book, including that portion that encouraged the faithful not to worry about the profane details of their lives:*So, don't worry, thinking what will we eat, or what will we drink, or what will we wear? For everybody in the whole world does that, and your father knows that you need these things. Instead, make sure of his rule over you, and all these things will be yours as well.*

James followed up with a remarkable homily regarding the trust in the Father that was expected of the followers of the Way. Paul was impressed with the simple honesty that emanated from this frail, crippled man. While he was not learned in the sense of the sages, such as Gamaliel, he did possess a charisma that gripped those who heard him; it was a charisma that sprang from an authenticity, a simplicity of understanding, and a grasp of a kind of spirituality that gave life to the body of Jewish tradition within which he found himself.

The day after Passover, Paul asked John if he and Barnabas could meet with Kephas and James to discuss some of the concerns that they brought from the Antioch assembly. John quickly returned with the suggestion that they meet after the noon meal and that some of the brothers of the Jerusalem assembly would also like to join in the meeting.

The weather had turned cold and drizzly, so Paul, Titus, and Barnabas remained in their room, sitting around a charcoal brazier for warmth, and discussed the various issues that brought them to Jerusalem. The authentic piety of James heightened their concerns about the central issue of the methodology of admission to the Chosen People. There had not been a single Greek at the Seder yesterday except for Titus. This meant all the Jews who were in attendance were either Galilean or Judaean Jews from birth, so the issue of the position of converts to the Way was not one that was particularly burning for the Jerusalem assembly.

After a light meal of dates, nuts, and figs, John came to the room to invite the three visitors to follow him to the large assembly room in the house, where they had celebrated Passover the day before. When they arrived, they saw about a dozen other men assembled on cushions in a large oval, with James and Kephas in the center at one end. Three cushions were arranged at the opposite side of the oval from James and Kephas.

"Welcome, brothers," James rasped with firmness and authority. "You will, I hope, forgive an old, crippled man for not rising and offering you the kiss of peace."

"The Peace of the Lord be to you, James, and to all the brothers assembled here," Barnabas said, opening his arms to all. There were some smiles and nods, but no one arose at the entrance of the three visitors. Paul recognized several from the Seder, but there were others whom Kephas introduced who had not been at the house yesterday.

Following the formalities, and after everyone was seated, Barnabas began. "My brothers, there are some of you whom I have not seen for many years, since I left my beloved Jerusalem for Antioch. You know that I was born a Jew in Cyprus but as a child moved to Jerusalem with my father who was a successful merchant. It was Kephas himself who baptized me and who became my spiritual father. You may know that it was the farm I inherited from my father that I gave to the saints in Jerusalem, as a gift provided by our Father in Heaven. So you are all extremely important to me. I hold you all in the highest level of love and affection."

Heads nodded.

"We three have traveled for many days and have endured hardships both on sea and on land in order to greet you and to ask your guidance in maintaining harmony within our assembly. As you probably know, we call ourselves *Christians* in Antioch, acknowledging that Jeshua, the brother of James, Our Lord, was the Anointed One promised by the Prophets of Old. It was he who had been promised, and whom we acknowledge that God raised from the dead as a sign of His favor."

More nods.

"My son in Christ, Paul, and I traveled to Asia four years ago, bringing the Good News to both the Jews and the Gentiles. While there were some Jews who opened their hearts to Jeshua's message, there were many more Gentiles who changed their lives, who acknowledge Iēsoûs as the Christ, and who await his return in glory. They have become brothers, with their families, and give honor to God for the gift of His Son, the same as we do."

Fewer nods; a couple quizzical looks. Kephas's eyes downcast. James' face impassive.

Barnabas took a deep breath. "There have been some who have held that the brothers and their families who have been baptized need also to be circumcised, after the Law of our Fathers, to become followers of our Way. My brother Titus, who was brought to holiness by Paul, is a Greek who loves the Lord, who is zealous to share the Good News with the entire world, but who is not circumcised. We have brought him here, today, before you, to ask that you confirm his brotherhood in our Way and to demonstrate thereby that one can become a part of our Chosen People through baptism alone. My brother Paul will explain our reasons for this request."

Silence. Several heads turned to look at James. His face was impassive. Kephas's eyes still downcast.

Paul arose. He could feel a tightness in his chest; his knees quivered slightly; his throat was dry. John looked at him, a small smile turned up the corners of his mouth, and he nodded slightly, offering the only sign of encouragement from the Jerusalem assembly.

"You all know that I am the least worthy to stand before you. You know that I was born a Jew, of the Tribe of Benjamin, raised in the tradition of the Pharisees. I lived in Jerusalem with my aunt and uncle from a young age and studied Torah at the feet of Gamaliel. I was in Jerusalem when Iēsoûs was crucified and heard, with my own ears, Gamaliel contend that Jeshua was a just man and ought not to be killed. But others more powerful than he prevailed, and Our Lord was hung on a cross, a cross of Glory."

The last phrase caused quizzical frowns. James' face remained the same.

"Yes, it was a cross of Glory because only then could God raise the Lord Jeshua as a sign, and this sign could be for us the source of our faith. For this is what makes us, here in this room, and all of our brothers and sisters in faith, different from everyone else in the world, Jews or Gentiles: that we are made right with God through our faith in the Risen Lord.

"Consider our father, Abraham. He was justified by his act of faith in God *before* he circumcised himself. From this we can learn that being chosen, being a part of the People of God, is made possible first and foremost by an act of faith, not by a ceremonial act. And if faith is the primary means of becoming part of God's People, then for those who are not circumcised as we are, we should permit them to become part of us, part of our people, through baptism alone, and not require circumcision."

Paul sat. Silence. Kephas stood up, being helped by John at his side.

"Moses brought us the Law. God wrote it with His own finger on the tablets. he said that he would be with us forever, provided we kept his Law. Each time we abandoned his Law, he left us, and we suffered. I walked Galilee with Jeshua. He was my friend. He called upon us to repent, that the Kingdom of God was at hand; he brought us to a simple life, but one centered in God. He knew God as Father, as one who loves us, who provides for our needs, and who is ever anxious for our well-being."

"In the earliest days after Iēsoûs was taken into heaven, we baptized our Jewish families with the understanding that of the first few days after he was taken from us we admitted some foreigners so that this would bring the Holy Spirit into our midst. With that exception, there was no attempt to baptize Greeks or Egyptians or Persians. He was a man of the Law who came to fulfil the promises of the prophets. If anyone wants to become a follower of the Law, let him follow the Law as our Father Moses has commanded. Let him be circumcised like any other proselyte; we will welcome him, and he will become a brother."

Nods. Heads turned toward the three from Antioch.

Paul again arose, quickly, moving toward the center of the oval.

"I did not tell you of how it came to be that I changed from my persecution of the followers of the Way to my present life of preaching the Lord Jeshua. I was on my way to Damascus, intent upon stamping out deviance from the proper observance of the Law, when I was struck to the ground by a powerful, unseen force. My sensation was one of utter peace. I felt at one with the universe. I looked to the south and the shimmering lake took on a golden hue, the rays streaming out of the water toward me. The vision snapped around to the north, and I saw the snow-capped peak of Mount Hermon suddenly begin to move toward me, becoming larger and larger, closer and closer. Yet I felt no fear. It was perfect, serene peace. I understood everything. The world was transparent; the white, puffy clouds seemed to part; and the sun spread out over the entire sky, sending gold streamers from horizon to horizon. Then the lights seemed to dim, slowly, gradually, until the experience stopped.

"Those around me saw something different, which was later described to me. They saw me stop and turn rigid as my eyes slowly rolled back in my head. Then I fell to the ground, my face contorted horribly, my eyes reopening, bulging out of my head. I frothed at the mouth, and my body began to convulse uncontrollably. My fellow travelers stopped, looked, and jumped back in fear.

"He is possessed by a devil, and if we don't leave him, the devil will possess us too, commanded the leader. Quickly. Stop looking and move on. Go on, move! Go ahead. Forget him. Move on. And the group solemnly proceeded."

"A man and two daughters were working in the field next to the road. They witnessed my fall and abandonment by my fellow travelers. They rushed over to me, made a sort of stretcher out of boughs of wood, and carried me to their house, which was close by in Capernaum. They cared for me until I recovered lavishing love on an unknown traveler."

"After a couple days, I recovered, thanks to the nursing skills of one of the man's daughters named Judith. I expressed my need to her to continue to Damascus, in spite of the fact that I found her very attractive. No sooner had I resolved to leave the next day than I came down with a severe case of malaria. At that point my body temperature became very high, and once again I lost consciousness. I had the same kind of feeling of utter peace that I had on the road several days before. I looked up, and there was a blinding light, and a voice came to me, saying, 'Saul, Saul, why do you persecute me?'

"I said, 'Who are you, Lord?'"

"And the voice responded, 'I am Jeshua, whom you persecute'."

"What would you have me do, Lord?" I said.

"Go into Damascus, present yourself to Ananias, and he will know what to do."

"Thereafter, having received the Lord Iēsoûs, I left Damascus and went to Arabia for a time. And while I was in the wilderness, the risen Lord Iēsoûs was revealed to me, and His Gospel was given to me directly. He instructed me and sent me to all the nations. He made me his apostle."

"So my mission was not given me by any man; I was, in fact, called in my mother's womb to be the apostle of Iēsoûs Christ to all nations. Not only to the Jews, but also to the Gentiles."

"Preposterous." came out of the oval, sotto-voce.

"Paul, you are turning our world upside down," said Kephas, remaining standing. "We Jews have always invited Gentiles to become followers of Abraham and Moses, and we invite them to become followers of

Iēsoûs. But the way to become a follower is clear. If we first ignore circumcision, then what about the Sabbath? What about the balance of the commandments? Shall we then decide that we shall merely overturn the Law and live like Gentiles? Circumcision has marked us out as the People of God forever. It is not for nothing that Iēsoûs was born a Jew, selected Jews as his disciples, and showed himself to Jews after he was raised from the dead. He came not to destroy the Law but to fulfill it."

"No, Kephas, I am not turning the world upside down; I am merely obeying the commandment of Iēsoûs, the risen Lord. It is not *my* Gospel; it is his! Can't you see, after his death and resurrection, the entire world has changed? Nothing is the same! You want to keep an outmoded way of living; he wants us to include the Law, but by surpassing it."

"A demon must be speaking, shouted Kephas. "I walked with the Lord for almost three years; if it was his Gospel, I would have heard it! And I never did! No one can surpass the Law. You are close to blasphemy! Silence!" Kephas' eyes blazed at Paul. His fists were clenched, pounding his knees as he sat cross-legged.

"Blasphemy, you say!" Paul shouted. "You bumpkin, you can't even read. You have never studied the Law. You would not know blasphemy if you stepped in it!"

"Brothers, Peace, peace," James said, his outstretched hand resting on Kephas's taut arm.

Barnabas offered the same gesture to Paul.

"I would like to spend more time with Paul alone," James said. "He and I will talk, and then we will all meet again. We must not have this kind of dissension in our midst. My brother loved Kephas, and it was his wish that he continue his work. As his closest heir, I want to make sure that this happens. But more than anything else, his work remains, continuing the life that he lived, the life the Father intended for us to live, loving one another and avoiding the unseemly conflict characteristic of the Greeks."

Titus started at this last comment, but merely looked at Paul with wide eyes. The comment was certainly not made with any consciousness of an offense, especially considering the context. He was simply startled at the totally unconscious sense of bias.

Paul, in turn, nodded ever so slightly to Titus, as if to say, "Don't worry, my friend. I heard the comment too, and I will handle it alone with James."

In his return tiniest movement of the eyes, Titus tried to ask many other questions: Why did no other men sitting in the oval express their opinions? They were utterly silent, except for Kephas. They merely nodded at the expressions of James and scowled when Paul spoke. In Antioch, when there was a discussion, everyone participated. Debate would occur, and action would take place, generally in accordance with an expression of consensus. Things were different here in Jerusalem.

Kephas helped James stand and handed him a walking stick, on which James leaned heavily, each step giving him pain. The two men went through a door at the end of the room, and Kephas looked over his shoulder, indicating that Paul should follow. He did.

CHAPTER 7

Dialogue

THE NEXT ROOM WAS SMALL, with a tiny window high in the wall that shed a gray light from the street, mingled with snatches of passing conversations, animals being beaten into motion, laughter, children, and gossip. The room had a mat in the corner, toward which Kephas helped the grimacing, emaciated man. Kephas lowered him to the mat; a sigh of relief escaped the ascetic's lips, and he urged Paul to sit on the cushion adjacent to the mat.

Kephas left without looking at Paul.

"I remember your last visit well, my son,..." James said.

"*Son,*'*Son,*'" *no less* thought Paul.

"You were so anxious to learn; you could not understand that I had not followed my brother in Galilee. It was not until after his death that I realized that I had missed the remarkable opportunity to be with him when he was his best. But that is in the past. I could see, years ago, that you would be a potent force in making sure his life continued in our new family."

"Thank you, Father," Paul said, doing the man honor.

"But I also saw that you would offer many problems. You think too much. You are quicker than we are. You have read the Word of God and all those other books that lawyers and schoolmen read. You ask too many questions. We are simple people, and don't know how to deal with the things you think are important. My brother lived a simple, but powerful, life. He said that love knew no national boundaries. I think I understand that, but most people don't."

Paul nodded, not wanting to interrupt the flow of his thoughts.

"You are like some of our Jewish brothers from Alexandria; Apollos, for instance. He has read many books about the end of the world, and God's judgment, and the separation of the Sons of light from the Sons of Darkness. He believes Iēsoûs will come again as the leader of the sons of light. It is too complicated for me. Iēsoûs was simple. He spoke so that everyone could understand him. You and Apollos speak so that no one can understand you. That is why Kephas becomes angry. He can't understand you. You use words of a lawyer, not words like we Galilean peasants use. We are simple people of the land. So was my brother. When he came here, he was like a fish in the desert. He should never have come to the city."

"Father," Paul said softly, "it is not my intention to use big words; but the message Iēsoûs revealed to me is so powerful, so compelling that I must try to express it in a way that both peasants and lawyers can understand. To a peasant, I must become like a peasant; and to a lawyer, like a lawyer."

"That is a good thought, my son, a good thought."

Silence.

"Now," said James, "I must speak clearly the fears that we all have here in Jerusalem. I know you were born in Tarsus in Cilicia, and I know that many Greek philosophers come from there. The school is well known throughout the world. Its knowledge is pagan. They exercise nude, even wrestling nude after being oiled. Many Jews who live in Asia are really more Greek than Jewish. They attend the theater; they stand while incense is being offered to Dionysus; they dine with pagans. They introduce pagan ideas into our way of life."

"But, Father, there are many Pharisees in Asia, like my family."

"I am not accusing you, my son; you have proved your devotion to the Law."

Paul wondered if this was a trap. He had spoken to only a few trusted people about his idea of a New Covenant, a new relationship with God that superseded the Covenant of Moses. He had spoken with Essenes, years ago, who claimed that they were the recipients of a New Covenant, brought by the Teacher of Righteousness. Now Paul realized that the true New Covenant was that which Iēsoûs had brought to humankind. It was a radical idea, too radical for Jerusalem. But how would James have heard? Patience, patience.

"As he said, 'Don't judge and you won't be judged.' But I have heard that you are trying to express the simple way of life we lead in the language of the Greek cults. The Greeks love 'mysteries', they love to think their god becomes present to them when they perform certain magical acts in a temple. They like to think that they are washed clean of sin by baptism. They think that if they are enlightened by a priest in an expensive ritual, then they will have a higher place in the life hereafter."

Paul was surprised that this peasant knew so much about Greek mystery religions. The desire of the populace to engage in such religious experiences was evidence to Paul that they had a desire for a higher level of truth, that brought by Iēsoûs. Hence, Paul would simply provide them with what he could see as being the essential truth of Iēsoûs' life, death and resurrection, and his imminent return in glory. The Greeks were open to this truth; many Jews simply were not. Just as James was not. Even Iēsoûs' own brother did not understand what had really happened!

"Father, you mentioned 'baptism.'"

"Yes."

"We baptize not as an act of Greek religion, but as an outpouring of the Spirit."

"The followers of John the Baptizer continue that tradition. They preach repentance, renewal. They preach a life similar to ours," said James.

"But without Iēsoûs," Paul said, "without a baptism of the Spirit."

"Baptism is acceptable for women who become Jews, but not for men. It is Greek and an abomination. And I don't know what 'Spirit' you are talking about," James said with some heat.

"I am talking about the Spirit of Iēsoûs the Christ, his outpouring of himself and his continued presence among us in our assembly."

"You see, you are talking with those big words again. What is this 'outpouring,' this 'continued presence'?"

"He revealed to me that the End Times have begun. he has conquered death and remains with us until he returns in glory to deliver a sanctified world to the Father."

"Yes, my brother was our 'Moschiach,' our deliverer, or what you call 'Christ.' But only because he taught us that God is our Father, and he loves us; that we should love each other; and that since he loves Gentiles as well as Jews, the Good News should be brought to the Gentiles as well."

"But enough Gentiles will not follow our Way if we require them to be circumcised," Paul responded through clenched teeth. "Our Way will die out, and Iēsoûs will have died in vain. Look how few Gentiles become Jews."

"The yoke of the Law is not light; it is not for the weak. God will provide enough people for the Way to continue."

"But you know that sometimes men die from circumcision. And if they don't die, they are in pain for months. They can't walk for three weeks, at least. What is suffered easily by an eight-day old baby brings the strongest grown man to his knees. Why else are there so many 'God-fearers' in the world? They follow our Law but refuse to become circumcised. Why can women become Jews by baptism, but men not?"

"Because the Law is clear."

"Your brother brought the Law to a new level."

"But he did not say not to circumcise. He said, 'Love the non-Jew'."

Paul responded: "Did he not also say, 'A student is not better than his teacher; it is enough for a student to be like his teacher.' And as he, himself, plucked grains on the Sabbath, as he ate with prostitutes and non-Jews, must we not be like him?"

"He did that to give us the example that all men and women are loveable, not that we should ignore the Law of Moses. He was observant; he went to Jerusalem for the Passover; he observed Shabbat. But our Fathers would pull an ass out of a pit on Shabbat or bandage a wound."

Paul felt it was hopeless. The raspy-voiced, frail man was quick and alert to each point; he had never been trained in the Law, but he had a sure grasp of the essentials. He needed another perspective. Perhaps…

"Father, let me ask you, do you have many poor in your assembly?"

"You know we do. Many sold their belongings and gave us the money, especially those who followed Apollos. They expected Iēsoûs to return with angels. And when he did not come, they had to turn to begging to live. Many have left the Way, angry. Why do you ask?"

"God promised Abraham that his descendants would be as many as stars in the sky. And it is true. But there are almost as many Gentiles as there are sands on the shore of the Lake in Galilee. If they were to join the Way through baptism, it might be possible to acknowledge the gift of faith from Jerusalem with a gift of material goods. Think of how you could help the poor in Jerusalem. But if you require circumcision, there will be so few who join the Way that it would not be worth the trip to carry the coins to you."

James thought.

Those who did the work of the Lord deserved their wages. The faithful provided for James and Kephas and John and their families so that they could continue the life that Iēsoûs had started. But were it not for Paul's benefactor, Barnabas, their little community would be bankrupt. Having sold or given away most of their worldly goods, their community was penurious. The tiny offerings that arrived barely paid for food. And many who brought portions of their own food to the house did so even though they were hungry. If there were rich Gentiles who might wait for the return of Iēsoûs without selling their worldly goods and who might send donations to Jerusalem, the poor members of the assembly might be brought out of their poverty. Such an act might even bring back those who had left the community having felt betrayed. It would be an expression of that generosity that Iēsoûs had taught. James remembered last winter, after the summer of no rains, how the faithful of Antioch had sent food to the hungry brethren in Jerusalem. That was a remarkable practical application of Jeshua's words, 'I was hungry, and you fed me'."

But no. None of that matters. Ever. The Law is clear. *You shall circumcise your foreskin, and this shall be the sign of My Covenant with you. The uncircumcised male, whose foreskin has not been circumcised, such a man shall be cut off from his people: he has violated my Covenant.* That is the Word of God. For countless generations the Covenant had been kept; that was a condition of being part of God's People, his people, his chosen ones."

"Paul, I am tired. I must pray. I must think. It takes me longer to think than you. You are a problem to me. But you do not anger me. I am of the land, and our ways are different from those of you born and raised in the city. Tomorrow, tomorrow. We'll talk again tomorrow."

Silence. Moments passed. Silence.

Paul realized that James had disconnected himself; his eyes were riveted on a spot on the floor; he was still as a stone. Paul rose, looking for a touch of permission to leave; but there was none. James was no longer part of this room; he was somewhere else. Paul backed out of the room; James never moved.

CHAPTER 8

A Conversation
Late at Night

KEPHAS AND JAMES SAT TOGETHER in the latter's small cell. The solitary oil-lamp cast flickering but indistinct shadows on the bare walls. There was dead silence in the dark street outside. The men had been talking for several hours.

Kephas: He told us to remain together as a family, to bring his Good News to all the tribes of Israel. But it is just you and me and John now; the others are scattered to the four winds, and except for Philip, we don't know if they have continued in the Way.

James: That is the problem. Paul saw that our numbers are small. We don't know when he will return; it has been almost twenty years, and his delay has caused many of our brothers and sisters to lose faith in his Way. You and I know that when he does come, it will be in the same manner as he left, quietly. And He will come to us, the people of the land.

Kephas: Yes. Not like that nose-in-the-air Alexandrian, Apollos, says, with all his angels and trumpets and clouds.

James: Tell me again, Kephas, about that time he called himself 'Son of Man.'

Kephas: That was when Zev bar Jonah said, 'Master, I will follow you everywhere you go.' And the Lord said, *Foxes have dens, the birds of the sky have nests, but the Son of Man has nowhere to lay his head.*

James: And did he tell you what he meant?

Kephas: No, not really. But that was when we were in the north of Galilee, and we had not slept inside a house for weeks. It was not long after Andrew and I had left our nets on the shore. But he used to call himself "Son of Man." I don't know why.

James: Did anyone ever read the Book of Daniel to you?

Kephas: I have heard some of it, I think.

James: Last week, I had John read part of it to me. There, Daniel said that he saw a vision, someone who came on the clouds of heaven, like a "Son of Man." He came to the one of Great Age, who I think is God, and God conferred upon him sovereignty, glory and kingship. Then all the peoples, nations, and languages became his servants. Daniel said that his sovereignty would be an eternal sovereignty and shall never pass away, and that his empire would never be destroyed.

Kephas: The Prophet Daniel said that?

James: Yes. John read it to me many times so that I could remember it clearly.

Kephas: Was he referring to Jeshua?

James: What do you think? He was referring to 'Son of Man'.

Kephas: No. Maybe. I don't know.

James: We know that Jeshua is the one who will redeem Israel, but he will redeem it if it follows his Way. Redemption is not through force of arms but through the Spirit of God that Jeshua brought. But maybe, just maybe, God will allow him to return as King, ruling the earth in justice and peace.

Kephas:	You sound like the Alexandrians.
James:	This points to one of our problems. We have had scripture read to us, but we can't read it ourselves. We have used those portions that we have heard as proof that Jeshua is Lord, that he is the one Israel has waited for. But there may be many more prophecies about him that we have not yet read.
Kephas:	You don't mean that we, at our ages, should learn to read!
James:	Of course not; but it means that some of those who have read the scriptures themselves may see something about Jeshua that we never saw.
Kephas:	I saw all I needed to see. I saw him heal. I heard him speak of the Kingdom of God. I don't need to read anything.
James:	Then who was he, really.
Kephas:	You ask me who your own brother was? You spent almost thirty years with him. I spent a couple and you ask me?
James:	I was almost ten years older. By the time he was four years of age, I was working in Sepphoris. I really didn't know him when he was a child. He and Judah were only a year apart; they were inseparable. But he died of gangrene from a building construction accident, only a year after Jeshua did. So I never was able to talk much to him.
Kephas:	He was a holy man sent by God. He was a Savior for Israel, if only Israel would listen.
James:	Could he be for all the nations.
Kephas:	For the Gentiles?
James:	Yes. For Israel first, but also for the Nations.
Kephas:	Who really cares about the Gentiles? They are God's curse upon us, a punishment inflicted upon us when we stray from his Holy Commands.
James:	But Isaiah said, *Foreigners who have attached themselves to the Lord to serve him and to love his name and be his servants, these I will bring to my holy mountain. I will make them joyful*

in my house of prayer. Their holocausts and their sacrifices will be accepted on my altar, for my house will be called a house of prayer for all the peoples.

Kephas: John has been reading to you again, (said with a smile.)

James: Yes. He does so every day.

Kephas: But those must be foreigners who are circumcised, who become part of the People of God. We have always accepted them.

James: When a foreigner is circumcised and adopts God's Law, he is no longer a 'foreigner', but a Jew.

Kephas: James, you are beginning to sound like that accursed Paul.

James: He may see more clearly than we do, my friend.

Kephas: I don't believe my ears!!

James: How many families who are followers of the Way do we have now in Jerusalem?

Kephas: Hundreds. I can't count how many.

James: Kephas, my old friend. At one time we had hundreds. But we now have maybe fifteen families, and we are a growing burden to them. It used to be that a shekel a year was all that was needed for our support from each family. You remember, almost fifteen years ago, we received gifts of over a thousand shekels? You yourself know that we received only one hundred twenty shekels last year, and some families gave fifteen shekels! If it weren't for Jacob, the potter; the widow Sarai; and her cousins, we would probably starve. God has sent them to us as gifts so that we might preach, but we are such a burden to these good people.

Kephas: James, what are you trying to tell me?

James: That our God is a God of foreigners as well as the God of the Jews.

Kephas: Of course.

James:	Uncircumcised.
Kephas:	No. Never.
James:	Kephas…
Kephas:	No. I will not hear this…
James:	Peace, my brother.
Kephas:	You have become senile in your old age. You have lost your wisdom. A demon has entered into you. (*Kephas rises from the cushion, his face flushed, fists clenched.*)
James:	Kephas…
Kephas:	God spoke to Abraham; God spoke to Moses; who has spoken to you? It could only be Satan.)
James:	Kephas…

(*But Kephas has turned on his heel and left the room.*)

CHAPTER 9

A Dream

FOR THREE DAYS, JAMES REMAINED in his cubicle, seeing no one. Kephas had not returned to his sleeping quarters the night of his interview with James, and cries of anguish were heard throughout the compound as his wife vented her agony at his disappearance. The community was totally disrupted; women hustled through the more public area of the central courtyard, venturing out to the community fountain and vegetable market, inquiring among other women friends to ask the men of their families for information about Kephas. It was nearly impossible for a man to disappear, since someone would have to feed him, which meant that some woman would be required to prepare the food. Men could not venture into the food markets or draw water at the fountains. They could not prepare food, as their presence in a cooking area was unseemly. Hence, the gender barriers so prevalent in the society made self-sufficiency impossible. But days passed, and no Kephas.

The fourth day after James and Kephas's discussion was Friday; and after sundown, the community of about twenty gathered in the largest room, men on one side of a temporary screen run down the longitudinal center of the room, the women on the other. James hobbled in, deeply bent, assisted by John. He assumed his position on a cushion on the extended centerline of the screen, so that those on both sides of the partition could see him. Paul, Titus, and Barnabas were among the men.

"The Lord be with you."

"And with you," the congregation responded.

Hear, O Israel, James intoned, and the congregation continued the ancient prayer in unison. At its end, silence.

"My brothers and sisters," James began softly, in a hoarse whisper, "I have sinned."

Silence; sobs from the women's side.

"I have driven our beloved Kephas from the house.

A door opened, and the space was filled with a familiar bulk.

"No, James, it was not you; it was Satan who tempted me," Kephas said, striding along the partition. He knelt in front of the wide-eyed leader.

Gasps could be heard from the women's side. James raised a hand and placed it on the shaggy, bowed mane in front of him.

"Where have you been, my brother?"

"At Qumran, with the Essenes. I prayed with them, and last night, God came to me in a dream. He was walking in the Garden of Eden; his face shone like the sun; young men dressed in white followed behind him, singing his praises. Some of the men were Jews, but most of them were Greeks, Egyptians, Persians, Armenians, Scythians from every tribe and every nation on the face of the earth. I fell on my face and adored."

The community hung on every word.

"When I looked up, there was no one except Jeshua. We were on the shores of the Sea of Galilee; he was sitting in my old boat. He handed me one end of the net, I rowed out into the lake, and returned down the shore, having let the balance of the net out. We then pulled the net to the shore, and it was filled with every kind of fish I have ever seen and many that I had never seen. Each fish I picked up had a gold coin in its mouth, and in the shortest period of time, there was a huge pile of coins. Jeshua smiled at me and then walked out into the lake. He motioned for me to follow, and I did. My sandals did not even get wet. 'Simon bar Jonah,' he said to me, 'fish for men.'

"Then he disappeared, and I felt myself sinking into the lake. I cried out for him and heard his voice from the sky *O you of little faith. I am always with you; walk to the shore.* And I did. Then I awoke, knowing that Jeshua came to save all men Jews first, but also Greeks."

James struggled to his feet, helped by John and Kephas. "He called you 'bar Jonah,' the son of Jonah, who was swallowed by the great fish but who, after three days and three nights, was vomited onto dry land. Kephas, why was Jonah at sea?"

"He was fleeing from God."

"And, where had God instructed him to go?"

"To Nineveh."

"A Gentile town."

"The town of Nineveh repented, changed its ways, and God did not destroy it."

"You are the son of Jonah; you have been sent."

"That is why I returned, after three days and three nights."

"But, my son, I shall not force you to go to the Gentiles. You shall be sent to Israel, and we will permit Paul to go to the Gentiles. We will have two missions, one to the circumcised, and one to the uncircumcised. We shall be one family, and the perhaps the gold coins found in the mouths of the fish will relieve the suffering of the poor in Jerusalem."

Paul nodded, stood, and walked to the front of the congregation. He held out his arms toward Kephas, and the latter engulfed the smaller man in a bear hug. When Kephas let him loose, Paul motioned for Titus to come forward. Kephas embraced him with the same enthusiasm.

"Welcome, brother Titus. May the Peace and Love of our Lord Jeshua Christ be yours," Kephas said in a loud voice, so that all could hear. "For my blindness, I ask your forgiveness."

The rest of the Shabbat service proceeded with a new level of joy and discovery. Afterwards, the entire community shared a meal, recalling the sayings and life of their Lord, with Kephas telling stories of their travels, of his teachings, of his parables, and of the joy of the open road.

The day after the Sabbath, Titus, Barnabas and Paul bade adieu to the Jerusalem Community, invited Kephas to visit Antioch, and headed for Caesarea Maritima and a ship to Antioch. The three walked confidently, stunned at the remarkable turn of events that God had wrought.

CHAPTER 10

Antioch

Autumn, 49 AD

THE SOFT BREEZE WAFTING UP the Orontes River cooled the city as the sun sank in the west. Antiocheans strolled on the quay, which was crowded with every conceivable form of watercraft. Silk from China, teak from India, bags of spices from Ceylon, linen from Egypt, bitumen from lower Palestine, goods of every description were piled along the wharf. Kephas, Titus, and Paul walked unhurriedly among the crowd, laughing at the seven-year-old boys who chased one another, dodging artfully through the older folks. They paused to watch a juggler performing on the deck of one of the Egyptian ships and applauded with the rest of the crowd as he kept four, then five, balls rotating in a perfect circle. Then he switched to knives and held the small group electrified. At the end of the act, small coins were tossed by the smiling public, including Kephas and Paul, and the three men continued down the quay, past the open gate and lounging sentries of the III Gallica Legion. A wave by Titus was returned by one of the soldiers.

"There will be wonderful weather for the celebration tonight," Titus .
"Leah said the she heard from the women that over fifty people would be coming."

"I hope that Menachem will provide the wine," Paul responded.

"You bet. I know that he got several amphorae of Lake Mareotis wine from Alexandria last week," Titus said, always knowledgeable in river traffic.

"I have not tasted that wine," Kephas offered.

"If you are lucky, you will tonight," Titus . "I have tasted wines from Italy, both from Seti and from Falernum. Those wines are rich and full and can be drunk when they are ten or fifteen years old. But the wines from Lake Mareotis are different. They are actually sweet. I think that Menachem will share those wines with us tonight."

"I still feel a little unusual, dining and drinking wine with Greeks. I can never be sure about whether the food has been offered to idols," Kephas mused.

"Kephas, you said it yourself...*It is not what goes into a person's mouth that defiles him; it is what comes out,* Paul quoted.

"I know, I know," Kephas responded. "But I still feel strange. And, tonight, such a large party. I hope that there will not be any...any... abominations," he stammered.

Titus and Paul laughed. "Most of those who will be celebrating Silas' retirement from the III Gallica Legion are Christians, like us," Paul offered.

"That is another thing, calling us *Christians*," Kephas said.

"How better to describe us," Paul continued. "Iēsoûs is the Christ, the Anointed One, and we follow him. Why not call us by that name?"

"I am just used to being called a *Nazarene*," Kephas said.

"But no one in Antioch knows where Nazareth is, or what it is famous for. But many know who *Iēsoûs Christos* is," Titus said.

"It is all so strange, so different. I now know how a landlubber feels when he first sets foot in my boat," Kephas laughed. "It is hard for me not to get seasick in these Greek waters."

Titus and Paul chuckled with Kephas, with Paul clapping him on the back as they walked along.

"And the women will not be veiled tonight," Paul added.

Kephas looked at him, surprised.

"Remember, this is a Roman party. A Roman officer is retiring after twenty-five years in the legions. He is one of us, and it would be unseemly if our women were to be veiled. The Greek women would think that our women are not beautiful."

"I am less concerned about the Greek women than about the Roman soldiers," Kephas responded, a frown on his face. "I have heard about what happened in Alexandria about twelve years ago, during the riots there. If that Alexandrian rabble had not seen the beauty of our women, they would not have killed so many of our men and left our women helpless before their lust."

Virtually every Jew had some relative or other who lived in Alexandria and who had related through letters and eyewitness stories from friends and family the absolute horror not only of the first week of riots, when Jews were forced from their homes, their belongings stolen by mobs, the men killed and the women and girls raped, but of the months after when they were forced to live packed into a tiny corner of the city, with many even surviving in a tent-city in a cemetery. For those observant Jews who lived a life of ritual purity, this latter insult, producing cultic uncleanness, was intolerable. And it had been only with the accession of Claudius, nearly three years later, that conditions returned to anything like what they had been prior to the riots. Paul had spoken of the riots with Apollos, an educated and brilliant follower of the Way who had left an important post under the famous Jewish customs collector Alexander Lysimachu (sometimes called the *Alabarch*) in order to travel to the Diaspora to preach the Lord Iēsoûs. Apollos had been there, had been beaten and left for dead and had witnessed the atrocities firsthand. Indeed, for him, they were the precursor of the End Times, evidence that the Son of Man was about to return in glory, announcing the arrival of the Kingdom.

After a few moments, Paul responded to Kephas, "My friend, there is a great difference between *never* wearing a veil and being unveiled in the intimacy of one's home or the home of a close friend. The latter our women do all the time. In this case, we are simply extending the boundary of *home* to include a celebration with non-Jews, many of whom are Christians. And while the place is actually part of the Roman camp, the commander is one of us, who has provided for our church(Paul used the Greek word *ekklesia* to refer to the group of Antiochene Christians) for many years. I don't think our women are truly at risk, or we wouldn't let them attend."

"Well, we have already accepted the invitation," Kephas said. "Not to appear would be to cause you to be dishonored. I will join you."

The three continued their journey, but their spirits had been dampened by the mention of the Alexandrian atrocities. They all felt their ultimate vulnerability. Being different and having different foods and traditions often created social hostility. Fortunately, the Jewish population, though a minority, was sufficiently large as to produce a feeling of safety, as long as one chose to ignore the fact that hostility between Jews and non-Jews lay always just beneath the surface and could erupt without warning at virtually any time. And while the Emperor Claudius had decreed that the rights of the Jews were to be respected throughout the empire, anti-Jewish sentiment was part of the very atmosphere of that time.

The three men continued silently until they reached a narrow alleyway off the main quayside road. There Titus took his leave, promising to be on time for the celebration at nightfall, and continued down the quayside. Kephas and Paul turned into the alleyway. They walked single file past two intersecting streets and stopped before a small shop with a wooden sign next to the door carved with an image of a tent.

The door was open, and two young men looked up from their sewing; they wore leather gloves that had the thumb and forefinger cut out, and used long needles that fit into a leathern notch in the palm of the glove for forcing through the stiff fabric. It was a new fabric woven by Paul's father in Tarsus from a thread made from hemp grown in the interior of Lycaonia, several days' journey northwest of Tarsus. It was far stronger than linen, repelled water, and was vastly lighter than the leather tents used heretofore. Paul had trained the two men in the use of this new fabric and he would sell the tents to the merchants who traveled overland out of Antioch.

"Peace," Paul smiled at the men.

"Peace, brothers," the men responded, continuing their sewing.

Paul led Kephas up the small staircase at the rear of the shop to the second floor, where they entered a sparsely furnished room with an iron bed at one end and at the other, a cot at whose foot lay a traveling bag.

"Shall we visit the baths?" Paul asked Kephas.

"You may go, but not I," said Kephas.

"It is really customary," Paul continued.

"Maybe for Greeks, but not for me," Kephas responded firmly.

"Well, if you feel uneasy about nudity, I would be glad to ask one of my workers to bring up a bucket of water."

"When we were on the road with Jeshua, we almost never bathed. We distinguished ourselves from the Pharisees by *not* bathing. The Law requires bathing after a nocturnal emission, but today there is no need for that. I will go to your dinner party as I am, with my clean garment. But no, I will not wash."

Kephas had arrived in Antioch yesterday and had not changed the sweat-stained garment, nor combed his beard or hair, nor washed his hands before eating. For him, it was a matter of principle, and it was clear that Paul would not be an instrument of change.

"Very well, my friend, I shall be back in about an hour. Then we should leave without delay." Paul removed a clean orange robe trimmed in brown from a small chest at the foot of his bed and headed for the public baths at the end of the street.

As he made his way through the crowd of homeward bound workers, he could not help but reflect on what he saw as a profound puzzle. Here was Kephas, the person who was recognized as occupying a place of great importance in the body of Christians, second only to Iēsoûs' own brother, but he was an illiterate peasant! He was utterly provincial in his outlook, given to essentially nonreflective action such as the absurdity of refusing to wash his stinking body. Paul had known wandering charismatics who called themselves *Cynics* followers of Diogenes, who owned a single cloak, who did not wash, who lived generally outdoors, in poverty, and relied upon the charity of townspeople for their daily bread. And, in many respects, Iēsoûs followed a lifestyle that was similar. But the difference in the messages of the Cynics and Iēsoûs was enormous. The profundity of the paradox of Iēsoûs' death on a cross, which made possible the permanent overcoming of sin; the mysticism of Iēsoûs having left this earth but remaining present in those who are admitted to the Saved of Israel through their acts of faith in him. These insights distinguished the Iēsoûs believers from the often crude Cynics. Yes, Kephas continued the charismatic tradition of unconcern for the present, for material goods. He certainly continued the tradition of Iēsoûs as Messiah; but he had no clue regarding the world-shaking theological insights that were being revealed to Paul on a daily basis. When Paul prayed, he would *see* what Iēsoûs meant; he knew, directly, as though Iēsoûs were speaking directly within his thoughts, that until the promised End Times, Iēsoûs would be present in the community of believers. But each time that Paul began to discuss what he saw so clearly and distinctly, Kephas was totally unable to engage in discussion. He did not have the intellectual ability to conceive of the problem of the Chosen People of Israel relying upon an enormously complex Law as a means of achieving righteousness in God's eyes. If he could not even conceive of the problem, how could he really acknowledge Paul's solution that entrance to the People, for Gentiles, required only an act of faith in the Lord Iēsoûs? And *this* was the person who the Lord had chosen? It made no sense.

Lord, why do you delay? Return now, before it is too late! Your holy assembly awaits you in faith. Bring history to a conclusion. If you wait, your holy assembly, under the influence of Kephas, will collapse out of ignorance. I know I am your chosen one, your prophet. You called me from my mother's womb. you speak through me. I know that, and I thank you. Come now, come now!" Paul prayed, shouting silently as he entered the crowded public bath.

CHAPTER 11

Kephas Prays

As Paul walked out the door, Kephas reached into his travelling bag, pulled out his prayer-shawl and phylacteries, put the shawl over his head and shoulders and the leather straps around his forearms, faced the wall, and prayed:

> *Father, Abba, listen to your servant. I am a simple man. Your Son called me to fish for men, and for that I left my nets. I know I am doing your will. But I am so afraid. Why have you taken me from the lake I knew so well, where I knew every cove, every submerged rock, when and where I could find fish? There I was at home. But you have sent me to cities, which I hate. Why? When our Father, Abraham, spoke to you, you answered; won't You just speak a little to a poor fisherman?*

Kephas continued his rocking back and forth from the waist and listened intently for several seconds. Nothing.

And not only cities, but Gentile Cities. And not only Gentile Cities, but eating with Gentiles and their unveiled women. I want to go home. I want to fish on the lake with Andrew. But James said I had to come here, to get to know Paul, to understand what he says about your son. And I don't understand him. He talks in riddles. He laughs at me behind my back. He looks down upon me. But I don't care, if it is your will. Am I doing what you want? Won't you tell me?

Rocking, eyes closed, hands outstretched, palms up. Silence.

I have heard that he says he is the apostle to the Gentiles. The gall! That he should claim the same mission that your son gave to us who lived with him. He is more Greek than Jew! I don't know how he convinced James, but he did. It must have been your will. Going to the public baths, no less! Where boys romp naked in front of grown, lecherous men! Oh, the abomination! These Greeks! And Paul would have them as brothers? He, a supposed scholar. Didn't he ever hear You shall not lie with a man as a woman, for that is an abomination? *Scholar? Rubbish!*

Rocking, eyes closed, a pleading expression on his face, beads of sweat forming on his brow. Silence.

Won't you send Your Son in Glory? Now? Let the end come now. Your holy assembly in Jerusalem is ready. We have been faithful to Your Son's teachings. We are ready for the Kingdom. If You don't send your Son back soon, Paul will ruin our work. When Your Son returns, looking for the faithful remnant of Israel, He will not find it, for it will have been destroyed by the Greeks. They will ignore the Law you gave to Moses, which your son fulfilled. He did not come to destroy your Law! How could he?

But Paul. Paul will bring desolation upon Israel. Come, Lord, Come. Your remnant waits with tears on its cheeks. We are faithful, but the meaning of faithfulness is beyond the understanding of this poor fisherman. Why did you take me from my nets? Won't you come and explain? I am so alone. I am so afraid. Abba, help me. In your son's name, help me. Help me. Speak to me.

The tears dripped onto his ample belly. For a few moments, he continued his rocking, then slowly stopped, unwound the phylacteries, removed the prayer shawl, and stowed both in the traveling bag. He hauled out a relatively clean, grey homespun robe, swished the stained one off and donned the clean one. Then he slumped in the single backless chair against the wall. He said he would return, like a thief in the night. *Of course the Father would not speak to me* Kephas said aloud to the four walls. *Who ever heard of a thief who announced when he would come to rob a house,* Kephas chuckled out loud. *Why did He pick me? I forget half of what he said, and the other half I don't understand. Why me? Oh well, when He returns, I will ask Him.*

He closed his eyes. His chin dropped on his chest, and in seconds, a regular wheezing snore filled the room.

A pink shaft of setting sunlight focused itself on the belly heaving synchronously with the rhythmic rumble as Paul re-entered the room, his skin shining with olive oil, his thin hair brushed. Paul stopped in the doorway, crestfallen.

Another night of being kept awake by that noise, he thought. *Maybe I'll help nature with a little more wine than normal. Last night I got no sleep. Look at that. This is the one James sent to us? And I have to present him to the brothers and sisters tonight? Ohhhh.* He lifted his hand to his forehead in the universal expression of incomprehension.

He slammed the door shut, and Kephas awoke with a start. "Oh, you're back so soon."

"It has been about an hour. I hope you had a pleasant nap. But now we must leave, as it would not be polite to keep our host waiting."

Kephas struggled out of the chair, self-consciously smoothing his beard and hair with his hands, as though to make himself presentable to the urban world through those brief motions. As Paul opened the door, having tossed the soiled garment on his bed, Kephas assumed an air of majesty and strode down the stairs into the dim abandoned shop. Paul caught up with him and opened the door to the street, holding it as Kephas exited. The stench of old sweat enveloped the massive hulk and was nearly intolerable close up. Paul winced and turned his head slightly aside as the moving cloud of odor swept by.

Stay upwind, Paul thought as he closed the door.

CHAPTER 12

The Knight

EVEN THE EXTERIOR OF THE home of Menachem was aglow with hundreds of oil lamps. The door to the atrium was open, with two sentries in burnished ceremonial battle dress smartly at attention, one of whom held the standard of the legion. Kephas averted his eyes from the images that he knew the Roman soldiers worshipped.

Abomination! he thought, amazed that Paul walked right up to the sentry holding the standard, addressed him by name, and wished him peace. A couple friendly words, and the sentry nodded both Kephas and Paul through the open door.

The atrium and peristyle garden were ablaze, almost as if it were day! Kephas had never seen so many lamps, and the crowd was overwhelming. The atrium was filled with men in white togas, the center of attention of which was one with the purple stripe of a knight. Around the edges of the atrium were other men in multicolored and richly embroidered robes. Paul's robe, while vastly simpler and more modest, fit well with the dress of the other men. And in the garden to the rear, the women were assembled, standing in small knots, chatting animatedly, and laughing together. Kephas blinked in disbelief at the exposed arms, necks, and cleavage of the women. He was about to make a comment to Paul, suggesting that it would be better if they were to depart this pagan place, when Menachem spotted them. He took the arm of the portly knight and steered him to Paul and Kephas.

"Paul, greetings," Menachem called out, unable to see the quizzical expression on the knight as he looked at the dingy, clearly out-of-place robe on Kephas.

"Peace, brother," Paul , embracing the soldier. "Menachem, I should like to present Kephas, from the community in Jerusalem. Kephas, this is our patron and our brother, Menachem."

"My Lord, Kephas, I thought it might be you," Menachem said, taking Kephas's grimy hand, bending, and reverently kissing it.

Turning to the astonished knight, he said, "My Lord Cumanus, I should like to present Kephas, a holy man who is visiting us from Jerusalem."

Cumanus, with an oval, fleshy face and ring of closely cropped hair between his ears and the polished sandstone dome of a head, bereft of a single hair, caught a whiff of Kephas and registered the involuntary reaction to that unpleasantness.

"I am not a 'holy man.' I am a poor fisherman whom the Lord Iēsoûs Christos has selected to preach the Good News," he mumbled.

"Is that the same 'Chrestus' that the Jews in Rome rioted about," Cumanus asked.

"Rioted?" Menachem and Paul blurted out simultaneously.

"Yes. In fact, Claudius expelled all the Jews from Rome because of the dissention about this Chrestus. I just got the news today in the military dispatches. I sent a cohort to Jerusalem as soon as I heard, fearing that there might be similar disturbances there."

"Impossible," Kephas insisted. "Our Lord, Iēsoûs, was a man of peace; it was he who said that *if one strikes you, turn the other cheek*; it was he who taught that if someone takes your cloak, give him your shirt. There is no place for rioting among the followers of Iēsoûs the Christ. It must have been someone else."

"Well," said the Knight, looking directly at Menachem, "the primus pilus of the Auxiliaries in Caesarea remembered a riot about twenty years ago in Jerusalem, at the time of what you Jews call the Passover a man named Iēsoûs of Nazareth turned over money changers' tables and attacked your own Temple. The primus primus remembered that he called himself a king, the poor, deluded fool. Fortunately, he was caught and crucified before he could organize his followers in revolt. I hope that your friends are not part of any group that claims any allegiance to him, since anyone who calls himself *king* without the leave of our beloved prince Claudius, asks for death at these hands." He stretched out a pair of fat hands with stubby fingers, whose nails had been chewed into virtual nonexistence.

"My Lord Cumanus, let me assure you that everyone in this room is loyal to Rome and to our Prince Claudius," Menachem said as he steered Cumanus away from Paul and Kephas and back to the safer knot of white togas. When he was out of earshot from Kephas and Paul, he continued. "You know these holy men. Never bathe, never wash or anoint themselves. All in response to a call from God to reject the world and to preach salvation. The holiest have to be the most extreme, so that by the time the ideas get translated, they find the golden mean that you and I know is the standard. After all, without extremes, there would be no mean, no?"

"Menachem, I am only a visitor in Antioch, and you have provided me with invaluable assistance with the cohorts in Caesarea. I look upon you as a friend. Let me give you some advice. Don't get too close to these people. They are dangerous. That one in the orange called you *patron*. If you need to provide them with something to retain their loyalty, that is fine. But I smell trouble."

"That is not all you smell," Menachem laughed.

"Oh, by the pantheon of Greek gods, I don't know why those wandering holy men have to impose their barbarism on us who are civilized," Cumanus chuckled in return. "Now, pour me another cup of your Mareotic wine. I have developed a liking for its taste. Does it travel well over open sea?" And with that, Cumanus and Menachem picked up a few guests in togas and strolled to the rear of the atrium next to the peristyle garden.

CHAPTER 13

The Dinner

IN THE MEANTIME, A CROWD was forming around Kephas. Barnabas had arrived just as Cumanus and Menachem finished their conversation. Barnabas greeted Kephas warmly, and Menachem approached the group, extended his hand and instead of offering a typical Roman grasping of forearms, he kissed the holy man's hand. Other men followed Menachem's gesture, kissing Kephas's hand, considering the stench a sort of incense that emanated from a holy man. One man thrust an arthritic hand toward Kephas and begged him to cure it. Kephas took the hand in his and prayed: *May the will of God become your will; and if it be his will that your hand be cured, in the name of Jeshua of Nazareth, let it be so.*

Kephas stood amazed at the attention and deep respect offered him. Some genuflected as they kissed his hand; some touched his garments. Then Deborah, Barnabas's wife, and Sarah, Menachem's wife, noticed the crowd about Kephas and left the garden to enter the customarily segregated atrium. Sarah was dressed in a canary-colored silk stola, a draped gown that was clasped above the right shoulder only, with the left shoulder bare. A twisted gold girdle was cinched tightly just beneath her shapely breasts, and the gown flowed to the floor in carefully arranged folds. A single pear-shaped ruby hung from a jewel-studded gold choker. Her red hair was piled up on the top of her head, surrounded by a tall gold circlet studded with small sapphires. Deborah followed Sarah, but was dressed modestly in a white, sleeved linen stola. Her black hair was piled on the top of her head in a fashion similar to Sarah's, but obviously done unprofessionally, and held in place by a silver circlet.

The crowd of men parted as Sarah approached. When Kephas saw her, he blanched. Sarah walked up to him, silent, knelt at his feet; and kissed the hem of his sleeve. She looked up, and Kephas saw tears streaming down her cheeks, making furrows in the thickly applied makeup. Deborah knelt beside her, took the other sleeve, and pressed it to her lips.

Kephas staggered backward, wideeyed. "What are you doing? Get up, get up. Oh, my."

"Lord Kephas, give us your blessing," Sarah asked, stretching her arms upward toward the dumbfounded fisherman, completely unaware that she was inadvertently exposing vastly more bosom than Kephas had ever seen, except (only once) on his rather dowdy wife.

Kephas stood still, blinking. Not a sound came from his mouth.

Paul understood and quickly stepped between and behind the women, gently helping them to their feet.

"Sisters," he whispered in their ears, "Kephas has never seen such beautiful women, and he is speechless. After dinner, when he has become more comfortable with our customs, I shall personally bring him to you, and you will be able to converse with him. Now, would you join the other ladies?"

Dejected, the two women departed, returning to a group of women who were clearly interested in the holy man but who had not the courage to violate the rule that while the sexes could attend the same social function, conversation was generally restricted to those of the same sex.

The cluster of men around Kephas parted again, and a tall, gray-crew-cut, sad-faced man clothed in a white toga that tended to slip off his skinny shoulder approached. Paul's eyes lit up.

"Silas, my friend," Paul cried out.

A hint of a smile broke through the sagging features of the long face, and the droopy eyelids softened slightly, creating barely distinguishable crow's-feet at their edges.

"P...P... Peace," Silas stammered. "I came to br... bring greetings to Kephas." And he followed the now-established custom of kissing Kephas's hand.

"My brother Paul has spoken well of you," Kephas said with a bit of authority, warming to the role of being the center of attraction of the powerful and the beautiful. "I continue to be amazed at the faith of the Antiochene followers of The Way. Even a poor fisherman can see the strength of your faith."

"While you are in Antioch, you must tell us of your memories of Our Lord Iēsoûs. You must share with us exactly what he said, how he prayed, how he died, and how he looked when he arose from the dead," Silas said, towering over Kephas and especially Paul.

How important it is to these people, Paul thought, *to meet someone who shared Iēsoûs' life, who was a disciple during his earthly sojourn. They think this peasant, who spent about three years with Iēsoûs without understanding anything, who is reputed to have denied even knowing Iēsoûs the night he was killed, to whom Iēsoûs has revealed less than he has to me. They think he is the most important person in the world! Amazing!*

A servant ringing a silver bell announced dinner in the next room.

The dining room, twice as long as it was wide, was draped in red and gold, and had a raised platform in the very center. A low lattice fence ran across the short dimension through the center platform, to the right of which the women congregated and to the left, the men. The center platform had six couches arranged in two back-to-back U-shapes of three couches each. On the men's side, Cumanus strode to the center couch, the place of highest honor. Menachem assumed the couch at his head; Silas that to his feet. Small rectangular tables were placed just in front of the couches. Similarly, on the women's side, Cumanus' wife assumed her place at the center couch, which was back-to-back with Cumanus.' Sarah took her place at the couch next to her head. And Silas's daughter, since he had no wife, assumed her position at the couch at the feet of Cumanus'wife.

The balance of the guests sat on cushions, cross-legged in the Eastern style. Eight cushions were arranged on a colorful, thick carpet around a low circular table, and stewards steered guests to the appropriate group, obviously by their status. The officers of the legion were shown to the highest places, and the balance of the guests were directed to carpets somewhat less plush, with ten cushions sharing a table rather than eight. Kephas, Paul, Barnabas, and Titus shared the rank of the lowest class. As they were seated, stewards brought wine for each guest. Paul tasted his and commented that it was certainly not Mareotic; in fact, it had been watered more than the custom, perhaps to mask the fact that it was about to become undrinkable vinegar.

Cumanus arose, and a hush came over the room.

"It is my good fortune that the Legate of Syria, Cassius Longinus, commander of all the Roman forces in Syria and Palestine, invited me to report to him this week. And it is my better fortune that he was unable to attend this grand dinner and that he asked me to represent the Senate and People of Rome tonight. Hence, I have the honor to offer to the gods of Rome, and all the gods of Syria and Palestine, an opening libation, begging them to keep our beloved Prince in good health and to preserve the peace and order of every country in loyal subjection to him." And with that, he tipped his cup, and a thick, red drop splattered at his feet. As he did so, everyone did the same, except Kephas. But no one noticed.

"And now, Menachem, call the standards!"

Menachem stood. "Standards, HO!" he barked.

The doors at the opposite side of the atrium from where the diners had entered flew open. A blast of military song filled the room as ten cornus, their long horns wound around their bodies, tramped into the room. Six drummers pounded out the beat. A troop of twenty soldiers tramped to the beat in shining cuirasses, sporting red horsehair on their brass helmets and carrying silver-tipped parade spears. Finally came the standard bearer, proudly carrying the legion's standard topped with a golden eagle, the III GAL. insignia emblazoned on a sign just beneath the eagle, a disc with the image of the two-faced god, Janus, and a series of four rectangular plaques inscribed with the major battles in which the standard had been carried.

As the standard entered the room, every soldier and guest at the gathering stood and cheered. Except Kephas. Paul, Titus, and Barnabas noticed. They exchanged a worried look. If it should be noticed that Kephas did not rise when the standard entered the room, there might be trouble. Paul looked at the sentry standing at the rear of the room. He, too, had noticed. But he was a Christian, and he made no move. Paul and Titus shared a sigh of relief, saying nothing but understanding everything.

"To the gods that protect the III Gallica!" Menachem intoned, tipping his cup so that the drop fell.

"To the gods," the crowd , offering their libation.

Kephas was aghast. He could not see that the Christians had been silent and had moved their cups but had not let a drop fall. In this way, they had not participated in a pagan sacrifice; nor had they engaged in behavior that would have been remarkably provocative and insulting if they had all remained seated when the standard had entered the hall.

Paul sat as quickly as he could, aware that not all the men in their group were Christian.

"Kephas, I know you are incensed at what seems to be our participating in pagan practices. But I beg you, in the name of the Lord Iēsoûs, to wait until we arrive back at my home to discuss it. If you engage in an outburst, as I fear is about to happen, you will probably destroy the assembly in Antioch. Please hold your tongue, I beg of you."

Immediately, stewards began bringing the food. Two pheasants, their plumage perfect, were brought on large silver platters and set before the diners on the raised platform. The crowd applauded. The majordomo, with a long, sharp carving knife in his hand, took the bird by the head, snipped a few threads with his knife, and, with a flair, pulled off the entire plumage. Steam rose from the golden-brown stuffed carcass beneath, which he expertly carved and set before the diners on the platform.

A roast was brought for the diners in the next rank below, and was carved and piled in silver bowls in the center of the table. And a large bowl with a rich-smelling combination of barley and cubes of meat was placed in the center of each of the lowest-class ranks. A platter of pita bread was passed around, and two bowls of sauces were laid next to the large bowl.

"That looks like meat," Kephas said.

"Yes, indeed," Paul responded. "Smell those sauces! Menachem has some of the best chefs in Syria." He dipped the pita bread into the sauce and then into the barley-meat mixture.

"What if that meat has been offered to idols?" Kephas asked.

"Don't worry; it hasn't," Paul said.

Titus and Barnabas nodded their agreement.

Kephas followed the other diners at the table, commenting on how delicious the combination was. Barnabas had told the non-Christian diners that Kephas was a wandering holy man and that they were fortunate to dine with such a man! He had even explained that Kephas had never dined with anyone but adherents to his cult, and not to expect him to speak with them. Since wandering Cynic charismatics were not uncommon and rarely dined in a social environment, the presence of Kephas was a curiosity but not a threat.

When the bowl was wiped almost clean, two stewards appeared, one with a ceramic ewer and the other with a tray containing ten cups.

"My Lord Menachem has asked that we offer this Mareotic wine to his guests at this table."

Paul and Titus looked at each other and smiled. Kephas raised his cup, half filled with the sour excuse for wine. The steward looked at Paul, who gently took the cup from Kephas's hand, motioned to the steward to fill one of the clean cups, and gave it to Kephas.

"I have read in a collection of Iēsoûs's sayings that *one does not put new wine into old wineskins.* You will know why he said that after you taste this," Paul said gently.

"I never heard Iēsoûs say that," Kephas said. "But I will try the wine."

Instead of sipping it, he threw the whole cup down. "Oh, that was good! I'll have some more."

The steward complied and continued to serve the balance of the table. Paul smiled.

The diners at adjacent tables noticed the special attention being given to Kephas's table; they could conclude only that it must be because of the holy man who was seated there. But he was drinking wine, which was not usual for most Cynics. Indeed, when the first ewer was emptied, a steward returned with a second ewer and left it on the table.

The wine helped mellow Kephas, and he became more talkative and less inhibited. As multiple courses were being served to the guests on the dais, simpler courses were served to other diners. Kephas' table received a course of fruits and nuts, and finally a platter of sweet cakes. Plus another ewer of Mareotic.

Kephas became the center of the conversation, because as he mellowed from the wine, he told stories of his youth as a fisherman on Lake Galilee. His stories were not only entertaining; they were humorous. Some were slightly off color but hilarious. Both Christians and non-Christians were rolling on their sides in laughter, Paul included. Once he got started, he got better and better. He told of the nomads from the desert who had never tasted fish but who were known to pay for goods with coins that had been devalued by chipping metal from the edges. Kephas and his friends had agreed to bring them fish one evening at an agreed price per unit weight. The nomads left with their fish, laughing at how they had taken the bumpkins with their devalued coins. Kephas and his friends allowed that they would have loved to see their faces when their wives cleaned out all the gravel stuffed down their gullets!

The evening lasted until quite late. The guests gradually began to take their leave, but Kephas continued to regale his table with his genuine wit and simple humor. Even Paul's sides ached from laughter.

They were almost the only ones left, except for a small knot of women on the far side of the lattice. Paul urged Kephas to stand and helped steady him as he steered him toward the women. The women approached the lattice barrier. Menachem and Sarah, along with Barnabas, Deborah, Titus, and Leah, gathered in a single group with the lattice as a visible but meaningless barrier.

"Thank you for that wine, Menachem," Kephas said. "I never tasted such as that."

"Your table was rather raucous," Menachem offered, smiling. "I was almost forced to share my Mareotis with the rest of the company!"

"I know, I know. When I catch a really fat female longheaded barbel so full of roe she's ready to pop, I strap that baby to my leg and throw my long cloak on so my wife and I don't have to share the roe with the neighbors. When my old lady sees me walking stiff-legged up the street, she knows what that means. Yes sir, I understand. And I appreciate you sharing your fine wine with a poor fisherman."

"Lord Kephas, will you celebrate the Eucharist with us on Sabbath? Will you tell us stories about Iēsoûs?" Leah asked.

"Yes indeed, yes indeed," Kephas responded warmly. "I plan to stay some time, now. And I almost forgot. The saints in Jerusalem thanked God for the food you sent last year during the famine. Our suffering was terrible. God closed the heavens. It didn't rain in Galilee or Judea for nearly a full year! We had no grain, no fruits. Herds of sheep and goats died; it was terrible. The bread and fruit you sent saved us from starvation. We'll never forget your generosity."

"You have sent us the Light of the World. It is nothing that we should send you a little of our excess," Deborah said.

The other women knew, however, of the immense effort that had been involved in collecting huge quantities of food, organizing pack-trains and recruiting armed men to travel from Antioch to Jerusalem. Twice bands of marauders attempted to hijack the food; twice the caravan successfully fought them off, at the loss of two men to wounds received in the highway battles. The Antiochene Christians cut their food consumption in half to help their brothers and sisters in Jerusalem. And this was the first acknowledgment of that gift. However, everyone knew that receiving a gift of that sort imposed an obligation to respond in some equivalent fashion in the future; the Jerusalem saints were indebted to the Antiochene saints. It was nice to hear that debt acknowledged.

It was clear that the evening was ended. Kephas and Paul, along with Menachem, Titus and Barnabas headed for the atrium, where the family units connected, and the women donned veils for the trip through the dark streets to their homes. They said their good nights at the door; Sarah, Menachem's wife, stood next to Kephas, touching his garments inconspicuously, her heart full of love for the man who lived with Iēsoûs, her Lord. And, as Kephas sensed her presence, as he glanced her way, afraid to let his eyes devour her beauty for any period longer than an instant, he felt a stirring in his loins the likes of which he had not felt for twenty years. And it frightened him. *Perhaps she is possessed by a demon. she is so beautiful, so tempting.* As he turned to say good night, she took his hand gently, kissed it, and held it to her cheek.

"Oh, no, please," he said, using this excuse to examine the expanses of white flesh, the cleavage between her breasts, her long, thin neck. "I am just a poor fisherman, and I spread the Good News of Iēsoûs, the Lord. You must not think that I am anything...anything except an unworthy messenger." And with that, he turned sharply and bolted out the door, his member erect for the first time in many, many years.

Paul and Titus glanced at their host, who shrugged as though he could never fathom a holy man, nor should he. They waved goodbye, Titus calling to Barnabas to see Leah home, and both followed Kephas, running to catch him.

The three men, in high spirits, walked down the deserted quayside; sailors slept on the decks of the ships tied up on the wharf. Cats prowled silently. A light breeze from the north raised little wavelets, which lap-lapped at the wooden hulls.

"Paul, you knew that the meat we ate tonight had not been offered to idols. And you too, Titus. How did you know?"

"Let's just say I knew. And I do. Don't worry," Paul said, his arm over Kephas's shoulder, the wine having built a feeling of camaraderie that spanned the gorge of the differences between the men.

"No, I want to know. How did you know?"

"Kephas, I would not ask you how you knew a longheaded some-thing-or-other had roe inside, but you know. Right? OK. So don't ask me how I know what I know. I do."

"But there is no law that governs longheads. But we both know what Torah states. So, I want to know. Tell me."

"Well, all right. But don't forget, you forced me."

"OKOk. Now, how?"

"Kephas, the Gentiles only offer oxen, lambs, and birds to their gods; never swine."

"You mean we ate pork?" Kephas shouted, incredulous.

"Yes. That delicious meat was pork."

Kephas gagged. He grabbed his belly. "PORK!"!!!"

"Shaddap" came a cry from the ship a few feet away.

"Agggghhh." Kephas doubled over, retching, the mass of his dinner spewing forth on the quay, on his gown, on his feet.

"Paul, you son of a whore! How could you? PORK!" And he retched again.

Paul and Titus laughed uproariously. They doubled over. They held their sides.

"Kephas, you said it yourself. It is not what goes into a man's mouth that defiles him, so don't worry. You will not find salvation in the Law; you find it in being part of the community that awaits the Lord."

Paul felt remorse then. Kephas was down on his knees, weeping, vomit down the front of his robe. They must have drunk too much of that Mareotic wine; Paul remembered the first time he ate pork; it had felt so strange to change a lifelong habit, not of diet, but of thought. He began to feel that he should have told Kephas in advance, but then he never, never would have joined them. And it had been so worthwhile for the Antioch community to have Kephas in their midst, when one of their own was being honored.

Titus and Paul put their arms under Kephas's armpits. He let himself be helped, and the three of them walked silently down the quay to the side street and then down the side-street to Paul's dark shop. They lit a single oil lamp, struggled up to the second floor, and dumped Kephas in his bed. He didn't move. Paul silently waved good night to Titus, and he collapsed in his own bed and fell into a dreamless sleep.

CHAPTER 14

A Changed Man

THREE MONTHS PASSED.

Kephas was a transformed man.

First, he had moved from the cramped quarters above Paul's shop into a suite of rooms in Menachem's house. Ostensibly, since the large room in which the faithful met was part of the house, Kephas would be immediately available to all the faithful. Second, his hygienic habits had changed. The Roman camp had a bath that was used by the officers, and after some urging, he adopted the habit of regularly entering the hot room, where he would sweat with the six or eight military men who might be there at the same time. Then the attendant used a strigil to scrape over the moist skin to remove dirt. Then followed the normal plunges in the hot, tepid and cold pools after which came a rubdown by the officers' masseur. And after about an hour, Kephas was treated to the application of fine, light olive oil. Menachem had provided a number of well-made linen robes so that Kephas would not have to wear the tattered, stained robes he brought from Jerusalem.

This physical transformation brought him closer to the growing congregation of believers. He reveled in his newfound preeminence. The majority of Jews in Antioch had adopted Greek social customs, and to have modified his behavior as he did endeared him to the Antiochenes. And, given their unqualified acceptance of him as being authoritative, he became remarkably self-confident; and this, in turn, unlocked the personal qualities that had been hidden from view. His homilies on

Shabbat were simple, poignant, and effective. He utilized his natural sense of humor often to bring laughter to the liturgy, something that neither Paul nor Barnabas ever did. Finally, the man who thrust his arthritic hand in Kephas's face at the banquet for Silas showed everyone who would look how the swelling had gone down, how the knuckles were gradually returning to their original shape, and how the pain was almost gone. Hence, people came to the assembly room at all hours of the day or night seeking cures for a multitude of ailments. In each case, Kephas told them of Iēsoûs, of his emphasis on that part of the teachings of Torah that emphasized love of God and love of neighbor, and how He would return soon in glory, at the end of ages.

All the leaders of the assembly, including Paul, developed a deeper sense of Kephas's mission. Paul saw a certain homespun wisdom that spoke to the simplest, the poorest, the broadest base of Antiochene society. Hence, the numbers of members of the assembly grew substantially in an extremely short time, so that the room Menachem had provided was too small to hold the entire assembly at once.

CHAPTER 15

Men from Jerusalem

THE LEAVES HAD FALLEN FROM the trees when the two men from Jerusalem arrived at the room of the assembly. Kephas was sitting with a group of Greek catechumens, *(those receiving instruction)* quoting Torah that he had learned from Paul and Barnabas. They had developed a sequence of teachings that would be presented to all groups interested in following The Way. The texts began with Torah then moved to several readings of the Prophets and Writings. Finally, Kephas spoke of Iēsoûs' life, His healings, His teachings, His death and resurrection, and finally His promise to return in glory. The entire series of discussions took several weeks, after which Barnabas would administer baptism, and the catechumens would be admitted to the People of God. Paul and Barnabas were seated in the far corner of the assembly room at a table on which a small scroll of parchment was illuminated by several oil lamps.

Two men stood in the dim background, since the overcast sky provided little light through the single window, and several oil lamps were clustered near Kephas. They listened to what Kephas taught. They were surprised at the authority with which he spoke, at his simple and heartfelt conviction, and at his warmth and apparent love for those at his feet. This was a different man from the Kephas they had known in Jerusalem. His beard was neatly trimmed; his hands were clean; his hair combed and cut. He had finished his prepared remarks and now was answering questions. Another surprise. The answers he gave were more penetrating than either of the two men would have given themselves.

For they, too, were teachers. They looked at each other and raised their eyebrows.

When the questions had ended, the group, men and un-veiled women sitting on the appropriate sides of an imaginary line, rose and either ambled toward the door or continued conversing in smaller groups. It was then that the two men walked into the dim light of the oil lamps.

Kephas recognized them at once. "Elihu, Rechab. How good to see you," he said, arms outstretched.

"May the peace of our Lord Iēsoûs, the Christ, be with you," Elihu responded, a little mechanically. Instead of giving Kephas a full embrace, he grasped him by the upper arms, offering a half embrace, more ceremonial than heartfelt. His partner responded in essentially the same manner.

"Have you just arrived? Where are you staying?" Kephas asked, not giving them a chance to answer.

"We arrived not an hour ago."

"I thought shipping had stopped already."

"We did not come by ship. We joined a caravan that was headed for Sinope on the Black Sea. Its route came through Antioch; it took us only eight days."

During this exchange, several of the catechumens remained standing around the group; they clearly wanted to meet other Christians from Jerusalem.

"Oh, my. I was so excited I forgot my manners." Kephas then introduced the catechumens to the visitors, who merely nodded to each but did not extend their hands or embrace them.

"Paul, Barnabas, come over here. We have guests from the Jerusalem assembly."

The exchanges of Peace were formal.

"We bring a message from James that we must deliver."

"Of course, of course. How is James? And John?"

The group of students drifted out the door, giving Kephas and the visitors some privacy. Kephas sat on one of the cushions, motioning the others to sit. They declined.

Elihu pulled out from his robe a small scroll attached to a leather thong that had been hanging around his neck. He handed it to Kephas, who handed it to Paul.

"Shall I read the document now?" Paul asked Kephas.

"No, we will consider this in private and will contact the brothers from Jerusalem in the morning" said a visibly shaken Kephas.

Where are you staying?" addressing the visitors.

"With Ya'akov ben Levi," Elihue said.

"You may return here if you like. I shall not put myself in the presence of Ya'akov." And with that Kephas pushed himself to a standing position, turned on his heel and walked out. Paul and Barnabas nodded to the visitors and ushered them to the street outside.

The three men walked back to the table where Paul and Barnabas had been working.

"Don't be afraid, my friend. The Lord has brought you here for a purpose. Let us read what he intends for you." Paul embraced the trembling Kephas.

From James, servant of God and of the Lord Jeshua Christ, to his brother Kephas, Greetings. The grace of our Lord be upon you as we anxiously await his coming. You know how highly the entire assembly of saints regards the two who bring this letter. For you know that they love you, as I do. We have, however, heard reports which, if true, we consider to be scandalous. The entire assembly prays that they are false, the work of Satan who prowls the world seeking to do mischief. But, rather than permit either falsehood or sin to continue, these faithful brothers lay before you the rumors that are afoot. It is rumored that you have abandoned the ways of your fathers laid down in the Law given by God to Moses for our guidance. It is rumored that not only do you dine with Gentiles, eating flesh that may have been offered to idols, but eat unclean foods forbidden by our Law. It is rumored that you participate in public sacrifice, frequent the baths with their abominations and sin, and actually live in the house of a Gentile and his wife. If these rumors are false, our trusted brethren will see for themselves that they are the work of Beelzebub, and they will return in joy to announce the truth to all. But if they are well-founded, then as brother of the Lord, and as leader of the assembled

faithful in Jerusalem, I abjure you to come to your senses and return to the obser-
vance of the Law in Jerusalem. Farewell.

Blood rushed to Kephas's head. He felt the same confusion he had felt three months ago when he first set foot in Antioch. Here he was now appreciated, looked up to, honored as one who had walked with the Master. Here he was given respect, modest but well-made clothing, good food, the comforts of having servants attend to his needs, and most of all, a warm community centered around this room. While he had been here, he had even seen the barriers between Sarah and the other sisters disappear; she even walked in the streets, veiled, with them to the marketplace and fountains in the city. They were different from other Antiochenes: Look how they loved one another.

As though Paul and Barnabas could read his heart, he continued aloud his internal debate: *Paul, they want me to return to Jerusalem! To stop eating with friends! How can this be?*

He silently answered his own question: *James is the leader. He has authority. To disobey would involve consequences I could not even visualize. I cannot t stay here forever. I have a wife in Jerusalem, grandchildren in Galilee. I was first and foremost a disciple of the Lord Iēsoûs Christ. But Iēsoûs' brother is the head of the community, and disobedience is unthinkable.*

He put his head in his hands, his elbows on his crossed knees. He rocked side to side, trying to change the facts. But he couldn't.

"Paul, I am exhausted, Kephas said. "I would like to sleep now and we can talk more in the morning." And with that he got up and went to his sleeping quarters.

"We must be with him in the morning and help him formulate his response to James," said Paul" For him to be influenced by those two from Jerusalem would constitute a significant loss. Most importantly, we must avoid his being alone with either of those two."

"I agree, Paul. We must help him,"

The two friends wished each other good night and retired.

Unbeknown to Barnabas and Paul, Kephas tossed and turned for several hours, unable to sleep and almost unable to pray. Hence the depths of the night, Kephas got up and silently walked to the house of prayer presided over by Ya'akov ben Levi. He knocked on the door several times with that response, but as he turned to leave Elihu opened the door and invited Kephas in. Lamps were quickly lit and Rechab appeared quickly, greeting Kephas warmly.

"I never thought I was seeing the day when I walked into the assembly room of my enemy.

"No, he is *Paul's* enemy said Rechab. Paul is preaching freedom from the Law in the assembly meeting in Menachem's home, and he was punished! And rightly so. It was agreed that Gentiles could become part of the People of God through baptism. But all Jews must follow the Law, and those faithful who are baptized must follow the Law except for circumcision. My Lord, James, is even questioning the wisdom of having given in to Paul and Barnabas on the issue of circumcision. Just what he feared would happen is happening, and of all people to you, acknowledged as a leader of the Jerusalem assembly subject only to James."

"I must speak. Paul and Barnabas have been extremely good to me and I must leave in such a way that our relationship in the Lord is not destroyed forever."

"No. There is to be no discussion. Remain with us without conversation with Paul or Barnabas, or we depart immediately for Jerusalem and announce that you have died to the Lord in the land of the Gentiles."

"Let me get my traveling bag," Kephas said. "I will reside with you and Ya'akov and will return to Jerusalem next spring."

"We will accompany you," Rechab said. "Ya'akov is expecting us for breakfast. We can be sure of what we are eating."

CHAPTER 16

The Message from Jerusalem

With sundown Shabbat began, and the congregation crowded into the assembly room. The cold outside demanded that the small window be closed, and the large number of people made the room stuffy and uncomfortable. Kephas was not permitted to preside at the Friday Shabbat service, but was given a separate chair next to the presiders chair. This evening the chair was empty. It had been five days since the two men accompanied Kephas from Menachem's house, and no one had seen him since. Ya'akov, however, had sent word to Menachem that henceforth, Kephas would be lodging with him.

Paul and Barnabas sat on stools to the right side of the presider's chair. Since virtually the entire congregation was assembled the "communal clock," that unconscious sensitivity of what "time" it was, had properly functioned. It was time to begin. But no Kephas.

Then the door opened. Kephas, flanked by Elihu and Rechab, walked in. He was strangely silent, not returning the greetings from the congregation but seemingly intent upon completing an unpleasant task. He did not greet Paul and Barnabas. Elihu and Rechab remained at his side as he reached the front of the room, and turned, facing the community.

"My brothers and sisters, before we begin our Shabbat service, I have to say a few words. You know how I have come to love each one of you, with the same love that our Lord, Iēsoûs Christos loved his disciples. And, as He would sometimes correct us when we needed correction, so I must tonight correct you."

The congregation stirred, sharing questioning expressions. Paul and Barnabas frowned at each other, concerned.

"Our Lord, Iēsoûs Christ, was born into the Law. He was circumcised on the eighth day and lived a life of holiness, praying in synagogues and at the Temple. He corrected those who misused the Temple, but never attacked the holiest of our institutions."

"The Law was given to Moses so that the People of Israel might be saved, might become righteous in the eyes of God. He has promised that we would be his Chosen People as long as we obeyed the Law that he, himself, had given. This is not the Law of man; it is the Law of God. To ignore the Law is to depart from God's People."

More stirring.

"Everyone knows that I am simply a poor fisherman. Everyone knows that I don't read but that I love God and His Son, Jeshua Christ. Everyone knows that I preach this Son of God as the one the Prophets foretold, as the one who would bring salvation to Israel and the whole world. The Jeshua I knew, and the Jeshua who walked the length and breadth of Galilee and finally walked to Jerusalem to be crucified so that the Scripture could be fulfilled, this Jeshua called sinners to Him. And I am one of those sinners! I confess that to you here and now. Not only did I deny Him in His hour of agony, I denied him in Antioch these last three months. Yes, denied Him! How? By denying the Law! Let me tell you how I denied the Law:

"First, I ignored the Law of foods by eating forbidden foods and not being cautious as to whether the food had been offered to idols."

"Second, I participated in pagan worship, honoring the gods of Rome."

"Third, I frequented the public baths, the place where abominations abound. I freely confess these sins and shall atone for them when I return to Jerusalem by making the prescribed sin offerings in the Temple."

"Now I must speak of the sin in this assembly."

"Women, you must no longer purchase your food in the markets of the Gentiles. You must buy only from Jewish vendors, since they have gone to great efforts to make sure that none of their food was grown by Gentiles, none was tithed to a pagan god, and that it is pure and bears no uncleanness. Further, you must eat only those foods that are not prohibited by the Law; never must you eat the flesh of a swine, of a fish that has no scales, of shellfish, or any of the other foods that bring pollution upon you."

"Men, you must no longer give any honor to a pagan god. Remember what God said:

I am the Lord your God who brought you out of the land of Egypt, out of the house of slavery. You shall have no gods except me. You shall not make yourself a carved image or any likeness of anything in heaven or on earth beneath or in the waters under the earth; you shall not bow down to them or serve them. For I, the Lord your God, am a jealous God and I punish the father's fault in the sons, the grandsons and the great-grandsons of those who hate me; but I show kindness to thousands of those who love me and keep my commandments.

"You must rid your houses of your statues and paintings of men and animals; you must offer no libations to the Roman gods or the gods of this city. For you must not become hateful to God, the Father of our Lord Jeshua Christ."

"Finally, neither men nor women ought to frequent the place where nakedness before others abounds. For the Lord has written that *Shem and Japheth walked backward to avoid looking upon their father, Noah's nakedness. And the Lord blessed them for that.*

"The saints in Jerusalem have agreed that you, Gentiles, could become part of God's Chosen People through baptism. But the Law was given so that His Chosen People could be distinguished from all others and that in following the Law, we will see salvation. So, you must make the Law your own. Be subject to it in everything you do, from rising in the morning to falling asleep at night. And if anyone says otherwise, let him be anathema."

There was a stunned silence. Then people began turning to their neighbors and whispering the same question: "What are we to do?"

Barnabas arose and walked to the place where the leader always stood.

"Brothers and sisters, we have been a family for many years. And we have always sought to do God's will. My brother Kephas has opened my eyes. For I, too, was born a Jew and kept the Law as being God's glory. But when I came to Antioch more than fifteen years ago, I gradually fell away from the full observance of the Law. It happened so slowly that it was almost imperceptible. But I am one of those sinners who has permitted the distance from Jerusalem to create a distance from the ways of God. I thank God that He has sent his servant Kephas, like a prophet of old, to remind us of what God has intended for us." Then he returned, sat on the stool next to the president's chair, and bowed his head deeply.

"NO! You are both wrong!" It was Paul who stood, hands clenched, the force of his words shocking the assembly.

"You simply don't understand the meaning of Iēsoûs' death on the cross and His resurrection! He has created a New Covenant for us. I have spoken of it for years. It is this that Iēsoûs Himself revealed to me. I was selected by God to preach this New Covenant; before I was born, He selected me in my mother's womb. This is not something that I, Paul, say to you. It is the word, the Good News of the Risen Lord. This New Covenant creates the People of God, and it is open to all men and women, first to Jews, then to Greeks. And, since many Jews reject this Covenant that God Himself has created, I, Paul, bring it to you, the Greeks of the world."

"And, as to the demands of Kephas, let me tell you why our way is better. If a Jew cannot eat with a Gentile, then we cannot share the Agape together. Jews would have one, and Gentiles the other. But are we not now all one in Christ? He died not only for Jews, but for all men and women, and He has promised to remain with all of us until the final days. Does he remain with the Jews in one way and with Gentiles another? Can Christ be divided? No, God forbid! Is that love different for Jew and for Greek? Of course not. If Kephas will allow Gentiles into the New Covenant without circumcision, admitting that one portion of the Law does not apply, then why does he insist that the entire balance of the Law must apply? Once one portion is recognized as not applying, there is nothing to suggest that the balance must apply, including the dietary rules."

"Kephas, if you insist on your position, you will destroy this assembly of those who love the Lord Iēsoûs. And Barnabas, I am surprised at you, yielding so quickly. The future of the Good News is not with the Jews; it is with the Greeks. And while we await His coming, our lives must be formed by faith in Iēsoûs Christos, not by sterile adherence to a Law that is dead!"

Menachem stood and faced Kephas.

"I am a military man. I command seven thousand troops in Syria and know that if the commanders disagree before their troops, chaos will result. The troops will not know whom to obey. Whatever their assigned task, they will fail."

"As for Sarah and me, we were introduced to the Lord Iēsoûs by Barnabas. It was he who baptized us, and it was he who showed us the way to salvation. But he never said that I must cease being a Roman soldier! He never said to me, 'Leave your station in life and take up farming or fishing.' And I have provided for the community of Christians because I recognize that I am who I am through His grace. But He made me to be a Roman soldier, not a Jewish merchant. Would you, Kephas, insist that I resign my commission as a Roman soldier? Because part of my duties includes giving honor to the standard of the legion. Yes, they are 'graven images,' but I know that no god resides therein. I confess the One God."

"But the soldiers who know no other god until they are converted to the Lord Iēsoûs they must honor the standard above everything else.

Otherwise, the barbarians outside the borders would make quick work of us!"

Yes, I offer a libation to the 'god' of the standard, and since there *are* no gods, I do no harm. I am sure that it is better for me to engage in this…this charade than to have the barbarians swooping over the borders, burning your towns, stealing your crops, and raping your women! Indeed, you were happy to accept the hospitality of the Roman army for many years until these troublemakers arrived from Jerusalem. If you ask me to give up my life, I say no. And that goes for my entire household."

"That is what I meant, Menachem," Kephas said softly, but so that everyone could hear. "The Lord Yeshua once met a rich young man who asked what he had to do to receive salvation. The Lord said to follow the Law. The young man said he already did that. Then Yeshua said, *Sell all you have and give it to the poor, then come and follow me.* With that, the young man left, sorrowing."

"And all the troops that are Christian?"

"They, too," Kephas said.

"Then there will be few people in the assembly of Christians in Antioch." And with that, Menachem walked out of the room, followed by Sarah and by those soldiers who were Christian.

"Kephas, Kephas, consider what you are doing," Paul exclaimed.

"Paul, Kephas has spoken, and he speaks with the authority of Our Lord's most prominent disciple," Barnabas interjected.

Paul stood up and walked directly to Barnabas. "Can't you see, Barnabas, that Kephas walked with the Lord for three years but never understood Him? The Risen Lord revealed, directly to me, the Gospel I preach. And I do not lie! There must be no division in Christ; there must be neither Jew nor Greek. There must be one body anxiously awaiting His return. And when we celebrate the Lord's Supper, there must be no division, with one group eating one food and another group eating another."

"Paul, you would create chaos. First, no circumcision for Greeks. Second, no dietary laws. Third, you would permit the honoring of pagan

gods. Next, you would permit fornication, sodomy, extortion, and rob-
bery! The Law is our bulwark against the disorder and confusion that
Satan would sow. The brothers at Jerusalem agreed with you on circumcision. But that is as far as it is possible to go!"

Paul heaved a great sigh and, with his eyes lifted toward heaven, proclaimed, "My forefather, Jeremiah, wrote:

Thus says the Lord:
'Stand by the roads, and look,
and ask where the good way is; and walk in it,
and find rest for your souls.'
But they said, 'We will not walk in it.'
I set watchmen over you, saying
'Give heed to the sound of the trumpet.'
But they said, 'We will not give heed.

The powerful of the time gave no heed to Jeremiah. But we know now
that God spoke the truth through him. And like the powerful of old,
you cannot see the truth. Thus, you and I can no longer share the task
of bringing the Gospel of Iēsoûs Christ to Jews and Greeks alike. You
follow Kephas, bringing the Good News to those in Judea. There will be
no issue, then, as to whether the Law is to be followed. I shall bring it to
the Greeks of Asia, and perhaps to Greece and Macedonia, and, Lord
willing, even to Europe."

Kephas rose again. He looked at the severely diminished numbers;
over three-quarters of the congregation had left with Menachem. He
could see the troubled expressions on the faces of those who remained.
But more importantly, he realized that virtually all those remaining
remained because of their close ties with Paul. There were Silas and Titus
and their families, and several others who were bound by ties of friendship to them. But there were few Jews besides Barnabas, Paul and himself.

"Brothers, brothers," Kephas said, "There must be no division in
Christ. I have a proposal to make. I shall return to Jerusalem and call

the brothers together to discuss this matter. I would propose that we require only a few important items of Gentiles who are baptized into Christ, for instance, that they avoid fornication, that they avoid food offered to idols, that they avoid blood and meat from any strangled animal. And that the Gentile churches remember the poor in Jerusalem. I can promise nothing but will recommend it to the brothers."

Paul responded, "I am ready to agree that all the Gentile churches would remember the poor in Jerusalem. As to avoiding fornication, of course. Would anyone join Christ to a harlot? And other behavior such as behaving truthfully, avoiding drunkenness, feuds, jealousy, and wrangling, all these come from the Spirit that is received in baptism. They do not come from the Law."

"As to the issues of food, that which is offered to idols and that of blood and strangled animals, I must pray for enlightenment. I must ask the Lord Iēsoûs to show me His answer. Then I shall be able to respond, if the brothers in Jerusalem suggest those as requirements. By the time a letter is received, the Lord will have shown me the correct answer. And I beg of you, Kephas, to encourage the brothers in Jerusalem to pray mightily, lest in your zeal for the Law, the body of Christ be damaged."

And with that, Paul nodded to Barnabas and Kephas, turned and walked out of the room of the assembly. Titus, Silas, and their friends followed him out. Kephas, Barnabas, and the two men from Jerusalem were the only ones left in the room.

"I feel seasick," Kephas said weakly. "I feel as though I am in my boat in a huge storm, with clouds pressing on the tops of the sails, the shore is invisible. Huge waves break over the bow of my small boat, my nets have snapped, and the entire catch has returned to the sea. A short time ago, the biggest problem was how to get the entire catch back to port and to receive the honors and praise of my fellow fishermen. Now I must struggle to keep the boat afloat, as well as to gain some bearings as to how to steer. And to make all this impossible, I am seasick. I cannot concentrate. I want only for the pitching and rolling to stop. I would give anything, anything for the calm. Lord, where are you?"

CHAPTER 17

Choices

THE NEXT DAY, MENACHEM ARRIVED at Paul's closed shop shortly after day-break. He pounded on the door, which was presently opened by a sleepy, disheveled Paul.

"I have been unable to sleep all night," Menachem blurted as soon as the door cracked open. "I must speak with you."

"Come in, come in."

They went to the rear of the ground-floor workshop, and Paul rummaged around in a small alcove that served as a tiny kitchen for the workmen, producing in a moment a handful of figs from a light leather bag. He tossed a couple to Menachem, who popped one into his mouth and pulled up a stool on which to sit.

"What do we do?" Menachem asked.

"Continue the work of the Lord."

"But how? Kephas…"

"Kephas is an ass! He doesn't understand anything. He is a plague upon us that we must survive."

"I have served under asses before; but they were my commanders, and they had authority. A soldier does not ignore orders from a superior, ass or no ass!"

"Menachem, listen to me. The fact that Kephas spent three years or so with the Lord and understood nothing… NOTHING…does not give him authority! The Lord Himself has revealed to me exactly what we are to do…EXACTLY! Now, listen to me. First, the Good News is intended for Greeks as well as Jews. We shall bring that Good News to both Greeks and Jews.

Second, the Lord revealed to me that our salvation is not through the Law, but through the Grace of Iēsoûs Christ. Ours is the New Covenant, for which the Law is merely preparation. In fact, my friend, the Law leads to death! I have not shared everything that the Lord has revealed to me, since the community was not ready yet. But the true Gospel is this: faith in Iēsoûs Christ supersedes the Law, completely and totally. You and our entire community are free of the yoke of the Law. We are subject to that higher Law that is imposed upon us by faith. Circumcision. Food. Even the Sabbath restrictions. All the works of the Law produce only sin, only death. You are freed from this death, Menachem. Freed! Have no fear; the Lord has chosen you. You are His. Indeed, as commander of the III Galicia, you have no choice to make. The Lord has made it for you. You are his, and you are free!"

"Paul, I have heard mutineers say the same thing. 'Slay...Slay the general; then we will be free.' But I knew that it was wrong to act against authority. And I was correct. How do I know who has authority?"

"If you can see clearly, CLEARLY, that a particular order of a Senator would cause not only the loss of your legion but the loss of the war and the loss of Rome itself, and if you could see clearly, CLEARLY, that an alternate course of action would bring certain victory and glory to you, your legion, and Rome, would you not disobey the senator and follow your better vision, confident that a successful outcome would give you the opportunity to justify your contrary order? Would you not rely upon your success to justify yourself to the emperor? Would you not risk your life?"

"If I could see clearly, I think I would," Menachem quietly uttered.

"Precisely! That is what I am doing!" He stood inches away from Menachem, taking him by the shoulders, speaking into his eyes. "I can see clearly that Kephas is wrong, dead wrong. James is wrong. The entire group in Jerusalem has no vision. They are peasants. But the Lord has provided me with the vision that the entire world is called to become the People of God! And if the orders of Kephas and James are followed, Satan will triumph! All will be lost! But if the entire world, Jews and Greeks alike, are brought to the Throne of God by Christ, and if God becomes all in all, then we will be able to explain why we did not follow their mistaken order! When you and I stand with the Christ before the face of God our Father, we will justify our act because we are right! Kephas and James will bring death and failure. We will bring life and success!"

"But what if they don't recognize us as brothers?"

"They will, they will. I told you last spring that I agreed to remember the poor in Jerusalem? I shall. You shall. The entire Greek world shall remember the poor. We will bring from all over the world a great collection of money to James and Kephas and all the Jerusalem saints. Every assembly from every city will contribute, and representatives from all the churches will bring it to their feet. The moment they accept our money, they will acknowledge us as brothers. We will be partners, equals. They will be to us as the church in Antioch is to you. Beholden! They will offer us the hand of friendship, despite the separate tactics in our battle."

"But what if they refuse the donation?"

"They won't. They see that the work of the Lord cannot be accomplished if the saints starve! Our contribution will permit them to continue the Lord's work. Without it, the entire work might be jeopardized. They won't refuse."

"As a military man, Paul, let me advise you. You are taking a huge risk. If they do refuse the donation, then there will be no way to heal the rift. Kephas is a peasant, indeed. And rather stupid. But my best sergeants have been of peasant stock. Once they set their minds to a task, nothing sways them. They don't see different strategies, as generals do. They plow ahead, head down, never looking right or left. That is Kephas."

"But James is different, Menachem. He is a peasant, but brighter. He will not let the Church of God be given over to Satan just because of Kephas's stubbornness."

"I don't know James..."

"I do. They will accept the money. Especially if it is a *huge* amount! Especially if it comes from the entire church, all over the empire."

"Paul, I am with you."

"I give praise to God that your faith is strong, Menachem."

"Now, what shall we do?"

"Here is the plan that the Lord gave me. I shall leave with Silas this week to revisit the churches that Barnabas and I founded in Asia. But we will go farther. To Macedonia. To Greece. To Athens. To Corinth. Perhaps to Rome or even Spain. We shall preach the freedom of Faith in Iēsoûs Christ to the entire world, to Jews and Greeks alike. No distinction. One faith, one people. And the collection will be an expression of unity of all of us in Christ Iēsoûs."

"And the church in Antioch?"

"Let Titus be the elder."

"And Barnabas?"

"He has cut himself off. He will not remain here. He will either return to Jerusalem with Kephas or will go back to Cyprus. For there is no church here except that which is made up primarily of Greeks! There are not enough circumcised Christians to make up a minyan so that a synagogue service can be held. It is a matter of numbers, Menachem. You should understand that!"

"And how do I help?"

"You help by speeding me on my way. Help Silas and me travel through Asia. We will need money. The Lord will acknowledge your gift to us. And keep faith with the church in Antioch. Help Titus. Remain strong."

"You can count on me."

Menachem rose and embraced the thin man with the blazing eyes. He now knew what Julius Caesar must have felt as he crossed the Rubicon. This was a watershed moment. He felt a rush of adrenaline as he realized that it was a historic moment. He was playing a critical role in the battle that raged through the spiritual universe. He had placed his life on the line with this General of the Sons of Light. The critical battle was now underway. They would succeed. They would annihilate the Sons of Darkness and, using this bold strategy, preserve the unity that Paul knew had to be maintained. It was risky. But what battle had no risk? He could feel the mantle of glory and honor that would be his as he stood with Paul before the Throne of God on that last day, triumphant, victorious! This was why he had been born. This was why he had been trained as a soldier, so that on this auspicious day, he could share the vision with Paul, the general. He knew!

He released his grip on Paul and, with tears in his eyes, left hurriedly to run home and share the news with Sarah.

Printed in Great Britain
by Amazon